DAUNTING DAYS OF WINTER

DAUNTING DAYS OF WINTER

GETTING HOME WAS JUST THE BEGINNING

RAY GORHAM

CONTENTS

PROLOGUE

aunting Days of Winter picks up the story where *77 Days in September*, originally released in May of 2011, leaves off. *77 Days in September* is the story of Kyle and Jennifer Tait, an ordinary couple surviving extraordinary circumstances.

Kyle, a supervisor with an electrical power company, has been in Houston helping with recovery after a major hurricane. As he prepares to fly home to Montana, terrorists launch a massive EMP strike against the continental United States, successfully destroying the electrical and computer infrastructure of the nation. Kyle's plane crashes upon take-off, and he barely escapes the burning wreckage, only to find himself stranded in a country where technology has been wiped out and modern-day people are left struggling to survive in a primitive world.

Forced to devise a plan to get himself home, and with the help of a fellow airplane survivor, Kyle builds a handcart to haul the meager supplies he needs to attempt the 2,000-mile journey from Texas to Montana on foot.

Across the country, Jennifer and their children, David, Emma and Spencer, face unimaginable challenges of their own. With no power, communication, or modern conveniences, life in rural Montana is not as carefree as the family is used to. Grocery stores are looted, doctors are unavailable, and law enforcement is unreliable, if not nonexistent. The residents of the Tait's small community band together to deal with the new reality in which they live, forming councils and structure, but quickly realizing that life will be far more difficult than any of them care to imagine.

While Jennifer toils to protect and provide for their family, Kyle and his handcart slowly move northward. He encounters stranded motorists, hostile gangs, highway bandits, and extreme weather conditions that threaten his safety and his very life. But he also finds evidence that, despite the dire circumstances, goodness and mercy still exist. In neighboring Wyoming, Kyle is saved from certain death by Rose Duncan, an attractive and independent woman isolated from her family and with whom Kyle quickly bonds, testing his resolve and his dedication to his family to the extreme.

With Kyle completing the last leg of his journey home, Jennifer's trials escalate and her family's safety is threatened after she repeatedly rebuffs the unwanted advances of Doug, the local law enforcement officer whose sanity and stability are slipping away. At Doug's mercy, Jennifer faces violence and assault during a series of events that culminate in the death of Doug and the potentially fatal stabbing of the Tait's son, David, leaving Kyle to return to an empty, blood-stained home before finally reuniting with his family.

Daunting Days of Winter begins the day of Kyle's miraculous reunion with his family and takes you further into the experience of post-EMP America. Enjoy the adventure.

1859

The impact of an EMP on the modern world would change life beyond imagination for the average "civilized" person. It would take us back to a time before electricity, computer chips, and satellite communication. It would take us back to a year like 1859.

In the century and a half since 1859, the world has seen change on a scale inconceivable to any previous generation of people. We've progressed from man, wind, and animal powered forms of transportation, to cars, airplanes, nuclear submarines, and space shuttles. Health and medicine have progressed from bleedings and wooden teeth to heart transplants, genetic engineering, and brain surgery. The availability of knowledge has transitioned from elementary primers that remained current for decades, to computer tablets that store thousands of books, update daily, and show live video feeds from around the world.

And yet, the citizens of 1859 saw change as well. Trains began to challenge steamboats for commercial superiority, electrification was being developed (though the first public generating station wouldn't be built until 1881), dental hygiene improved with the patent of the toothbrush in 1857, and medical and scientific breakthroughs were occurring at a breakneck pace around the globe.

For the average citizen, however, everyday life wasn't much different from what it had been when Columbus crossed the oceans or King Arthur's knights roamed the countryside. Life expectancy was just over forty years for a newborn child, three in ten children died before the age of fifteen, and a woman who bore eight children (a common family size for those times due to the manpower needed for the family farm and ineffective birth control) stood a better than ten percent chance of dying during childbirth. Two-thirds of all men worked as farmers, clearing the land, sowing by hand, and herding the animals, as well as helping to provide the local defense. These farmers were supported by a spouse who, in addition to helping in the fields, spent a large portion of her day cooking, sewing, teaching, mending, washing, hauling water, doctoring children and animals, gardening, and taking the wagon to the general store.

Compared to today, life was difficult and challenging in a host of ways. The Oregon Trail was the transcontinental highway of the time, having been used, at that point, by nearly 400,000 brave pioneers who walked or rode in a wagon across the continent, many who would end up buried in unmarked graves along the way. That same trail would continue to be used for another decade by immigrants heading for Oregon, California, Utah, and other places in the West, until the first transcontinental railway was completed in 1869.

Bank robbers and highway bandits plied their trade during these years with relative immunity, escaping afterwards into the unmapped and uninhabited countryside or to towns where word of their deeds hadn't reached. On those occasions when the law did catch up with these outlaws, justice was swift and harsh, and often at the end of a hangman's noose.

Diets were bland and variety was limited. Farm animals provided the protein, supplemented mainly by whatever could be grown locally, usually corn, potatoes, apples, grains, and a few other staples. Soups and breads were regularly served in most households, while ice cream, chocolate, potato chips, and Coca

Cola either hadn't been created yet or were such luxuries that the average person had never experienced them.

Clothing was typically handmade and passed down from one child to the next, and furs were often worn out of practicality, not as a fashion statement.

Mail delivery was slow, unreliable, and inefficient, making long distance communication difficult. The Pony Express, offering Missouri to California delivery in the unbelievable time span of just ten days and achieved by way of 120 riders using 400 horses and covering 1,900 miles, wouldn't begin its eighteen months of operation until the next year, in April of 1860.

Politically, James Buchannan was president, Oregon was admitted into the Union, and a fifty-year old lawyer named Abraham Lincoln was building his reputation as a presidential candidate. An English naturalist named Charles Darwin, who few in America had heard of, published a book proposing a radical theory on the origin of species. And John Brown, a militant reformer, tossed a proverbial match into the gas can of slavery by way of a failed uprising at Harper's Ferry, Virginia, paying with his life just six weeks later at the conclusion of a short trial.

One other event from 1859 also deserves mention. On September 1st of that year, Robert Carrington, while watching the sky from his private observatory in London, observed a flare on the sun of such unusual brightness and intensity that he diagramed and made note of the event. For the next two days after the flare, the world was awash in unusual phenomena. Northern Lights, observed as far south as Jamaica, were so bright in parts of America that tradesmen, lacking watches and alarm clocks, went to work thinking it was morning, and people across the Northern Hemisphere believed neighboring towns to be on fire. Even birds were fooled into thinking that it was daytime and began singing during the night.

A few telegraph operators witnessed sparks leaping from their equipment, while others saw papers ignite. In Boston, operators unplugged their telegraph equipment batteries and were still able to operate on the current provided by the aurora. In other areas, telegraph wires shorted out and fell to the ground, triggering isolated wildfires.

The solar anomaly of 1859, a mild curiosity at the time, has since become known as the Carrington Event and has been determined to be the most powerful geomagnetic storm on record. Because the world was technologically primitive at the time, the impact was limited to a heightened aurora, damaged telegraph equipment, and some unexpected shocks for a few telegraph operators.

Historically, such storms occur about once every hundred years. If one were to happen today, most scientists predict that the impact would be similar to that of a global scale EMP, causing trillions of dollars in damage worldwide. Beyond the damage and the dollars, however, the loss of our electrical and computer infrastructure would be devastating. It would impact the world significantly, and send every nation back in time, perhaps to a lifestyle not unlike that of 1859.

CHAPTER ONE

Friday, November 18th
Deer Creek, MT

Kyle gently stroked the back of Jennifer's hand. "I still can't believe I'm actually home. I've dreamed about this so many times that I'm terrified I'm going to wake up." Emotions remained close to the surface.

Jennifer laughed. "You keep saying that. We're real, Kyle. Believe it. Our family really is back together again." She grabbed his hand, squeezing warmly with both of hers and kissing the back of it. Spencer had fallen asleep on the couch between them with his head resting in Kyle's lap, and he stirred, mumbling something that neither of them could make out, then wiggled his shoulders and drifted off to sleep again.

"He's gotten taller."

Jennifer nodded. "You said the same thing about Emma and David. Also told us we all look skinnier. But you can say it again if you want. You can say anything at all, as long as you promise never to be gone again." She could feel tears bubbling up and dabbed at her eyes as her voice trailed off.

Kyle squeezed his wife's hand and rubbed her foot with his. He tried to make eye contact with her, but she was looking out the small window, staring at the sliver of a moon that hung in the night sky. "Don't worry. I don't ever plan on being away from you again. Besides, my legs are so tired from walking, I don't think I could go another mile, especially if it's away from you."

Jennifer let out a long, deep breath and closed her eyes, pressing Kyle's hand against her cheek. "Your hands are rough. I don't remember them being like this," she said, her voice soft and sleepy.

"You should have seen the blisters I had the first few weeks. I didn't realize how soft I was before all this happened."

"I like them. I know why they're rough; it means something to me." Jennifer tried unsuccessfully to fight off a yawn. "Have I mentioned how good you look with a beard?"

Kyle nodded. "A couple of times. I don't agree, but who am I to question your taste."

Spencer stirred again and moaned, then rubbed his eyes as he shifted positions. Emma sat on the other side of Kyle, leaning against the armrest with one leg draped over Kyle's leg and an arm behind his back.

"I'm tired," Emma said, yawning. "But I don't want to go to bed."

The fire in the fireplace cracked and popped and lit the room in a dancing, honey-yellow hue. "You can stay up as long as you want, Em. It's not every day your dad gets home after walking across the country. He'll be here tomorrow, too. Isn't that wonderful?" Jennifer paused, then continued in a halting voice. "So don't think you have to stay up all night."

"I won't stay up too late," Emma answered. "Just a little while longer."

Kyle turned as David pulled himself out of the recliner he was resting in. "The fire needs more wood," he said as he stood.

"I'll get it, Son. You sit down. Don't strain yourself." Kyle started to gently move Spencer off of him, but David protested.

"I'm fine, Dad. You're just like Mom and Mrs. Jeffries. They worry about me all the time. My wound doesn't really even hurt anymore. I can get the wood. I'm not a cripple."

"I know. I know. But if you tear it open, it could be dangerous. You know as much as anyone what the situation is."

David smiled. "Got it, Dad. You can go back to staring at Mom. I'll put more wood on the fire so there's enough light for you to see her."

"Maybe we don't want the lights on," Jennifer said playfully, her emotions temporarily back under control.

Emma made a gagging sound. "If you guys start kissing again, I'm going to be sick. I've never seen so much kissing in all my life."

"Emma, you're nine," David said as he placed a log on the fire. "I'm guessing you haven't seen much kissing, besides Mom and Dad."

"You're one to talk, David; you don't even have a girlfriend."

"How do you know I don't have a girlfriend? You follow me around all day?"

"Kids. Cut it out," Jennifer said, giving them a look. "Dad didn't walk all this way to listen to you fight. I'm sure he could have stayed in Texas and found some other kids to do that."

Kyle grinned. "This feels normal. Not you guys arguing, well, okay, I guess that is kind of normal, but just being together, talking, listening, touching. This feels normal. It feels right." Kyle choked up, and Jennifer's eyes glistened in the firelight.

"Mom cries a lot too. So don't feel embarrassed," Emma said matter-of-factly. "We've all gotten used to it. Didn't know it was contagious though."

"You're such a ditz, Emma," David said as he returned to his seat. "Mom, why couldn't I have had two brothers?"

Kyle reached out and pulled Emma into him, burying her face in his chest. "Don't say that about my only little girl, David. She might be a ditz, but she's the only ditz I've got, so you'd better treat her well."

Emma let out a muffled yell.

"Am I smothering you?" Kyle asked, relaxing his embrace. "Or is my smell killing you?"

"A little bit of both, actually," Emma said as she leaned back against the armrest. "But you're not the only one who stinks."

Kyle laughed as he tussled her hair. Jennifer leaned forward and glared warmly at her daughter, her lips hinting at a smile. "What? He does kind of smell."

"What's gotten into you, little girl? I can't remember the last time you had this much spunk. Are you feeling alright?"

Emma shrugged. "I'm just glad Dad's home."

"I'm sorry I smell so bad, Em. It's been a few days since I had a bath. For some reason the motels were all closed. Maybe I can get cleaned up a little better tomorrow. Hopefully Carol won't mind if I make an even bigger mess of her bathroom."

"You smell just fine to me," Jennifer said as she leaned back into the couch. "And Carol has repeatedly told us to make ourselves at home here."

"I spit bathed with a wet towel a couple of times this week, but the river was awfully cold, so it was short and sweet. Those clothes I was wearing, they should probably be burned just to keep us safe."

"We're not burning any clothes. We make everything last. We'll set you up with a real bath tomorrow. There's a crew that brings water up from the river every morning. It's not our day for bath water, but I'm sure they'll make an exception. Your showing up here has really made a difference in the mood of the community. I actually saw a lot of people smiling for the first time."

"I think I met most of the community today, but I really don't know these people. How's it been?"

Jennifer shook her head from side to side in a slow and deliberate motion as she searched for the right words. "It's been difficult, but you seem to have given a lot of people hope who had lost it. You– making it back from so far away–it's amazing. I still almost don't believe it. I've prayed for it and dreamt about it, thought about it every hour of every day, but I was losing hope, just like everyone else."

"I prayed for it more than Mom did," Emma interjected in a sleepy voice. "Every night before bed I said my prayers and asked for God to bring you home. Mom said I needed to do that every day."

Kyle rubbed Emma's leg. "I prayed to make it home, too, sweetie, and it had been a long time since I'd said any prayers. I guess God got tired of hearing from us, huh?"

Emma nodded, her eyes barely open. "But He listened, didn't He?"

Jennifer smiled at Kyle as he turned back to her. "Your daughter really missed you. I can see a change in her already." Emma's eyes closed. "This whole thing has been really difficult, Kyle. I know you've been through a lot, walking so far and somehow making it home. But being here every day, seeing our neighbors slowly die, being hungry most of the time, the weather getting colder, and the nights longer..." She shook her head. "It's hard. Sometimes you just want to give up. I think a lot of people had gotten to that point. We had gotten too used to easy; hard is taking some adjusting."

"Do you think we're safe here?"

Jennifer nodded. She glanced at the fire, watching the flames swirl and dance. "We're safer here than any place else I can think of. I think you're the miracle we needed, both for our family and the community. You've reminded us of what a person can do if something is important to them, if they don't let the impossible stand in the way."

"I didn't know what I'd find when I got here, Jenn. You can't imagine how I felt when I found blood in the house." Kyle wiped at his eyes. "But we survived. We're together, and we'll make it. I don't know what it's going to take, but we've got to promise that we'll never give up. Okay?"

"I promise," Jennifer said, her eyes still focused on the flames. "I don't know what it's going to take, but I promise."

"David, do you promise?" Kyle asked his son.

"I promise, Dad. If you can make it home, we can do this."

"How 'bout you, Emma."

Emma nodded, her eyes still closed. She mumbled faintly. "If David can do it, I can. I promise."

Kyle glanced down at Spencer, who was sound asleep and breathing deeply. "How about you, Spence? Are you ready to face whatever comes?"

CHAPTER TWO

Saturday, November 19th
Deer Creek, MT

Unable to sleep, Kyle lay on his back staring at the ceiling as he listened to the steady breathing of his family. Jennifer slept beside him on a hide-a-bed mattress laid out on the basement floor in front of the fireplace. Emma and Spencer slept on cushions from the couch that were placed on the floor beside the mattress, and David slept in the recliner, the same one he'd spent so many hours in recuperating from his stab wound.

Kyle's mind drifted back over the previous eleven weeks. The fact that he was lying beside his wife, in Montana, with all three of his children alive and mostly well and in the same room was almost more than he could believe.

He was thrilled to be home, so thrilled he couldn't sleep. It struck him that for the first time in almost three months he faced a day with no predefined purpose—no town or mile marker to get to before the sun set, no far off family that he was pushing himself to return to. The family was here. The walk was over. And now he wondered if the hard part was the journey he'd just survived or the unknown future ahead of him.

He watched the burned logs in the fireplace, the embers still glowing faintly orange. The room was beginning to chill, but firewood was limited, so Kyle resisted the urge to put another log on the fire. David had explained that while there was plenty of wood in the area, there were limited numbers of saws and axes available to cut and split it. Most of what they were burning at this point was deadfall that was thin and dry enough to break by hand, but once winter intensified, the denser, better wood would be essential.

Kyle rolled onto his side. The foam mattress, while adequate, reminded him of the countless semi-truck bunks he'd slept on over the past weeks, and he made a mental note to retrieve a better mattress from their house in the morning, once he was cleaned up. At least with that he'd have a purpose for the day.

Jennifer was silhouetted in the faint light from the fireplace, and Kyle reached out, putting his hand on her shoulder and giving it a light squeeze. Jennifer jerked and let out a shrill noise, breaking the heavy silence of the night. Before he could react, Kyle felt Jennifer striking him. "Get away from me!" she shrieked. "Get away!"

Kyle shielded his head with his arms and rolled off of the mattress. He heard David's groggy voice and the recliner swing back into the sitting position. "Mom! What's wrong?"

Kyle leapt to his feet, avoiding Emma and Spencer while trying to figure out what was wrong with his wife. "Jenn?" She had stopped yelling but was now gasping loudly. Forgetting about a short coffee table next to him, Kyle took a step backwards to give Jennifer more space and hit his leg on it, sending him tumbling over the table in the darkness. He fell with a dull thud, groaning as he hit the floor.

"Dad, was that you?" David asked. "Mom, are you alright? What's going on?"

"Yeah, that was me, David," Kyle said rubbing his elbow. "I don't know what's going on. Jennifer?"

Jennifer's breathing had slowed. "What happened?" she asked.

"That's what we're trying to find out. You started yelling and hitting me. All I did was put my hand on your shoulder."

"Kyle? I'm sorry."

Kyle heard Jennifer start to cry. "Is there a light or something we can turn on?"

"Just an old flashlight, but it's pretty much dead," David answered. "I can put more wood on the fire if you want, but it will take a few minutes to catch."

Carol called out from up the stairs. "Everything okay down there?"

"I think we're okay. Not sure what happened, but I think we're fine," Kyle answered. He crawled around the table to where Jennifer sat on the floor. "Can I touch you?"

"Yes," Jennifer said in a voice that was barely audible.

"Do you want me to put more wood on the fire?" David asked.

"I think we'll be okay without it. Spencer, Emma, you guys awake?"

There was a sleepy "uh huh." Kyle couldn't tell who it was.

"Sorry we woke you up. Mom just had a bad dream, I think. Go back to sleep." Jennifer was shaking, and Kyle wrapped his arms around her. "Jenn, what's wrong? I've never seen you like this. Are you okay?"

Jennifer rubbed Kyle's arm and laid her head on his shoulder. "You scared me; that's all. Not used to having a man in my bed I guess. Can we just forget about it?"

"You just want me to forget this?" Kyle released his wife and leaned back, trying to read her expression in the inky blackness. His right arm still tingled from the fall, and he flexed his fingers to work out the pain. "I suppose we can for now, as long as you promise not to beat on me again." Jennifer let out a weak laugh, but Kyle noticed a glint of light reflect off her cheek.

Jennifer dabbed at the tear. "I'll try, but I don't know if I can promise you that, at least not yet. Give me time." She spoke in short, halting sentences, fighting to control her emotions.

Kyle took her hand in his and caressed it. "This has something to do with what happened in our house, doesn't it? This is why you won't go back home."

"Kyle, I'm so sorry. It's just...," her emotions overwhelmed her, and she began to sob uncontrollably.

"Jennifer," Kyle said, leaning in close. He wrapped his arms around his wife and held her tight. "Jennifer, please. It's okay. Don't apologize."

"But... it shouldn't...be like... this, Kyle," she sobbed. "It's your first night home, and I'm a basket case. I'm sure this isn't what you expected, or what you deserve after all you've been through."

"Jennifer. Stop. It's okay." He pulled her gently down on the mattress and drew the blanket over her shoulders. "It's getting cold. Let's just try and go back to sleep. I'm already forgetting what happened, just like you asked."

"You thought you were coming home to a normal, stable wife, didn't you?"

Kyle brushed away the strands of Jennifer's hair that rubbed against his face and kissed her on the forehead.

Jennifer drew back a bit. "You thought you were coming home to a normal wife, didn't you?" Her tone was more urgent.

"I didn't know what I would be coming home to." He paused to reflect. "I went eleven weeks with no contact, in a world screwed up beyond recognition. I didn't know what to expect. It was total hell."

"Are you disappointed with us? With me?"

"No! Never! Don't ever think that. Today was the best day of my life. I can't describe how happy I am to be home with you and the kids. I've walked fifteen hours a day for two and a half months, with next to no one to talk to except myself. That gives a person too much time to think. I hoped everything would be perfect and imagined things would be normal, with no problems, but then I would catch myself thinking about far worse outcomes, too. It was a long walk."

"Did you forget mom had me here to take care of her?" David asked, his voice bright and alert.

"Are you listening in on us?" Kyle asked, trying to see David in the darkness. "We're trying to have a private conversation here."

"You're ten feet away. Mom woke up in the middle of the night yelling, and you flipped over a table, and I'm supposed to fall back asleep in two minutes?"

"Well, no, it's just dark, and I forgot you were there. Your sister went right back to sleep."

"No I didn't; I'm still awake." Emma's voice was soft, but alert too.

"You listening in on us, too?"

"I'm not trying to, but you're just right there, talking."

Kyle shook his head. "Spencer?"

"What, Dad?"

"Nothing, bud. Just checking." Kyle laughed. "I may as well have the video camera recording this for posterity."

"Camera doesn't work," Emma piped up.

"Thanks for the information, little girl." Kyle could hear Jennifer giggle beside him, and he laughed, too. "A thousand hours walking, and I can't say that I pictured my first night home like this. And in response to your question, David, I didn't forget you were here to take care of your mother. I knew you were, and you exceeded my expectations."

"Thanks. Hey, wait. Was that a compliment? At first I thought it was nice, but now I'm not sure."

Kyle smiled. "Let's just say, my son who lived for video games, music, and friends has made his father unbelievably proud, as has his sister and little brother. Now how about we try and get some sleep. The sun will be up early."

"No it won't." Emma said. "Night lasts forever. I always wake up before the sun comes up."

"Okay, fine," Kyle said, trying not to laugh. "How about we just try and get some sleep? Good night, everyone."

"Good night," they replied, nearly in unison.

Kyle pulled Jennifer tight against him, feeling her shiver as he did so. He moved his mouth close to her ear and whispered. "You're the most beautiful, wonderful, amazing woman a man could want. There is nothing about you I'd change, except for maybe what you're wearing. I had pictured something a little sexier than sweatpants."

"That's sweet, Dad, but we're not deaf. We can still hear you." David said, fighting to suppress a laugh.

"Yep. We sure can," Emma added. "You can hear everything at night, like Spencer, when he farts all the time. It's disgusting."

"I do not fart all the time, Emma. Don't say that."

Kyle heard Spencer hit his sister.

"Kids!" Jennifer said, nearly shouting. "I am really sorry I woke you up, but it's probably well after midnight. I don't want to kill any of you, so to prevent that, how about everyone quiet down and go back to sleep. Agreed?"

There was a murmur of agreement, and the room became still once again.

CHAPTER THREE

Saturday, November 19th
Deer Creek, MT

The day was overcast and cold, but that didn't deter the steady stream of well-wishers from dropping by to welcome Kyle. Word had spread quickly through the small community and surrounding homes, and Kyle's return, after such an amazing journey, had given him a quasi-celebrity status in the few hours he'd been home. Finally, after recounting his trip home for the ninth time before lunch, Carol hung a note on the front door explaining that Kyle was exhausted from his trip, but that he would share his experiences with everyone at the community meeting the next day.

With the visits halted and Kyle no longer feeling like he needed to spend every minute at Jennifer's side, Kyle began to address his hygiene needs. An extended bath was followed by a haircut, after which Jennifer's sewing scissors were put to good use on his beard. A trip to his house to gather the rest of his clothing had Kyle dressed in familiar clothes and feeling human by dinnertime.

Seated in a patio chair on the front porch, Kyle heard the front door open and looked up to see Jennifer motioning for Spencer to come in. "Looks like it might snow," Kyle said, indicating a front of clouds moving in from the west with a dip of his head.

Jennifer nodded. "It's got that chill. We've only had one big dump so far, plus a couple of skiffs of snow some mornings. Hope winter isn't in any kind of a rush to get here." She followed his gaze. "What are you looking at?"

"I don't know. Just looking. A part of me feels like I should be moving on. That's what I've been programmed to do for so long. It'll take me a few days to get back to normal, whatever that is. Carol's been nice to let you stay here; how long do you think we're welcome?"

"When we moved over, she didn't put a time limit on it. Seemed to indicate we should just plan on staying. Why?"

"That was before I showed up. She doesn't know me, so who knows how long this will work."

"Where do you think we should be?"

"At our house. Most of our stuff is still there. Seems kind of silly to be hauling things this direction."

Jennifer's back stiffened. "You're thinking about moving back home?"

Kyle nodded. "If you give me a couple of days, I'll have things cleaned up good. I've been thinking about it. That's our home, Jenn. It doesn't seem right for us to not be there."

"You don't think I could've cleaned the blood stains?" Jennifer looked at Kyle, incredulous. "I'm not afraid of scrubbing the walls or the carpet. It's not the blood." Jennifer shuddered. "I came to tell you dinner's ready. It's beef stew. Let's eat, it should be good."

CHAPTER FOUR

Wednesday, November 23rd
Deer Creek, MT

Kyle walked south, along the bank of the small creek from which the community got its name. The creek was at its smallest size this time of year, a slow trickle barely four feet across at the wider points. The channel itself, which had been cut over the centuries, was over thirty feet wide and a good eight feet below where Kyle walked. Water flow was steady and reliable, but because the creek emerged from the valley directly into the Shipley Ranch and through their cow pastures, the water was unsuitable for most everything but irrigation. Still, with the steady supply of water, the vegetation in the creek bottom and along the banks flourished, and the creek was lined with tall trees, including native pines and firs, along with a variety of maples, cottonwoods, poplars and fruit trees that had been planted by the residents who owned the surrounding land.

The thick vegetation was inviting to wildlife, and while raccoon and beaver were a nuisance year round, deer, antelope, and the occasional elk also made appearances in the winter. Black bears were also known to be in the vicinity, and many of the long-term residents had at least one tale to tell of encountering a wandering bear during their time in Deer Creek. Kyle and his family had walked along the creek a few times the previous summer, but had yet to see any of the larger wildlife.

It was the stories of bear sightings that explained the pistol strapped to his waist, but the purpose of the day's journey was to try and bag dinner for Thanksgiving. With his twelve gauge slung across his back, Kyle was heading south into the mountains in search of turkey, if he could find it, or pheasant, if no turkeys could be found.

It had been daylight for forty-five minutes, but the sun was yet to clear the mountains to the west, and the air still held the crisp, icy chill that was common for November. In the few days since his homecoming, the weather had been cold and snowy for a couple of days before warming up to the upper 40's, leaving the ground sloppy and muddy. Most of the snow had melted off the day before, but this morning it was cold, and Kyle's breath was visible as he walked.

A path led to the creek bottom, and Kyle followed it. He crossed the creek on a fallen log before tracing the path back up the far bank. The barbed wire fence marking the north boundary of the Shipley Ranch was just ahead, and Kyle slipped through, briefly snagging his jacket on the wire before tugging loose. As he continued south along the creek bank, he could see a half-dozen men attacking large, round bales of hay with pitchforks, then hauling the loose feed to the fields where it was quickly consumed by the hungry and impatient herd.

Kyle waved to the foreman as he crossed the pasture. David would soon be working on the ranch again, his position held for him by Mr. Shipley while he fully recovered from his stab wound. Kyle had added his name to the list of people willing to work at the ranch, but currently there were more available hands than work to be done, so he was currently without a job.

The morning before he'd gone to his old home to continue salvaging items that would be useful in their new residence at

Carol's, followed by an afternoon of feeling cooped up, making today's jaunt a welcome relief. Ten weeks of walking had gotten Kyle so used to being active that the past few days of hanging around the house, despite the joy of being home, had made him antsy and uncomfortable.

Sunday had been the town meeting where Kyle had spoken and answered questions for over forty-five minutes, giving a recap of his journey and, at Jennifer's suggestion, trying to inspire people to persevere. He wasn't sure how inspirational he'd been, but a lot of people had come up afterwards to shake his hand and thank him.

That had been followed up on Monday with Kyle and David joining the new militia. Sean Reider, the head security person and man putting together the protective force, had announced after Kyle spoke that they had to start organizing and training, and had urged and cajoled as many community members as possible to join. Sean's efforts had been rewarded with fifty-three individuals showing up for the first meeting, ranging in age from David, at fourteen, to Tom Hanson, at sixty-nine. Kyle had been surprised by the number of weapons in the community, but pleased, under the circumstances.

The militia members had been broken out into companies, training had been scheduled, and strategy discussed. Being expected to fight for the community, to prepare to actually shoot at people, was an uncomfortable thought, but Kyle knew that was the only option they had and was likely the only way they'd make it through the winter intact.

Regardless of participating in the militia and his new responsibilities there, it felt good to get out and stretch his legs, and walking without a backpack on or a cart to pull made progress fast and effortless, despite the uneven terrain. The creek meandered back into the mountains, and Kyle followed it for a couple of miles as the sun slowly climbed overhead, finding comfort in the solitude and thickening pine trees, and enjoying the change in scenery from the paved roads he was used to. The creek split, and Kyle followed the narrower arm of it east to where it came tumbling gently down the hillside, splashing between small boulders and tree roots, leaving delicate icicles hanging from the bushes growing along its edges.

Kyle stopped in a small clearing and took his hands from his gloves and rubbed them on his face to warm his cheeks. He listened for the telltale sounds of wild turkey, but heard only the wind as it gently rocked the pine trees back and forth. He glanced back towards Deer Creek and could see sections of the freeway north of it, but the forest hid the community itself. There was a cut in the forest above him, so he headed that direction.

The slope of the mountain was gentle, and with weeks of conditioning and a good breakfast fueling him, the climb was easy and enjoyable. He reached the ridge, about 1,500 feet above the valley floor, followed it for a half mile or so, then dropped down the east side and continued exploring, finding an old logging road near an empty one-room cabin that was missing windows and looked to be decades old, as well as several four-wheeler trails. He saw a few deer off in the distance that, had he had his rifle with him instead of his shotgun, he could have taken, along with a number of pheasants, but no turkey. Kyle stopped occasionally to reset his bearings, then, determined to impress everyone with a turkey, he pressed on.

About six miles south of Deer Creek and deep into the mountains, Kyle found a maintained gravel road and followed it westward, along the south side of the mountain. After a good mile, he was about to head back home when he heard something that sounded very much like a turkey. He stopped and listened. With a lull in the wind, the trees quieted, and he could hear the deep guttural wallowing, the distinct sound of a Tom turkey. He followed the sound further west, stopping every couple minutes to listen.

Kyle noted that the sun was past vertical and on its downward trajectory, and estimated the time to be around 1:30 in the afternoon. He pulled out a small chunk of jerky and tore off a chunk, popping the piece in his mouth as he glanced around for the turkey. As he savored the flavor of the meat, he realized that it actually had little spice, but because of his limited diet of late, that little bit of beef fat seemed like a rare treat. As he chewed, the distinct sound of turkeys came to him again, this time from the south, downhill from where he stood.

Kyle grabbed his shotgun, checked the chamber for a shell, and gingerly climbed through the barbed wire fence that lined the side of the road. The snow on the south-facing slope had mostly melted off, but the undergrowth was thick, forcing Kyle to carefully pick his way downhill in the direction of the noise.

A hundred yards from the road the ground leveled out and the trees thinned. The turkey sounds seemed to come from behind a football field long outcropping of sandstone that lay up ahead of him. Kyle put his gun to his shoulder, eyed the sights, released the safety, and crept forward ready to shoot. Then he heard a different sound, definitely not a turkey. He paused and listened, trying to identify it. It was a bleating sound, like livestock.

As he stood, paused and listening, he detected a faint smoke scent. Kyle sniffed the air, but couldn't be sure. The turkeys wallowed again, definitely from behind the rocks. He crept forward as quietly as he could. A large juniper bush grew alongside the rock outcropping, and Kyle moved silently in behind it. He peered through the bush and noticed movement.

Up ahead, three large turkeys, their feathers fanned out, paced back and forth in a clearing in front of the rock. Kyle raised his shotgun and aimed at the one nearest him. As he was about to pull the trigger, movement in the background caught his attention. He lowered his weapon just as a goat walked towards the turkeys. It had a chain around its neck that was tethered somewhere back towards the rocks. Kyle lowered his gun and stepped out from behind the bush, peering carefully around the rocks.

The goat's chain was attached to a stake embedded in the ground about ten yards from the rock face. A fifty-foot radius around the stake was grazed down and nearly clear of brush. Closer to Kyle, up against the rocks, was a wire cage, ten foot by twenty, where a female turkey and at least half a dozen good-sized chicks were caged, the hen being the obvious object of the male turkeys' attentions. Kyle looked around, searching for further evidence of domestic animals or the presence of people. He saw neither.

Kyle approached the turkey pen, distressing the male turkeys, which circled around behind him making a series of strange, alien-like noises and rushed him when he turned his back. The turkey pen had a thin layer of waste in it, but was otherwise clean and well tended. Kyle looked at the goat, which was eyeing him as it chewed lazily on a clump of dry grass.

"Hello!" Kyle called out, then waited, but there was no answer. He turned his attention back to the male turkeys, which were as large as he could ever remember seeing. Their heads and necks were bright red, and long flaps of skin hung down over their beaks and swung from side to side as they assaulted him vocally. Kyle wondered how something so ugly could taste so good. He grabbed at the closest one, but it retreated beyond his reach as it warbled threats at him.

Kyle looked around again, still not seeing any signs of humanity beyond the obvious ones in front of him. He looked back at the turkeys and thought how nice one of them would taste for dinner. He raised his shotgun again, pointing it at the nearest turkey, but just couldn't pull the trigger. Kyle knew what wild turkeys looked like, and these weren't them. This breed was domestic and obviously belonged to someone.

Kyle lowered his gun and slung it back over his shoulder, took a deep breath, then turned and retraced his steps around the end of the rock outcropping, heading back towards the road. He had just rounded the end of the rocks and turned back to take one last look at the turkeys, which were following him, when a gunshot rang out and a bullet whistled by, ricocheting off the rocks a couple of feet above his head. Kyle dropped to the ground and rolled up against the rocks, then crawled behind the bush he had crouched behind earlier. Another shot rang out, the bullet striking the rock nearby and showering pieces of sandstone on him. Kyle's head swiveled from side to side, trying to locate the shooter.

"Stop shooting!" Kyle shouted. No response came. He looked towards the road, gauging how long it would take him to sprint that far. He pulled his handgun from its holster and turned so that when he leapt to his feet he'd be moving in the right direction. He was about to make his move when a voice called out.

"Drop the gun and stand up." It was a man's voice and came from somewhere in the trees, not too far distant.

Kyle weighed his options. He realized he'd been pretty vague with Jennifer about where he was headed, and if something were to happen to him, there was no way help would show. He tried to figure out where the gunman was.

"I'm not going to shoot you," the man called out to him. "If I was, you'd have been dead fifteen minutes ago when you squeezed through the fence at the road. Drop your shotgun and pistol and stand up, then I'll show myself."

The voice came from behind a clump of bushes forty yards away. Kyle could make out a shape, but was unsure if he was seeing a person or a rock. He quickly weighed his options, then pushed up onto his knees, took his shotgun off, and laid it on the ground, then put his pistol down beside it. He looked back towards the bushes and cautiously rose to his feet.

Kyle waited, but nothing happened. He crossed his arms and nervously leaned back against the rocks. He waited in that position for a couple of minutes until a man slowly emerged from behind the bush, followed closely by a German shepherd. The man carried a military-style assault weapon and wore tan pants and a large camouflage jacket. A green wool hat was pulled down over his ears, and a full beard, more gray than black, covered his face. A pair of glasses glinted in the sunlight.

The man approached slowly, and the dog ran ahead of him, approaching Kyle with a deep, threatening growl that sent shivers down Kyle's spine. Kyle looked from the man, down to his own guns on the ground beside him, then at the dog, which was now just a few feet away.

"Don't make any sudden moves, and the dog won't hurt you. If you go for your gun you'll lose an arm," the man said in a matter of fact tone. "Stand still while Copper sniffs you for weapons."

The dog hit on Kyle's pocket and growled again. "Do you have another weapon?" the man demanded.

Kyle shook his head. "I have more shells for my shotgun, but that's it."

Kyle was instructed to put the shells on the ground. The dog sniffed him again, then returned to his owner and lay down on the ground.

The man crouched and rubbed the dog's head. "Why are you up here?" he asked as he stood back up.

"I was hoping to find a wild turkey, for Thanksgiving dinner tomorrow. I didn't realize I was trespassing. Thought this was all National Forest land."

"It is for the most part. I have a ninety-nine year lease on the land. What's your name, and where did you come from?"

"Kyle Tait. From Deer Creek." Kyle began to relax a little. "Who are you, and do you mind not holding me at gunpoint?"

The man looked down, realizing his gun was still pointed at Kyle. He lowered the muzzle towards the ground. "Sorry about that. Can't be too careful nowadays. Not a lot of law and order to be found. My name's Frank Emory." He coughed a couple times, then turned to the side and spit. "Why didn't you shoot my turkey?" he asked as he wiped his mouth with the back of his hand.

Kyle shrugged. "I could tell they weren't wild birds. I'm not desperate, so I'm not going to kill someone else's animals." Kyle paused a second. "If my family was starving, I'd have shot it. We're lucky. We're not there, at least not yet."

Frank smiled for the first time. "You're honest, boy, on multiple fronts. I respect that. Did you prep for all this?"

Kyle looked confused, and Frank restated the question. "You said your family isn't starving. Were you ready for the EMP attack? You must have known it was coming."

Kyle shook his head. "No. Can't claim to have done anything to prepare for this, unfortunately. Guess we got lucky and bought a house in the right place. You? You look pretty prepared."

"Damn right I'm prepared. Spent the last eight years getting ready. Would have liked to have a couple more, but yeah, we're in good shape."

"We?"

"You're asking too many questions. Maybe I got a militia. Maybe I have five sons with their guns leveled on you right now. Maybe I ..."

"Oh Frank, relax. This one's harmless." A female voice came from above and behind Kyle, startling him.

Kyle lurched away from the rocks and jerked his head over his shoulder, causing Copper to growl and spring to his feet, ready to lunge.

"Down Copper!" Frank ordered. The dog slowly lowered back down to the ground. "You surprised him, Brenda. Good thing Copper's on his best behavior today. Kyle, this is my wife, Brenda; she's part of the we."

Brenda scaled nimbly down the rocks and dropped to the ground beside Kyle. "Hi Kyle," she said, extending her hand. "It's nice to meet you." She smiled brightly and seemed sincerely pleased to meet Kyle. Brenda was short, just a little over 5', with short blonde hair, freckles that covered a nose that was bent noticeably to one side, gray eyes and dimpled cheeks. She wore tan pants and a camo jacket similar to Frank's, but had a much slimmer build than her husband. Her jacket was unzipped, and Kyle could see a leather holster holding a weapon in addition to the assault rifle slung across her back.

Kyle took off his glove and shook her hand. "Nice to meet you, too," he said.

"Can I get you something to eat?" she offered. "I know you said you weren't desperate, but you sure don't look to be packing any extra weight either."

"I'm fine, really," Kyle said. "But I appreciate the offer."

"You have kids, Kyle?"

He nodded.

"Wait here. I'll be back in a minute." She smiled at Frank and headed down the hill.

"Damn woman's too nice," muttered Frank. "I try and scare the hell out of people, and she's Mrs. Claus. Don't let here fool you though, she's a better shot than I am. She can take down a deer at over a thousand yards."

"Can I pick my guns up?" Kyle asked.

"Do you like your arms, the ones attached to your shoulders?"

Kyle nodded.

"Then I suggest you leave your weapons there. You can take them when you leave, but for now it's best that only I'm armed. You are on my property after all."

"Fair enough," Kyle answered, less nervous but still wary. "So what all do you have here, Frank. I can't see much beyond a few animals, but eight years of prepping is a lot of time. You must have quite a bit."

"Kind of nosy, aren't you?"

Kyle shrugged. "Just making conversation."

"That's not information you need to have."

"Sorry. Forget that I asked. Can I ask how you knew this was going to happen?"

"You can ask that. Let's go sit down." Frank motioned Kyle around the front of the rock outcropping to a dry patch of grass where he could sit. Frank sat on a rock, and Copper lay down at his feet. "How much do you want to know?"

"I don't know, enough to make sense, I guess."

"Hmm," Frank stroked his beard as he thought. "I guess the beginning it is." Frank leaned forward, looking directly at Kyle. "You have any military experience?"

Kyle shook his head.

"I do. Joined straight out of high school. My dad and grandfather were army, so I decided that was the place for me. I spent time in Kuwait, helping to kick Saddam Hussein's ass out of that country. Stupid Iraqi army had no idea what hit them. Anyway, after that they thought I was smarter than some of the other grunts, so they sent me to school, and I ended up in military intelligence. Last ten years there I was analyzing the Middle East and its threats. You do that long enough and you understand that we're screwed."

"That's a bleak assessment, don't you think?" Kyle asked before catching himself. "Of course, I guess we kind of are screwed, aren't we?"

"Five months ago people laughed at me when I shared my concerns. 'America this, America that,' they would say. And they were right, to an extent. We had an amazing military, still do for the most part, but they didn't understand our enemy. The damn Muslims don't think like we do. When mothers send their own sons out to blow themselves up, then celebrate when they do, that's an enemy that should scare the stuffing out of you."

"Scare the stuffing out of you?"

Frank shrugged. "Brenda doesn't like me to swear. I have to use substitutes."

"Got it."

"Anyway, when the women think like that, that's one screwed up culture. The leaders have no constraints. They can put their soldiers or the entire flipping country at risk."

Kyle snickered.

"Shut up, Kyle. I could blow your damn head off if I wanted to."

Kyle looked at Frank and raised his eyes.

"She lets me say damn," he replied. "And hell, too. So I hope I don't offend you with my French."

"I'm sorry," Kyle said, trying to hide his amusement. "Please continue."

Frank cleared his throat and spit again. "I can stop talking, if you'd like. We can just sit here and wait for Brenda."

"No, no. Please. Go on."

Frank wiped at his nose. "You need to excuse me. My system doesn't love this cold weather. But as I was saying, the Muslims don't think like us. They are willing to sacrifice everything in this life, for the promise of what's in the next. When you couple that with an absolute hatred of the West, it was obvious to me that they would forever do everything they could to bring us down, and an EMP was their best shot to get us. They paid a heavy price, but what do they care. They're up there with Allah."

"What kind of a price? I haven't heard any news for weeks."

"About three weeks ago the CIA traced the ship that launched the bomb back to Iran. Once we had sufficient proof, we went in there hard. Unloaded a hell of a lot of missiles on them. Any place suspected of having anything to do with their government or military is now a pile of rubble. Israel had already taken out Syria and Egypt and kicked Iran between the legs, but now with Tehran gone, the whole Middle East is in chaos. I sure as hell would hate to live in Israel right now, because there's a butt load of angry Arabs. Those Jews always seem to be able to handle themselves though." Frank laughed for a second. "To be honest, I bet right now the Jews are pretty glad that they aren't Americans. At least they've got flush toilets and electricity."

"So how did you end up here? Missoula isn't exactly a hotbed for military intelligence."

"I put my twenty years in, qualified for retirement, and got out. I was tired of all the PC bullcrap. Couldn't say squat about the Muslims anymore." He shook his head in disbelief. "Those damn Jihadists are our number one enemy, the ones we've spent over a decade at war with, and we have to go to sensitivity training classes to make sure we don't say anything to hurt their feelings. And it wasn't just that."

The turkeys had come around after fleeing the earlier gunfire, and Frank threw a couple of rocks to shoo them away. He took a cough drop from his pocket, unwrapped it slowly, and put it in his mouth before continuing with his story. "To top it all off was the whole gay issue. They got rid of the 'don't ask, don't tell' policy, which was tolerable, but all of a sudden there's a concerted outreach to homosexuals, and I just couldn't take it. I know I sound like a bigot, and maybe I am, but that was too much. I don't care what a person does in their bedroom. Hell, a couple of the best analysts I worked with seemed to bat left-handed. But as soon as they dropped that policy, the military became some big social experiment. Gays needed to be hired, gays needed to be promoted, gays needed to be on all the important analyst teams. Everything was being re-oriented. Being straight became bad for your career. Once I knew the date I qualified for retirement, I gave notice and was gone. We were all happy. I was out, and they could hire a homosexual who liked Islam."

Kyle noticed Brenda coming back up the hill. "My brother was in the service. They put him through college, then he put in the years he needed to pay that off and left. He didn't love his military experience either, but not sure it was for the same reasons."

"It's so frustrating," Frank said as he threw another rock at the turkeys. "We have so much might. We dominate the world, but it's run by politicians, not soldiers. I really don't care that much about gays, but the politicians want to look good for the voters, not do the hard things needed to win militarily. Affirmative action isn't the best policy for defense of the country. That has to be merit based, and even then there's no guarantee. I left when I knew our leaders didn't have the spine to do what needed to be done, that they'd leave us vulnerable while the Jihadists plotted behind their backs. What a waste of a good country." The contempt in Frank's voice was thick.

"Hi Boys," Brenda said, rejoining them. "What are you two talking about? You didn't get him going on politics, did you?" she asked Kyle as she handed him a small package.

"I suppose I did," he answered. "I asked him what made him get so prepared."

"It's like taking a sip from a fire hose, isn't it?"

Kyle nodded.

"We don't get a lot of visitors up here, so Frank tries to get as much talking in as possible when the opportunity arises."

"I can understand. I spent a few weeks alone on the road. It feels good to talk." Kyle turned back to Frank. "So what did you do when you got out of the service?"

"Border patrol. My background made it easy for me to get hired. I'd found this property a few years before leaving the military, then got myself assigned to the Canadian border. Four and a half years ago I was in an accident and lost the sight in my left eye and hurt my back, so they retired me on disability. I do, or I guess did, custom ammo to make some extra money, so between that, my disability and retirement, and Brenda's income as a nurse, we did fine. We didn't have any debt and put everything extra into the property."

"The one problem," Brenda said. "Is that it's lonely, and too quiet. We chose this place because the remoteness made it safer, but I do miss people."

"You'll have to come visit down in Deer Creek. It's a small community, but it's safe, and there are good people there. I didn't take a direct path here, but I don't think it's too far."

"Seven miles on foot," Frank answered. "Almost ten if you drive. There's an old dirt road that winds around that you can take, but the only decent road around here goes south and takes you the back way into Missoula."

"Do you have any neighbors?"

Brenda shook her head. "There are a few cabins, but they're all seasonal. Summertime is busy between them and the campers at the lake that's a few miles down the road, but by the time hunting season is over, it's quiet. This year especially so."

"I can imagine. Listen," Kyle said, glancing at the sun. "I should probably be on my way. I hear it's seven miles back home, and I'm not familiar with the route. It's probably best that I get home before it gets too dark."

Frank rose from the rock he sat on and groaned as he straightened his back. "It was good meeting you, Kyle. If you're back up this way and can find us, feel free to stop in."

Brenda smiled and nodded. "It was good to see a different face. I love Frank, but a little variety now and then is nice. I hope you like Oreos." Brenda spoke in a rapid, staccato pace, and Kyle had a hard time breaking in. "I put a sleeve of them in the bag, along with a couple of MREs. You look so skinny."

Kyle grinned. "My kids will be ecstatic." He thanked them for their generosity, got directions for the most direct route, then began the journey home, bagging two pheasants and a rabbit along the way.

CHAPTER FIVE

December
Deer Creek, MT

After the euphoria of Kyle's first weeks home lessened, life in Deer Creek soon settled into a boring routine. Having been absent from the community for the first months of the crisis, and with all of the essential jobs taken, Kyle struggled to keep himself busy. He participated in militia training three time each week and took regular hunting trips, but the training only took twelve hours a week, and with the deer population thin and Shipley beef available, it didn't make sense to haul a deer five miles on foot strictly for the sake of having something to do.

With forest fires being a concern for the next year's fire season, the community organized a cutting crew to clear a hundred foot ring around Deer Creek, and Kyle worked on the crew for the two weeks it took to complete the project. What would have taken a pair of bulldozers a day or two to complete instead took a team of sixteen men two weeks to finish. It was hard, difficult work, but was greatly aided by two teams of four horses that were used to both pull the felled trees to town after they were de-limbed and to pull the stumps from the ground once the roots were cut.

Days were short from a daylight sense, but long from a work perspective. With Deer Creek being a rural area, Kyle was surprised at how few axes were available. The first day the roar of chainsaws echoed through the mountains, but by the end of the day the fuel was exhausted and the balance of the work became an act of manual labor. After a thorough petition of the residents, the community had only been able to round up a total of twelve axes, four hatchets, a pair of two man saws that had hung decoratively over barn doors, and a handful of wood saws, hacksaws, and heavy pruning shears.

One of the retired veterans had spent a day combining an electric grinder with an exercise bike so blades could be sharpened each night, a two-person job requiring one to peddle while the other honed the blades. By the time the firebreak was finished, the axes were coming out razor sharp each morning and making quick work of the trees.

The tree project had been beneficial on a number of fronts, the most obvious being the town's safety. Additionally, it had helped the men get to know each other outside the militia and had provided a huge source of fuel for the homes that had woodstoves or fireplaces, to which all the residents had combined and relocated to for the winter months.

Felled trees were hauled to a central location, cut in sixteen-inch lengths, then split and stacked to season. Deadfall was cut and stacked separately so that the already dry wood could be burned first. Half of the gathered wood was divided among the sixteen men on the cutting crew. The balance went to a community pile to be sold, traded, or given away, depending on the needs of the residents or outsiders who came to do business. The residents of the home where the wood was stored were put in charge of wood security and disbursement, in exchange for an allotment of wood after giving a weekly accounting to the community board.

One thing that had amazed Kyle since arriving home, and even on his journey, was the improvised economy that was sprouting up and how people were coping. In Deer Creek, the important barter items were food, wood, gasoline, and labor. Thanks to the cattle at the Shipley Ranch, no one there would starve, though diets would be protein heavy. With the forest around them, wood was readily available as well. Gasoline was worth its weight in gold, leaving labor as the most often exchanged commodity.

Beyond the commodity items, there were a host of other tradable goods and services. Ammunition wasn't as big a commodity as Kyle had expected it to be, though much of that had to do with the fact that hunting wasn't essential, and Sean Reider, militia head, encouraged conserving ammo as much as possible for defensive uses. 22LR shells were abundant, but there weren't so many of any other caliber that they could be shot indiscriminately. Once the weapons were sighted in, target practice was rare and limited mostly to 22s.

What little propane was left in the community was now being strictly allocated to hot water heater use. Dan Livingston, an enterprising resident with a cistern and generator, had found enough material over the past few weeks to get both his water pump and water heater going, which meant there was one home in the community that could be used as a bath house. It wasn't luxurious by any means, but it did allow for people to trade for up to three short, but hot, showers a week. Payment was made in propane, food, wood, gas, or labor, the labor used for relocating propane tanks, hauling in water, cleaning showers, or whatever else Dan needed done. It was apparent, to whoever cared to observe, that Dan was quickly becoming wealthy by Deer Creek standards.

What made a person wealthy had been redefined. There were a few silver coins and one-ounce pieces floating around the community, but since you couldn't eat them or burn them, they were of little value to the average resident. Dan Livingston, the shower man, Bryan Shipley, the rancher, Anderson West, whose well stocked construction business hosted Sunday meetings, Carol Jeffries, the doctor, and Kyle's neighbor, Grace, along with Gabe

Vance, who were both Mormons and had followed their church's counsel to store quantities of non-perishable food, were the individuals who could best be described as the wealthy, though that was all relative at this point.

Kyle felt good about how his family was fairing. Jennifer taught on a regular basis at school, he and David were both part of the militia and able to do a lot of the physical jobs that were available, plus David had his job back working for the Shipleys. Grace and her food supply had relocated to Carol Jeffries' home with the Taits, so they had food, shelter, medical care, and good companionship. Once spring rolled around, Grace's expertise in gardening would be a huge boon to the community, but none would benefit more than the Taits, as Emma and Spencer could be put to work to help provide much needed food resources.

Life wasn't anywhere near perfect, but all things considered, Kyle and Jennifer were feeling lucky.

CHAPTER SIX

Thursday, December 22nd
Deer Creek, MT

A week had passed since the completion of the wood-clearing project, and Kyle had moved on to his next work assignment. Within the militia, the organization had changed somewhat, and Sean asked for volunteers to work overnight patrols on a permanent basis rather than rotating teams through the less desirable overnight shifts. Unable to find regular work at the ranch, the area's biggest employer, Kyle leapt at the opportunity to have something permanent to do. The opportunity came with increased meat allowances and extra showers for his family, and that, along with adequate wood for the winter, put them in a comfortable position.

The nights on shift were long and cold. According to the calendar it was December 22nd, and the time from sundown to sunrise was at its longest duration. Factor in the impact of the mountains around the community and daylight in Deer Creek was in unusually short supply. And while the community didn't have a curfew, the lack of lighting and the colder winter temperatures meant most people were inside to stay once the sun dropped behind the mountains. Most people, that is, except the nighttime militia.

Kyle knocked on the door of the house that had become the militia's de-facto garrison. "Who's there?" came the voice from inside.

"Seahawks," Kyle replied. It had been decided that they should use code words to add a layer of security and give warning if a non-militia person approached the house or one of the patrols in the dark. With NFL team names being familiar to all of the men, Seahawks, Broncos, Cowboys, Patriots, and Colts had been adopted by the various militia teams.

Kyle heard the deadbolt, then the door opened, and he was let inside. He removed his gloves and briskly rubbed his hands together as he moved over to the fireplace. "Cold one out there tonight," Kyle said, to no one in particular. "Thermometer says 25 degrees, but the wind makes it feel worse."

Kyle had just finished his first patrol, and Ty Lewis was bundling up to take his place. "How cold do you think it'll get?" Ty asked. Ty was thirty-two years old and had been a science teacher at a high school in Missoula. He had moved to Montana from Atlanta a year before the Taits, fulfilling his childhood dream of living in the Rocky Mountains. "My body isn't built for these cold temperatures. Should have listened to my mom and stayed in Georgia." Ty said it with a grin, but Kyle couldn't help but think there was some truth to it. Not only was the Montana weather tough if you weren't used to it, but Kyle wondered how bad the culture shock had been for Ty, as a black man in Montana. Additionally, it hadn't been very long since Ty and his wife had gone through the pain of losing their seven year-old daughter, who had drowned while on a family vacation over the summer. Their family had just barely returned from her funeral in Georgia when the EMP hit. Ty had been through a lot, but was still amazingly positive and easy to be around.

"Just wait until winter really gets here," Kyle said, unzipping his coat.

"We were here last year, so unfortunately I know what to expect. I'll see you in an hour." He pulled his hat on, and let himself out the front door.

Kyle dead-bolted the door, picked up a book, and dropped into the chair by the fire to read. The house the garrison used was located on the extreme western edge of town, between the two roads leading into Deer Creek. It was an old, two-story farmhouse, and had been the residence of the family who had first farmed the area. It had sat empty for more than a dozen years, but its location and the presence of a wood-burning fireplace made it the perfect set-up for the militia. The windows of the upstairs bedrooms had clear views of both roads coming into Deer Creek, providing a good vantage point for the watchmen positioned at the windows each night. A third man watched the roads while walking the loop from the house, to the bridge, to the barricade on the east road leading to Missoula, and back to the house.

The night shift consisted of the three men monitoring the roads, four doing loops like Kyle and Ty were, another stationed at the Shipley Ranch, and the ninth hunkered down in the lookout spot up the mountain. The men on duty took turns rotating through the assignments. Of the tasks, Kyle preferred walking the perimeter, his body and mind accustomed to the walking and the solitude.

After twenty-five minutes, the next patrol arrived back at the garrison, gave the password, and Kyle was off on his next round. The route was pretty standard. East along the river to the mountain, southwest for a mile and a half to the ranch's fence, west to the mountain, then northwest back to the garrison. Each night the direction of the route was chosen based on a coin toss, with the men walking the same paths and seeing the same scenery, just from a different angle.

Kyle was a little over halfway through the loop and passing the firewood lot when he heard a noise. He brought his gun to the ready position, and stopped to listen. Occasionally he'd come across a raccoon on his rounds and thought that might be the case, but wasn't sure.

Kyle cupped his hand to his mouth. "Anyone there?" he called out. No answer. "Anyone there?" he called again, this time a little louder. Still no answer, and no animals scurrying away.

Kyle began to walk back between the piles of wood. He shuffled his feet and kicked at pieces of wood to make noise, hoping to scare off any animals that might be hiding. The woodpiles were six feet high and stacked in rows that were twenty feet long. The faint light from the crescent moon made dim shadows play tricks on his eyes. Twice he was ready to shoot at what he thought were black bears, before realizing it was just shadows he was seeing. Kyle had just rounded a corner to walk the narrow aisle between two stacks of wood when there was a scrambling sound, and a wall of logs collapsed on him, knocking him sideways.

He spotted a dark figure emerging from the shadows as he fell, which threw an armload of wood at Kyle, then took off running towards the river. The wood wasn't heavy, and in a matter of seconds, Kyle had extracted himself and his weapon from the pile and was pursuing the figure out of the woodlot. He chased the figure across a horse pasture, then through the trees along the creek bank. Kyle had closed the gap to ten feet when the figure jumped down the bank, ran across the ice on the creek, and began to climb the opposite bank.

Kyle, yelling "stop" at the person throughout the chase, paused a second, jumped down the creek bank and followed across the creek, catching the runner by the foot when he slipped climbing the far bank.

"Leave me alone!" the man cried breathlessly.

Kyle pulled him by the ankle, jerking him down from the top of the creek bank. The man kicked out with his free foot and caught Kyle solidly on the side of the knee, dropping Kyle to the ground. Kyle let out a pained yell, but didn't release his grip on the man's ankle. He twisted hard, spinning the man around onto his side. Kyle lunged at the man's head, but caught a fist on his own cheek instead.

Kyle grunted, tasted blood in his mouth, and moved his hands to protect his head. The man beneath him swung again, the blow grazing off of Kyle's ear in the dark. Kyle steadied himself. He was straddling the man's torso and could see the arms swinging at him again. Kyle deflected the blow, then unloaded a series of punches to the man's face. After four solid blows, the man quit fighting back. Flooded with anger, Kyle was pulling back for one last punch when he heard another voice nearby.

"What's going on down there?"

Kyle immediately recognized Ty's voice. "I'm over here," he answered. The man he sat on moaned and shifted beneath him. Kyle unclenched his fist and frisked the man, then got up and retrieved his own weapon from where he'd dropped it.

"Is that you, Tait?"

Kyle could see Ty walking on the creek bank above him. "Yeah, it's me." Kyle pointed his gun at the man on the ground. "You have any weapons?"

The man groaned but didn't respond verbally. Kyle knelt down and frisked him again, finding only a small pocketknife and a dead flashlight.

Twenty minutes later, Kyle stood in Gabe Vance's living room with Sean Reider and the wood thief, Dale Briggs. Dale wiped blood from a cut below his left eye with a damp rag that Lori Vance had given him as Kyle explained what had happened.

Gabe looked at Dale and shook his head. "Anything to say for yourself?" he asked.

Dale shook his head.

"Go home, Dale," Gabe said. "It would have been easier for you to go cut down a tree."

"I don't have an axe," Dale mumbled as he turned towards the door and let himself out.

Kyle looked at Gabe, embarrassed. "Sorry about disturbing you like this. Guess it wasn't that big a deal."

"You're fine," Gabe said, waving his hand. "I wasn't sleeping that well anyway, and that kid deserved to get his butt kicked. Maybe it will knock some sense into him."

"I've never seen him before," Kyle said. "Thought maybe he was a looter from out of town."

Gabe shook his head. "No, well, yes. I guess he is a looter, but he's one of ours. His mother is Lois Briggs. Good lady. Teaches with your wife at the school. She's a single mom, and Dale's her youngest. She worked for an architect in town while Dale went to college. He graduated a couple of years ago with a degree in literature, but a job was never handed to him, so he just hung out at home being a nuisance to his mother. She makes excuses for him. Says he has depression, but I think he's just a lazy bum."

Sean zipped up his jacket. "I tried to talk him into joining the militia, but he went off on a tirade about guns. Glad now he didn't join. We don't need to have some kid there to babysit."

Gabe nodded. "You're better off without him. It would take two guys to hold his hand. I should probably be nicer, but he ticks me off. Doesn't help his mother at all, and I know she splits what food she gets with him, so she's going without. Stealing that wood was probably the most initiative he's taken in the last year. Maybe there's hope."

CHAPTER SEVEN

Thursday, December 29th
South of Deer Creek

Kyle cupped his hands around his mouth and shouted. "Hello!" He waited and listened, but only the turkeys trailing behind him responded. He waited a few seconds more and called again. This time he heard a dog bark, and he retreated to a rock outcropping, climbing on top.

Copper bounded up the hill, heading straight for the boulder that Kyle was perched on. "Copper, sit!" Kyle commanded, but the dog ignored him, circling the rock and growling. Kyle looked down the hill and saw Frank walking warily towards him, his gun drawn.

Frank shouted something and Copper quit pacing and sat down.

"Kyle!" Frank exclaimed when he got close. "I'm sorry. My vision's not so good; I should have recognized you," he said as he lowered his gun. "Get down off that rock. Copper probably won't eat you; I've already fed him today."

Kyle watched the dog as he cautiously climbed down. Copper growled but didn't move towards him.

"What brings you to these parts?"

It was late December, unseasonably warm, and Kyle, who worked ten days on and four days off, was in the middle of his days-off period. "I wanted to invite you to a New Year's Day party."

"Is it that time already?" Frank asked. "Guess I don't pay much attention to the calendar."

Kyle nodded. "Well, three days from now it is. We've invited the folks from the town of Clinton to come. I thought maybe you and Brenda would enjoy coming and meeting some people. It's all dependent on the weather of course."

Frank raised his hand to cut Kyle off. "I think we're going to have to pass on this one. I know Brenda would love to go, but she twisted her ankle pretty bad last week. She's up and hopping around now, but I don't think she'd be up for a party." He paused a second. "I guess I shouldn't make the decision for her. Why don't you come down to the house and ask her. I know she'd enjoy seeing you again."

Kyle followed Frank down the mountainside. They took a left after eighty yards and walked past a stand of pine trees. Frank came to a stop. "What do you think?" he asked.

Kyle looked for a small cabin, but didn't see anything, then noticed a pair of windows in the rock face. "You live in the hillside?"

Frank beamed. "It's the most expensive cave in Montana, or at least I'm guessing it is. Actually, it's not really a cave, and I have no idea how it compares cost wise, but it sure as hell wasn't cheap. Come on in." Frank led Kyle to a steel door, painted to blend in with the rocks, and pushed it open. "We got company, honey. Hope you're decent," he called inside.

Kyle followed Frank into his home, letting out a low whistle after his eyes adjusted to the lighting. "Wow!" he said. "This is amazing." Kyle's eyes swept the room. "This is not what I was expecting. How'd you do this?"

Kyle heard a door open, and Brenda emerged using a crutch for support. Her hair was pulled back in a ponytail, and she was dressed comfortably in sweat pants, a t-shirt, and bright yellow socks. She greeted Kyle. "I know you're the Deer Creek guy, but I'm sorry, I've forgotten your name."

"Kyle," he said. "It's nice to see you again."

"You'd think I'd remember. It's not like we're swamped with visitors. Come. Have a seat. Frank must have given you the stamp of approval if he's exposed our hideout. Whatcha think?"

Kyle shook his head as he continued looking around. He was in a large room, forty feet wide by twenty feet deep. If he'd been blindfolded and led inside, he'd have thought that he was in a modern house because other than a shortage of windows, it looked like a completely modern dwelling. The room he was in had a reclining, leather sofa, a large ceiling fan hanging from a ten-foot ceiling, and a home theater system centered on one wall and surrounded by shelves filled with books. The room was sparsely, but nicely, decorated with rugs, paintings and photographs. The kitchen and dining area were on the far end of the room and had modern cabinets, slate floors, a gas stove, and a dishwasher. Three separate pine doors at the back of the room, leading deeper into the hillside, were closed.

"I'm speechless. Thought I'd be in a cave with water dripping from the ceiling."

Brenda laughed. "When I married Frank and he said he wanted to live in the mountains, I was thinking a little cabin with a nice porch. Didn't think he meant literally 'in the mountains'. It took him a bit to convince me this was the way to go, but I'm glad we did."

"This must have cost a fortune."

"Not as much as you'd think, but it all depends where your priorities are. There's over $90,000 worth of concrete and rebar here. The rest of it wasn't that much since the labor was free. It's not going to win any architectural awards; it's just a big square with five rooms, but it has everything we need."

"This is nicer than my house."

"I wouldn't go that far," Frank replied. "We do without some things, though not as much as you might expect. There's no AC, but being in-ground keeps our temperatures fine in the summer. Water's a bit of an issue. We have two cisterns further up the hill, one fed by a small year-round spring, the other by a stream that runs March until August most years. The spring gives us twenty gallons a day, so we're not hurting, but we can't take baths or irrigate with it, and we only flush a couple times a day." Frank stroked his beard and thought for a second. "I had more working solar panels than we do now, but the EMP took them and the better charge controller out. Fortunately we have some old equipment that we're running off of, but it's not full power. There's some other stuff, but you get the idea."

"I'd love to have something like this. It's fantastic."

Frank motioned for Kyle to sit, then walked towards a woodstove. "Can I get you some coffee?"

Kyle's eyes widened. "I think I've forgotten what coffee tastes like. I'd love some."

"Milk? Sugar?"

"You've got milk?"

"It's goat milk, but it's good."

"Both, please," Kyle said, watching expectantly as Frank poured the hot drink while Brenda retrieved the milk and sugar. Kyle took the mug from Frank and cradled it in his hands, sipping slowly, savoring the warmth and flavor. "I may never go home. A pot of real coffee would be worth a mint down there."

"Didn't you have anything stored?" Frank asked between sips. "A case of coffee, some MRE's, anything?"

"No, I mean, we'd stock up in the winter a little bit, in case the weather kept us snowed in for a few days. But Jennifer, my wife, she worked in town, so she could get to the store easily."

"Can't get to the store now, can you?" Frank said, staring intently at Kyle.

"Brace yourself, Kyle. The lecture's coming," Brenda said, then shook her head at Frank. "He's a guest, dear. Don't be too rough on him." She turned back to Kyle. "Our son got this lecture all the time, as did all our friends, family, you name it. They've all heard it. That's why no one comes to visit."

Frank looked at his wife and gave her a defensive look. "No one comes to visit because they didn't listen to me, and they're probably dead or dying. Prior to September, they laughed at me behind my back. Thought I was a fool. Thought that the blood and sweat I put into this place was a waste of resources. 'Buy a condo,' 'go on vacation,' 'get a boat,' they'd say while they flushed their money away. You ever been to Hawaii, Kyle?"

"No," he answered. "We wanted to, but couldn't afford it." Kyle heard Brenda catch her breath.

Frank took off his glasses and cleaned the lenses with his shirt. His good eye was bloodshot, and his cheeks were getting red. "I've never been to Hawaii, Kyle, but I didn't want to. Do you know that for the price of a vacation in Hawaii you could buy a year's worth of food? Half our friends went on fancy vacations every year, but didn't have jack squat for food storage."

Frank was talking faster, his eyes darting between Kyle and his wife. "Do you smoke, Kyle? Or I guess I should say did you smoke? A lot of people went cold turkey this year."

Kyle shrunk back in the couch and shook his head. "No. Tried it once, but it made me sick."

"Good," Frank said. "Nasty habit, and a waste of money. Do you know that if you smoked a pack a day for ten years you would have spent enough to buy food for your family for two years and enough guns and ammo to fight off a small army."

"Frank, Kyle didn't come up here to be lectured. Besides, this doesn't do anyone any good at this point." Brenda's eyes were pleading but warm as she spoke to her husband.

"Relax, dear. I want him to think a little on his walk home." Frank's tone was icy cold. He turned back to Kyle. "Eat out much?"

"I don't know. I guess if you count lunches, probably seven, eight times a month."

Frank's eyes bugged out. "That's at least $100 a month wasted. Just as bad as cigarettes." Frank took a deep breath, trying to calm himself. "Look, you can tell by looking around that this stuff is important to me. Promise me something."

"Sure, what?"

"You're young. Promise me that when things come back around, because they will, and you'll still have lots of life to live, promise me that you'll think a few years down the road. It doesn't have to be another EMP. It could be a pandemic, or a war, or a solar flare. Shoot, Mother Nature has half a dozen things up her sleeve that she could use to really mess us up. Promise me that you'll get ahead of the game."

"Okay, Frank, that's enough. Let poor Kyle up for air."

Frank grunted. "Wait here, Kyle." He got up and walked through the far door.

Brenda smiled weakly at Kyle. "Sorry about that. He took a lot of grief from everyone about all this," she motioned around the room. "I think he wants to be able to gloat. Don't take what he said personally."

"He is right, you know," Kyle said, looking Brenda in the eyes. "I've thought about it a lot. There's a ton of stuff I could have done differently. What you've got is way out of my league, but I could have been a lot more prepared."

"Well, you're still alive, so you must have done something right."

"I don't know. God must like me, or something. By all rights I should be dead."

"You didn't come up here to be lectured, Kyle. Is everything okay?"

"Things are good. I actually came to tell you about a New Year's party."

Kyle was filling Brenda in on the details of the party when Frank returned holding a plastic baggie filled with white powder. He tossed it on the table in front of Kyle. "Take that," he said. "It'll help you out."

Kyle looked at it uneasily, reaching out to touch the bag. The consistency of the powder was a little finer than table sugar.

"That's okay," Kyle said. "I appreciate it, but I think I'll pass."

Frank looked puzzled. "Take it. It'll help you get through this. If you have younger kids, it'll help them, and the older, weaker folks too. But you don't have to share if you don't want to. You can use it all yourself. It's up to you."

Kyle was shocked at Frank's suggestion. "Hey, really. I appreciate the gesture, but I've got to say no. I admit I tried weed a couple times when I was younger, but I stayed away from the hard stuff. It's not my thing."

Frank's expression switched from curiosity to amusement as Kyle spoke, and he began to laugh loudly. Kyle looked at Brenda, who was covering her mouth. He could see in her eyes that she was laughing as well.

"I'm guessing that's not what I thought it was."

Frank shook his head, his laughter calming. "This is to make your water safe. It's bleach, or actually it's swimming pool shock – calcium hypochlorite. Same thing as bleach, but this will last forever. Liquid bleach degrades fairly quickly; this won't. I wrote the mixing instructions on a paper in the bag."

"So it's not crack then, huh?" Kyle confirmed, embarrassed.

Frank shook his head. "No drugs here, Kyle, at least not that kind. Did you tell Brenda about your party?"

CHAPTER EIGHT

Monday, January 9th
Deer Creek, MT

David pulled the collar of his jacket tight around his ears as the wind blew cold and steady, as it so often did at night up in the observation nest, pelting him with flecks of ice scoured from the side of the mountain. The militia had constructed an observation post on top of the western mountain, where they had the best views of the valley below, and David's assignment was to scan the area for threats. The outpost was crude, consisting of a shallow, twenty-foot trench with dirt and rocks piled around it to block the wind and shield the observer. At night, and on especially cold days, a tarp could be drawn over the top of the trench as a shield from the wind and to retain heat from a small fire the sentries kept burning by their feet.

Once he was resituated, David grabbed the binoculars with his gloved hands and scanned the roads below him. He had a good view of the freeway, from the east side of Missoula all the way to Clinton, but the view of the smaller road on the south side of the river was partially obstructed. From the east, he could see the road clearly until it was almost directly below him, then an outcropping of rocks and some trees blocked the view for nearly a mile, until just a couple hundred yards from the militia house.

David swung the binoculars from east to west, then back east again, pausing on every rock, shadow, and tree that caught his attention. He noticed movement along the far side of the river and twisted the focus knob to sharpen the image. A buck stepped gingerly onto the ice and snow, dipping its head down to the water, then raising it up quickly, looking back over its shoulder. David watched it turn from side to side, then dash off across the freeway and up into the trees on the facing slope of the opposite mountain.

He continued to swing the binoculars east, past the bridge, along the road, past a couple of abandoned homes on the far side of the river, and then into the town of Clinton. His gaze lingered on the town, wondering which home belonged to Amy Carpenter, the girl he'd met the week before when she'd come with her family, and most of the residents of Clinton, to Deer Creek's first annual New Year's event.

The party had started at noon and lasted about 4 hours, with food, games, a children's production of *Toy Story*, dancing, trading, and a lot of socializing. David had noticed Amy during the games. They had been on different teams during the relays, and she was one of the few teens who had kept up with him. During the last hour of the party, a well-intentioned band from Deer Creek had provided music, and David had asked Amy to dance, giving him an opportunity to learn her name and get to know her.

The fire at David's feet popped, and he felt a coal bounce off his pant leg. He pulled the canvas back to check the fire, then grabbed a piece of wood, knocked a chunk of snow off of it, and carefully set it on the fire. Sparks danced upwards, and he waved them away with his hands while watching the tiny embers die in the cold wind. On nights like this, the fire was the only thing that made the lookout post bearable. He couldn't complain too much though, because he'd volunteered for the assignment, and he did like that he didn't have to sit around and talk with the old men in the house, or walk twenty plus miles each night.

So far there had only been three nights that David hadn't had to make the climb to the outpost: twice, when it was snowing too hard to see anything, and once, when the temperature was ten below zero, and it was highly unlikely that anyone would attack under those conditions. As David watched the fire to make sure the wood caught, his thoughts drifted back to Amy. She was fifteen years old and a year ahead of him at the Catholic High School. Her hair was dark brown hair, her eyes brown and very pretty, and she was more shapely than most of the girls her age. She was slim, like everybody else these days, but not so skinny that she looked unhealthy. Her hair had been pulled back in the standard ponytail, and she had smelled really good, a pleasing combination of soap and good perfume.

The piece of wood caught fire, and David arranged the canvas back over the hole before picking up his binoculars and training them back on Clinton. Amy had described where her house was, and David thought maybe he'd found it. In the light of the full moon, he could see smoke coming from what he thought was the Carpenter's chimney. He smiled to himself, trying to imagine what her house looked like inside.

A twig popped somewhere behind him in the trees. David spun around, startled by the sound which was amplified by his fear of being ambushed, or, the more likely event, being eaten by a bear. He put his gun to his shoulder and aimed it towards the woods, leaving the binoculars swinging from the strap around his neck. Unexplained noises were pretty common, something he should be used to, but they never ceased putting him on edge. He waited cautiously, but heard and saw nothing, so turned back around.

He trained the binoculars on the road just west of Clinton and continued to scan towards Missoula. He could see a figure walking on the Deer Creek side of the river, one of the militia-men on their rounds. He knew they were militia because most of them walked the same path every time, despite instructions to the contrary. The militia house came into view, along with the bridge, the trees and rocks below him, the road on the south side of the river, and a strange, dark shape. He swept past the object before its strangeness registered, then quickly swung back, trying to spot what had caught his attention, but it was right at the point where trees obscured the road.

He climbed out of the foxhole, ran a few steps west, and refocused on the road below him. Just as David zeroed in on the shape, it seemed to break apart and move towards Deer Creek. He only had an instant before the trees blocked his view again, but it had looked like a group of people. He wasn't positive though, because he'd seen it so briefly. It could have been deer, geese, or even some of the abandoned dogs that were packing together.

David's heart pounded as he stared down at the road. He swept the binoculars further west then back to where the trees blocked his view, but saw nothing unusual. He grabbed the gun he had been issued, an AK47, and four thirty-round magazines, and ran west along the ridge, trying to find a better vantage point.

Tripped up by a rock in the darkness, David fell to his knees, dropping his gun and bruising his shins. Recovering quickly, he picked up his weapon, ran a few more feet, and aimed the bin-oculars back down on the road. What little extra bit of the road he could see was empty. Directly below him, he knew there was a plywood sign, painted with a warning:

Guarded community!
Do not approach after dark, with weapons,
or in groups larger than three.
Violators will be considered hostile.

Similar signs were posted on the bridge, on the far east end of town along the river, and south of the Shipley Ranch, facing the old gravel road coming down from the mountains.

David ran back towards the trench. He looked through the sights of the gun and found the truck hood that hung between two trees in the backyard of the militia house. With limited communication, if the lookout couldn't give a warning in person, their signal in the event of an emergency was to shoot the hood hanging in the yard. David had made this shot many times during training and knew that the hood rang like a bell, audible all the way to the far end of the community. He'd also been reminded many times that when he shot it, there would be fifty-three militia members running his direction, ready to fight.

David swore under his breath and lowered his gun, all thoughts of Amy long fled. He heard a sound, maybe voices, and froze in place, terrified that people were coming up across the top of the ridge. He waited, straining to hear anything that was out of place, but heard nothing. He ran down towards the militia house, crouching low and carefully avoiding making any loud noises.

He'd taken this path dozens of times and knew it well, but it had never been this dark, and never under this kind of stress. Part way down the hill the trail led south, away from the road, so David cut north, off trail, towards the road. It was dark in the trees, but his eyes had adjusted enough to the moonlight for him to be able to jog, dodging branches and rocks as he ran. His heart raced, both from the running and from the fear that what he'd seen was something threatening.

A thick cluster of trees lay ahead, and he slowed to push through it, sliding through the branches as silently as possible. He was almost through the trees when his left foot fell out from under him. David clutched for branches as he began to fall, realizing, to his horror, that he had emerged through the trees at the top of a fifty-foot cliff, a sheer drop to the rocks and boulders below.

He grabbed desperately for the branches, branches that scraped at his face as he fell, his left foot sliding over the edge, his right leg still on top. His momentum carried him forward and downward, and he gasped, panic stricken, as rocks and pinecones tumbled down the cliff, bouncing with echoing cracks off the boulders below.

As he continued his slow motion slide over the precipice, his right hand grasped a fat tree root curled tightly around a weathered rock, and his right leg wedged between a tree trunk and a small boulder, bringing his fall to a halt but still leaving him dangling precariously over the edge. He let out a deep breath and opened his eyes as sharp pains shot through his right leg. Terrified, he held tight for a second, then used the root to carefully pull himself back up, finally rolling back over the edge into the trees, with sweat rolling in cold beads down his forehead.

He groped in the darkness for his rifle, which he'd dropped near the edge. His right hand bumped against the barrel, and he snatched it up with hands shaking so hard from the near fall that he could hardly get his finger on the trigger. He edged back towards the cliff top, this time much more carefully and slowly. From this new vantage point, he could see the militia house to his right and the road down below, and he watched the road, searching for movement.

Something shifted in the trees below, and he leaned forward, tense, only to see a deer scamper off towards the river. David waited and watched for what seemed like an eternity. His rapidly beating heart had slowed, but his bruised leg throbbed, and the chill of the winter night was beginning to work its way through his thick, sweat-soaked jacket. He shifted side to side on still shaking legs and swung his arms back and forth to get the blood flowing. Finally convinced that it had been a false alarm, David was about to retrace his steps back to the top of the hill when he definitely saw movement by the river. Looking harder, he spotted two figures crouched low and trotting towards the bridge. He scanned the road directly below and saw two more figures moving stealthily towards the militia house with what appeared to be weapons in their hands.

David brought the AK47 to his shoulder and turned to shoot the truck hood to warn the others and bring the rest of the militia to help. The words his dad had said to him the first night he went up the hill echoed in his head. "You've got our lives in your hands, Son. Don't let us down."

The hood had been hung so that it was directly facing the nest at the top of the hill. Now that he had run back towards the house, however, his angle to the target was considerably different, shrinking the target size in half, despite his being closer to it. He looked down at the road. The men there had paused in a ditch to talk; he couldn't see the men by the river. David took aim at the hood and pulled the trigger.

The perfect silence of the late evening exploded with the gunshot, the sound ringing so loudly he was sure the dead would rise from their graves, but there was no ringing warning from the truck hood and how far the sound of the shot had carried he didn't know. David fired again, aware that the sound and the flash would alert the men crouching in the ditch below him that he was there. Again there was no ringing of the hood.

"Dammit!" David whispered. He glanced at the window of the house where he knew a guard was posted and saw movement and a rifle sticking out. At least they're on alert, he thought. He aimed again, noticed a flash from the rifle at the window, then rocks and pine needles exploded in the dirt just behind him as the pop of the weapon reached his ears. "Damn! Damn! Damn!" he exclaimed to himself, realizing he was taking friendly fire, and that the sound of weapons this far away wouldn't be enough to rouse the community.

David scrambled ten feet further up hill, saw another flash from the window, and heard the bullet hit a tree close to where he had knelt just seconds before. Once again he took aim and pulled the trigger, and once again he missed his mark. Another flash from the window of the house was followed, almost immediately, by a flash from the side of the house. One of the shots hit a few feet above David, but the other zipped by close enough for him to hear it whistle past before bouncing off a nearby rock.

David dropped to his stomach and edged forward to look over the cliff. The men hiding in the ditch appeared to be looking up at him, then they started crawling out of the ditch, back in the direction they had come from. David realized the gunfire was scaring the intruders off before anyone in the community found out about them, and with his luck, he'd be killed by his own militia before he could alert them.

Adrenaline coursed through his body, making his hands shake again. He again took aim, but this time at the figures on the road, who were much closer than the hood and seemed to fill the scope of his weapon. Another shot sounded from the house, with the bullet crashing through the branches above his head. David took the forward shape in his sights and began to put pressure on the trigger, then paused. His mind raced. That was a real person down there, someone who felt pain, someone who had a life and a family. David had killed countless aliens, Nazis, zombies, and gangsters on his Xbox, but this wasn't a video game. This time they were real.

Another shot rang from the house, and the bullet struck below him on the cliff. With hands still shaking, David looked through his gun sight, aiming dead center on the man's chest, and pulled the trigger. The gun roared, but he was used to the sound, and it no longer fazed him. He quickly recovered from the kick and drew the sights back on the men now scrambling back to the ditch. Calmer, he pulled the trigger again and saw his target fall while thinking to himself, "I've just shot a living person." It didn't seem real.

The second man pulled his wounded comrade into the ditch, and David took aim at him and fired. The man screamed and fell to the ground. The scream made it real. David pulled back from the edge and began to cry.

He'd barely retreated from the edge when a volley of gunfire erupted, and the air above him came alive - bullets spinning by, ricocheting off rocks and trees, branches falling. It was as if World War II had erupted on a Montana mountainside. David wiped his tears on his coat sleeve and crawled further from the edge, knowing the cliff protected him from the incoming fire. He climbed to his feet while trying to stifle sobs of fear and grief and ran downhill, crouching low, searching for another spot, knowing the darkness and the trees made him as safe as he could hope for.

He stopped twenty yards downhill, crawled back to the edge, and looked down. Two shots came from close to the river, the flash of light exposing the shooters' positions, but they hit far from David, and returning fire would have just given up his new location. He focused on the militia house and saw guns sticking out of the upstairs window and a figure on the porch, crouched behind a barricade. He glanced down at the hood and saw that it was facing him. Blinking, he looked again. The hood was hanging from only one rope and had turned so that he had a square shot.

David quickly brought his gun to his shoulder, took aim, and pulled the trigger. Ring! The sound of the bullet striking the target was more welcome than anything he could ever remember hearing. He fired again. Ring! The hood slowly spun around, and David waited until just before it squared up and fired once more. Ring! Fresh tears came to his eyes and blurred his vision, but this time they were tears of relief.

Gunfire continued below, and David shrank down low to the ground, but no more bullets screamed overhead. He waited for two minutes before looking up again. Men were running towards the militia house from the direction of town. Someone shouted commands. Voices were shrill.

The figures in the ditch were shooting towards the militia house now, and David heard glass break. He could see that they were trying to work their way towards the river, but moving slowly, neither able to help the other due to their injuries.

As David watched, he saw more flashes of gunfire from the river area. The trees and bushes were thick there, and providing excellent cover. Undeterred, he took aim at a spot a rifle's length back from the flash and pulled his trigger as fast as he could, until his weapon was empty. He released the empty magazine, jammed in another thirty rounder from his jacket, and looked back at the river. Gunfire from there had stopped, but he wasn't sure if it was because the target had been hit or was moving, so he watched and waited.

David was starting to feel the cold again when he saw movement. A lone figure emerged from behind the trees onto the ice where the river was frozen over, dark stains marking his footprints as he attempted to reach the far bank. David shuddered as he once again shouldered his weapon and lined up the figure in his sights. He could see that the man struggled to walk, and knew that he had probably caused the man's injury. This didn't feel anything like a video game. This was real blood, suffering, anger, terror and guilt, all mixed together. This was more awful than anything he could imagine.

The man was halfway across the river when he suddenly turned back towards the shore he had come from, then stopped. David grabbed the binoculars that still hung from his neck and pressed them to his eyes. The right lens was broken, so he closed that eye and watched the man through one eyepiece. The man pushed at the ice in front of him with one foot, found it stable, then moved carefully ahead, repeating the process.

David knew what the man was doing. The ice on the river was thick at the shore, but the further out you got, the more the water underneath carved out thin spots. The week before, David had stepped out a few paces onto the ice to retrieve his hat that had blown off, and the creaking of the ice had sent him scrambling for the edge.

The injured man moved a little further, testing the ice as he went. From his perch, David could see that the militia was gathering at the garrison. Close to twenty people were there, and they likely weren't aware of the person on the ice. David looked back at the man, grabbed his gun, and took aim, but it was hard to shoot now that the fear and adrenaline were gone and no one was shooting at him.

Just as he was about to pull the trigger, the man slipped and fell. He tried to rise but lost his footing once more. His movements became more frantic and uncoordinated, and David realized that the man was slipping on wet ice, ice that was thin and breaking up around him. David could see the urgency in the man's movements, then a dark line appeared in the ice beneath him, widened, and the man's legs dropped into the water. He clawed at the ice, frantically trying to pull himself out of the water, but each time he started to escape, more ice broke away, and he slid back down again.

The scene hypnotized David. Tears ran silently down his cheeks as the man's arm movements became slower and slower and his life drained slowly away. Finally, after a couple of minutes, the movements stopped altogether, and the body was slowly pulled from the ice by the current, disappearing in the darkness of the river.

A heavy shudder ran through David's body, and he noticed how really cold he was. The wind whistled in the trees and blew on his face, making him shiver violently. With the threats gone, he stood, backed away from the edge, and headed back to the trail, numbly picking his way around rocks and trees, intent on heading back to the lookout post and the warm fire he hoped was still burning. Just as he got back to the trail, he heard footsteps moving quickly in his direction.

David quickly hid behind some rocks, certain he was going to have to face at least one more person fleeing from the militia. He readied his gun and waited as the person drew closer, then saw a dark shape run past him up the hill, breathing hard and moving fast.

"Stop!" David shouted, his finger on the trigger, ready to shoot. "Stay where you are!"

The figure stopped, raising its hands. "Seahawks!" a man shouted.

"Dad?"

"David?"

David jumped up from behind the rocks. "Dad, I'm here!" he sobbed as fear and relief hit him all at once.

Kyle ran towards David and grabbed his son in his arms. He was panting and could barely talk. "David! I was so worried," he choked out. "I could see the shots coming from up here." He gulped for air and pressed David's face against his shoulder. "I should have been here for you. Are you alright?"

***

The remainder of the night and the next morning were a blur of events that Kyle shielded David from as much as possible. Because David hadn't seen the group as it approached Deer Creek, he hadn't been able to say for sure how many men they were looking for. Once he had explained to the militia leaders all that he had seen and done, David had been relieved of duty for the night and sent home, and recon teams had been organized and sent out to the two places where David had seen shooters, as well as along the road and up the hillside, where David's view had been blocked.

By the time the sun was well up, the recon teams had found no evidence of other men, although without knowing exactly where and what to look for, they couldn't be sure they hadn't missed anything. The body of the man who had fallen through the ice on the river had been located just over a mile downstream. He only had one bullet wound, but it had done significant damage to his lower abdomen. Carol had commented that the temperature of the water, combined with a significant loss of blood, had sped up his death, and that his chance of surviving more than a couple of hours without extensive surgical repair would have been slim. The second man found by the river was dead. Of his six bullet wounds, three would have proven fatal under most circumstances.

Two men had been found in the ditch. One was dead, shot in the neck, but the second man was still breathing. He was bandaged and taken to the militia headquarters, where he drifted in and out of consciousness most of the night, mumbling incoherently.

The four men appeared to be between twenty-five and forty years of age and had been well armed. Among them had been found two Bushmaster assault rifles, two Remington deer rifles, a Lugar 9mm with a silencer, and a laser sited Glock 45 semi-automatic, plus each carried a knife of one description or another. Additionally, one had carried pepper spray, another bolt cutters and a crow bar, and a third was armed with a sledgehammer.

The Deer Creek militia had not escaped damage. Luther Espinoza, stationed in the upstairs window, had taken a shot to the shoulder, right in the joint, and was in a lot of pain. Carol had examined him, cleaned out the wound, and stitched his shoulder up as best she could, but the damage to the bone and joint was severe, and she worried that he might never regain the full use of his arm.

The final issue to resolve was what to do with the surviving shooter. A meeting of the militia was called, and the man's fate debated, with the discussion lasting for close to four hours and ending with a decision that he would be executed. That same afternoon, the man was carried from the militia house, taken out of sight of the town, and shot. Since no blanks were available, all four volunteers on the firing squad had used loaded weapons, and the man was hit four times in the chest.

The actual decision to execute the man had only taken the militia a little over an hour to decide, but the discussion had then gone to what merited such a sentence, as the only people who had been killed were the assailants themselves, since they had been unsuccessful in taking any lives. Based on the nature of the assault and the weapons they'd carried, all had agreed that the invaders were planning and prepared to kill. Thus the sentence had been passed, along with the agreement that in the future, murder, attempted murder, and anything similar would be handled in like manner.

The next full militia meeting was scheduled for two days later, and twenty-seven new members attended, which, coupled with the loss of Luther due to his injury, swelled militia membership to seventy-nine individuals, twenty-two of them women. The increased membership allowed for two additional people on the overnight shift, another up in the observer's post, and a dedicated patrol along the river. During the days, more energy was spent on digging trenches, building fortifications, reinforcing the militia house, and being more prepared in general, should the need to combat hostiles arise again.

CHAPTER NINE

Wednesday, January 18th
Deer Creek, MT

J ust as the sun was dipping below the mountains, a weak knock sounded at the front door. Kyle answered it and was greeted by a frail, elderly woman who he vaguely recognized. She wore a bright red, wool coat that seemed to swallow her up and stood in stark contrast to her white hair. Kyle could see two spindly legs sticking out from the bottom of the coat capped with a pair of well-worn slippers that were wet with snow and ice.

"Hi," she said, forcing a smile, her voice shaking and hurried. "Is Dr. Carol here? I think my sister has died."

"I'm so sorry, ma'am," Kyle responded, ushering her in. "Let me get Carol for you." He turned to run up the stairs, but Carol was already on her way down.

"It's for you," he said, indicating the woman at the front door.

"Hi Sherry," Carol said sympathetically. "Did I hear you say that Penny passed away?"

The old woman nodded as tears formed and rolled slowly through the maze of wrinkles on her face. "I believe so," she answered. "She started coughing and couldn't stop. I went to get her a drink of water, and that's when I heard her fall. When I got back to her she was already gone. I tried to check for a pulse, but," she paused, tears still flowing, "but I couldn't feel anything. I tried to do CPR, like you showed me, but I'm just not strong enough."

Carol quickly found her jacket and put it on, then wrapped a comforting arm around the woman. "Lets go see if we've lost her." They hurried out the front door, closing it tightly behind them.

Kyle looked at Jennifer, who had emerged from the kitchen nibbling on a small piece of bread. "Who was that?" he asked

"Sherry Williams. She lives down the street with her sister, Penny. Moved in a couple of years ago when her husband died. I think they're both close to ninety."

"Should I go with Carol or something? I feel like I should be more helpful."

"Let's just wait and see. Sherry suffers from dementia, or Alzheimer's, or something, and her medications ran out long ago. I think this is the third time that Penny's died, so it might not be an emergency, but Carol's said it's just a matter of time for either one of them."

Kyle stroked his beard. "Do we do funerals, when people die?"

"Yes, Kyle, that's usually when we do funerals," Jennifer answered, laughing. "They don't like it so much if we do it before then."

"Ha-ha-ha. Good one." Kyle held his sides in an exaggerated laugh. "That's not what I meant. I was just thinking about those guys last week. We just dug some holes by the road; there wasn't a service or anything. Nobody from town has died since I got back, so I was just curious how we handle it."

"Yes, we have funerals. Gabe does them, and they've been nice, all things considered."

"Gabe? Isn't he a plumber?" Kyle looked at Jennifer, his brow wrinkled. "Does he make flushing sounds when they lower the body into the ground?"

Jennifer let out a laugh, despite the shocked look on her face. "Stop it, Kyle. That's sacrilegious or something."

"I'm serious. Why do we have a plumber do the funerals? Seems weird."

"Gabe's a Mormon. Grace says he's a Bishop in their church, so he's done weddings and funerals and that kind of stuff. I guess in that church they're only asked to be the Bishop for a few years, so they keep their regular jobs."

"Do they have to be plumbers?"

"I doubt it. Any job is probably okay, as long as it's legal."

"How about a doctor?"

"I'm sure that's fine."

"That would be strange. 'So, Mr. Tait, please turn your head and cough, and I hear you've been having lustful thoughts. Tell me the truth or I'll probe deeper.'"

"You're terrible," Jennifer said, smacking him on his shoulder. "Ask Grace if you want to know more; I don't know the details."

"How about a gynecologist. 'Mrs. Tait, please put your feet up in the stirrups. Now, I've been wondering why you haven't been at church lately.'"

"Drop it, Kyle. I would guess that they don't do exams at church on Sunday, but I don't know. Ask someone who does. You work tonight, right?"

Kyle nodded.

"How soon 'till David will be ready to go back?"

"I'm not sure. Sean says he can take as much time as he needs, but I don't think they'll put him back on nights."

"Good. I was nervous about him being up there before, but no way I want him up there now. He can walk around town during the day, but I don't want him out at dark anymore. It's too dangerous."

Kyle gave Jennifer a hug then slowly slid a hand around to her chest but found it quickly pushed away. He bit his lip in frustration and took a step back, trying to look her in the eyes. "He's a big boy, Jenn. There were lots of fourteen year olds fighting in World War II, and they managed. But you're right, and Sean agrees. David will be on days, at least for a while. Sean was pretty concerned that David let those guys get so close."

The front door opened, and Carol stepped back inside, with Sherry tucked under her arm. "Kyle?" Carol said as she pushed the door shut. "Could you go get Gabe? We need to arrange for a funeral."

Kyle offered condolences, then hurriedly pulled on his coat and boots and was out the door. The sun had set, and the wind was picking up, dropping the temperature noticeably. Kyle wrapped his scarf around his neck as he hurried to Gabe's house.

They returned to Carols' house together, chatting briefly about the community and the funeral. Kyle hurriedly put on an extra layer of clothing and grabbed his weapons before rushing off to work, already late for his shift.

By the time he arrived at the militia house his preferred assignment, walking along the river, had been taken, leaving him with everyone's least favorite assignment - walking the town interior. Even though it provided a little variety because there was no defined route to patrol, it was further from the garrison and tended to be the one with the fewest opportunities to warm up.

The night was cold but passed without incident, and soon after sun-up, Kyle was home and in bed, dead to the world. He had been asleep for just a short time when he felt someone shaking him.

"Kyle," Jennifer said, tugging on his arm.

Kyle blinked, shook his head, and looked at Jennifer. "What?" he mumbled, trying to get his bearings.

"Sean's here. He needs to talk to you. Says it's important."

Kyle swallowed, cleared his throat, and sat up. "Alright. Tell him just a minute." He already had his sweatpants on, but grabbed his sweatshirt that he kept on the fireplace hearth and pulled it on before going upstairs.

Sean sat on the couch in the living room. His cheeks were red, and he wore a thick, olive green jacket. "Morning, Kyle," he said, sounding like the drill instructor Kyle was used to. "Sorry to wake you."

Kyle shrugged. "What's going on?"

"There's a girl from Clinton that's missing. According to her father, she came over here to visit that Briggs kid, Dale, the one you caught with the wood. Anyway, she came over for a visit last night and never made it back home. Dale said she left at midnight, and he's the last one that saw her. I understand you did the interior patrol last night?"

"I did," Kyle confirmed as he fought off a yawn. "But I didn't see anyone. It was cold and quiet."

"You're sure you didn't see anyone, or hear anything out of the ordinary?"

Kyle shook his head. "It was cold, and I took a couple of longer breaks, but everything seemed fine. I'm positive I didn't see her last night."

"You ever see the girl before?"

"Yeah, I think so. Couple of nights after the News Year's deal. There was a girl on horseback heading home along the river on the east end of town, about a couple hours after dark. Does she have some nose loops?"

Sean nodded. "Her dad says she has some piercings, tattoos on her arms, dark hair, about 5'3" tall. He wasn't sure of her weight, but says she's skinny."

"Sounds like the same girl, but it was cold, and she was bundled up, so I didn't notice any tattoos. She seemed nice enough. Was real cheerful when I asked her what she was doing. Do you need me to come and help search?"

"No. You go and sleep. We need you on patrol tonight. But if you remember anything, have someone find me. They've got a search party going in Clinton, and I'll get this morning's militia and some volunteers going on our side of the hill. Hopefully she'll turn up. Maybe she was upset with Dad and didn't go home, stayed at a friend's place, or something."

"You should look in the hills between the towns," Kyle offered. I've walked them a few times while out hunting. You can get turned around and heading the wrong direction pretty easily, especially at night."

CHAPTER TEN

Wednesday, January 18th
Central Wyoming

Rose Duncan gave her horse a soft nudge in the flanks. "Hurry up, Smokey," she encouraged, keeping on eye on the column of gray smoke that was rising in the distance. The smoke was dark and thick, and more than normal for this time of year, and for the area. Further more, it was coming from the general direction of her home, just not quite in the right location, but its presence made her nervous.

She'd been uneasy this entire trip, more so than any time in the past. Since the beginning of November, weather permitting, she'd been making a biweekly loop to the surrounding farms and ranches, for social reasons and to check on her neighbors' welfare, as well to talk security and do some trading. The first time around it had taken her just a day to complete, but this time she had been gone for two nights and covered in excess of forty miles. Some of the folks she visited were neighbors, while others were acquaintances from real estate dealings and rodeoing. A few others she had met when she began her trips.

Despite the fact that they had already made it halfway through the winter, Rose had noticed that there was a sense of depression with most of the people she'd visited, more so than during her earlier visits. One of the ranches had been abandoned. At another, they were preparing to leave. And at a third, a widow had given up and was just waiting to die. Rose had spent half a day splitting wood and trying to talk the woman out of her depression, but there were few encouraging words to say, and Rose was sure that the next time she stopped by there wouldn't be anyone to talk to. Most of the others, while not quite as discouraged, had similar gloom and doom outlooks and didn't want to do much more than hunt and wait for spring to arrive.

The tree-speckled hill up ahead overlooked her valley, and she spurred Smokey to a trot, anxious to discover the source of the smoke, but Smokey's breathing quickly became labored. The deer carcass draped over his shoulders, though gutted and decapitated, added to his already heavy load, and so Rose eased up, her concern for her horse's exhaustion overriding any anxiety she felt.

Once they crested the hill, Rose could see across the valley, past the freeway, and up the far hill to the source of the flames. Her neighbor's hay barn was fully engulfed, the fire raging furiously and well past any hope of containment. She tried to see if anyone was trying to fight it, but was too far off and there was too much smoke to make out any movement.

Rose continued home at a faster pace, and with a little over a mile to go, she heard an unfamiliar sound in the distance. "Whoa, boy," she whispered, reining Smokey to a stop. Rose held her breath, trying to place the low hum she could hear over Smokey's labored breathing. The pitch of the sound changed, and Rose realized that it was a diesel engine, a sound she hadn't heard for months.

She caught her breath and felt her heart pounding. Her hands shook on the horn of the saddle. Unsure why she was so afraid, she shrugged her shoulders and patted her horse firmly on the flanks. "Let's go home, boy." Smokey lurched forward and hurried along the familiar trail, sensing rest and feed were soon at hand.

The sound of the engine drew nearer, and Rose swung Smokey south, veering from the direct path home into the forest that bordered her property instead. The trees were thick, but Rose knew the forest well enough to navigate through to a place she could observe her home undetected.

Rose listened to the engine as she dismounted, heard it slow then accelerate again, knowing from the direction and distance that the vehicle was approaching her house. She heard a dog and recognized Max barking at the approaching vehicle. Sensing something bad, she dropped the reins and quickly untied the two rifles on her saddle, feeling for the box of ammo in her pocket as she ran the thirty yards to the edge of the tree line. Max had accompanied her on the first trip, but between his age and ailing hips, she had chosen to leave him home from subsequent trips with a supply of bones to chew and food to eat.

She reached the tree line at the same time an old, red pickup truck with four men inside appeared in her driveway. It approached her home at a crawl, taking two minutes to drive a quarter mile, then pulled to a stop a hundred feet from her front door. Rose held her breath as she waited and watched, her chest tight and her stomach churning. Max was on the front step of the house, watching the vehicle.

The driver's door opened, and a man stepped out of the truck and bent down. The angle of the truck made it difficult for Rose to see what the man was doing until he stood back up again with a rifle, rested it on the door of the truck, and aimed it at Max. She gasped, wanting to shout at the man and call Max away, but she knew she shouldn't draw attention to herself.

The passenger door of the truck opened, and a second man emerged. He was carrying a rifle as well and motioned to the first man, who lowered his weapon and straightened up. Relieved, Rose let out her breath and watched the second man approach the house, walking slowly and motioning to the dog. Max stood and approached the man, hesitant and slow, the pain from his hips making him limp as he walked.

Rose knew Max was protective and likely growling, but she also knew that he had slowed with age and was limited in what he was able to do. "Stop, Max," she said under her breath. "Come here, boy. Please!" Max and the man were an arms length apart when the man stopped. Max hesitated as well, sniffed in the direction of the approaching man and barked, backing up a step.

Before she could react, the man took his gun by the barrel and swung it quickly overhead, striking Max across his head with a savage blow. Max tried to dodge but was too slow. The blow dropped him to the ground on his side, where he writhed in pain. The man lifted his rifle again and brought it down across Max's head a second time.

Rose gasped and staggered backwards as the man swung a third time, shocked at the brutality of his attack. She laid one rifle on the ground, lowered herself to a knee and brought the other rifle into firing position. She found the man in the scope of the gun as he turned and motioned to the others. He was laughing as he looked back down at Max, lying immobile at his feet, then he stepped forward and kicked the dog viciously.

Rose brought the crosshairs to a point at the base of the man's throat and pulled the trigger. With the rifle sighted in for one hundred yards, the bullet dropped over the longer distance and struck the man just below his ribcage, entering with a dime-sized hole and knocking him backwards onto the ground in front of the pickup.

Rose chambered another bullet as she turned her attention to the men at the truck. The other two had gotten out and began approaching the house while Max was being beaten. Now they scrambled back towards the truck, unsure of where the shots were coming from. Rose took aim at one of the running men and pulled the trigger, but only heard the distant thud of a bullet striking metal.

A gunshot rang out, and branches a few feet away from Rose cracked and fell as the bullet cut its way through the forest. She scrambled to the cover of a tree as she chambering another bullet, then peered out from behind her cover. The three men had retreated behind the vehicle, rifles visible and leveled in her direction. They appeared to be talking, the first man motioning to the far side of the house where barns and fences would provide cover almost to the tree line five hundred yards to her right. If any of the men were to make that far Rose knew she would be in a precarious situation.

Shielded by a tree, Rose trained her rifle on the man taking directions and followed him through her sight as he rushed towards the back of her home. Attached to the corner of the house was a six-foot chain link fence. When the man stopped to remove the chain on the gate, Rose fired twice, working the bolt like a professional, striking him in the hip with the second shot. The man clutched at his hip as he fell, twisting on the ground in pain. Rose could see that the wound wasn't fatal, but knew it would take him out of the action for the foreseeable future.

In Rose's mind, the men were not only responsible for Max's death but also for her neighbor's barn being burned and for the general sense of fear and hopelessness she'd encountered on her recent visits. These people, neighbors and friends, families that had been independent, self-sufficient, hard-working and decent, were being driven from their homes by these bandits, these rats, these putrid pieces of scum who felt justified in terrorizing good people simply because they were hungry, had weapons, and hadn't found anyone able to stop them. Well Rose was going to stop them. And if it meant burying four bodies in her front yard, so be it.

The passenger door on the truck slammed shut and Rose heard the engine start. Through her scope she saw the driver's hand on the steering wheel, but his head was out of sight. She stood for a better view of the driver, but he was still hidden, so she took aim at the truck instead and fired. The bullet left a hole in the lower half of the truck door but was too low to do damage. The pitch of the engine dropped, and the truck rolled forward, then stopped, blocking her view of the man on the ground.

Rose's rifle was empty; she quickly grabbed her other gun and prepared to fire. This rifle, a Savage 223, didn't have a scope or the dropping power of her Mossberg 30-06, but it was loaded and ready to shoot. She could see movement behind the truck, but only occasionally did a head pop up above the hood, and never long enough or still enough to justify taking a shot from this distance. Impatient, she fired a couple shots into the door of the truck, then set the gun down and hurried to reload her Mossberg.

She heard the truck moving and watched it circle across her front yard, then take out the rail fence and head back towards the road. Rose fired the three shots she had loaded, striking the truck twice and noticing that it jerked to the side after her second shot before it could retreat towards the freeway. As the truck disappeared, she sank to the ground, a wave of nausea sweeping over her. The smell of gunpowder hung in the air, and the acrid stench burned her nostrils and made her angry that she had had to kill, angry that she was alone, and angry that people around her were giving up.

The image of Max's crumpled body drove her to her feet. She ran back to her horse, now skittish from the gunfire, and mounted, whipping him with the reins to hurry him home.

The body of the first man was still in the driveway, just a few feet from where Max lay. She approached him slowly, her rifle readied. The body lay in a circle of red, the rocks and sand now dark with the stain of spilt blood. His arms were spread out wide, his mouth and eyes both open, and one leg was cocked at an awkward angle. One hand still clutched the rifle he'd used to bludgeon Max.

Rose pushed the man's head with the tip of her rifle, and it rolled limply to the side, releasing a thin stream of blood from the corner of the mouth. Rose kicked the gun from the man's hand then moved slowly towards Max, her dear friend's lifeless body bringing on a flood of emotion. His head was distorted and bloody, but she reached out and stroked his shoulder, treasuring the softness of his fur and the comfort of his presence, knowing those things would just be memories, yet another part of her life that had been ripped away by this disaster that never seemed to end. Rose buried her face in Max's still warm side and wept.

When she was cried out, Rose removed the deer carcass and pack from Smokey, got back in the saddle, and spurred her horse towards her closest neighbors where the smoke was coming from. The mile and a half ride to Fanny and Lloyd's home took longer than normal, as Rose had never felt so vulnerable or as much of a target. The fear of vengeful men willing and ready to shoot her, or worse, plagued her thoughts and made her jump at every unexpected movement or sound.

By the time she reached her neighbors' farm, the fire had mostly burned itself out, the hay barn now a smoldering pile of ash that stirred in the breeze and left dark blots of ash on the patches of snow that surrounded it. From the drive she could see a spray of dark splatters on the white vinyl siding, along with a mound behind the rails of the front porch. She knew what she would find, but approached the house anyway.

The bodies lay to the side of the front door, Lloyd on the bottom, his rifle beside him, and Fanny sprawled face down on top of Lloyd, their blood pooling together on the weathered deck boards. Fanny's long, gray hair fanned down and covered Lloyd's face. They had celebrated their forty-fifth wedding anniversary the previous June with a cruise to the Bahamas, and Rose had been sure they'd have many more, but that was before. Now nothing was sure. The world was in a slow motion collapse, and not only couldn't she stop it, but she couldn't even get off.

As she walked back to her horse, Rose assessed her situation. Her dog was dead, as were her closest neighbors. The surrounding ranches and farms were being abandoned. There was a dead man in her driveway and men somewhere nearby who were injured, angry, motivated to kill her. Everything was changing so fast. Her existence, boring and mundane as it was, was shredded and wrenched from her control in the course of a morning, thrown into the hands of others who didn't know or care about Rose Duncan. But she still had the freedom to choose, and they could only take that from her if she willingly gave it up. She refused to let that happen, refused to give anyone control over her.

The body was still in her driveway when she returned home, just as it had been an hour before, and she stared down at it from her saddle. "You will never win!" she sneered, her voice low and powerful. "You can threaten my life, but I will never, ever give you my spirit." She spit at him, her saliva splattering on the man's blood-drained face. Rose smiled for the first time all day.

CHAPTER ELEVEN

Wednesday, January 18th
Deer Creek, MT

Jennifer hurried down the basement stairs, the scared look on her face alerting Kyle that something was wrong. "Kyle, some people are here to see you. Sean, Gabe, and a couple others."

He'd been drifting in and out of sleep for twenty minutes before Jennifer's footsteps had roused him. "What do they want?"

Jennifer shook her head. "Just said they need to talk to you, but something doesn't seem right. Their faces, it's just, I don't know. Hurry, okay?"

Kyle dressed and was quickly upstairs. "Hey," he said, addressing the men. "Jennifer said you wanted to see me? What's up?" Sean, Gabe, Ty Lewis and a man Kyle didn't recognize stood uncomfortably in the living room.

"We found the girl from Clinton," Sean said, looking from Kyle to Gabe.

"Is she alright?" Kyle asked, but he knew the answer. Four people didn't show up to give you good news.

"We found her body, Kyle," Gabe said. "A couple of hours ago."

"Oh no. I'm really sorry to hear that," Kyle said as he dropped into a chair. "What happened?"

Sean shook his head. "We don't know for sure. Still trying to figure that out. Thought maybe you could help us."

Spencer bounded into the room. "Dad!" he shouted, jumping up on Kyle's lap. "You're awake! Can we play a game?"

Kyle gently pushed Spencer off his lap. "Not now, son. Go find your mother. I'm a little busy." He turned back to Sean, his heart beating a little harder. "I don't know what to tell you more than what I said this morning. It was pretty quiet last night, but cold. Was it exposure?"

The men looked nervous and hesitant, their eyes not willing to meet Kyle's. "Kyle," Ty finally spoke up. "We found her body in your house, your old one. It appears she was raped and strangled." Ty's gaze dropped to the floor as he spoke.

Jennifer gasped from the doorway of the kitchen, and they all turned to look at her. "You found her where?"

Sean answered. "In the basement of your home, the empty one. Her pants were down around her knees; it looks like she was sexually assaulted."

"Wait," Jennifer interrupted. She led Spencer and Emma out of the kitchen and down to the basement. The men waited in silence for her to return. "Go on," she said as she walked back into the room.

Kyle could see her hands shaking. He smiled at her and mouthed, "It's okay," but he felt a dead weight in his stomach and didn't know if he believed it himself.

"I forgot your kids were in there," Sean apologized.

Jennifer shook her head, but didn't say anything, her voice lost.

"A searcher saw her through a basement window, but the house was locked. Her pants were down around her knees, and there was bruising on her neck. We don't know if she died from the cold or from an assault, but it wasn't accidental."

Kyle tried to swallow, but his throat was too tight. "Do you need the key? Is that why you're here?"

"It's not," Sean said, his voice nervous. "They broke in, the searchers. Thought she might still be alive. We're here for you, Kyle. We need you to come with us."

"What do you need Kyle for?" Jennifer asked, her voice uneven and rising. "He already told you he doesn't know anything."

"Jennifer, we're sorry," Gabe said as he stepped towards Jennifer. "This is just a real bad situation. We need to talk to Kyle, in private."

"But he's already told you…He doesn't even get paid anything to do that stupid job. You think he had something to do with this?"

"Jennifer! It's okay," Kyle said, stopping his wife. He wrapped his arms around her and kissed the top of her head. "I didn't do anything; they'll figure that out. It's going to be fine!"

She was crying, wiping at her eyes with her hands. "You just got back. Don't go," she pled. "Just stay here. Please!"

"I have to go. If I don't, it'll look bad. I trust them." He looked at Sean. "What do you need me to do?"

"Do you have any weapons on you?"

"No," Kyle said, lifting his sweatshirt.

"Then put on your jacket and shoes and come with us." Sean pointed to the fourth man in their group who hadn't said anything to this point. "This is Don Anderson from Clinton. He's the community rep from there."

Kyle nodded at him warily, then dressed and followed the group out the door. To his surprise there were four more men waiting outside for them, all with rifles, none looking happy.

"You guys think I was going to try and run off?" Kyle whispered to Ty upon seeing the armed escort.

"They're from Clinton," Ty answered. "Friends of the girl's family. Not very happy about what's gone down. No one is. Not in Deer Creek, Clinton, or anywhere. It's got everyone shook up."

The procession silently made its way down the street towards the militia house, a rare spectacle for the bored residents of Deer Creek that drew gawkers and the curious outside their homes. The mile long journey took fifteen minutes, and the party arrived well before sundown. As they approached, the door was opened from inside, where three more people were waiting.

"You didn't cuff him?" an unfamiliar face inside the militia house asked.

"No," Sean answered. "No need. He came without any problems, like I told you he would."

"Humph," the man said. He sneered and glared at Kyle. "Don't go thinking that helps you at all."

Kyle heard undisguised derision in the man's voice and stopped just inside the door. "Have I been arrested or charged with something that I don't know about?"

The man focused his glare on Sean.

Sean held his hands up in front of him. "His wife and kids were there; he was cooperating. I didn't see the need to escalate the situation. He's here, isn't he? Besides, we haven't even questioned him yet."

Kyle froze and looked around the room at the people that were gathered. "You think I killed that girl, don't you." Kyle shook his head and spoke directly to Sean. "This is unbelievable. I've done nothing!" He turned as if to leave, but the four men from Clinton blocked the door, their weapons at their hips, their fingers poised on the triggers.

Kyle took a deep breath and turned back inside. "What else do you want me to say? I've already told you everything."

CHAPTER TWELVE

Wednesday, January 18th

Central Wyoming

Rose struggled with the zipper of her old duffle bag. It hadn't been used in years, and the metal teeth were unwilling to let the zipper head slide easily along. "Need to oil this," Rose muttered, aware of her growing tendency to talk to herself, a habit that had recently started to worry her. She pulled the open end of the bag tight with her free hand, pressed down on the zipper and yanked, finally drawing it closed.

Smokey was hitched to the post by the back door and grazing on some of last year's grass that was visible through the melting snow. Dusty, Smokey's mother and the first horse Rose had acquired upon moving back to Wyoming, was tied to Smokey's saddle and loaded with gear for Rose's escape. Before arriving home, Rose had determined that not only was she no longer safe in her own home, she was now likely a target of the thugs who'd been there that morning, and she was sure they'd be back. She didn't plan to be there when they returned.

Rose walked to the open front door and listened for the sound of a motor while scanning the road. Nothing. She hurried out the back door with the bag, tied it to Dusty's saddle, then went back inside for more. She already had a tent, two sleeping bags, containers of food, and her duffle filled with clothing secured to the horses, along with both rifles and all the ammo she could find.

A map lay open on the kitchen table. Rose hurried over to it and took another look. Circled in red on the last fold of the Montana map was Deer Creek. "Hope you're ready to return the favor, Kyle," she whispered. For a couple of weeks after Kyle had left, she'd thought about following him to Montana, but there had still been people in Wyoming for her, and Max couldn't have made the trip. Eventually, she'd chalked the notion up to a school-girl crush and fragile emotions and brushed it aside.

With her current situation, however, traveling to Deer Creek crazily seemed like her best alternative. The length of the journey, far longer than any pack trip she'd ever taken, scared her, but she couldn't think of any more inviting options. She had no strong ties in Denver, where she'd lived long ago. Plus, a large city wasn't exactly the smartest place for a person to escape to. She had no family around, with one of her sons overseas, and the other in Atlanta, and a distant husband that hadn't been a part of her life for a long time. None of her neighbors seemed willing or prepared to take her in long term. Her associates in the real estate profession were just that, associates. She belonged to no church, and lived too far from town to have belonged to a bowling league, or anything like that, and it wasn't like you'd move in with someone you bowled with, at least not for more than a night or two. Looking back, Rose realized her life was disappointingly shallow, consisting of just her kids, her horses, and her job.

By her reckoning though, Kyle owed her. At great risk to herself, she had saved his life, and in their short time together, he'd become as good a friend as she'd had in the last ten years, maybe longer. If he turned her away, she'd figure something else out, but she didn't see that happening. He'd had every opportunity to use her and lead her on and hadn't. He was decent and sincere. He'd broken her heart, but for the best reason she could think of for a man to break a woman's heart. No, he wouldn't turn her away. Be surprised to see her? Of course, but she was sure he'd find her a place to stay, at least temporarily, and help her with food and friendship and be someone to talk to.

Beyond her connection with Kyle, Deer Creek had sounded like a good place to be—rural, but still with a sense of community, a river, mountains, and nice people—an ideal location and base from which to rebuild. Rose stuffed the map in her pocket and circled her house, looking for a few last-minute things to take. Pictures of the boys, her driver's license, address book, and first aid kit were all tucked into her bags. She was making a final sweep of the house when she heard the bone chilling and unmistakable sound of an engine.

"Why so soon?" she cried out to herself as her stomach sank and the strength drained from her legs. She ran to the front door on weak legs and scanned the road. A couple miles away she saw the red truck heading her direction, followed closely by a white SUV. The vehicles approached slowly, their occupants probably cautious, unaware that it was a lonely, middle-aged woman who'd done so much damage. The vehicles stopped, and Rose watched briefly as men piled out, two from the truck and four from the SUV. "I love you, Max," she shouted at his lifeless body still lying in the driveway. Then she hurried for the back door.

Smokey whinnied as she ran towards him, sensing her anxiety. "Easy boy," she said as she untied his halter and rubbed his nose. "We have to go, pal. I need you to hang in there for me." Bags tied behind the saddle made mounting difficult, but she got her leg over, swung the horse's head to the side and kicked hard with her heels. Smokey turned and started away from the house. Dusty resisted as her lead rope pulled tight, then she too made the turn and followed behind Smokey.

The direct trail to the trees was in full view of the parked vehicles. Rose swung south of the house to avoid being seen, down into the creek bottom and up the far side. She was fifty yards from the trees when she heard the two vehicles draw closer. "Lets go, Smokey," she urged, coaxing him to a run. The rope connected to Dusty pulled tight on Smokey's saddle. Rose knew her horses' loads were heavier than usual, but they needed to get into the cover of the trees in a hurry, or things would go bad fast.

She bounced in the saddle as the horses cantered towards the trees. The packs slapped against the horses' sides, making noise, but not enough to drown out the whine of vehicles accelerating towards the house. Tires skidded to a stop in the gravel of her driveway, followed almost immediately by slamming door and a flurry of shots. Rose shrunk down low, certain bullets were coming her way. Instead she heard glass breaking at the house as countless weapons were fired, then someone shouted. With her horses nearly galloping, Rose hurried to take a final look at her home as they reached the shelter of the trees.

A single shot echoed as she turned, and a bullet careened by overhead. She spotted one of the men with his rifle aimed in her direction. "Go!" she screamed as the horses slowed for the trees, kicking hard and willing them into the safety of the forest. They plunged headlong into the growth, the branches clawing and slapping at her, trying to pull her from her mount as she broke virgin trail through the heavy branches. Rose gripped the saddle and tucked her head behind Smokey's neck while kicking furiously as more shots rang out.

They were deep into the forest before she reined the animals in, allowing them to pick their way more carefully through the trees. She wiped blood from a scratch on her cheek as she drew the horses to a stop and listened. No more gunshots, but she could hear the dreaded engines sounding closer. "Please, no!" she cried, spurring the horses forward yet again.

The vehicles were moving towards her, likely following an old trail her sons had cut with their 4-wheelers years back, one that led from the house up onto the ridge overlooking the valley. The trail was narrow, bumpy, and hard to follow, especially after years of disuse, and unfortunately, it went in the direction she needed to go and would bring them far closer to her than she wanted.

"Move it, Smokey!" she urged, once again kicking him in the flanks. The gunshots had him on edge, and he lurched ahead, almost throwing her from the saddle. They pushed through the trees, picking their trail better than in the mad dash into the forest, but fear and urgency still overtook caution, and Rose endured a steady pummeling from low hanging branches.

Smokey pressed forward, sensing Rose's panic and needing little coaching from her. He avoided the narrowest paths between trees, as the abuse from the branches was no more enjoyable for him than for her. Sweat lathered on his shoulders, and his breathing was labored. The trail was just ahead and visible to Rose. She glanced towards the house and saw nothing, despite the loud echo of the vehicles rolling through the trees.

She took a deep breath and drove forward, emerging from the trees and onto the trail before turning right. Free of the trees, Smokey and Dusty quickened their pace, the open space allowing them to run freer and faster. Rose was headed for a trail that cut across the side of the mountain a half-mile further up the hill. It was the trail she used to visit her neighbors and was familiar to her and her horses, plus it was winding and rocky, and far too narrow for any four-wheeled vehicle to follow.

Maybe there was a chance she could find that trail if she avoided the exposure of the road, but a rocky bluff cut across above them, and she wasn't sure that she could pass it anywhere other than through a gap that the road used. She made a quick decision and stayed on the trail. They had galloped for two hundred yards when Rose felt Smokey suddenly surge ahead. She looked back to see Dusty falling behind, the lead rope dangling close to the horse's feet. "Whoa, Smokey!" she shouted, reining him in and turning him back downhill towards his mother. He fought the change in direction, sensing the danger behind them, but Rose forced him back to Dusty, now walking slowly towards them.

Rose quickly leapt from the saddle, landing awkwardly and stumbling into Dusty before catching herself on the pack. Rose snatched the end dangling from her saddle and tied it to the other end of Dusty's halter. The horse eyed her as it breathed deeply, the air billowing in front of her in great silver clouds. "Time to go, girl," Rose said as she remounted Smokey. A glance downhill told her that the white SUV, mostly obscured by the trees, was bouncing along the trail just three hundred yards back.

"Quick Smokey," Rose said, urging him forward. "Before they see us." They took off once again, driven harder by the glimpse of their pursuers so close behind. As they rounded a curve in the trail, Rose saw the path she wanted fifty yards ahead. The road they were on made a steep climb through the cut in the bluff, then turned right and ran along the ridge for a couple of miles before dropping back down on the far side of the woods in the direction of the highway. Rose's trail cut left where the road turned right, followed the ridge for a distance, then dropped down on the far side into the cover of the trees, and angled away from her house and towards a neighboring ranch.

Rose held her breath as the horses slowed for the steeper climb to reach the fork where the trail and road diverged …thirty yards…twenty yards…ten yards. She was breathing a little easier as they turned onto the horse trail when she saw the vehicle round the bend fifty yards back and come into full view. She made eye contact with the driver, then saw the front seat passenger point towards her. The vehicle accelerated, bouncing wildly on the rough road and throwing its occupants hard against the roof.

Smokey was breathing hard, but Rose had to ignore his discomfort and drove her heels into his sides. "Last time, boy. Let's go." They raced down the trail, the horses rushing hooves on the rocks sounding like a stampede of a dozen animals. Behind her, Rose could see the SUV, an old Ford Bronco, rocking side to side as it accelerated up the steep section of road, going far faster than she imagined it could. "Run!" she screamed, knowing Smokey was approaching his limit. She felt one of his hooves slip on the rocks and he started to go down, then miraculously he caught himself and dashed forward, straining at the bit in his mouth.

They raced ahead, Rose ducking low, afraid to look back. From the sound of the engine, she knew the Bronco was fighting the steep grade of the last section of road. She could see, just a little further ahead, where the trail turned and dropped down, hidden from her pursuers by the trees, where they would be safe, out of range, and impossible to follow except on foot. The Bronco's engine went quiet, then doors slammed and men shouted, followed by gunshots just as Smokey turned into the cover of the trees.

Having struggled to breathe since the Bronco came bouncing towards them, Rose finally let out a lungful of air as they rushed headlong into the cover of the trees, and further down the hillside, quickly putting more and more distance between them. Her whole body shook, and she hunched forward, grasping Smokey's mane in her hands, squeezing, pressing tight with her legs to stay in control, knowing she didn't have the luxury of allowing her emotions to take over.

They rode non-stop for thirty minutes, gradually slowing as Dusty labored more and more to keep up. The sound of the vehicle had faded in the distance, and the ensuing silence was a welcome relief. They approached a stream where the horses could drink and rest, miles from the men chasing her and safe from the threat of gunfire.

At the stream, Rose dismounted and stretched her legs. It was dark and cold, but there was less ice than was typical for mid-January. Rose rubbed Smokey as he dipped his head to the water. "Good boy. Good boy," she repeated, briefly resting her forehead on his shoulder. After untying Dusty, Rose led the mare to the stream, noticing a limp as she turned. "You okay, girl?" she questioned while patting Dusty's neck and checking the saddle. A dark streak on the right rear leg caught her eye, and Rose reached out to inspect it, drawing back fingers that were wet and sticky with blood.

Rose looked closer at the wound, finding that it was round and raw and big enough to fit her index finger in. Dusty shied away as Rose probed the edges of the wound, fresh blood still draining from it. "You poor girl."

A short walk up the path revealed a spotty trail of blood in the snow as far back as Rose could see. Tears pooled in her eyes as she walked back to her horse. "I didn't know you were hurt," she said, stroking Dusty's nose. "I'm so sorry I did this to you. You poor girl; it's just not right."

CHAPTER THIRTEEN

Wednesday, January 18th
Deer Creek, MT

Hearing a tapping on the front door, Jennifer jumped from the couch and quickly swung the door open. "Hi, Ty," she said, looking past him as she stifled a yawn. "Where's Kyle? Isn't he with you?"

Ty Lewis shook his head. "It's just me. Can I come in?"

Jennifer stepped to the side, allowing him to enter. "I went down there, you know, but they wouldn't let me in. Said he couldn't have visitors."

"I know. I saw you. That's why I'm here. Thought you needed to know what's going on."

Jennifer dropped anxiously onto the couch and motioned for Ty to do the same. "When are they going to let him come home? He will come home, won't he?"

Ty pressed his clasped hands against his mouth and took a deep breath. "I don't know how much I should say, but things look, well, they don't look good, Jennifer. I hate to say it, but I'm more than a little worried."

"But he didn't do anything. How can things be so bad?" Jennifer hurled her words at him, her hands balled into fists.

The room was dark, and the moon, being the only source of light, cast long, gray shadows over everything. The whites of Ty's eyes stood out in the darkness, flashing each time he blinked. "Listen, I'm with you on this, but it's not about you and me. The girl that died, her daddy is a big shot over there. He had a little grocery store and a couple other businesses, so he's really taken care of the town for the past few months. They're all pretty riled about what happened, understandably so."

"It doesn't matter who her family is. Kyle didn't do anything." Jennifer was nearly shouting, her voice echoing in the room.

"Hey, I believe that," Ty said softly, holding his hands up in protest. "I believe that, but the situation looks all wrong. Kyle was in the wrong place at the wrong time. The body was found in his house, and he was the one on patrol that night. Dale and his mother both swear the girl left by midnight. No one else saw or heard anything."

"He would never do anything like that," Jennifer said, still worked up. "I know Kyle. He might have a bit of a temper. Everyone does. But he'd never hurt anyone that way."

Ty looked directly at Jennifer. "There's going to be a trial. It'll probably start next week. It'll be over quick, maybe two or three days."

"Will he come home after that?"

"If they find him innocent."

"What if they don't?"

Ty took a deep breath. "Jenn. It's rape and murder. It won't be good."

CHAPTER FOURTEEN

Thursday, January 19th
Central Wyoming

Lou Thompson knelt over the injured horse, shaking his head slowly. "It's no good, Rose. There's nothing I can do for her." The sun was just coming up, and the wind that swept down over the hillside and howled through the trees was cold and biting. Lou's worn cowboy hat was pulled down tight on his head, the collar of his jacket turned up to block the wind. "She won't stand, and it looks like she's been laying here for quite some time." He turned towards Rose. "She isn't going to make it."

"Are you sure?" Rose stood next to Lou, her hands pushed deep in the pockets of her heavy coat, watching while he examined Dusty.

"It's a miracle she made it this far. Look how big the wound is, and there's no exit hole so the bullet is still inside, probably lodged in her hip. Horses have a lot of muscle there, which probably slowed the bullet enough to keep from shattering the bone, but that tissue is all damaged, and she's lost a lot of blood. The fact that she walked this far is incredible, but that's the end of the miracle. It's only a matter of time and how much we're willing to let her suffer." The wind gusted again, pelting them with snow and ice. "Let's go inside where it's warm."

They walked to the big ranch house in silence, shielding themselves from the weather with their arms. Once inside, Rose took off her boots and dropped down hopelessly onto a couch near the fireplace. "It's just not right, Lou. That horse shouldn't have to pay for my mistakes. I should have left sooner."

Lou slowly took off his coat and hung it on a stand by the front door. He was a fourth generation rancher and owned one of the largest spreads in their part of Wyoming. Just under 18,000 acres of his own, along with 6,400 acres of federal land leases, gave him miles of solitude and security. At 55 years old, Lou still looked like he was in his early forties. Other than a six-inch scar on his right cheek he was movie star handsome, standing six foot two and built long and lean, as if he trained for marathons instead of running his ranch. He was showing signs of aging, though, as his long mustache was a little grayer each time Rose visited, and his head a little more bald.

As a little girl, Rose had dreamt about growing up, getting married, and living on a ranch, and both Lou and his property, from a physical standpoint, more than exceeded everything she'd aspired to. It was his wife, Sonja, however, who Rose really felt a kinship with. She was Nordic pretty, intelligent, witty, and such a catch that Lou had gone against his father's wishes in marrying her, then a waitress in her immigrant parents' restaurant, when he was just twenty-one and not yet done with college.

Lou continued dryly, unmoved by Rose's emotion. "I don't know about the blame, but we probably shouldn't wait too long on the animal. That injury will keep her from standing, and the longer we wait, the more she'll suffer. If you want," Lou said, approaching the fire with his hands held out to warm them. "I can shoot her for you, or you can do it. It doesn't matter to me. I'll have to cut her up and take her away from the house though, so the carcass doesn't draw the wolves in. We have enough problems with them as it is."

"Good heavens, Lou," Sonja said, emerging from the bedroom. "Show a little empathy. Dusty isn't an old car or one of your steers; she's a part of Rose's family. You're so business-like when it comes to the animals." She shook her head and rolled her eyes, giving Rose an apologetic look.

Lou turned away from Sonja and closed his eyes. "They're all just things. If you let yourself get attached to them, then you have problems like this. I am sorry though, Rose. I guess maybe I was a little insensitive."

Rose gazed numbly into the fire. "It's okay. You're not the one who put her at risk."

"You can't blame yourself," Sonja said. "This is bigger than all of us. That we've made it this long says something about us. Lou, you just go take care of Rose's horse for her."

"No," Rose interrupted. "Dusty is my responsibility; I should do it. Just give me a minute to get my head right."

"I'll go work on some breakfast," Sonja said as she excused herself, giving Lou a stern look.

A few minutes later the sound of the front door closing was followed by a lone crack from a rifle.

CHAPTER FIFTEEN

Tuesday, January 24th
Deer Creek, MT

Jennifer walked as close to Kyle as she could get. He was flanked on both sides by guards, with two more following close behind. The guards were all well armed, but with a mismatch of weapons that reflected the improvised nature of the community's operations. A small crowd trailed behind, and Jennifer could see people up ahead, heading towards the community building from all directions. The trial was to begin that morning and was the most anticipated, talked about event the community had experienced since the EMP, almost five months before.

"Looks like it's going to be a full house," Kyle said to the guard walking between him and Jennifer. The man was from Clinton, a friend of the victim's family, and treated Kyle like a leper. He gave no reply, just stared straight ahead.

"How are you holding up, Kyle?" Jennifer asked, half jogging to keep up.

Kyle smiled. He'd spent the last four days and nights in the crawl space of the militia house, only coming out to speak with his counsel, the prosecutor, or his family, when they were allowed to visit. As luck would have it, the assistant District Attorney, a bright, powerful woman, lived in Clinton, knew the victim's family, and jumped at the chance to do something more than chop wood and scavenge for food.

On Kyle's side, Boyd Kelley, a sullen, unpleasant, estate attorney, still harboring a grudge from losing out to Gabe for the job of community head, had been drafted to represent him. Knowing how the two attorneys would appear to the jury had Kyle feeling like he was spotting the opposition two touchdowns and a field goal before the game began. "I'm doing alright, Jenn. How about you guys?"

"Not so good. We're all really worried, and we miss you a lot."

The last four days had been the longest of his life. He'd been adequately fed, and the crawl space was tolerably warm, but sitting around doing nothing, while being so close to his family and in such unbelievable circumstances, was testing the limits of his sanity. "I miss you too, Jenn, and the kids. Can't wait to come home." He smiled bravely, but having spoken to both his counsel and the prosecutor for hours, Kyle wasn't sure that was going to happen. "How's Spencer?"

"Not good. He's having a hard time with all this. He doesn't understand why you can't come home, but you saw that yesterday when we visited."

"Tell him I love him, okay?" Kyle struggled with his emotions.

"I do. Every day."

They rounded the corner and approached the building where most events happened: church, community meetings, militia training, and now murder trials. A group of people was waiting to go in, more than Kyle had ever remembered seeing there. Many, he assumed, had come from Clinton for the trial. "Quite the crowd," he observed. "We should have sold tickets."

"Not much else for people to do; I suppose they're curious."

"Guess I'd be here if it wasn't me on trial. Do you know I love you?"

Jennifer nodded. "I do, but it's always nice to hear you say it. Think they'd take the handcuffs off for a hug?"

Kyle looked at his escorts questioningly, knowing they'd heard his wife. No one responded or even looked at him. "I think that's a no. How about a rain check?"

Jennifer tried to keep from crying. "Only if you promise it will never expire."

"I promise," he replied, finding it hard to talk. "Just give me a couple days." They arrived at the makeshift courthouse, and the people crowding the entrance stepped back to allow the entourage to enter. The inside of the building was packed, standing room only, and the two men bracketing Kyle grabbed ahold of his coat and steered him through the crowd, both to ensure that they weren't separated from him and so he could get through the throng.

Kyle was led to the front of the building, where an improvised court had been set up. The judges' table was a tall dinette draped with a black tablecloth, at which Gabe Vance and Don Allen, the respective mayors of the two communities, co-presided. To their left, and Kyle's right, was the jury of five locals, two from Deer Creek, two from Clinton, and a man who lived between the two towns and hadn't attached himself to either community. The prosecutor's table was closest to the jury, and the table for the defense, where Boyd Kelly sat, disheveled and pale, was to Kyle's left. The guards led Kyle to a chair beside his attorney, removed his handcuffs, then positioned themselves in chairs just off to the side.

Grace Anderson had arrived early and taken a seat directly behind the defense table, saving a seat for Jennifer, who slipped in quietly beside her friend.

The dull roar of conversation quieted as soon as Kyle sat down, then Gabe rose to his feet. Neither he nor his counterpart had any experience with running a trial, but had taken direction from the two attorneys on the best way to proceed under the circumstances.

"Good morning," Gabe shouted as the crowd quieted. A murmur rolled through the crowd as the proceedings commenced. "We will begin the trial of Kyle Tait, represented by Boyd Kelly, for the rape and murder of Leah Smith, who is represented by the family's counsel, Helen Markham."

Gabe delineated the trial's proceedings, explaining the rules of the courtroom and the decorum expected of the spectators. This was followed by the agenda for the trial, most of which had been whispered throughout the community already, but Gabe reiterated it for the benefit of anyone in attendance who hadn't heard. The first day of the trial was for opening statements, followed by the prosecution's case and witnesses. The next day, Wednesday, was for the defense to present their case, followed by any rebuttals, then closing arguments on Thursday. At that point, the trial would be turned over to the jury, with their deliberations to last until a verdict was reached.

Gabe noted that the schedule would be fluid and adjust as needed, but most people expected a verdict before sundown on Saturday.

Gabe finished his explanations, then asked the prosecutor for her opening statement.

Helen Markham, shoulders back and head high, smartly dressed in a red blouse and black skirt, walked to the front of the room, turned, cleared her throat, and smiled. Kyle guessed that she was in her early forties, maybe a little younger, but he didn't really care. Her brown hair was shoulder-length and styled neatly, and although Kyle didn't find her particularly attractive, she wasn't ugly either. Her voice was low and gravelly, more suited to a radio personality than what you'd expect from a courtroom attorney.

"Good morning," she began. "It's with deep sadness that we've gathered in this court today. The tragedy that befell our communities last week is hard to fathom. Leah Smith, a vivacious young woman, the joy of her family, brutally raped and murdered. Her body left to rot, hidden in the basement of an abandoned home. And Kyle Tait, a father of three young children, husband, local militia member, heroic survivor of an almost impossible journey home, sits here charged with her murder. Mr. Tait is also the owner of the home where the body was found, the man not only on guard duty the night the victim was murdered, but the one with specific responsibility for the area of town where both the victim was visiting and where her body was found.

"I know this is going to be a difficult case for everyone. Both the victim and the accused are members of our communities, so we've all been touched by the crime in one way or another, directly or indirectly. And it's going to be difficult, too, for our jury. We've been so conditioned by the news reports and dramas we watched on TV to expect every crime to have irrefutable evidence—fingerprints, DNA, video of the perpetrator, incriminating emails, GPS data from cell phones—all high-tech pieces of a puzzle that would lead us to an inescapable conclusion of the accused's guilt. Well, we don't have those things anymore, do we? No DNA, no fingerprints, no video—none of it. So what do we do? Do we throw out all hope of discovering the truth and let the accused go free? Or do we do the best we can with the information we have at our disposal?" She paused and looked around the room, stopping to look each of the jurors in the eye.

"That's what we are asking you to do today, this week. This is not the first jury to hear a case under difficult circumstances. It's only been in the last hundred years that fingerprint evidence has been allowed in the courtroom, let alone DNA or GPS evidence. No, good people on honest juries have been making difficult decisions for over a thousand years, weighing evidence, listening to witnesses, assessing the cases presented, and rendering a verdict. I'm confident that as we proceed through this case, you'll find it to be straightforward and will be able come to a conclusion as to what happened.

"Leah Smith, young, sweet, pretty, leaves the home of her boyfriend at too late an hour. It's dark out, not much of a moon that night. She leads her horse quietly through town, trying to make it back home without being seen. But before she gets very far, she's stopped. It's a man with a gun, the only person in the area. She's unarmed. He questions her. She explains she just left her boyfriend's, and the thought arouses him. He speculates as to what this pretty, young girl and her boyfriend have been doing, and he propositions her, or maybe she flirts with him to try and get him to let her pass. Late at night, with no one else around, she's scared enough that she agrees to what he asks when he promises not to hurt her, and she follows him into the basement of his own home, explaining why there was no screaming and no witnesses.

"Having second thoughts, she says she's going to tell his wife, or her father, someone, or maybe he just fears that she will. The thought of losing everything he worked so hard to save makes him fearful. Family gone, reputation shot, ostracized from the community with nowhere to go. He starts to worry. He tells her to be quiet. Maybe she laughs. He strikes out, hits her. She screams, and he panics, grabs her, covers her mouth, and pushes her down to shut her up. But he stays on her too long. He's no monster, but in the heat of the moment, things have gone way too far. She's no longer breathing, and he realizes what he's done.

"He hides the body and locks the door to his house, knowing he needs to check in back at the militia house. For the rest of the shift he's worried, knows if anyone sees him with a body, it's all over. He decides to wait, to give it a few days until the heat dies down then dispose of the body, hoping that it looks like she ran away, or that an outsider will be blamed for her disappearance. But someone found the body and ruined his plans." Helen pauses again, allowing the sobs from Leah's father and younger brother to amplify. Two members of the jury dab at their own eyes.

The prosecutor turns back to the crowd. She works the jury and the spectators, continuing to paint a picture of a tragic crime and a young life snuffed out too soon, describing Leah's childhood, her grief at the divorce of her parents, her successes in school, her job, and her despondency after the EMP, before finding happiness again with a boyfriend in Deer Creek.

Her statement takes just over an hour to finish, a powerful, emotional, and convincing narrative that Kyle himself finds absorbing. And with every minute she speaks, the cold despair that clutches Kyle's chest tightens its icy grip on him.

CHAPTER SIXTEEN

Tuesday, January 24th
Central Wyoming

Rose pushed the door of the ranch house closed behind her, the warmth of the room a sharp contrast to the chilly outside air. "Well, everything's loaded and strapped down tight. I guess I should be off now."

Sonja smiled and gave her a hug. "You understand you're welcome to stay longer, don't you?"

"I do, but I hadn't even intended to stay as long as I have. I so appreciate you letting me be here, coming unexpected like I did."

"It's the least we could do for a neighbor and a friend. I just wish all this wasn't happening. I'm not sure what things will be like when it's all over, but I fear they'll never be the same," Sonja said wistfully.

Lou stood from his chair in front of the fireplace. "Wish those thugs would have followed you here. The ranch hands and I would have made short work of them, and made things a little safer for you."

"It'll be alright, Lou. They'll avoid places like yours as long as they can, at least until they run out of the smaller places. I'm lucky I was left alone as long as I was."

"Well, we'll be ready for them if they do show up. They'll have to bring a small army along if they want to take what's mine."

Rose smiled knowingly. "Thank you again for your help, and the supplies, and the horse. You're truly a life saver."

Lou shook his head. "Don't thank me yet for that horse; she's got a bit of an attitude. If I didn't know who her parents were, I'd swear she was part jackass. And anyway, we have more animals than we need, so it's not much of a sacrifice. Worst case you can shoot and eat her."

The Thompsons walked Rose outside, waiting to wave when she finally rode off with her two horses loaded down with supplies. Three inches of fresh snow from a storm the day before covered the ground. It had delayed her departure, but today was clear and the temperatures were warming, with water already dripping from the eaves of the house and snow sticking to the horses' hooves.

Rose took a deep breath, waved goodbye to the Thompsons again, and turned the horses towards the road. It had been a few years since she'd been to the ranch by this road, six years in fact, when she'd been Lou's real estate agent and sold off a third of his ranch so that he could pay the estate taxes from his father's passing. The sale had been the largest real estate deal and commission of her career, but had unfortunately come from difficult circumstances, as Lou had not only just lost his father, but had also had to give up a sizeable chunk of the ranch that had been in his family for almost one hundred years in order to pay the death taxes.

Since that sale, Rose had passed through, stopping at the Thompson's ranch, once or twice a year on horseback, but theirs had mainly been a professional relationship. Lou's willingness to help her as much as he had was a surprise to her, as she had hoped for and expected nothing more than a place to spend a night or two before beginning her journey to Montana. Instead, both Lou and Sonja had been extremely generous, replacing her horse and providing supplies she hadn't had time to gather before fleeing.

She knew her journey was high risk, but at least with Lou's assistance, her odds had increased somewhat.

Rose guided Smokey through the open gate and towards the driveway under skies that were a vivid blue with a few wispy clouds to the north. Miles of undisturbed snow surrounded her, and the glare of sunlight on the snow made it unbearable to look around. Rose dug out a pair of sunglasses Sonja had insisted she take, plunked them on her nose, and gave Smokey a slap. The lead rope from her new horse, Blitz, pulled tight, and Rose looked back to make sure that the chestnut-colored horse was securely attached. Blitz, who was six inches shorter than Smokey and named for the lighting-shaped patch of white on her forehead, snorted and pulled against the lead, twisting her head from side to side then, temporarily accepting the futility of the fight, fell in behind Smokey.

CHAPTER SEVENTEEN

Tuesday, January 24ᵗʰ
Deer Creek, MT

Boyd Kelly walked to the front of the room. He paused and gave Kyle a nervous smile. The prosecutor had just concluded her opening statement, leaving the crowd buzzing. Boyd waited for the crowd to settle down, then, when it was finally quiet, he cleared his throat, pulled a notecard from his pocket, and began his opening statement.

"Jurors," he started, his voice cracking and wavering. "You'll find I'm not as eloquent as Ms. Markham. I apologize for that."

Kyle leaned forward and rested his elbows on his knees. "This is bad" was the only thought that ran through his mind. He glanced at Jennifer, with her bloodshot and swollen eyes, but she was watching Boyd.

Boyd went on at the front of the room. "I'm an attorney, but my specialty is estates - helping people plan for their own demise, not trying to keep someone from facing theirs. This whole situation is not fair. Not for me. Not for you. Not for Kyle Tait. And certainly not for Leah Smith." His initial nervousness seemed to lessen, but his voice was still whiney and weak, a stark contrast to the powerful, confident tones of the prosecutor.

"Leah deserves to be alive and to live in a town and a place and a time where she could call 911 if she felt threatened, or drive her car home, or text her boyfriend at night instead of sneaking home on horseback. Kyle deserves a real attorney, not a close to retirement desk jockey like me. He also deserves a real investigation.

"Helen told you quite a story. It almost brought tears to my eyes, but it was a fairytale. Once you scrape away all the emotion and the storytelling, the only facts she told you were that a girl died, and that she was found in the basement of a home that Mr. Tait owns. Those are things you already knew. The rest was nothing but speculation, conjecture, make believe.

"Please remember that fact as we go through the trial. There will be no DNA, or video, or fingerprints. Not even witnesses to any crime, or confessions, or wounds on the accused. It's all conjecture, and a man's life hangs in the balance. Please don't make a decision based on sorrow and emotion that you'll regret for the rest of your life. Thank you."

With that, Boyd returned to his seat. A stunned silence filled the room, the expectation being that his opening would be as lengthy as the prosecutor's. Gabe looked at Boyd to confirm that he was done, and Boyd nodded affirmatively.

"The prosecution will now present their witnesses," Gabe said, indicating a lone chair set up between his table and the jurors. "The time is yours, Ms. Markham."

Helen stood, facing the front. "Thank you. For my first witness I call Carol Jeffries."

Carol walked to the front, gave her name to the court, was sworn in, then sat in the witness chair. "Ms. Jeffries, what can you tell us about the body?"

Carol looked nervous and fidgeted with the hem of her shirt as she spoke. She described the condition of the body, the injuries on the neck, the burst blood vessels in the eyes that indicated strangulation, and the disheveled clothing.

As there was no contention regarding the fact that Leah was dead and how she was found, the prosecutor had only a few questions for Carol. Boyd cross examined, but did not bring anything new to light as there was no disagreement on the points at hand.

The next witness was Sean Reider, head of security and defacto policeman/detective of the community. He reiterated what Carol had already stated with regards to the body then Helen changed her line of questioning and delved into his interactions with Kyle.

"How long have you known the accused?"

"Just a little over two months."

"Any issues?"

"None whatsoever. He's done a great job."

"So you'd say he's an exemplary individual?"

Sean nodded. "Yeah. I don't see any reason not to."

"How'd he act when you told him Leah was missing?"

"I'd woken him up, so he was sleepy. But he told me he hadn't seen anything."

"Did he offer any suggestions? Give any clues?"

Sean thought a second. "He suggested we look over on the mountain between our two towns. Said it was easy to get lost up there."

"Where is that in relation to where the body was found?"

"It's the far side of town, but it made sense. I already had a couple of people looking that direction, so it …"

Carol cut him off. "I don't need your interpretation of his suggestion, sir. My question was, where is the area he directed you to in relation to where the body was found. You said it was on the far side of town. Is that correct?"

Sean confirmed the fact.

"Is there anywhere else, within this little community, that is farther away from where Leah was found than that mountain."

"No, there isn't, but it was the most logical place to look."

Helen glared at Sean. "Thank you, sir. I believe the relevant part of your answer is 'no'. There is no place further from the crime scene than the location to where the accused directed you."

Helen asked Sean a few more procedural questions then yielded the witness.

Boyd began his cross-examination as he walked towards Sean. "How did Kyle act when you informed him that the body had been found?"

"He looked shocked. He seemed very surprised that she had been found dead. I think we all expected her to have just gotten lost on her way home. I know I did."

"Did you physically examine the accused?"

"Yes."

"Was there anything on his body to indicate he'd been in a struggle?"

"No. He had a few scratches on his arms, but they were older, scabbed over. He said he fell when he was hunting."

"Did Kyle ever make any comments about raping or killing anyone?"

Sean shook his head. "Nothing at all like that."

"Did you ever worry about him patrolling at night, unsupervised?"

"No. I have a lot of confidence in all the guys who work at night. It's a good crew."

"All right, thank you," Boyd said, concluding.

Helen asked for a redirect and returned to face Sean. "You said his wounds were old. I'm just curious. What physiology class have you taken that would give you the expertise to make such a statement?"

Sean looked at the prosecutor, his disdain for the question obvious. "I've not had a physiology class, ma'am. But I did receive medical training in the military..."

"So you haven't had specific training in this area. Correct?"

"Not specifically, but I had medical training when I served in the military. I've been…"

"Mr. Reider," Helen interrupted him again. "Just answer my questions. I understand you want to help Mr. Tait, but you are speaking out of line."

"Look," Sean said, straightening up in his chair. "I realize we are not the expert scientists you are used to having as witnesses, but I'm not stupid. I don't need training to know what an old scratch looks like."

Helen smirked at him. "Thank you, Mr. Reider. Nothing more. Please don't leave the court, ah, this building. I may have more questions for you later." She stepped over to her table and consulted her notes. "My next witness is Dale Briggs."

Dale strode to the witness chair with his chest puffed out, but looking like he might throw up at any second. Once sworn in, he focused his attention on Ms. Markham, who asked a series of questions about his relationship with the deceased. Dale described how they'd first met at the New Years party, their first "date," the sexual nature of their relationship, how much he'd cared for Leah, and what had happened the night in question.

While Dale poured his heart out as he described his lost love, Helen casually strode over to the defense table. When Dale was finished, she waited for him to compose himself then asked, "Can you describe for us your relationship with Mr. Tait?"

"I don't have a relationship with him," he retorted. "He's an ass."

Helen lingered by the table, and Kyle's heart sunk, knowing where the questions were heading. "Any past dealings with Mr. Tait?"

"I guess you could say that. He beat me up a few weeks ago." Whispers rolled through the room, and Helen paused for effect, waiting for them to subside.

"Please elaborate."

Dale smirked at Kyle. "It was about four weeks ago. It was really cold that night, and my mom and I needed some wood, so I went to the wood lot when it was dark and took some. He caught me there and chased me down. Beat me up pretty bad. I still had a black eye at the New Years party."

"Were you entitled to the wood?"

"Well, we live here, and the trees don't belong to anyone, but they wouldn't give me any. So I guess in their eyes I didn't deserve it. I dropped it all when I ran off, but he still attacked me."

Helen had been watching Kyle during this exchange, then very dramatically turned to the witness. "Did you fear for your life?"

"I did," Dale answered, now on the verge of tears. "Another guy came and stopped the attack, but I thought he was going to kill me, all for an armload of wood."

"Anyone else know about this?"

"He does," Dale said, turning and pointing at Gabe. "And the last witness, he did, too. And the guy who stopped Kyle from attacking me, the black guy, he does. I don't know his name."

"Thank you, Mr. Briggs. I'm so sorry for your loss. I have no further questions."

Kyle whispered a few things to his lawyer, who then stood for cross-examination. "Mr. Briggs. I'm sorry for your loss, but I do have a few questions for you. When the Smith girl left your home, did you walk her to the corner?"

Dale shook his head no.

"Did you watch her ride down the street?"

He shook his head again in the negative.

"Did Leah ever indicate she had any problems with the militia?"

He thought a second. "No, not that I recall."

"So you were the last one to see her alive, didn't escort her anywhere, are an admitted thief, and we should take your word on all of this?"

Dale shifted uneasily. "Look, I know the wood wasn't mine, but nobody was going to be hurt by the little bit I took, and my mother will tell you that Leah left my house, and I didn't."

"When you stole the wood, who initiated the assault?"

"I don't remember."

"Did you throw the wood onto Mr. Tait?"

"I'm not sure."

"When it came to blows, did you punch and kick Mr. Tait after you pushed a wall of wood on top of him and before he struck you?"

"I...I...I can't be certain. It's possible. But none of that even hurt him. I had black eyes and a fat lip."

"Just because you can't fight, that doesn't mean Mr. Tait is guilty of anything." A chorus of muted laughter came from the crowd. Boyd asked several more questions about Dale's background, revealing little, then sat down.

Helen stood. "I'd like to recall a previous witness. Mr. Reider, would you please come back to the witness chair?"

Sean returned to the front, his face blank. "Mr. Reider," Helen began. "I asked you just a few minutes ago if you'd had any issues with Mr. Tait, and you said no. Correct?"

Sean agreed.

"The last witness, Mr. Briggs, tells us of an incident where the defendant assaulted him and of which you were directly aware. Why is it you chose not to inform the jury of that event?"

"I just forgot about it. It wasn't a big deal. You know, we recently saved this town, and likely yours, from armed infiltrators. We had to bury four of their guys and one of ours got shot up, and you expect me to make a big deal about a punk thief who got a fat lip?"

"It's not about the fat lip, sir. It's about a man you put on patrol who seems to have a problem with his temper, with his self-control. You see, the problem is when you don't tell us stuff like that and when you make it so obvious whose side you're on, it makes the jury think you're hiding something, and that you're trying to protect the accused. Frankly, I think that myself. Now, why is it you didn't tell us about the incident with Mr. Briggs?"

"I told you. I forgot. And besides, I don't think Kyle did any more than most people would've done. We're figuring this out as we go. I'm not a trained policeman. We don't have nightly reports that we fill out and can refer to. We're just trying to keep you people alive. That doesn't make us nefarious."

Helen rolled her eyes. "Thank you. Please, work on your recall in the future." She waited as Sean returned to his seat. "For my next witness, I'd like to call Audrey Welch."

A woman three rows back stood, hesitated, then walked to the front of the room, her gaze directed at the ground. Kyle turned to Jennifer and whispered, "Who's that?"

Jennifer shook her head slowly. "She lives on the other side of town. Don't know why she'd be called to testify."

When Audrey was seated, Helen faced her. "Do you know the defendant?"

Audrey looked at Kyle. "I know who he is, and I know his wife a little, but I can't say that I know him."

"When did you first meet him?"

"Just after he got back. It was pretty exciting, like he'd returned from the dead. I mean, after that much time, with everything going on, to have him show up alive was remarkable. We left to get to the meeting early, because we heard he was going to tell about his experiences."

"When you say 'we', who do you mean?"

"It was my son, Shane, and I that went."

"Did Mr. Tait disappoint when he spoke about his experiences?"

Audrey shook her head vigorously. "No. Not at all. It was fantastic."

"Did he say anything that disturbed you?"

She hesitated, looking nervously at Kyle and Jennifer.

Helen stepped between them, breaking the line of sight between Audrey and the Taits. "Did he say anything that disturbed you?" she repeated.

Audrey exhaled and made eye contact with the prosecutor. "Like I told you the other day, my son is a little impulsive. He asked Kyle if he'd killed anyone on his trip home..."

Kyle's mind instantly flashed back to his first Sunday home. He'd spoken for about thirty minutes at the town meeting and was answering questions when an impish boy of about twelve had questioned him about killing people. Kyle had intentionally left out any mention of the shootout in Colorado while speaking, but asked point blank about it, he had been caught off guard and his vague answer had clearly given the impression that he had taken a life. Afterwards, he'd wished he'd just said 'no' and moved on. He hadn't provided details, other than to say his own life had been on the line, but the damage was done, enough to make people look at him just a little differently.

"And?" Helen asked, prodding.

"Well, he didn't come right out and say it, but the implication was pretty clear that he did. Even my twelve year old got that. It bothered me when he said it, but how can I say if it was wrong or right? I don't know..."

"Thank you, Mrs. Welch. I don't need your interpretation of Mr. Tait's intentions. I just needed to know what he said about killing people on his way home. So, to summarize, Mr. Tait tacitly admitted, in front of the town, that he killed in order to make it home, correct?"

Boyd stood. "I object your honor. Leading the witness."

Gabe, wide-eyed, looked nervously at Don, his co-judge. "Boyd, I'm not sure what to say, exactly, but I was there. I don't think she's making Mrs. Welch say anything out of line. Perhaps on your cross you can clarify things."

Helen looked back at the witness. "Did he admit to killing, or not?"

"He didn't say those words that I remember, but I took it as an admission."

"Thank you. Nothing further."

Boyd stood, but didn't move towards the witness. "Did he say the words 'I killed x number of people?'"

"No, he did not say the words 'I killed someone.'"

Boyd hadn't been at the meeting she was referring to and hadn't been able to question Kyle about it, so was unsure how far to push the questioning, so he thanked the witness and sat down.

Helen smiled as she stood back up. "I now call Steven Lee as a witness."

Kyle's heart skipped a beat when he heard the name. Jennifer noticed his distress and gestured for an explanation, but he just closed his eyes and stared at the floor.

After Mr. Lee was sworn in, Helen began her questioning. "How do you know the defendant?"

"I've worked the guard shift at night with him for a few weeks."

"Do you get along?"

"Yeah. Haven't had any problems. He's been a good guy to work with."

"Did you work the night of the murder?"

"Yes."

"Did you see anything unusual that night?"

Steven hesitated. "I'm not sure. It didn't seem like it at the time, but with everything that happened, there might be more to it."

"What do you mean by that?"

"Well, that night I had a job similar to Kyle's, patrolling the interior, but in a different section. It was kind of cold, and I was heading back to the militia house to warm up when I saw movement up by a house. I had my gun out and had him raise his hands before he identified himself. It was Kyle."

"Why do you find this unusual? I'm sure that situations like that happen on occasion."

"Yeah, it's happened a couple times in fact. The thing that concerned me was, the next night I realized that it was his house that he was near when I saw him, where the body was found."

An audible murmur came from the crowd.

"You're saying you saw him by the front door of the house where the body was found, correct?"

Steven nodded sheepishly. "Yes. I suppose so."

Helen paused and looked at the jurors, who were jotting notes. When they looked back up she asked a handful more questions, then returned to her seat.

Boyd stood for cross-examination. "That's all very interesting. I wonder if you saw Kyle go to the house?"

Steven shook his head. "No. I just saw him by his house. I was just walking down the street, keeping an eye out for stuff."

"Did you see him with a body?"

"No."

"Did you hear a woman's voice?"

"No."

"Did you see the victim's horse?"

"No."'

"Did Kyle seem nervous?"

"No, not especially. Maybe just a little startled when I spotted him."

"Did he have blood on his hands, or his pants down? Anything that would indicate he had just committed or was preparing to commit a murder?"

"No. If the body hadn't been found there, I probably wouldn't have thought about it again. It wasn't until after the girl was found that it stood out to me."

"Are you sure it was the night of the murder that you saw Kyle near his house?"

Steven nodded. "I am. Kyle usually has the patrol along the river, not the interior, but he was late getting to work that night. So I'm positive it was the night in question."

Boyd asked a few questions about the work they did at night, then, finding no other fruitful veins to explore, excused the witness.

The prosecutor next called a string of witnesses, which included the girl's father, the man who had found the body, two other militia members who had worked the night the girl disappeared, a neighbor Leah had spoken to about her new boyfriend, and a teacher from Leah's childhood. The prosecutor concluded just after sunset, having artfully painted a tragic picture of an innocent girl cut down by a heartless opportunist.

CHAPTER EIGHTEEN

Wednesday, January 25th
Deer Creek, MT

Small pellets of snow fell quietly to the ground, but inside the metal court building the pellets hit the roof with the volume of a tropical monsoon unleashed. Don Anderson, the Clinton mayor, was forced to shout to be heard over the ruckus when he opened proceedings for the day. "Thank you for coming," he bellowed to the crowd, which was larger than it had been the day before, with people sitting in their own camp chairs wherever they could find space. "We will proceed according to the schedule announced yesterday. The defense will now present their case. Mr. Kelly, the time belongs to you."

The defense's case would be followed by closing statements if time permitted, then, once they concluded, the jury would be sequestered until they reached a verdict. Due to the nature of the situation and the lack of resources for sequestering a jury for an extended period, everyone involved in the trial had agreed that a four-fifths verdict would be acceptable.

Boyd stood and smiled at the jury. "Thank you, Mr. Anderson. I will call Mr. Kyle Tait as my first witness." The din of the pelting snow drowned out his voice, but when Kyle stood and moved towards the witness chair the crowd became animated.

As soon as Kyle was ready to testify, Boyd moved close to the jury. Kyle and his attorney had talked yesterday after court and discussed his testimony and whether or not it was needed, but with no forensics or witnesses to make his case, they both felt it might come down to Kyle and his believability. His taking the stand was, both agreed, essential. They hadn't had time to rehearse answers, but Kyle knew the direction Boyd was headed.

"Mr. Tait," he began. "You're here today to answer a charge of murder. Would you relate to the court and the jury what your criminal history looks like."

Kyle smiled and looked the jurors in the eye. His hair was combed, his beard neatly trimmed, and he wore his newest jeans and the one dress shirt and tie that he owned, delivered to him at the militia house by Jennifer. The storm and the accompanying ruckus let up just as he began his testimony. "Yes, Mr. Kelly. I don't have much of a criminal record. I've had a couple of speeding ticket and one for a late registration, but that's it."

"Anything from your childhood?"

Kyle blushed a little. "Ah… my friends and I…"

Boyd looked slightly panicked.

Kyle continued. "We got caught stealing a case of beer from the grocery store. I was a senior in high school, so seventeen years old. My mom told the police to teach me a lesson, so I spent a night in jail and was sentenced to fifty hours of community service. That's the only blemish from my high school days."

His attorney let out a relieved breath. "Anything more serious than that?"

Kyle shook his head. "Nothing."

"What about the event that was alluded to yesterday, where it was alleged that you confessed to killing someone?"

"That was a terrible thing." Kyle looked right at the jurors, like Boyd had instructed him. "Yes, I killed a man. I still have nightmares about it. I was in a situation where it was kill or be killed, and I didn't want to die out on the road, away from my family." He stood up and removed his shirt and tie and held up his arm where the scar from the bullet wound was still clearly visible. "I tried to do everything possible to avoid it. This is where I got shot before I killed the guy. I was forced to take his life, or else I wouldn't be here today." He put his shirt back on before sharing, in detail, what had happened on the road in Colorado.

Boyd paused when Kyle finished, giving the jurors a chance to think about what they might have done in the same situation, then cleared his throat before asking the next question. "The young girl who was killed, Leah, had you ever seen her before?"

"Not on the night in question."

Boyd looked surprised. "Had you seen her before that?"

"Yes," Kyle confirmed. "About a week before she died. I was on patrol and saw someone on horseback coming towards me. I waited behind a tree until she was almost to me, then I confronted her."

"Anything unusual happen."

"No. I surprised her a bit, but she told me where she was going. I just told her to be careful and not be out so late. It wasn't a big deal, just unusual because people aren't out at night much."

"Did you attack her?"

"No. Absolutely not."

"Did you hurt her?"

Kyle shook his head. "Not in any way. If I had done anything to her, I'm sure she would have told someone, but nothing happened."

"Why do you think she was found in your house?"

"I don't know why she was left there, other than the fact that it's empty. Maybe with the house's history whoever killed her might have thought people would avoid it. I just don't know."

"Did you put the body down there?"

"No. I didn't kill her, and no, I didn't put the body down there. I had nothing to do with it. Besides, why hide the body in a room with a window. Someone who knew the house would have concealed her better."

"The night Leah went missing, did you see or hear anything?"

"Nothing out of the ordinary. I mean, there are always a few noises—you'll hear dogs, and owls, the river, stuff like that, but screams, or fights, or something to indicate a problem? Nothing like that."

"Did you fall asleep during your shift?"

"No. After the gunfight that happened a couple of weeks ago, I don't think anyone could sleep on duty. I went back to the militia house to warm up a couple of times, for maybe fifteen or twenty minutes, but other than that I was out there the whole night."

"Why did Mr. Lee testify that he saw you by your house on the night of the murder?"

"It was about halfway through my shift when I noticed the front door of my house was open, so I closed it. I had gathered some stuff from there the day before, so when I saw the door open I just figured I hadn't closed it tight. I closed and locked the door, then stopped to relieve myself by a bush. I was coming from the front of the house when Steven saw me. That's it."

"Do you notice many doors open at night?"

"Not really. It's pretty dark out there at night, but I'm familiar with my own house and noticed the door cracked open."

"Why didn't you tell Sean about it when he talked to you the next day?"

"Because I didn't think we were looking for a body. I was sure she was lost, and I didn't think she'd be lost in my basement."

Boyd asked a few more basic questions, then it was Helen's turn for questioning. She stood, a smile on her face, and turned to Kyle. "Kyle, how hard is it to kill a person?"

Kyle swallowed hard before looking at the jury. "It is the hardest thing you can imagine doing, but when your life is threatened, like mine was, you do what you have to do. You never forget about it though."

"So, say someone was going to report to your wife, or Mr. Reider, that you raped them or coerced them into having sex. That would threaten your life, or at least threaten your life the way you know it, right?"

"I'm not answering that. I know what you're trying to do. That didn't happen."

"Okay, fine. I understand. Let me rephrase it for you. You took off your shirt and dramatically told the jury how you killed a man because he was going to keep you from getting back to your family. What would have happened to your family if your wife found out you made it with some twenty-year-old, let alone that you forced her to have sex with you? Would that have threatened your family's happily-ever-after?"

Kyle stared ahead, refusing to answer. Helen waited, putting on a show for the jury with her patience, but Kyle stayed silent. "Fine, Mr. Tait. I understand you don't want to address that question. Let me move one. You said you met the victim about a week prior to her death, correct?"

"Correct."

"Nothing happened at that time, right?"

"Nothing happened."

"Was she cute?"

"Pardon me?"

"Was Leah cute? You've got a twenty-year-old girl walking around by herself late at night. Did you think she was cute?"

"I wasn't thinking about that. I just wanted to know what she was doing. Besides, everyone is all bundled up at night. You can hardly even see what people look like."

"So you'd just met this woman, 5'3", about a hundred pounds, cute face, sneaking home late at night from her boyfriend's house. What did you think about the rest of the evening?"

"Just work stuff—glad that I hadn't shot her as an intruder, hoping that someone wasn't going to jump out of the shadows and kill me, or someone else I work with, or do something to my family. That's what I think about. What do you think about late at night when you're on patrol, protecting your town?"

"My," Helen said, a smirk on her face, ignoring Kyle's query. "You are quite the man. You must have amazing control to spend hours alone every night with no one to talk to except an occasional wandering twenty-year-old woman, and think of nothing but work. No conjecturing what she had just been doing, or what she looked like with her bulky clothing off. No hoping you might run into her again some night. No thoughts at all about her. Simply amazing. Wish my ex-husband was that disciplined."

Helen strode over to her table and sat on the edge of it. She lowered her voice from mildly shouting over the weakening storm outside to a more conversational tone. "You think about hiding bodies often?"

"No."

"I was just curious, because in your earlier testimony you said that there were better places to conceal a body. I'd like to know how often you actually think about concealing dead people."

"That's not something I normally think about. It wasn't until after all this that a thought like that even crossed my mind."

"So it's safe to say that prior to the morning of January 19th you hadn't thought about the best place to hide a dead person in your basement. Is that correct?"

Kyle paused, not sure how to respond, knowing how she was turning his answers against him. The jury shifted in their seats, watching and waiting intently for his answer.

"I never planned out where to hide a body. That's not something I've ever needed to do."

"Why?" Helen responded, almost at the top of her lungs. "Because the people you kill, you just leave them to rot in the middle of the road? Is that it?"

Kyle didn't respond.

Helen continued after an extended pause. "So, we can take it from your testimony that before the night of January 18th you had never given thought to where to put a dead body. The fact that Leah is found in a less than ideal location in your basement," she said, putting heavy emphasis on the word 'your,' "shouldn't surprise us at all. Should it?"

Kyle rubbed his face. He was finding it hard to breath. "I didn't do it. I know this all looks bad, but it wasn't me."

"Yes, I've heard you say that numerous times, Kyle, just like all the defendants I've put in jail in the past. They deny it all, too. If we only locked up the ones who admitted guilt, we wouldn't have a need for very many jails. It's my job to help the jury see past your denial. Leah died the night you were on shift, her body is found in the basement of your house, and the searchers had to break in your door to get to her, even though there was no sign of forced entry prior to that. Do you just leave your home unlocked all the time? So people can help themselves to whatever?"

Kyle looked at the jury and then at his interrogator, his voice shaking as he answered. "Listen, I've been moving stuff from our old house to where we're living now. My wife said we weren't going back, so I had collected everything that was useful. I don't usually lock the doors, because there's not much there anymore."

Helen rose from the table and took a couple of steps towards Kyle. She shook her head slowly from side to side. "I have no further questions."

CHAPTER NINETEEN

Wednesday, January 25th
Deer Creek, MT

At the end of the sixty-minute lunch break, Kyle huddled with his attorney as the crowd filed back into court. Because the jurors were unable to leave, other than to go to the bathroom, lunch had been brought to them and they had eaten in the courtroom. They looked nervous and uncomfortable and avoided eye contact with Kyle while chatting amongst themselves. The weather outside had turned sunny, but there was still a steady drone inside as the spectators discussed the case.

Boyd had initially planned to call Dale Briggs' mother as a witness, but had found her to be depressed and uncooperative in an earlier visit, and then she hadn't shown up for the trial at all. That left Sean Reider, who had testified previously, and Jennifer as his only remaining witnesses.

What had started out as a bad dream for Kyle had quickly devolved into a terrifying nightmare that he was anxious to awake from. The prosecutor was doing her job too well, catching every little word and twisting it to her advantage. Kyle understood that that was her objective, but being in her gun-sights terrified him. The night before, one of the guards had reminded him that execution was the punishment if he was found guilty. At first, knowing he was innocent, the thought had only mildly worried him, but with the direction the trial was going, and the possibility of a guilty verdict growing, that same thought made him absolutely sick to his stomach.

Kyle saw Gabe and Don coming down the center aisle, and the buzz in the room quieted. There was no formality of a government court, but the people in attendance were just naturally respectful, and grateful that they hadn't been needed to fill any of the difficult roles in this drama.

Don resumed the session, and Sean Reider was put back on the stand. Boyd asked Sean questions about procedures and militia responsibility, which he answered effectively. Then Helen countered, forcing Sean to admit that there was next to no record keeping, that the militia's efforts were focused on defense, not policing, and that the majority of what any individual militia member did was based on their own discretion and not on formal protocol.

Next, Jennifer was called to the stand, and Kyle was so nervous he couldn't look her in the eye. He knew what she was going through and he had to fight to control his emotions. He watched as his wife raised her shaking right hand and was sworn in, her voice sounding stronger than he expected. He forced himself to make eye contact, and she smiled.

Boyd walked towards Jennifer, stopping halfway between the defense table and the witness. "Mrs. Tait. Thank you for being here today."

Jennifer nodded and smiled. Kyle could see her legs bouncing nervously.

Boyd continued. "I know this must be difficult for you, but you know Kyle better than anyone, and you saw him in the hours before and after his shift on the day this terrible tragedy occurred."

Jennifer's back was straight, and she watched Boyd with a warm confidence. "I think it's important for me to be here today. I want justice to be served."

"How long have you known Kyle?"

She beamed at the crowd. "It's been eighteen wonderful years."

"How long have you been married?"

"Sixteen years, five months."

Boyd laughed a little, then continued. "In all the time you've know Kyle, has he ever hit you?"

She shook her head vigorously. "Never. We've had our disagreements, and he's gotten mad at me before, but he's never even threatened to strike me."

"Has he ever hit your children?"

"They've had a few spankings, but that's it. Just a couple of swats on their backsides, to get their attention."

"Any legal issues he's had to deal with?"

"None that I knew of. The situation with the beer in high school was news to me. I'm going to remember that one for a while and use it to my advantage." A couple of the jurors laughed along with Jennifer.

"Has Kyle ever done anything that would make you think he had the capacity to commit the crime he's accused of?"

"Nothing at all. I'm 100% sure he would never do anything like that."

"When he came home last Thursday morning was there anything out of the ordinary about his behavior? Was he acting strangely?"

She thought a second, then shook her head. "It was a normal morning. He was tired, he had a little something to eat, then he went to bed. It was just like most mornings."

"Did he act nervous? Frightened?"

"No."

"Did he ask to get up early, so he could go hide evidence?"

"No."

"Any injuries?"

"No."

"Did he act sore or uncomfortable?"

"He said his toes were cold because the temperatures were pretty low that night, but that's it."

"How did he act when he found out Leah's body had been found?"

"He was completely shocked, especially when we were told the body was found in our home. I could tell it caught him completely off guard."

Boyd continued questioning Jennifer for twenty more minutes before concluding and turning her over to Helen. Jennifer smiled confidently. Her testimony appeared to resonate with the jurors. Kyle felt a huge weight lifting from his shoulders.

Helen clasped her hands in front of her and smiled at Jennifer. "I can tell you really love your husband."

"I do, very much."

"Couples so much in love are a dying breed. Anything you wouldn't do for your husband?"

"No. I'd do..." Jennifer paused. "I love him very much. Everything I've said has been the truth. I wouldn't sell my soul for him, if that's what you're insinuating."

Helen stepped casually towards the jurors. "I understand you've suffered some pretty traumatic things over the past few months."

Jennifer studied Helen closely and thought about her response. "Yes. I think we all have. I don't know that I'm that different from anyone else."

"Oh, come now, Jennifer. I think it's been pretty rough for you, even by current standards. Your husband gone, your attempted rape, and that unfortunate situation where you had to kill a man. Now Kyle accused of this terrible crime. I don't know anyone who comes close to your struggles."

Jennifer nodded. She looked at Helen intently but remained silent.

"Rape is a pretty intense experience. I've worked with a number of assault victims and know that it can take a long time to recover from the trauma."

"It does. It's been more difficult than I would have hoped, but having Kyle home has helped tremendously." Jennifer glanced at Kyle, whose eyes were locked on her, and she smiled at him just a little. It spoke volumes to him.

Kyle mouthed, "I love you," to his wife, and she turned away, feeling the tears building in her eyes.

Helen paused for a second, then pressed on. "This is a personal question, and I'm sorry I have to ask it, but when was the last time you had sex with your husband?"

Jennifer paused. "I beg your pardon?"

The prosecutor cleared her throat. Every person in the courtroom got quiet, the room so silent that you could have heard a snowflake land on the roof. "I asked when you last had sex with your husband. Sometimes it can take months, or even years, for rape victims to be comfortable with intimacy again. It's a terrible crime. Much more than physical scarring takes place, as you no doubt know. In your case, it would be even worse, with your daughter there and your son nearly being killed."

Jennifer's mind spun; she looked at Kyle, panicked.

Kyle could see the turmoil on her face. He closed his eyes, held his breath, and felt his heart pounding.

"And remember, Jennifer," Helen said, stepping closer, her tone warm and understanding, like a longtime friend. "Remember that you've sworn to tell the truth. I know this is a personal question, but it's important for us to understand everything. Maybe let me rephrase the question. How many times have you had sex with your husband since the EMP occurred, FIVE months ago?"

Jennifer felt the room spin as she formed the answer. "Once," she said, her voice trembling and barely audile, even in a room full of people straining to hear her reply.

"I'm sorry," Helen said, stepping back. "I don't think our jurors could hear that. Could you repeat your answer, a little louder?"

She closed her eyes. "Once," she said, loud enough to be heard most of the way to the back of the room. Jennifer's mind raced back over the two months since Kyle's return. That he was interested was not in doubt. The comments, the touches, the looks were obvious, but something in her had changed. Doug's escalating harassment and the intense foulness of everything he'd done to her that night, David's nearly bleeding to death in her bedroom, and Emma's trauma had all made that part of her dry up. Compound that with the reality that their children slept in the same room, showers were rare, birth control was a calendar, toothpaste was a distant memory, and she felt like she resembled a starving prisoner of war. All of it had resulted in not just an absence of desire, but an aversion to the thought of it.

Once, about a month ago, she had forced herself to respond to his caresses, but Kyle had known it was difficult for her, to the point that he had apologized afterwards. She had hoped it was satisfying for him, but with his apology, she'd burst into tears and been depressed for the remainder of the day. For his part, Kyle had been wonderful, telling her how beautiful she was, reminding her what she meant to him, never pressuring her for anything more than a hug and a kiss. Now this. Her hang-ups made him look deprived and guilty.

"So, Mrs. Tait." Helen paused and looked at Jennifer, at Kyle, at Leah's family, then back at Jennifer. Indecision marked her face, and she took a couple deep breaths. She looked back at Leah's father, then her jaw tightened, and she continued. "If I understand this correctly, in the ten weeks your husband's been home, you've had sexual relations with him only one time. Correct?"

"Correct."

"A healthy, sexually-active male. How'd he take the neglect?"

Jennifer swallowed, her eyes glistened, but she didn't answer.

Helen pushed on. "I also understand he was gone for about three months prior to that."

Jennifer nodded, her throat too tight to speak.

"So, in five and a half months, he's had sex one time that you know of. At his age, that's got to be pretty difficult, wouldn't you think?" Again no answer. "Is he a eunuch or something?"

No one in the room laughed.

Helen turned to the jury. Their eyes were riveted on her. "You think a man quits wanting sex because you don't feel like it?" Her voice was rising, her pace quickening. "You think he'd quit wanting food if you stopped feeding him? We already know he killed at least one person on his way home from Texas. How about rape? We can't be sure about that, other than what he tells us. Crossing the country, armed, no witnesses. Who knows what kind of trail he left in his wake. Then he gets home, his wife, unable to perform, and no hookers around. What would you expect?"

Jennifer sobbed from the witness chair, her shoulders rising and falling, her face buried in her hands, a muffled "I'm sorry," heard through the tears.

"Stop it!" Kyle jumped to his feet and glared at the prosecutor. "Stop it right now! She doesn't deserve this; she's not on trial." Boyd tugged on Kyle's arm but Kyle batted his hand away. The two guards positioned behind him jumped to their feet and grabbed ahold of Kyle's arms. Kyle began to pull away but stopped as a murmur rippled through the courtroom.

Helen stepped back and looked nervously to the front, towards Gabe and Don.

"Kyle, sit down!" Boyd hissed, looking uneasily at the jurors.

"Jennifer, don't be sorry," Kyle pleaded, eyes locked on his wife. "You have nothing to be sorry for." He jerked an arm away from one of the guards and glared at them, then dropped back into his chair.

Helen caught her breath. "Temper, Mr. Tait. Try not to lose control," she taunted, before turning her attention to the jurors. "Hopefully you can disregard that little bit of drama. You never know what a trial will bring, especially under conditions like these." She turned back towards Jennifer, her tone less combative. "Let me conclude, Mrs. Tait. Your husband's sexual activity has been pretty minimal the last six months, has it not?"

Jennifer wiped her eyes on her sleeve and nodded. "It has, but that's my fault, not his."

"It doesn't matter whose fault it is. When a man is starving, he will go looking for food, don't you think?"

"Not Kyle."

Helen looked at Jennifer, admiring her devotion. "I have no further questions." She clasped her hands together and smiled sincerely. "I'm truly sorry for all the stress you're under. You're a brave woman."

CHAPTER TWENTY

Wednesday, January 25th
Deer Creek, MT

Kyle heard someone in the room above him toss a log on the fire, followed by the sound of a poker scraping on the brick hearth. Kyle's sleeping pad was up against the fireplace's brick foundation, the warmest location in the crawlspace, and while the crawlspace was not as warm as the main floor, it was well above freezing and much warmer than he feared it would be when he had first been locked in his underground cell.

The defense had concluded midafternoon, allowing both sides time to present their closing arguments before the end of the day. The verdict was now in the hands of the jurors and would likely be decided soon, since the case wasn't long or complicated, and there wasn't much evidence to consider. As Helen had summarized, repeatedly, Leah Smith had been sexually assaulted, and her body had been found in the basement of a sexually starved, admitted killer, with whom she'd had previous contact, on a night he was working alone and couldn't provide an alibi.

Boyd had countered that there was no evidence linking Kyle and Leah, no witnesses to the crime, no confession, and no history to indicate Kyle would commit such a violent crime. Unfortunately, the defense attorney's dry, insecure approach had been tedious in comparison to Helen's practiced dramatics, and by Kyle's observations, the jurors' attentiveness was more evident when she spoke than when Boyd did.

Lying in the oppressive darkness of the crawlspace, Kyle tried to think of what he could have done differently, to avoid being where he was, to have prevented this whole mess, but came up with little. Maybe he could've made sure his house was locked, or taken a different shift. When it came down to it, though, there really wasn't much that would have made a difference.

Kyle heard more noises upstairs. A chair squeaked, followed by footsteps moving towards the front door. Grit dropped onto his cheek through a crack in the floor above, and he wiped it away. He heard voices and a muffled conversation, then footsteps approaching the hatch that accessed the crawlspace. The chest that secured the trap door scraped the floor as it was pushed away, followed by the rasping of stiff hinges being pulled upward. Kyle climbed to his feet and shuffled over below the door with his head ducked low, guided by the faint orange glow from the opening.

"Tait! You've got a visitor." The gruff voice came from one of the guards from Clinton who helped watch Kyle each night, a man whose name Kyle didn't care to learn.

"Who is it?" Kyle asked, his voice rising from the soupy darkness.

"It's me, Kyle," Jennifer said, peering into the opening.

Kyle's heart skipped at the sound of her voice. "Jennifer?"

"Can I come down?"

"Of course. Is it okay?"

"I told her it would be fine," Gabe said as he crouched by the hatch. "I walked her over here so there wouldn't be any questions. We can't allow you to come out until after the verdict, but I didn't think there'd be any harm in Jennifer spending some time with you here, assuming you're good with that."

Kyle quickly repositioned the stepladder he used to access his cell to a spot easier for Jennifer to reach. "You have no idea how good I am with that."

Jennifer sat on the edge of the opening and lowered her legs. Kyle lightly grabbed an ankle with one hand and guided it to the top step of the ladder; his other hand held the ladder still. Gabe and the guard stood ready to help her, but she found her footing and descended out of view.

"We'll come for you in the morning, Jennifer," Gabe said as they prepared to close the hatch. "Kyle, you have to stay here until the jury is ready. Have a good night." The hatch swung shut, and the chest was slid back into position. Kyle pressed the button on his flashlight, and a single, thin beam of white light pierced the darkness.

"A flashlight?" Jennifer asked. "Where did you get that?"

Kyle took Jennifer by the hand and led her over to his sleeping pad, carefully guiding her head to avoid the metal pipes that hung from the joists. "Ty gave it to me. It's LED, so it doesn't use much power. There's not much to see down here, so I only use it to find my bucket, or on special occasions like this."

Her eyes shimmered in the light, and Kyle could see she was on the verge of tears. "What's wrong?" He switched off the light and sat beside her in the darkness.

She let out a sob-laced laugh. "What's wrong? You're fighting for your life, and we're imprisoned in the cellar of a decrepit old house, and you ask what's wrong?"

"I'm sorry," he said, pulling her close and rocking her. "I'm sorry I'm putting you through this. I'm sorry that after everything else, that you have to deal with this."

"Oh, Kyle. You haven't done anything wrong. It's this whole screwed up world we're living in. I don't know what to do."

"What do you mean?"

"I'm terrified that I'm going to lose you. I think my testimony today sealed it. How am I supposed to live with that?" She wiped her eyes and nose with her sleeve.

"Don't say that, Jenn. I was so happy to be your husband today, just as I am everyday. I'd walk from Texas again just to spend one day with you, let alone ten weeks."

"I should've lied. Should've said we made love every day, till I couldn't walk anymore. Told them you begged me to stop. Instead, I made you look more guilty."

He could hear her sniffing, and he kissed her on the head. "I love you. Do you understand that? No matter what happens, good or bad, I completely, absolutely, one hundred percent, no hesitation whatsoever, love you."

There was a long pause before she spoke. "I know, Kyle, but I don't deserve you. You nearly die walking home, and instead of a loving wife you find some frigid, emotionally unstable waif posing in her place, someone who jumps at her own shadow or at a touch she isn't expecting. How can you still love me?"

"Oh, babe," Kyle said, fighting to control his own emotions. "Please don't say that. What do I have to do to make you believe that I'm completely, crazy in love with you? When we got married, I thought a man could never love anyone more than I did then, but I was so wrong. When I was walking home, every night I prayed for at least one more day with you, one more touch of your hand, one more kiss. Then when I made it, when I finally saw you, it was the most powerful thing I've ever felt. I didn't know it was possible to love someone that much. I remembered everything we've been through together, the easy times, and the hard. I knew for sure then, and still know today, how little I want a life that you aren't a part of. I love you so much more now than the day we got married because of what we've been through, because every minute we spend together makes you more a part of me. Please, don't ever ask me how I can love you."

His arms were wrapped around her, and he pulled her even closer, resting his head on hers, then kissing her cheek. She didn't speak, but he could feel her crying.

They sat together, feeling each other's warmth, rocking gently. After a long period of silence, Jennifer finally spoke. "I'm scared."

Kyle nodded. "Me too. Me too."

"What do I do if I lose you?"

"You'll never lose me, but if the worst happens, you'll be fine, Jenn. You'll make it. You're tough."

"I'm not that tough. If they find you guilty, you know they're going to shoot you, right?"

Kyle nodded, the lump in his throat growing larger. "Yeah. I try not to think about it, but it's crossed my mind a time or two."

"How do I live with that? How do I look at our kids everyday for the rest of my life, knowing that their father was murdered and I couldn't do anything about it."

"Try and think positive."

"How? How do I think positive? There's not a positive thing about this. That woman was too good. Your guy, Boyd, was serviceable, but she was a pitbull. She could have gotten Spencer convicted. There was no way to stop her."

"Whatever happens, you'll be fine. You have to be fine. Promise me that. You made it for months without me; you can do it again. This is still a good community. They'll help you. They can hate me, but they like you."

"Stop it, Kyle. I'm not that strong. When you weren't here, I didn't know where you were, so I could believe you'd be back, that I just had to hold on another day. That gave me strength, taking it a day at a time. If this happens, then all hope is lost. I'll have nothing to hold on to. They may as well shoot me, because losing you will kill me. I don't know how women do it who lose their husbands."

Kyle fought to compose himself. "You can't think that way. We have three children who need you. You'll find the strength; I know it. Besides, I'll be there. You might not be able to see me, but I'll be there. I know I'm not that religious, but if it's possible, if God will let me, I'll give up heaven so I can be at your side every minute of every day, until it's your time. I'll catch every tear that you shed. I'll be in every breeze that you feel. I'll hold your head every night when you fall asleep. I'll never, ever be gone from you. You just have to be strong until we're together again. Do you promise to do that?"

Jennifer couldn't speak. Sobs racked her body and sapped her strength. Kyle held her, rocked her, stroked her hair, kissed her forehead, and experienced her in his arms, praying the moment would never end. "Do you promise me?" he asked again when his own tears slowed.

He felt her head nod. "I promise," she managed when she could finally speak. "As long as you promise to always be there, I promise."

"I will always be there."

He felt her twist in his arms, and she pushed him down on his back. She leaned down and kissed him on the lips, a deep, warm, all-consuming kiss. "I love you, Kyle Tait," she said as she pulled away and sat up. He heard the zipper on her jacket, then felt her hands searching for his.

CHAPTER TWENTY-ONE

Thursday, January 26th
Deer Creek, MT

The jurors were back in their seats at the front of the room, silent, eyes down, arms folded tightly across their chests. The verdict had just been handed to Don Anderson, and the tension was thick. There were a few whispers and some sideways glances, but without exception everyone's attention was locked on the two men at the front.

Shortly after the first signs of daylight had peeked through the cracks in the foundation, the hatch had been opened and Jennifer told to leave, then Kyle had waited for seven long hours before being informed that the verdict was in, and he was to be taken to the courthouse.

When Kyle and his entourage arrived at the building, it was packed, with every seat full and more than a hundred people standing in the back of the hall. Jennifer waited in the first row behind the defense table, wearing her best dress. Their three children were next to her, all dressed in church clothes at least one size too small. Spencer grinned at the sight of his dad and ran forward to hug him. Kyle knelt down and winked, his arms still secured behind his back. "You sure look good. How are you doing?"

Spencer wrapped his arms around Kyle's neck. "I want you to come home, dad. I miss you."

"I want to come home, too, son. Maybe today. Would that be alright?"

Spencer nodded, his arms still tight around his dad. "Why are your hands tied up? What did you do?"

"I didn't do anything, Spence. People are just worried."

Jennifer peeled Spencer off of Kyle, and both father and son began to cry. Kyle stood up and proceeded to the front of the room. He smiled at David and Emma, who both sat there with swollen, red eyes. Jennifer slipped into her chair with Spencer and smiled bravely at Kyle.

Boyd pulled Kyle's chair away from the table and waited for him to sit. "How are you doing today?"

"Had better days, I have to admit. Hopefully things will improve."

"Lets hope so," Boyd replied, patting Kyle on the back.

Kyle watched as Don placed the envelope with the verdict on the table in front of them. Gabe looked up and addressed the jurors. "Is everyone in agreement on the verdict?"

There were nods and mumbled affirmations.

Don opened the envelope, took out the folded piece of paper, and he and Gabe read the verdict in silence. He then returned to the jury, where the foreman stood to receive the paper.

"Please read your verdict," Gabe said, his voice cracking.

The man nodded, unfolded the paper, and read. "We, the members of this jury, on the charge of murder, find the defendant guilty."

A roar of voices filled the room. Kyle heard Jennifer gasp, then Emma's panicked voice. "What does that mean, mom?"

Boyd put his hand on Kyle's shoulder and almost shouted to be heard. "I'm really sorry, Kyle. I thought we made our case."

Kyle stared at the ground, shaking his head vigorously from side to side.

The foreman waited for the room to calm down. Gabe banged on the front table with a hammer until it was almost silent and the foreman could continue. "On the charge of rape, we find the defendant guilty." Another roar went through the crowd, though not as long or as loud. The juror handed the paper back to Don and sat down.

All eyes were now locked on the two men at the front of the room. Don and Gabe whispered back and forth briefly, Gabe shaking his head as he spoke. Finally Don stood, and the room went silent. "Mr. Tait," he began, his voice shaking. "This jury has found you guilty of rape and murder. This was a vicious and terrible crime, and because of the horrific nature of it, you are sentenced to death." A smattering of applause could be heard as the room again descended into chaos. Several minutes and several pounds of the hammer later, the room got quiet again and Don continued. "The sentence will be carried out before sunset. We ask that young children not be exposed to this event." He took a deep breath and put his hand on the table to steady himself.

Kyle heard his family crying, despite the surrounding commotion, and Carol Jeffries trying to console Spencer and Emma. Kyle's head was spinning; he leaned against the table to steady himself. His guards stepped closer, nervously scanning the crowd. Gabe once again used the hammer to return order to the court. "Mr. Tait, do you have anything to say?"

Kyle took a deep breath as he sat up and nodded. Don motioned for Kyle to speak. He stood and turned to the crowd, which quickly went silent. Every eye in the room was glued to him as tears ran freely down his cheeks. "I just want to say," he looked at the Smith family, "that I'm sorry." An explosion of voices forced Gabe, once again, to use his hammer to settle the crowd. "Not," Kyle shouted, the noise decreasing. "Not because I hurt your daughter. I didn't. But I am sorry for your loss. I have children who I love very much, and I can only guess at the hurt and the loss that you're feeling. I hope those wounds will heal."

He looked at his wife and smiled. "I want you all to know how much I love my wife. And whatever you think about me, or this verdict, please don't hold this against her. She's an amazing woman who made me a better man than I ever would have been without her, but she'll need your help." He swallowed, the lump in his throat making it hard to speak. "I don't know who did this, but my death will not make you any safer. I do hope that at some point the guilty person will be found and that you will all be able to sleep safer at night." He thanked Don and Gabe and sat down, nearly collapsing into his chair.

Don dismissed the crowd, and chairs clattered on the floor as people hurried to the exit. Kyle felt arms around his neck and Jennifer's lips on his cheek. "I can't believe this, Kyle," she choked out. "I can't believe this is happening."

Kyle focused on his children. David was wiping his eyes on his sleeve, Spencer had his face buried in Carol's lap, and Emma, looking terrified, clung tightly to her mother's arm. Kyle broke down and sobbed uncontrollably, his emotions too much to control, his shoulders heaving as the magnitude of his sentence hit him. "I love you all so much," he wailed, his arms still secured behind his back, making it impossible to hug his children.

His guards stood a few steps back, watching the scene unfold, waiting to take him away, while the family huddled and wept together, broken hearted, and in unbearable pain. The room had mostly emptied, leaving just Kyle and his family, Carol, the four guards, and some curious onlookers. With no more words to say, Kyle and his family just sat, holding each other, being together for their final few minutes.

One of the guards finally spoke up. "I'm really, really sorry, Mr. Tait, but we need to go. We have to take you now."

Kyle looked up at the guard. "I understand," he said. He tried to stand, but his legs gave out, and he fell to the floor. Two of the guards grabbed his shoulders and helped him to his feet, supporting him on each side.

"We can escape, Dad!" David whispered urgently. "I'll get my gun; we can get away."

"No, David," Kyle said shaking his head. "Don't do that. No one else needs to get hurt. It's better to die innocent than kill to be free. Please, son." He waited until David looked him in the eyes. "You've got to be there for your mother. You understand? She needs you more than ever."

Tears streamed down David's defiant face, but he nodded his understanding. The guards began walking him towards the door, and Spencer started screaming hysterically. Carol held him in her arms to keep him from running after his father. Emma lay in a heap on the floor, her head cradled in Jennifer's lap, her eyes swollen and red. "David," Jennifer said, her voice faltering. "Hold your sister. I have to go with your father."

"No, Jennifer!" Kyle called out. "I don't want you to see this. I don't want you to have that memory."

Jennifer stumbled down the aisle between the rows of empty chairs, drying her eyes to be able to see. "I'll close my eyes or look away when the time comes, but I have to be there. I won't be able to forgive myself if I'm not there for you."

She numbly followed the group through town, back to the militia building where a short meeting was held, then to a small plateau part way up the mountain that had been scouted out and designated for this purpose, initially for the execution of the man from the raid. It was a private area shielded by trees and only a short distance from the community.

Jennifer was shocked by the number of people who had followed along, intent on seeing the process through to the end. Leah's father was there, as well as Gabe Vance, Don Anderson,

Ty Lewis, and three-dozen onlookers, only a few of whom she knew. She wanted to rant and scream at them and demand that they give her privacy, but it took all the strength she had just to stand there.

Two men zip-tied Kyle's ankles together, then looped straps through each elbow and to trees on both sides of him, so he couldn't attempt to flee. Kyle stared at Jennifer, tears running steadily down his cheeks. Once Kyle was adequately secured, a guard stepped forward, his hands visibly shaking, and slid a thick pillowcase over Kyle's head.

Kyle called out to his wife. "Jenn, I love you, and the kids! Always remember that!"

"I love you too, Kyle!" Jennifer answered back. She felt her legs go weak, and she started to sink to the snowy ground. Ty Lewis, fighting tears of his own, caught her as she fell and supported her.

"I'm sorry, Jennifer," Ty said. "He's a good man. This isn't right."

Sean Reider slowly walked to a position in front of Kyle, stopping fifteen yards away. He took a wide stance and inhaled deeply. His hands shook, and all color had drained from his face. Despite the cold temperature, a bead of sweat ran down his forehead.

Kyle's guards moved to a position between Jennifer and Kyle. Kyle stood straight and tall, his head erect, dignified, and strong.

"Why is Sean doing this?" Jennifer asked, her voice a whisper. "

Ty leaned close to her ear. "He has no choice. No one else would, not even the men from Clinton. Sean doesn't want to do it either, but Gabe and Don insisted that someone had to carry out the sentence. They argued about it for a long time while the jury was out." He shook his head. "I don't envy Sean at all. This whole thing is screwed up."

Sean raised his rifle, lowered his eye to the scope, hit the safety and slid a shaking finger onto the trigger. The only sound Jennifer could hear was her heartbeat. The spectators, the wind, the river were all silent, waiting for the crack of the rifle, the sound that would signify the extinguishing of a life.

Frozen, unable to breathe, and with everything around her paused, Jennifer watched Sean's hands, waiting for his one finger to move. She glanced at Ty. His eyes were closed, and he had turned away, tears staining his cheeks. Gabe knelt in prayer to the side of the group, his head bowed, shoulders heaving.

"I can't do this!"

Jennifer's eyes flashed back to Sean. His gun was lowered, and he faced the group, shaking his head.

"This isn't part of my job. You can shoot me, run me out of town, replace me, whatever you need to do, but I will not execute this man."

Jennifer shrieked. Ty's grip on her loosened, and she dashed past the startled guards towards Kyle. A roar of voices erupted behind her, and from the corner of her eye, she saw someone break from the crowd. She threw herself against Kyle, slamming into him, nearly forcing the air from his lungs. "Kyle!" she screamed as she pulled the pillowcase off his head and kissed his cheek.

A gunshot rang out. The bullet exploded at head level in the tree to her left, pelting Kyle and Jennifer with chunks of wood.

"Get off him right now! I'll kill the son-of-a-bitch myself if no one else will."

Jennifer turned her head to see the barrel of Mitch Smith's gun aimed at her. His eyes were blazing, and his mouth quivered, but his hand was steady, with his finger glued to the trigger of the gun.

"I should have known you people wouldn't serve justice."

"I'm not moving," Jennifer cried, turning to face him. "You want to shoot him, you put the bullet through me."

"Jennifer, get away!" Kyle urged, desperation in his voice. "He'll do it."

"Move!" Mitch bellowed. He shifted the gun slightly and shot again, the bullet slamming into the tree on the opposite side of her. "Next one's going through both of you. I'm not telling you again."

"Move Jennifer! Now!" Kyle insisted. "Don't do this."

"Mitch, put the gun down," Don Anderson pled. "This isn't the way."

"Then what is? I patiently sat through the trial and heard the verdict. You tell me what the right way is."

"I'm not moving!" Jennifer cried. "He's innocent. Please understand that."

"That's not what the jury said!" Mitch spat back. "They said he should die."

"They were wrong! He would never do what he was accused of."

"Mr. Smith," Sean said, turning his weapon towards Mitch. "I'm sorry. I don't want to shoot anyone. Let's just put the guns down and see what we can work out."

"What about Leah? What about justice for my daughter?"

"I'm not moving away, sir." Jennifer eyed the man. "I know you don't want to kill anyone. Please."

"You don't know what I want! I want him to pay! I want my daughter back! Don't try telling me what I want!" He re-aimed his gun at Kyle, right through the middle of Jennifer's chest. "I'll count to three, and then you're both dead. It's your choice."

Kyle's arms were still secured to the trees and his feet bound, so he pushed frantically at Jennifer with his head. "Move!" he screamed.

"One!" Mitch yelled. He stood five yards from Sean, a few feet from the group he'd come with, and directly in line with Kyle. Several people had drawn their guns, but they didn't know where to point them. At Mitch? At Kyle? At Security?

Don Anderson pleaded, "Mitch, don't do this!"

"You don't have the authority to shoot him," Sean threatened as he raised his rifle to his shoulder.

"Two!" Mitch continued, oblivious to the urgings of those around him.

"I'm not moving!" Jennifer said, taking a step forward. "You'll have to kill us both."

"Jennifer, don't!" Kyle screamed, frantic and desperate.

"Mitch!" Don urged.

"Three!" Mitch yelled just as Ty Lewis tackled him, hitting him at shoulder level and knocking the rifle upwards as the trigger was pulled. The bullet sailed over Jennifer's head, snapping nearby branches and bouncing off the mountainside behind them. The rifle fell to the ground as both men rolled to a stop. Mitch lashed out with a fist, catching Ty in the face and knocking him backward, then reached for his gun but was wrestled down by Sean and one of the men who had secured Kyle to the trees.

Jennifer turned back to Kyle, smiled wearily and fell into him, out of breath.

"I told you to move," Kyle said between sobs. "You were almost killed."

"I can't lose you, Kyle. I just can't do it."

CHAPTER TWENTY-TWO

Friday, January 27ᵗʰ
Deer Creek, MT

Kyle wearily eyed the stack of clothes on the floor. "This seems all too familiar, except the last time I did this was in Texas."

Jennifer pulled clothes from the clothesline that was strung across the basement. "This is a first for me, and I don't like it at all, but at least I know you're alive. That's a million times better than last time."

"My head's still spinning from yesterday. I still don't believe what you did."

"I don't want to think about it, but you keep bringing it up. Let's just forget about it right now."

They heard the front door slam, followed by footsteps pounding down the stairs. "Dad!" David exclaimed when he got to the bottom. "Mr. Shipley agreed."

"What did he want for it?" Kyle asked, incredulous.

David shrugged. "It doesn't matter. I got the horse, like you had hoped."

"That's fantastic, David, but what did it cost?"

"I just have to stay later, and work Saturdays, but I got a saddle, too. I offered to throw in Emma, but they said then I'd have to work Sundays as well, so I decided we'd just keep her."

"Shut up, David," Emma said. "You did not tell them that. You're a liar."

"Kids, your father's leaving. Let's not do this. Let's give him something good to remember."

"When do you have to be gone by, Dad?" David asked, turning serious.

Kyle's head whirled with everything that had happened in the last sixteen hours. The verdict, the chaos as he waited, being helplessly strung between the trees, then seconds from execution, all sent a shudder through his body. Once Mitch Smith had been disarmed and pacified, the execution group had moved back to the militia house, where both of the attorneys, the jury, and others were waiting.

All involved were in a quandary regarding what to do, seeing as they had a convict but no legal operative willing to kill him. Even Mitch had eventually calmed down and apologized for almost shooting Jennifer. Finally, Helen had spoken up and admitted that there was enough doubt in her mind to spare Kyle the death sentence, but not enough to just set him free.

A decision had finally been made when Kyle proposed a solution. "Let me leave. My parents live in Idaho. I'll go there now and send for my family in the spring. We'll be gone, and I won't be a threat to anyone. Just give me a day to pack up and leave."

Even Mitch, once Helen Markham had spent a few minutes with him and shared her reservations about the verdict, had reluctantly agreed to the new plan. Only one member of the jury, a man from Clinton, had expressed serious reservations. The four other jurors had readily agreed to the modified plan, having all felt a jolt that had surprised them upon hearing the gunshots thought to have been the execution, and had expressed remorse over the outcome. Seeing Kyle brought down from the mountain alive had lifted a burden for them.

Jennifer had taken the banishment well, even though the thought of Kyle being gone again upset and angered her. But compared to the alternative, the punishment was heaven sent.

In addition to clothes and weapons, the Taits gathered together and packed twenty pounds of food, mostly in the form of dried meat, a few first aid supplies, a butane cylinder and lighter, half a jar of petroleum jelly, a small spool of wire, David's two-man tent, some of Frank's powdered bleach, a sleeping bag, silver coins Gabe had brought over, and a knife. Kyle briefly wished he had his cart, but the procurement of a horse had improved the situation significantly.

When the gear was finally packed and loaded, some on the horse and the remainder in a backpack Kyle wore, the family had another tearful separation, though far less painful than the one from the day before.

"Good luck, Kyle. I love you! Be safe," Jennifer called out as he swung the horse away from the house. She watched and waved, along with their kids, Carol, and Grace, as Kyle rode away.

Too cried out from the past few days to shed any tears, Kyle smiled at his family and friends and waved back, blowing kisses and putting on a brave face until he was out of sight. One more separation, one more journey into the unknown. He shook his head to clear it, not knowing how much more of this primitive and unpredictable life he could take. The memories of normalcy haunted him. It all seemed so long ago, but it wasn't. It was so easy back then, and so easily lost.

Kyle was heading south through the Shipley Ranch when he heard his name called. Sean Reider was waving his arms and running towards him. Kyle stopped his horse and waited.

Sean was out of breath when he reached Kyle. "Kyle… thanks for waiting," he panted. "I want to say I'm sorry, for yesterday, for everything that happened."

"You're sorry for not shooting me?"

"No," Sean said, catching his breath. "I didn't think you were guilty, at least I have my doubts, but I shouldn't have even been willing to raise my gun at you. Guess I would have made a good Nazi."

"Nazi?" Kyle said, puzzled. "What's that have to do with us."

"So many of the Germans put their consciences on hold and just went along with what their leaders told them to do, no matter how repugnant. I really scared myself yesterday. I almost took your life trying to be good at my job, even when I knew it wasn't right."

"Don't be too hard on yourself. I don't know if I'd have done anything different in your position. We're all in a bad way right now, scared, doing things we don't know how to do, making it up as we go, not knowing when things will be fixed. It's a little overwhelming, isn't it?"

Sean nodded. "It is." He looked south towards the mountain and at the steep road winding up its side. "Well, I don't want to hold you up. It'll be dark soon. Why are you headed this way? I heard you were going west, to Idaho."

"There's someone I need to see. Hoping he'll put me up for the night."

CHAPTER TWENTY-THREE

Saturday, January 28th
Montana/Wyoming State Line

ose dismounted, then tied the horses to the fence that ran along the highway. She kicked at the snow, scraping some patches of grass bare with her boots so the horses could graze. With her hands on her hips, she stretched from side to side, swinging her arms one way, then the other, trying to work out the kinks in her back.

Fresh snow drifted from the sky but was fortunately not too heavy, nor was the air too cold, just a few degrees below freezing she guessed. The Montana welcome sign stood fifty feet away, riddled with bullet holes. She studied it and wondered how many people like her had passed it these past five months. Refugees seeking…seeking…her thoughts paused here like they always did. What was it she was seeking? What had the others who had passed through here been seeking?

She knew what Kyle had been after, and she imagined that had made the journey more bearable for him, but here she was, one week in and still unsure what it was she was expecting. It was the uncertainty that made things difficult, that and not belonging anywhere. At least Kyle had had a home to move towards, a place that, even if his family hadn't survived, was still his.

She, on the other hand, was homeless, the smoke she'd seen rising from her little ranch as she escaped through the trees assuring her of that. She was also heading to a place she'd never been, hoping for generosity from a person she'd known for all of five days. What if he wasn't there, or hadn't made it, or wouldn't help? What then?

What were the other people who passed by here doing? Seeking family? Escaping the cities? Fighting to survive through the winter? For what purpose?

Blitz whinnied and tugged on the reins. Rose patted the horse on her side, rubbed her nose, and whispered softly. The first two days had been a battle. Blitz didn't take to being pulled around by another horse nor walking in straight lines for miles on end. At one point, something had spooked her, and she'd broken free, bucking off her load and running away. It had taken Rose two hours to corral the mare, find her things, and repack the load. But as of late, Blitz seemed to be accepting her role without too many more protestations.

Smokey tore at the grass and chewed noisily, breaking the otherwise eerie silence. Silence was something Rose was finally getting used to. Before, there had always been noise, whether the TV, or radio, the furnace or the fridge, trucks driving by on the freeway, whatever. There was always something. Now it was so quiet you could hear the flow of blood in your ears and the sounds of nature that had been there all along but had been drowned out by the hum of daily life.

Living alone made the silence worse, a constant reminder that there was no one else there. Even her husband Bruce, as unfaithful and detached as he was, would have been someone to talk to, to listen to, to touch. Solitude was fine if you could call your friend or take a walk through the mall. Even getting spam emails at least let you know someone or something knew you were alive. But enforced isolation, with only a loyal dog and a couple of horses for company, just wasn't healthy.

Rose pulled out an MRE Lou had given her, tore it open, and bit off a chunk. It tasted slightly better than mud and had the consistency of cardboard, but she knew it contained the calories she needed, so she forced it down. With her meal complete, such as it was, she put the wrapper back in the pack, took a drink of water, filled a bottle with snow, and readied the horses to head down the road.

Based on the position of the sun, Rose estimated she had another four or five hours of daylight, and standing still thinking sad thoughts wasn't going to help, so she turned the horses, mounted up, and crossed into Montana.

CHAPTER TWENTY-FOUR

Sunday, January 29th
South of Deer Creek

Kyle stepped out of the shower and dried himself off with a towel that was warm, clean, and smelled fresh. He dressed quickly, brushed his teeth with real toothpaste, combed his hair, and exited the bathroom.

Brenda Emory was in the kitchen making breakfast while Frank put plates on the table. "Pancakes alright?" she asked.

"Sounds great," Kyle answered, putting his newly acquired toothbrush and toothpaste in his pack. "You don't know how much I appreciate you letting me stay while the weather blew through."

"Don't you mention it. After everything you've been through, we're glad you came here."

Kyle had arrived late Friday night, and despite nearly shooting him in the dark, Frank and Brenda had welcomed him warmly and insisted he stay. Saturday's weather had blown in cold and snowy, and Kyle had been convinced to wait out the weather and leave once things cleared up. By late Saturday afternoon, the system had blown through, leaving three inches of fresh snow and moderate temperatures.

Kyle spent most of Saturday helping Frank tend to the animals, clean snow from solar panels, and check traps for food, all while catching up on world events. Once back at the house, he was taken on a tour of the back half of the Emory's mountain-side home. Three doors led off of the main room. One accessed their bedroom, another the bathroom, and the third was a steel door that led through a concrete wall to a bunker within a bunker. Bigger and extending further into the hillside than Kyle had expected, the room was self-contained and, according to Frank, set up to get them through two years without leaving. "That," Frank assured him, "is assuming we don't kill each other in the meantime."

Not only were there several racks of emergency food, catego-rized by meal and food type, but also barrels of water, in case their spring ran dry, weapons and enough ammo to supply a small army, a HAM radio, cots, body armor, hand generators, surgical supplies, and everything else a person would need to last out the millennium.

"Why?" Kyle asked, trying to wrap his mind around every-thing Frank and Brenda had accumulated.

Frank looked back in disbelief. "You don't understand, even now?"

"But what kind of an investment would this take? I mean, there has to be a hundred thousand dollars worth of equipment and supplies here."

"That's close," Frank said, shutting off the light and leading him back to the living room area. "Why not do this? I couldn't afford to buy a farm in Chile, or an estate in Australia, so I did what I could. I have no regrets, but I bet you do."

Kyle thought of all the things he could have done differently or cut back on. Frank had lectured him before, and Kyle had given some thought since then to what he would have changed. For the most part, they'd lived frugally. But he could still identify a couple hundred dollars a month that could have been used more wisely. "Yeah, I've got regrets, now that you mention it."

Brenda had been reading a novel during the men's conversation, but she marked her place and put her book down, then looked at Kyle. "Saving our money to pay for all of this wasn't that bad, really, and I certainly wasn't sad when we moved out of the trailer and into the mountain. You always need a place to live, and we just considered our home to be our retirement fund, or 401k, without the tax advantages."

"Screw the taxes," Frank said, smirking at his wife. "My friends were always bragging about how well their Apple or Google stock was doing, and good for them. My stock is in that room," he jabbed his finger towards the back. "And it's worth a hell of a lot more today than anything on the NASDAQ."

"I don't think I could have talked my wife into it, to be honest."

"Because you never tried, Kyle," Brenda said, looking over her glasses. "Women are wired to want security and minimize risk. Once Frank explained what he wanted to do, I was sold 100%. We even started doing some things before we found this property – storing food in our apartment, reading literature, doing a community garden, growing tomatoes in a window – just what we could. The garden didn't produce enough to totally feed us, but I learned how to grow things, how to can food, and we saved money on groceries that we could then put into this place."

"*The Bible* never did much for me," Frank said, leaning forward and waving his arms around for emphasis. "I figured if God was really in *The Bible*, he'd have made it more interesting. Anyway, the problem with being atheist is you don't have an afterlife to look forward to. No harps and singing in the next life for me, so I decided to extend this one as long as I can. Thought about cryogenic freezing for about a week, then figured this was a better use of my money."

Kyle laughed. "I wish I could blame my lack of preparations on belief in God. It would sound noble, but it'd be a lie. I'm probably like most people, figuring tomorrow will always be like today, which was just like yesterday."

"To be honest, my parents thought I was nuts when I married Frank and we started doing all of this prepping. My dad used to ask me if I was in an abusive relationship and Frank was keeping me against my will. Even offered to help me escape." Brenda rolled her eyes, then continued a bit wistfully. "I hope they're alright. Dad and Mom live in Phoenix, not a good place to be right now I'm sure."

"We stored enough food for our family to survive with us," Frank explained, "Even though they gave us such a hard time about it, which is why we don't offer to let you stay permanently. We're sorry, but we still hope they might find some way to get here. I hope you understand."

Kyle nodded. "Don't apologize. I understand the need to know your family is ok. I'm hoping to find my parents alive and well. They're up near Sandpoint, Idaho and had been living on teacher's pensions, so they didn't have a lot extra. Hopefully they've made it so far."

Brenda gave Kyle a sympathetic look. "I know how you feel. I worry all the time about my folks, and Frank's, too. But you have to let people do what they want. My dad loved to golf, and he could do that year round down there. That's why they stayed in Arizona."

"Don't feel bad, Bren. You know we did our best to convince them to come up here." Frank looked back at Kyle. "One drawback to doing all this prepping is everyone thinks you're nuts, even your relatives. Bet they don't anymore. Built this place to get us through anything – famine, war, EMP, solar flare, pandemic. You name it, we can last it out here, except for maybe a direct hit from a nuclear bomb or an asteroid, you know, global destruction type things. Other than that, we're covered."

Their discussion rambled on for another couple of hours as they enjoyed both the social aspect of the conversation and the verbal repartee. They veered from one subject to another, going from prepping to life in Deer Creek, crime, loneliness, first aid, and a raft of other topics. They segued into Frank's HAM radio conversations with the outside world and spent the next thirty minutes filling Kyle in on the latest developments.

Kyle learned that a lot had happened in the five months he'd been out of the loop. Less than twenty-four hours after America had been hit by the EMP, Israel, along with limited elements of American armed forces, had launched a series of pre-emptive strikes, taking down the Iranian, Syrian, and Egyptian governments and militaries in devastating attacks. Cutting off the heads of those repressive regimes had thrown their countries into such severe chaos, that what little was left of their armies had been overwhelmed with the task of regaining some semblance of civil order, a task at which they were so far failing in their efforts.

In addition to the Israeli attacks, the U.S. was being blamed for a series of targeted cyber attacks against Russian and Chinese regions that headquartered political and military forces. Unable to retaliate in kind since the U.S. had already been crippled, what was still functioning of the Russian and Chinese governments had threatened military strikes as recourse for the attacks. In return, the American President, sensing little value in diplomacy, had dropped a small nuclear bomb over an unpopulated area of Siberia and promised hundreds more if either country made any aggressive moves.

With the three major powers in the world crippled and trying to regain their footing, multiple regional conflicts had erupted. India and Pakistan had come to blows with a limited nuclear exchange killing tens of millions and leaving untold thousands sure to die from their injuries. With the global economy cratered and U.S. dollars no longer flowing towards the Middle East to prop up their various allies, a schism within the different Muslim sects had also boiled over, leading to a regional war based on religious alliances. Several of the governments, including Jordan, Saudi Arabia, Libya, and Iraq had fallen, plunging those countries into deeper anarchy and mayhem.

Israel had been able to avoid the whirlpool of disorder to this point, parking all of its tanks on Israeli borders, mobilizing its reserves, and shooting any and all who approached. The strategy wasn't popular, but it was effective, and was thus far holding back the growing tide of destruction that surrounded it.

Europe had not been able to escape unscathed. While Israel hunkered down, many of the highly populated Muslim communities in Europe had risen up in response to the Jewish actions, pushing several countries to the brink of civil war. Eventually martial law had been declared throughout the European Union, and while a few pockets of resistance were still fighting back, it seemed Europe would eventually come out of the conflict comparatively intact.

The problem was, as Frank pointed out, that with Europe under martial law and dealing with internal threats, they were not in any shape to be of assistance to the United States, so we couldn't count on them to provide resources that would help us get back on our feet. Germany and Korea had been the source for the majority of the world's electrical generating equipment, and with Germany now offline, it would take Korea decades to provide even a fraction of what America needed to rebuild.

To this point, the Southern Hemisphere had been least impacted by the state of world affairs, though with much of the world's purchasing power in North America and Europe shut down, the ensuing depression had caused massive unemployment, unrest, and misery even there. Due to a combination of factors such as isolation, cultural stability, and national pride, Australia and Japan were the two least affected countries, even though many of their industries outside of agriculture were on the verge of collapse.

On the American front, conditions were as bad as, if not worse than, much of the world, with the most devastating destruction occurring in the Northeast, stretching from Washington, D.C., to Concord, NH. The mortality rate in those areas was nearing 50%, a result of lack of medical care, violence, starvation, and diseases stemming from failed sanitation systems. Combine that with fires that burned through entire neighborhoods, and it seemed that whole portions of the country were turning into massive refugee camps. A few pockets of stability were emerging in the Northeast, but it would likely be the end of summer before any sort of sustainable communities could be re-established. What had once been the economic hub of the world had been reduced, in the course of a few weeks, to a third world region where stealing a potato from a neighbor's garden could get you shot.

Other parts of the country were faring better than the Northeast, but most big cities were not too far behind in sinking to third world status. Northern cities, like Chicago, were struggling the most, as harsh weather was added to all their other problems. Southern cities, where a person could more easily survive the winter, uncomfortable as it may be, were fortunate to have less densely populated regions, allowing people room to grow food. The cities in the South also had sizeable agricultural regions that produced crops year round, in many instances, providing enough food to subsist on, even if it made for a one-dimensional diet.

To the west, the worst locations to be in were Phoenix and Las Vegas, primarily due to water shortages. To this point, the climate in those areas had been beneficial, but the absence of rain and the dependence on water treatment and pumping facilities that no longer worked resulted in the worst misery. Southern California was also a bad place to be, but mostly because of the human factor. Sanitation and violence were causing the greatest number of deaths, with many areas in the cities now armed camps, at war with neighboring gangs over control of limited resources.

From a national perspective, the Pacific Northwest was the only region in the country that could be described in any sense as having survived well the affects of the attack. The weather, though harsh at times, was survivable. Population density, outside of the Portland and Seattle areas, was tolerable. And, the region was naturally rich with agriculture, abundant wildlife, water, ranching, fishing, and a host of other resources that made survival more likely than not.

Throughout the country there were areas that ran counter to the trends, but as a whole, that was the disposition of the nation and the world in general, according to Frank and based on information gleaned from his HAM radio conversations.

Kyle came away from the discussion mildly depressed at the state of the country, and while he wasn't too surprised, hearing about it from someone who wasn't just speculating or repeating rumors was discouraging. Cut off from the rest of the world and focused on your own survival, it was easy not to think about what others were going through, then hard to hear that it was so bad. The only bright spot from his discussion with Frank was finding out that they were faring well in comparison to the rest of the country, which hopefully meant that he and his parents would have a better than average chance of surviving once he made it to them.

Conversation continued while Kyle and the Emorys ate their breakfast of pancakes with real maple syrup, fried eggs, and toast with jam, all flavors that had long been absent from Kyle's diet. Life for Frank and Brenda, from a convenience standpoint, didn't seem to be very different from life before the event. Daily routines had changed, and they were physically cut off from others, but they didn't worry about food, or heat, or water, or, most importantly, about tomorrow.

Yes, Kyle decided, if he could go back, there were things he'd definitely do differently. If only that was an option.

CHAPTER TWENTY-FIVE

Saturday, January 28th
Eastern Montana

The roadblock, positioned near an old weigh station in the middle of the highway, was visible from three miles away, and Rose approached it with hesitation. Crossing Wyoming and Montana had so far proven to be a pretty quiet endeavor, consisting mostly of wide-open stretches of farms, ranches and forests. A few towns that dotted the map were going to be hard to avoid though. Crow Agency up ahead was one of them.

Rose generally rode in the median or along the sides of the highway. A couple of times she'd used bolt cutters to cut fences and skirt wide of an area, until a property owner had noticed once and come after her waving a rifle, swearing and cussing about how she'd ruined his fence and made more work for him. She'd given him a box of shotgun shells and some fresh venison to appease him, apologized, and hurried on her way, grateful the man had limited his assault to a few choice adjectives.

Progress on her journey was steady, and the horses were doing better than expected, though good feed was scarce, and they were all just now getting used to trekking for hours at time. Both horses were shod, thanks to Lou, but to the extent she could, she still tried to stay off of surfaces that might damage their hooves.

The barricade was closer now, and Rose stayed alert as she drew near. Both of her rifles were loaded and easily accessible, as was the pistol in her saddlebag. She also had a small knife. Still, no matter how well armed she was, one person against a group wasn't a good situation.

"Stop!" A tall man in his late forties stepped out from behind the barricade, keeping her fifty feet away. He was dressed in a long, brown duster, his unkempt hair matted to his head. His face was dark and weathered and betrayed no emotion. A rifle hung casually from his left hand.

Already nervous, Rose jumped in her saddle at the man's voice. She reined Smokey in and waited for instructions.

"What are you doing here?"

"I'm just passing through, heading to Missoula," she answered warily, scanning the area for more people. She could see someone peeking out from behind the barricade and another on the far side of the highway.

The man whistled. "Missoula? That's a long ride."

Rose nodded.

"Are you alone?" he asked, looking past her and down the highway.

Rose watched him, cautious, unsure of the best response to give.

"That's not a tough question, is it? It means is there another person traveling with you?" A smile cracked the man's solemn face.

"I'm alone, but I'm not helpless."

"I see your guns; we know you're armed. We're just a small town here and don't want any troubles. It's dangerous traveling alone, you know."

"I'm very aware of that." Smokey danced anxiously beneath her. "Can I be on my way?"

He nodded. "We'll escort you through town, to make sure nothing happens to us or to you." He whistled and called out a couple names. Two girls carrying shotguns emerged a few seconds later from the house nearest the barricade and ran towards the man. The older girl appeared to be in her mid-twenties, the younger one maybe sixteen. The man gave instructions to the girls, then waved Rose forward.

"Ride slowly. My nieces will walk with you to make sure you don't stop. Any questions?"

"No," Rose said, shaking her head. "I just keep going, right?"

The man nodded. "Keep your hands on your saddle and don't reach for your guns. We've had some problems in the past so we're just being careful." He stepped back and motioned for Rose to pass.

Rose kicked, and Smokey started forward, his slow easy gait rocking her in the saddle. Rose rode down the middle of the road, while the girls walked about twenty feet on either side of her and slightly behind. They rarely spoke to each other, but when they did, it was in a language Rose didn't understand.

"Do you speak English?" Rose asked the older girl when they were about halfway through town.

She nodded. "I do. Do you speak Crow?"

"No," Rose answered. "Haven't had much use for it."

"I was a nursing student. Now look at me." She raised her gun in front of herself. "I'm a security guard."

"I was a real estate agent. Now I'm a refugee."

They walked in silence awhile longer, watching the road, thinking.

"Why are you traveling so late?" the girl asked. "Lots of people come through last year, but not so many now."

Rose explained her situation and need to travel. "Did anyone come through last year, around the beginning of November, pulling a cart?" The girl thought a minute. "I don't know dates, not sure what month this is now, but I think so. It was like a big wagon?"

Rose nodded.

"Yeah. I think so, but there have been a lot of people, just not many lately."

"How's your town doing?" Rose asked, looking at the bleak surroundings.

The girl shook her head. "Not good. Too many were dependent on their government checks and never learned to take care of themselves or think about tomorrow. You don't have to worry about working when someone gives you money every month. My uncle was on the tribal council, always warned about those things, but no one would listen. Now our people can't survive without the white man providing for us. Many of the old people have died, and the young ones have given up. Suicide happens a lot, and fighting, but at least the liquor is gone."

"I'm sorry," Rose offered.

The girl pointed to a faded billboard advertising Little Bighorn Battlefield. "In his time, Custer and the Army used guns to destroy us. Our people knew to fight against that. We were strong then. In my father's and grandfathers' generations, they've destroyed us with welfare, and we just ask for more, not seeing what it does to us. It's worse than the alcohol." She kicked a rock, rolling it across the highway. "Maybe now, with this," she waved her arm at the lifeless town. "Maybe our people will wake up, regain their pride, reclaim our heritage now that the free ride is over. If we don't, there will be no more Crow Nation."

"There may not be an American nation, if things get much worse."

The girl laughed contemptuously. "I think that was already gone before this happened. America lost its vision. It was money, and play, and more money. It didn't stand for anything. Our people had the same problem. We had nothing to strive for, so we became lazy and weak."

"You are wise beyond your years. Did they teach you that at school? Doesn't sound like nursing to me."

"School my ass." She spit on the ground and tucked her long hair behind her ear. "The university just kept telling me I should demand more from the government. But why? That's the poison that's killing us. Our father was an alcoholic, spent most of his government checks on beer, then he abandoned us. Our mother was killed in a car accident when I was eleven, so my uncle took us in and raised us. He says our great-great-grandfather was a chief when they took our people away. I think he exaggerates, but he's trying to inspire us to be free and great again, like our ancestors."

They were approaching a roadblock on the other end of town that was guarded by two men sitting in old, blanket-covered recliners. "Thank you for the escort," Rose said. "I was quite nervous when I saw your uncle, but it was actually nice to talk to you. What is your name, by the way?"

The girl held her head high. "My name is Tabitha Gray Eagle, and I am a Crow Indian."

Rose smiled and extended her hand. "Well, Tabitha, it was an honor to have met you. I hope you'll be safe."

Tabitha took Rose's hand and shook it. "What is your name?"

They were interrupted by one of the men at the barricade. He spoke Crow to the girl, and Rose didn't understand.

Tabitha said something in reply, directed a stern look at him, and gripped her gun.

The man got up and approached. He was a short man, older than the two girls, and dressed in a ragged coat and dirty jeans. He smiled at Tabitha, exposing yellowed and missing teeth as he rubbed a fresh scar on the side of his face. Then he focused on Rose, giving her a look that unnerved her. "You alone, lady?"

Shivers ran down her back. Rose pulled the reins to the right and gave Smokey a kick. "I need to be on my way. It was nice meeting you, Tabitha."

"Good luck, Miss," Tabitha said as she waved. Then she turned to her sister and motioned with her head back the other way.

The man waved as well, and Rose felt his eyes following her. "Goodbye, Lady!" he shouted before slowly ambling back to the barricade and dropping into his chair.

CHAPTER TWENTY-SIX

Monday, February 6ᵗʰ
Western Montana

A deer sprang out of a stand of trees and darted across the road in front of Kyle, startling his horse and causing Kyle to jump in his saddle. He reined the horse to a stop and studied the forest where the deer had emerged. "It's alright, Garfield," he said, rubbing the horse's neck. Garfield, named after the comic strip cat because of his unnaturally orange coloring, flicked his tail from side to side and wandered towards the trees where some taller patches of grass grew.

Kyle dismounted and stretched his legs, watching the horse as it tugged at the wild growth. Garfield had been a decent companion even though he was old and had a mind of his own, not wanting to walk too fast, go for too long, or pass a creek or stream without stopping for a break.

Riding wasn't foreign to Kyle. He'd done it a lot as a child, spending weeks in the summer on his grandfather's farm riding with his cousins. But grandpa had also had an old dirt bike, and rather than messing with saddles and halters, it was much easier to wheel the bike out of the barn, jump on, kick it over, and be off. Looking back, it would have been nice to learn more about horses, but as a twelve year old, he'd been more concerned with fun and adventure than in planning for any distant, doomsday scenario where a knowledge of animal husbandry might come in handy.

Kyle tied Garfield to a fallen tree, untied his canteen from the saddle and walked to the river to fill it. His knees popped as he squatted down at the river's edge and dipped the canteen into the water until it was full. He stood and shook each leg, one at a time, then dropped to the ground and did a set of pushups.

Garfield was nice to have, much better than walking, but Kyle sometimes wondered if his old cart would've been a better arrangement where he could've carried more and gone on his own schedule. But then again, despite his aching back and painful saddle sores, his body was taking less of a beating than when he'd walked, and he didn't need to eat as much food to make it through each day. Add to that the fact that traveling the river valleys meant there was plenty of food and water for both horse and rider, and this set up did seem to be the best overall under the circumstances.

Travel had been steady and easy so far. After leaving Frank's place, he'd traveled west, gone around Missoula, then hooked north onto State Highway 93, the route he usually took to visit his parents. He knew the road well, having last traveled it just before his business trip to Houston, but that was six months ago and things had changed a lot since then.

Where before it had been just a few hours travel time with food and fuel available along the way, it was now a three-week journey with limited food, no fuel, and questionable survivability. Traveling through towns on horseback was usually a straightforward event. Stop at the checkpoint on the southside, state your purpose, assure the sentries you had no evil intentions, then pass quietly through, sometimes escorted, other times not.

He felt like a cowboy in an old western movie, riding unannounced into town, a wary sheriff keeping an eye on him, the townsfolk nervous as children scampered out of his way, though in the movies the townsfolk never looked as hungry or as worried as they did now. Kyle had picked up a few letters along the way to be delivered to people in towns further along his route, the recipients' names and towns printed neatly on the outside of envelopes. There was no postage fee, but the senders usually offered some food, a couple of bullets, or something else of value for his troubles. To this point, Kyle had picked up sixteen letters and already delivered three of them to grateful family or friends, anxious for news from their loved ones.

Garfield snorted, and Kyle walked back to him and checked the straps of the saddle, making sure there were no saddle sores on the horse and that everything was secure. He took a few grains of Frank's powdered bleach and dropped them into his canteen, then closed the lid and shook it vigorously. "You ready to go?"

Garfield ignored him and continued to graze. Kyle circled the horse, checking the bottom of each hoof for embedded rocks, then mounted up and continued on his way.

CHAPTER TWENTY-SEVEN

Tuesday, February 7th
Deer Creek, MT

Ty Lewis knocked on the door, then stood back and waited. The door opened a few inches, and Jennifer peered out through the crack. "What do you need?" she asked, squinting in the sunlight.

"Hi, Jennifer," Ty said, rubbing his arms to ward off the cold. "I promised Kyle I would look out for you guys while he was gone, so I'm here. My daughter said you weren't at school today." She nodded. "Can I come in? I don't want to let all your warm air out."

Jennifer hesitated, then pulled the door open wide enough for Ty to come in.

Ty hurried in, and closed the door behind him. "Feels good in here," he observed. "Mind if I sit down?"

"How long are you planning on staying?" Jennifer asked, her arms folded tightly across her body, her head dipped low.

"I don't plan to stay too long, Jennifer, but we need to talk. What you're doing isn't healthy." He smiled and tried to make eye contact, but she wouldn't look him in the eye.

"How do you know what's good for me and what isn't?" she snapped. "Maybe this is how I like things. Maybe this is all I can do." A tear welled up in the corner of her eye, and she wiped it away. "Maybe you should just leave me alone," she said, raising her voice and motioning for Ty to leave.

Spencer heard his mother and ran up the stairs from the basement. He looked at his mother, then over at Ty, then wrapped his arms around Jennifer's leg, giving her a hug.

"Hi Spencer," Ty said. "You doing okay, buddy?"

He nodded his head innocently and looked up at his mom.

"He doesn't exactly understand why his father's gone. After Kyle's miraculous return, to have the town try and kill him then run him off is a little hard for this family to wrap our heads around."

"You want to come over to my house and play with Zettie tomorrow?" Ty asked Spencer. "You know her from school, right? I think she's your age."

Spencer nodded again. "She's in my class." He looked up at his mom. "Can I go?"

"That would be fine, if it's okay with Mr. Lewis."

"Of course it's okay, Spencer. When I get home, I'll tell her to get her room cleaned up. Hope you like to play with dolls," Ty said, flashing his teeth in a broad smile.

Spencer shook his head vigorously.

"How about trucks and legos and stuff? I love my girl, but I kind of hoped for a little boy, so she's got a few things like that too. Does that sound better?"

Spencer nodded shyly, and his mother rubbed his head affectionately. "That does sound better, doesn't it? Why don't you go back downstairs for a few minutes, while I visit with Zettie's dad." She watched Spencer leave, then turned back to Ty. "So why are you here?"

"I'm sorry it's taken me so long to see you. I stopped by a couple of times, but Carol said you weren't up to talking yet."

"She told me. I'm sorry to be such a bother. You don't need to worry about us."

"I promised Kyle I would, and I meant it. How would it look when he gets back if I haven't kept my promise?"

Jennifer looked at Ty with dead eyes. "What makes you think he's coming back?"

The look on Ty's face spoke volumes. He was about to say something when Jennifer raised her hand to stop him.

"I don't mean that he would choose not to come back, but what if something happens to him? The first time, I was so naïve thinking he could just somehow cross the country and get back to us. He did it, but he was so lucky. After listening to his stories, and thinking about what he went through, there's no way that should have happened. The world is all screwed up, Ty. My fourteen-year-old son has been stabbed, and he's had to kill armed invaders. I've killed someone, as has Kyle. That Smith girl was murdered, raped, and dumped in my house. This world is falling apart. How can I even hope that Kyle will make it back with everything that's going on?"

"You don't have a choice, Jennifer; it's not just you. You have your kids and your friends. People look up to you."

"Who looks up to me?" she retorted. "No one cares what I do. My kids, maybe, but I even wonder about them lately. I feel like I'm going over the edge, Ty, like I should be locked up in an asylum."

"More people than you know watch you. My wife and I… you don't understand. Last fall, this whole thing went down less than a month after we buried our daughter. We'd been home from Georgia for less than a week when the EMP hit. Our world was still spinning from losing her, and then all this?" Ty looked around the room, motioning to the dead lights and the condition of the house, then looked back at Jennifer. "We were ready to give up. I didn't want to go on. It was so hard. Trust me, I kind of know how you feel."

"What made you keep going?"

"There were a handful of things, but one of them was you."

It was Jennifer's turn to be puzzled. "Me?"

Ty nodded.

"What did I do? I only just barely remember seeing you at the town meetings. Did we even talk?"

"It wasn't anything you said, Jenn. It was just you, your spirit."

She still didn't get it.

Ty grinned and chuckled. "We watched you. For some reason, you were kind of like our beacon of hope. Someone, I can't remember who, told us your husband was gone, that you were all alone with your kids. Yet at the meetings, you always seemed so happy, so hopeful. My wife mentioned it to me one evening when I was really low. Said if Jennifer Tait could be happy and hopeful under similar circumstances as us, why couldn't we?"

Jennifer listened, staring at the floor.

Ty continued. "She was right. The next day the weather was really nice, and I took a long hike and asked myself what good it was doing for me to be walking around like a man half dead, feeling sorry for myself. Yeah, it hurt, and it still hurts more than I can describe to have lost our little Lonnie. I'm sure it always will, but hating life just made it worse. You helped show me that, Jennifer."

She shook her head. "I don't know if I believe you."

"You can believe it or not, but it's true. Come by and ask my wife if you'd like. Talia didn't go on the hike with me, but she knows the story."

"I was just naïve then. I didn't know any better. Sorry to let you down now."

Ty forced a smile and watched Jennifer for a minute, but she wouldn't look up. "Jennifer, you're a big girl. I can't tell you what to do. I understand how tough it is, but hating people isn't going to fix anything. I can't promise you things will be great or that Kyle will be back tomorrow, but I can tell you it's easier if you choose to smile. No one's out to get you. Everyone's just afraid and still figuring out how to deal with life. Give them some time."

"I'm the one that needs time, you know," Jennifer snapped before catching herself. "I will think about it though. I want to be happy, Ty, I really do, but with Kyle gone on top of everything else, it's too hard."

Ty took her hand and gave it a squeeze as he stood to leave. "I'm here to help if you'll let me. If there's something you need, please tell me. How about if I come by for Spencer after lunch tomorrow, okay?"

Jennifer nodded. "Thanks for stopping by. I do appreciate you thinking of me."

Ty let himself out, and Jennifer sat back down on the couch.

"So what are you going to do?" Carol asked from the kitchen.

Jennifer jumped. "I forgot you were in there."

"Didn't mean to eavesdrop, but I couldn't help hearing the conversation."

'It's your house; don't apologize."

"He made some good points, you know."

"I know," Jenn said, nodding. "But it's so much harder this time. I'm terrified Kyle won't come back. I keep thinking of him dead or hurt somewhere on the road, and it terrifies me. I really hate to say it, but if he'd been shot last week, at least the uncertainty wouldn't be hanging over my head every day like it is now. I understand why the families of people who go missing struggle so much. I think not knowing can almost be worse than death."

Carol stood in the doorway of the kitchen. "We all have tough things to deal with, Jennifer. I know you know that. Just realize that you'll make it through this. You've got a lot of friends pulling for you."

Jennifer nodded and went and helped clean the kitchen. She was about to go downstairs when someone pounded on the front door. She jumped to her feet and hurried to it, pulling it open. Ty stood on the front porch again, this time out of breath.

"Is Carol here? There's an emergency. We need a doctor!"

CHAPTER TWENTY-EIGHT

Tuesday, February 7th
Billings, MT

The road ahead looked like a World War II movie scene, with charred pieces of steel littering the highway, blackened vehicles on the road, and partially collapsed and burnt out buildings along the perimeter. It was just as the ranchers had described to Rose during her two-day stay with them while Blitz recovered from a leg injury, a deep gash inflicted by barbed wire buried beneath the snow.

Rose had met the ranchers, Paul and Mindy, at their home a few miles south of Huntley while seeking help for her wounded horse. The couple had been kind enough to take her in and help doctor the wound on Blitz's leg, which, fortunately, hadn't been too severe. Two days rest had done wonders for both her and her animals, but once refreshed, she had been anxious to get back on the road again, despite Paul and Mindy's concern for her wellbeing as a woman traveling alone.

Now picking her way through the debris, Rose was feeling uneasy. What lay before her was the most graphic depiction she'd seen of the destruction that had followed the September attacks. Two oil refineries on the south side of Billings had lasted three days past the event before erupting in a series of explosions that shook buildings for thirty miles and launched pieces of shrapnel thousands of feet. No one knew what had triggered the blast, at least no one who had survived the explosions and the ensuing destruction, and there was nothing to be done except watch the fires burn themselves out, leaving charred buildings as semi-permanent reminders.

Fires had raged for five days following the blasts, burning through entire blocks and killing an untold number of residents who were unable to flee quickly enough. Those on the periphery of the blast zone who had escaped from the fires had then found themselves in a desperate situation, as there were no relief services to step in and provide assistance after homes and all personal possessions had been lost in the destruction.

Churches attempted to help but were quickly overwhelmed by demand and unable to resupply, and their efforts soon fell short, resulting in a large homeless community that was struggling for survival against both hunger and nature on the edges of the Yellowstone River.

From the road, Rose could see makeshift shelters lining the river's edge, constructed of whatever materials the homeless had been able to scavenge: old cars, cardboard boxes, pieces of steel tanks that had been blown apart by the refinery explosions, sheets of drywall, and even fallen trees stacked to provide shelter from the wind, a scene more suited to the slums in some nameless place in India than a modern-day city in America. Rose half expected to see naked, starving children with distended bellies bathing in the river and likely would have, she thought, were it not for the sheets of ice extending from the shore, preventing access to the water except in a few isolated locations.

Smoke rose from several of the shelters, and people wandered from shelter to shelter, gathered wood, fished, or sat and stared vacantly at the tumbling water. She gripped her rifle in her hands, her eyes scanning the road for any sign of threats. Paul and Mindy had warned her about the community at the river, but to avoid the highway would have meant either going through the heart of Billings, or circling so far north or south that it would have added several extra days of travel.

A quick trip, armed and read, was Rose's response to the threat, and so far she had proceeded without incident. Smokey and Blitz were making good time, and most people had paid little attention to her, absorbed instead in their own struggle for survival.

Rose kept to the north side of the road, moving the horses at a brisk pace, and veering onto the pavement only when debris or interchanges required it. Her heart raced as they hurried along. The road, much as it would have been when the EMP hit, was filled with the heavy traffic of a holiday weekend. Cars, trucks, and semis, all obstacles that could easily conceal an ill-intentioned person, were everywhere. Even the shoulder of the road and the grassy area alongside it were not free of vehicles, making the journey a challenge for a person maneuvering two horses.

"Hey, can you help me?" She had made it most of the way through the city. In fact, she had just started to breathe easier as the city fell away behind her when she heard the voice call out. She slowed and looked around, not seeing anyone.

Rose had passed a blue pickup truck parked off the road halfway into the center median when she heard the voice again. "Help me, please." She paused, looking around again. The voice was strange, not distinctly male or female, and wasn't coming from anywhere she could identify. She raised her gun, her nerves on edge. The horses, sensing her tension, were skittish themselves. She spotted movement in the median to her left. A leg extending past the blue pickup twitched and kicked. "Help," the voice said again.

Rose couldn't see the rest of the body, but she didn't like the situation. "Go, Smokey!" she urged. As she prodded the horse forward she heard a noise and felt a hand on her arm. She turned to swing her rifle, but the person held her arm tightly and jerked her hard from the horse. Smokey spooked and lurched forward, further unbalancing Rose and causing her to fall from the saddle. Her gun roared as she pulled the trigger, but the un-aimed shot only served to make her ears ring and further startle the horses, sending them running, panicked by the noise and commotion.

"Nice try, bitch!" A man, his face, dirty and bearded, slammed his fist into her cheek and sent her crashing to the ground.

The blow dazed Rose, and her rifle fell from her hands, clattering onto the highway. "Stop!" she yelled, desperate and disoriented.

The man grabbed her jacket and pinned her to the ground, rising above her. He threw a leg over Rose to straddle her, using the weight of his body to keep her down, his hands holding her arms at her side as she thrashed helplessly. "Dangerous place to be traveling alone, lady," he said, leering down at her through squinting brown eyes, a perverse grin splitting his face. "Don't get many women in these parts, 'specially not pretty ones."

A shadow fell over her as another man approached. She assumed he was the source of the voice from the median. "You let the horses get away, you idiot!" the man accused.

Rose tasted blood in her mouth. She turned to try to see the second man. "Let me go," she insisted. "I haven't done anything to you."

He looked down at her and grinned. "No one said you did," he replied, spitting on the pavement. He wore a filthy, brown work coat, and a dark, unkempt beard covered his face, much like the other man's. He didn't strike her as being especially big, even looking up at him from the ground. "We've just embarked on a new career, and you just happened to pass through at the right time, depending on your point of view."

The man astride her looked towards the horses, which were still galloping away. "Sorry about the horses," he said. "But she had her gun out. You heard the shot. I had to grab her arms."

The other man shook his head. "Just shut up, alright. I don't care what happened. Now I've got to go chase them down." He pulled a gun from his waistband and aimed it at his partner. "You think you can handle her by yourself while I go get 'em?"

"No problem," he replied, nodding his head vigorously. "I'll have her warmed up and ready for you when you get back."

"You sure?"

He nodded again, his mouth drawn in a tight line. "I'm sure," he replied. The first man stood, jerking Rose upward and twisting her arms painfully.

With Rose back on her feet, the man from the median handed the pistol to his partner. "Take this. If she tries anything, shoot her, but try not to damage any of my favorite parts."

His partner took the gun and laughed. "Count on it," he said. "Do you want to check her for weapons before you go?"

He shook his head. "You do it. Looks like the stupid horses have stopped. I gotta go before they run off again."

Rose heard the man behind her grunt then felt the barrel of his gun press against her back and his hand press against her waist. His hand rubbed across her body, sliding from her waist to her thighs, then up across her chest and down her back. She shuddered during the search, her legs shaking and her breath coming in short gasps.

"You have any weapons?" he asked belatedly after physically probing far longer than necessary.

"Just the gun I was holding," she choked out, trying to sound calmer than she felt, which wasn't very. "There's another gun on the horse, but that's it."

"I'll check again when you get inside. If you're lying..." he trailed off ominously. He pushed her forward, his handgun still aimed at her, then swung his leg and kicked her hard in the thigh.

Rose attempted to block the kick unsuccessfully. The impact of the blow left her leg throbbing, but she didn't fall, only letting out a small whimper.

"So you don't try to run off," he said as he bent down and picked up her rifle, inspecting it quickly. "Nice gun."

Rose stared at the road and massaged her leg, but didn't respond.

"Walk to that motorhome," the man ordered, pointing to a forty-foot motorhome parked on the opposite side of the freeway and fifty yards back in the direction she had come from. "If you behave well, we'll let you go."

"What if I don't?" Rose asked as she limped towards the RV, not really wanting to know the answer.

"If you don't then, well, you won't like it, but Mickey says we got to conserve our bullets."

"So it's up to Mickey, is it?"

"I decide, too, but Mickey's in charge, so, yeah, I guess it's up to him. You have a problem with that?"

Rose shook her head. They were approaching the motorhome, and she slowed, awaiting directions. She looked over her shoulder and saw Mickey still headed the other way, the horses nearly a mile down the road, pacing nervously in the median and still tethered together.

"Open the door and get in," her kidnapper ordered. "Don't make me shoot you."

Rose reached for the door handle and tugged on it. The door stuck a little before opening, then she climbed inside, her eyes taking a few seconds to adjust to the dim light. The coach smelled of body odor and sewage. She tried to breathe through her mouth, but the odors were so strong she could taste them, and she fought the urge to vomit as she moved further into the RV.

As the man lumbered in behind her, Rose saw an open door at the rear and a woman dressed only in a sport bra and shorts lying on a bed with her back towards the door, arms bound behind her body, with fresh bruises and wounds on her back and arms.

The man shoved Rose onto the couch, stepped past her, and pulled the bedroom door shut. "My wife's sleeping. Try not to make any noise."

With the image of the woman in her mind, Rose was too terrified to respond, and her body started shaking.

Her captor turned towards her, leaned her rifle against the wall, and pointed the handgun at her head. "Take off your shoes and your pants."

"What do you want from me?" Rose asked, her voice barely audible, her mouth still tasting of blood.

The man laughed. "If you haven't figured that out already, there's no point in me explaining. Just do what I say."

Rose reached down and pushed off her boots, then, hands shaking almost uncontrollably, unhooked her belt and the button of her jeans. "Please don't do this," she begged. "Please."

"Hurry," the man ordered, glancing out the front window. Rose followed his gaze and saw that Mickey had reached the horses, but Smokey was making Mickey chase him to be caught. "I don't usually get to go first. I have to be done before he returns."

"No," Rose said, shaking her head. "I won't do it."

The man's face hardened, and he raised his gun, aiming it at Rose. "We can do this dead or alive. It's up to you. You cooperate, and you'll live. Mickey will get bored of you in a couple of weeks, and you'll get to go. Fight it, and worse things will happen to you."

"I'd rather die," she mumbled, her arms limp, her strength gone.

The man lashed out with his foot and kicked her in the shin, sending sharp pains shooting up her leg, then he shoved her backwards, and she tumbled onto the floor. "Listen!" he growled. "You're lucky I'd rather not put bullet holes in this thing, or I'd shoot you in the foot. Take your pants off now, or I'll make sure you're kept here alive for a lot longer than two weeks!"

Rose recoiled and began to cry, but still forced herself to push her jeans down. She lifted her hips and pushed on the waistband, scooting her pants down past her knees. She tugged her white thermal underwear up as she pushed her pants down.

The man laughed derisively. "Hurry it up," he demanded. "I don't have all day."

Rose kicked her jeans off, and they landed under the table across from her. The thermals were tight, probably a size too small even with all of the weight she'd lost, and they clung to her legs, revealing the curve of her hips.

"Nice. Now stand up and turn around."

Rose stood and turned, tears running down her cheeks. "Please don't..." she began, but the man cut her off.

"You're wasting your breath, lady. You don't leave 'til we get what we want. Understand?"

She nodded and slumped back down onto the couch.

"I didn't say sit down, did I?"

"No," Rose mumbled weakly, standing again.

"Take off your jacket."

Rose removed it.

"Now your sweatshirt and t-shirt."

She tossed her clothes on the couch, leaving just her bra and thermals.

"Very nice," he muttered, staring at her chest. "They real?"

Rose shook her head.

"Thanks for spending the money. That's why they're still big," he observed, grinning. "Not like all these other scrawny women who shrivel up when they get skinny."

Rose was numb, both physically and mentally, and didn't respond.

"Put your hands on your head," he directed, then smiled as she did so. "That makes them look even bigger, you know."

He removed his coat, then knelt down in front of her, still holding the gun in his hand, and reached for the waistband of her thermals with his empty hand. He tugged, but it hung up on her opposite hip. He looked up at Rose, clad only in thermals and a bra, her hands on her head, and felt his hormones surge. His heart raced, and his breathing became shallow. "Don't move."

Rose closed her eyes and braced herself, hands still resting on her head. As her hands slipped slightly, she felt the cold steel of the red-handled knife her neighbor, Lou, had insisted she take brush against her fingers. It took a second for Rose to remember what she was touching. She had promised Lou that she would keep it on her person at all times, and as her hair had gotten longer, she'd found it more convenient to use it to tie her hair up, than to carry it in a pocket or boot. She felt a second hand on her hips and realized her abductor had set his gun down. She looked out the front window and saw Mickey with Smokey in tow, but still nearly a mile away and struggling to get the horses to come back with him.

"I like black underwear," the man said as he slid down her thermals. "Lift your foot."

Rose lifted her left foot and felt him pull the underwear off. As she set her foot back down, she shifted her weight and coughed while simultaneously flipping the blade open, something she'd practiced doing while warming herself by a fire in the evenings.

"Lift this one," he ordered, tapping her right foot.

Rose looked at him as she lifted her foot, willing him to look away. He smiled at her with filthy, yellowed teeth exposed and stray hairs from his beard stuck to his lips with saliva. He extended his tongue and slowly licked his lips. She waited, both hands behind her head, blade extended, fingers trembling, trying to focus.

He kept his eyes locked on hers as he tugged the long underwear from her right foot. "This is as good as a hooker," he said, his smile growing.

Rose held her breath, still waiting for him to look away. She swallowed, wanting to scream, to lash out immediately, but needing to wait until he looked away. She knew if she failed, this nightmare, this hell, would get much worse and last much longer than she wanted to imagine.

"My name's Mantle," he said, laughing. "Get it? We're Mickey and Mantle, like the baseball player." He caressed her thigh, still looking up at her.

Rose gasped and looked at the ceiling. "Just do what you have to do, Mantle," she said, forcing the words out, wanting to vomit. From the corner of her eye she could see him grinning, almost giddy, then he leaned in and kissed her on the inner thigh.

This was her chance. She was either going to die trying or succeed in sending him to hell, both options far better than what lay in store otherwise. Clasping the knife in both hands, she swung it over her head and down as hard as she could, plunging the blade into the back of Mantle's neck just below the collar of his shirt.

CHAPTER TWENTY-NINE

Tuesday, February 7ᵗʰ
Deer Creek, MT

Jennifer took a step back from the door, startled. "What's wrong, Ty?"

Ty was breathing hard. "There's a girl, from Clinton."

Carol had already risen from the couch and moved to the front door. "It's not another murder, is it?" she asked.

Ty shook his head. "No. She's pregnant, ready to deliver. They're bringing her here because there's no doctor in Clinton. They were on the wrong street. I told them how to get here, then ran ahead to warn you."

Jennifer looked at Carol. "You deliver babies?"

Carol shook her head quickly. "Calves and puppies. Never human."

"Well, get ready, Carol," Ty said, as he looked down the street to where two people were leading a very pregnant young woman on a horse, "because you're about to get the chance."

"I've worried about this," Carol said anxiously, "but nobody in Deer Creek is pregnant. I didn't think about Clinton. Jennifer, get Grace. Ty, help get some water heating up."

Carol pushed the furniture back against the living room walls, then sent Ty and David to retrieve the box spring from the bed Grace used and place it in the center of the room.

Jennifer met the group from Clinton at the front door and helped guide the pregnant woman to the box spring on the living room floor.

"What's your name?" Jennifer asked as she helped lower the young woman onto her back.

"I'm Heather," she answered, gritting her teeth in obvious discomfort and struggling to get the words out.

"Hi, Heather. I'm Jennifer. Carol is the doctor. She's going to help you."

"I heard she was a vet," Heather gasped.

"I am," Carol said, as she emerged from the kitchen with a stack of towels. "Obstetricians are in short supply, so I guess it's me or your neighbor. I've delivered lots of farm animals, if that's any consolation."

"Do I have a choice?"

"Not at this point you don't." Carol checked the girl's pulse. "This your first baby?"

Heather nodded, relaxing a little as the contraction ended. "I had the ultrasound scheduled, but then everything crashed and I couldn't have it done. I don't even know if it's a boy or a girl, but I'm pretty sure it isn't due for a couple of weeks. I thought I'd have a chance to come and talk to you before now, but I haven't been feeling very good."

Carol patted her hand. "Well, just relax. How strong are the contractions?"

"Compared to what? They're pretty strong I guess, but I don't know. My water broke a little bit ago, then it felt like a snake wrapped around my belly and started squeezing. Felt like I needed to go to the bathroom too, but I knew enough not to push, at least not yet."

While Carol tended to the mother, Jennifer talked to the elderly couple that had brought Heather to Carol's. "Are you family?"

The woman shook her head. "Just neighbors. She worked at the truck stop in Clinton and rented our basement apartment. We've been trying to help her as best we can."

"Is the father around?"

The man shook his head and spoke softly. "He's a truck driver. No one knows where he was back in September, and he hasn't shown up. They weren't married." He paused, biting his lip. "I didn't really know him, but I always wondered if he was that committed to her. He'd go a long time between visits; she was always worried about their relationship." He frowned as he glanced over at Heather and exhaled faintly. "She's a sweet girl, but..."

His wife grabbed his arm. "Shhh, not now," she said, her eyebrows furrowed. She looked at Jennifer. "We'll do what we can to help Heather out. By the way, I'm Jane, and my husband is Gordon. What do you need us to do?"

Jennifer shrugged helplessly. "Carol, what do we do?" she asked, returning to Carol and Heather.

Carol issued orders, sending Jennifer and Grace after more blankets and rags, Ty to get one of the women in town who was an LPN, Gordon to get water, and Jane to help with Heather. Spencer had heard the commotion and come upstairs out of curiosity, so David was assigned to keep Spencer and Emma out of the way and to maintain the fire and keep the house warm.

"I feel another contraction coming on," Heather said, her voice rising as she gripped Jane's hand.

"Let me know when this one ends and the next one starts, and how strong they feel," Carol directed. "We need to track them as they get closer together."

Heather clenched her lips together and nodded, her face reddening as she absorbed the pain of the contraction. After twenty seconds she gasped, then took in several deep breaths. "Okay, it's ending, but they're getting stronger."

Carol lay a blanket over Heather and helped remove her pants and underwear. "I'm going to wash my hands and get some wet towels. I'll be right back." She hurried to the basement where two large pots of water sat on a grate in the fireplace, sprinkled in a few grains of the powdered bleach, and dipped her hands in the water of the smaller of the two pots. The water was still quite cool, and she grumbled under her breath before turning to David and Gordon. "I need it hot! Get the fire cranked up and monitor the temperature of the water. It might get real warm down here, but you'll have to put up with that."

Gordon added wood to the fire while David took Spencer outside to bring more wood in.

"Call me when the water gets hot to the touch. Understand?"

Gordon nodded. Carol dipped an old bath towel into the water, then wrung it out and ran back upstairs.

Jennifer knelt at the head of the box spring and stroked Heather's hair, keeping it pulled back from her face, while Jane held her hand and chatted with her.

"You feel the next contraction coming on?" Carol asked, seeing Heather shift under the blanket.

She shook her head. "No, it's just not very comfortable on this thing."

Carol bit her thumbnail as she assessed the situation. "I really want you on something firm, but maybe we can improve things a little." Carol grabbed some pillows from the couch and, with the help of Jennifer and Jane, set about repositioning Heather on the bed. When they were done, Heather was propped up with couch pillows, her hips on the edge of the box spring and her legs extending off, supported with pillows. As Carol commented under her breath, it was far from perfect, but it was the best they were going to manage under the circumstances.

CHAPTER THIRTY

Tuesday, February 7th
Billings, MT

ose felt the knife strike bone, the impact making a dull thud in the silence of the RV. Mantle jerked his head back and screamed as a thin trickle of blood began to drain from the wound. He pushed at her, but Rose clung fast to the knife anchored in his back, grasping it desperately with both hands and drawing the wound open as she fought to keep her grip.

He clawed for her hands as blood now ran freely down his back and splattered on the floor around him. "You stupid bitch!" he screamed, trying to jerk away, flailing at her with his hands.

Rose tugged at the knife, wanting to pull it out, but the blade, embedded deep in his bone, resisted. She stepped back with one foot, twisted the knife, and jerked it as hard as she could. Mantle fell forward with her pull, still screaming and twisting in pain as the knife pulled free.

Rose stared at her hands and the knife, scarlet red and dripping with blood. Mantle lurched away, and she saw him groping for his handgun with his free hand while keeping the other pressed against his neck, trying to staunch the flow of blood. Rose raised her foot and lashed out, catching him in the nose with her heel and snapping his head back.

"Stop!" he screamed, eyes watering and blood now gushing from his nose too. He coughed and sprayed blood on Rose's legs. His eyes were filled with panic, like an animal caught in a trap, knowing its fate but terrified of meeting it. "Don't kill me," he begged. "This wasn't my idea."

Rose could see that Mantle was still groping for the handgun, his fingers just inches away from it. She kicked at him again, but this time he grabbed her leg with blood slicked fingers, dragging her towards him. Rose slipped on the bloody floor, landing hard by Mantle. He struck her, punching her in the stomach and knocking the air from her lungs.

In spite of the pain, Rose could feel the gun pressed against her leg. She kicked it away from Mantle while slashing at him with her knife, cutting a deep, six-inch long gash in the arm he was using to search for the weapon. Her lungs ached for air, but she ignored the need and cut again, stabbing him in the thigh as she tried to crawl away.

He grabbed her leg, but with only one good hand to use, Rose pulled away, retreating from Mantle in the narrow walkway of the motorhome.

Mantle breathed heavily and glared at her. "Mickey's going to kill you, you know. You have no idea what you've done." The dirty, gray shirt he wore was now stained red, with only the shoulder opposite the wound still its original color.

Rose retreated further, then spotted her rifle on the floor against the couch, where it had fallen during the struggle. Mantle followed her gaze to the gun. He leaned to grab it at the same time Rose lunged, catching her in the face with a bloody elbow, and knocking her backwards, his size and strength still overpowering her. Rose fell back against the bedroom door, and Mantle snatched the gun from the ground and pointed it at her in one swift motion.

He struggled back to his feet, holding the gun in his crippled left hand, blood running from his forearm and thigh, his right hand pressed tightly against the back of his neck. "I might die, whore, but I won't be the only one. Get on your feet!" He spit at her, a red gob of saliva landing on her thigh.

Rose was breathing rapidly. She labored to get into an upright position, then stood up just a few feet in front of him. She stared at him, strong, defiant, unafraid. "Death would be far better than a week with you. Pull the trigger."

Mantle grinned, his teeth red with blood, and pulled the trigger.

The gun clicked softly, but didn't shoot. Mantle looked puzzled.

Rose still held the knife in her hand. She closed the eight-foot gap between them in two quick steps, plunged the blade in the left side of Mantle's groin, and pushed down before pulling it out again, severing his femoral artery. Blood spurted from the slice in his pants, sending a thick stream three feet in front of him and covering her legs and the floor in the warm, red liquid. She raised the knife again and buried it in his neck above the collarbone, leaving just the handle sticking out.

Mantle looked at Rose as she pulled back with the knife, his eyes wide, the color in his face draining quickly. He struggled to form words, but couldn't, and he dropped to his knees, the blood from his groin slowing to a small stream.

Rose yanked her rifle from his hand and stepped away. He gazed at her, his eyes rolling unsteadily in their sockets, but his expression was unmistakable.

She wiped off the blood covering her gun on a couch pillow, then held the weapon in front of him. "Bolt action," she demonstrated, chambering a bullet. The casing of the bullet Rose had fired when Mantle had pulled her from her horse fell on the vinyl floor and bounced with a metallic ring. "Now you go rot in hell."

She raised the rifle and brought the butt end of it down hard on the bridge of his nose, sending Mantle slumping backwards onto the floor of the RV.

Through the windshield Rose could see Mickey leading the horses back to the motorhome, only a couple of vehicles away. Rose moved forward, trying to avoid the blood on the floor while ducking low, grabbed the pistol, and set it on the table. Shivering in the cold, she hurriedly pulled on her thermals and shirt while watching Mickey lead the horses closer. She ejected the magazine from the handgun and inspected it, finding it empty with no bullets in the chamber.

"Didn't want to waste bullets," she said under her breath, disgusted. "You didn't even have bullets, you piece of trash." She tossed the gun on the couch and readied herself for Mickey's return.

Crouching down behind the driver's seat, she peered out the front window and watched as he tied Smokey to the guardrail on the side of the road. His face was expressionless, void of any emotion. No anger. No excitement. No fear. Just blank and soulless.

"Hey Mantle," Mickey shouted as he tried to see inside while crossing in front of the motorhome. "Hope you saved something for me." He paused by the passenger window, listening for a reply, but heard nothing. "Pretty quiet in there. Is she enjoying it?"

Rose could hear him laugh at his own remark, and the hair on the back of her neck stood on end. She leveled the gun at the center of the doorway, where she could see his silhouette through the opaque window in the door, and heard him tug on the door latch.

"You want me to wait for a few more minutes while you finish up?" he called through the door.

Rose's heart beat faster. She wanted a shot with no obstructions, both to guarantee a hit and to see his expression, but the longer he waited to enter without hearing anything from inside, the greater the chance he would be suspicious and come in ready to fight. She could see him lean close to the door, his head cocked sideways to listen.

Rose swallowed hard. She could feel the sweat forming on her forehead and along her spine.

"Mantle?" he called.

Rose rocked the camper back and forth and let out a deep groan loud enough for Mickey to hear outside the camper.

His head jerked back from the door. "What the hell?" she heard him exclaim. The door flew open and Mickey leaped into the RV, catching Rose momentarily off guard. His body had just filled the frame of the door when he saw her crouched behind the driver's seat, her rifle pointed straight at him.

His face betrayed his surprise and confusion as Rose pulled the trigger, the rifle roaring, the bullet striking Mickey in the right side of his chest, knocking him backwards out the door. Rose hurried to the open doorway as she chambered another bullet.

Mickey, looking terrified, lay on his back on the ground. He fumbled for a gun holstered on his hip, but Rose shot again, striking him in the stomach. He screamed shrilly when the bullet hit and clutched at the wound, gaping at Rose, half dressed and standing in the doorway. She watched him down the barrel of her rifle, her right hand working the bolt.

"Screw you!" he yelled defiantly, extending the middle finger of his right hand.

With his hand directly in her line of sight, Rose pulled the trigger, the bullet blowing off three of his fingers before striking him in the bottom of the jaw. His arm dropped limply onto the road, the bloody stump of his hand draining blood onto the pavement, his body motionless.

A violent shudder coursed through Rose as she stared down at the dead man. She didn't regret shooting him, she was sure he deserved to die, but the tension, the emotion, and the fear of all she'd been through in the last thirty minutes made her head swim, and she held the sides of the doorway for support.

Sobbing came from the rear of the RV and brought Rose back from her state of delirium. She remembered the woman in the back and turned back into the motorhome. She stopped at a bucket of water sitting in the kitchen sink and poured some of the water over her arms and hands, excising the vile, sticky blood from her body.

"Everything will be alright..." she called out before catching herself, unwilling to say something she didn't believe. She thought a minute. "They're both gone now. They're dead. I'll be right there."

She quickly dressed, putting her boots on last, then walked slowly to the back and knocked on the door, hearing only muffled sobs. "I'm coming in," she announced as she turned the doorknob and entered the bedroom. Even with the brief glimpse she had had of the woman when she first entered the coach, she was still unprepared for the scene before her.

The woman lay on the bed with her back to the door, her arms secured behind her with rope, her hands purple and swollen. Bloodstains marred the sheets, and when Rose leaned forward, she could see that the woman's face was swollen and bloody, and a sock had been stuffed in her mouth.

"What a nightmare this must have been for you," Rose whispered softly as she carefully extracted the sock. The woman took in deep breaths, but otherwise continued to lie passively on the bed, reacting very little to Rose's presence.

Rose's knife lay on the carpet outside the door, and she grabbed it to slice the bands from the woman's arms. "Do you have clothes here?" Rose asked, scanning the room for anything that looked feminine.

The room smelled of sweat and filth, and Rose found the odors difficult to stomach. "Let me get something to wipe your face," she said. She left the RV and walked quickly to her horses, where she knew some rags were tucked away in Blitz's pack, taking long, deep breaths as she walked. She wet the rags with water from a canteen, then returned to the RV. The woman still lay on the bed in the same position, but with her freed hands in front of her, rubbing her wrists.

"What's your name?" Rose asked, sitting down beside her. The woman didn't answer. Rose warmed the cloth in her hands before dabbing at the wounds on the woman's face. As she wiped, the woman flinched at her touch, and Rose wondered whether it was the temperature of the rag, the pain of her wounds, or the shock of a tender hand. Rose kept wiping, being as gentle as she could possibly be.

"I'm Rose. I'm so sorry for what you've been through. It must have been terrible, but it's over now." The woman gave no indication that she heard and was seemingly unaware that she was free, other than rubbing her freed hands in front of her face.

"You hungry?" The woman didn't respond, but Rose still went in search of food, finding only some canned goods and a little dried meat in a cabinet. She noticed clothes on the bunk over the driver's seat and grabbed some items that looked like they might fit the woman. "Here you go," she said as she set a blouse and a pair of pants on the bed.

"That's mine," the woman mumbled, her voice parched and weak. She extended a bony arm and grabbed the shirt, pulling it towards her. As she struggled to rise, Rose helped her into a sitting position, turning her on the bed so she could brace her back against the headboard.

"You seem pretty weak," Rose commented, feeling the bones of the woman's ribs as she propped her up.

The woman nodded. "No food," she said. "Just a little water."

While the woman slowly pulled her blouse on, Rose leaned back, noticing for the first time that the woman had long brown hair and light colored skin. Her face was swollen and bruised, her body skinny and emaciated, making it hard to tell if she was an older teenager or a young retiree.

"I'll try and find you some water and some shoes," Rose said. She returned to the bunk where she'd found the clothing, finding, to her horror, five pairs of women's shoes and some other changes of clothes. She grabbed them all, stopped in the kitchen area to find some water for the woman to drink, then returned to the bedroom and set the things down beside her. "Do you have a name?"

"Alayna," the woman finally replied, her voice lifeless. She reached for the water with weak arms and took a long drink.

"How long have you been here?"

Alayna stared at Rose with hollow eyes, nearly swollen shut from abuse, her expression vacant. "I don't know."

"You're free now. You can go home."

The woman flinched. "I don't have a home anymore. They killed my husband."

Rose looked away. "I'm sorry. Can I do anything to help you?"

Alayna wrapped a thin blanket from the bed around herself, her hair hanging in long, dark clumps across her face. "You don't need to stay…you can go," she said, her voice wispy and weak.

"I do need to go," Rose said, eyeing the setting sun. "I really don't want to spend the night anywhere near here. Will you be alright?"

Alayna stared right through Rose and didn't acknowledge the question.

Rose rummaged quickly through the cupboards, searching for anything that might be of value. She found blankets and dirty clothes and a few more cans of food, but nothing she couldn't live without. "I'm going to leave now," she said, slipping back to the bedroom where Alayna sat semi-comatose on the bed. "Are you sure I can't do anything for you?"

Alayna shifted her eyes and looked briefly at Rose, then silently averted her gaze.

"Good luck then," Rose offered feebly. "The dead man outside has a gun on him. I'll leave that for you so you'll have something to defend yourself with. I don't know if it's loaded, but even empty it has some value." Rose wanted to do more, but what could she possibly do, she asked herself. Society was broken down, and everyone was in a fend-for-themselves reality. No one was looking to take on a psych case if they could avoid it, Rose included. She turned and headed for the door, stepping around Mantle's body, and exited the RV.

A chilly wind blew from the west, and Rose estimated there was only an hour until sundown. After that, unwilling to push her horses any harder than she had to, she thought it would be too cold and pointless to proceed.

Rose rubbed Blitz and Smokey's noses reassuringly, then checked the loads, tightened her saddle a notch, and mounted up. As she swung Smokey around to the west, she heard a noise at the motorhome and saw Alayna, still wrapped in the blanket, exit the vehicle. "It'll be dark soon, and it's cold. You should put something on," she called out.

Rose prodded Smokey with her heels, encouraging the animals forward. They hadn't even made it past the first vehicle when the sound of a gunshot exploded through the crisp, cool air, startling the already skittish horses and sending them dancing sideways. Rose fought to regain control of Smokey, then turned, expecting to see Alayna, gun in hand, standing over the body of the monster who lay dead in the street. Instead, Alayna's crumpled form lay on the road beside him.

"Dammit, Alayna," Rose cursed as she leapt from the saddle. She rushed back to Alayna, kneeling quickly on the ground beside the body and avoiding the blood that drained from a gaping wound in the woman's head. "That's not why I left you the gun!" she yelled, clenching her fists.

"Why?!" Rose yelled, grabbing Alayna by the shoulders and knowing the answer even as she uttered the question. It wasn't like the thought hadn't crossed her own mind, fleeting as it might have been, and she was doing well compared to this poor woman. A dead husband, days or weeks of being brutalized, no one to help her deal with the hell she had just barely survived, plus nightmares and memories that would torment a person for years. What was there for Alayna to live for?

Rose let go of the woman's shoulders, gently brushed the hair from her face, and saw a peace in her still-open eyes that hadn't been evident in the last hour of her life. "I hope there's a God up there for you, Alayna," she whispered. "If anyone deserves or needs His love right now, it's you."

Rose covered Alayna's body with the blanket that she had been wrapped up in, took the handgun that had fallen from her lifeless hand, and searched Mickey's coat pocket for extra ammo. Then, newly supplied, she hurried away.

Mounting Smokey in one quick motion, Rose once again drove him west, refusing to let herself look back at the carnage she knew she would be seeing in her nightmares for years to come.

CHAPTER THIRTY-ONE

Tuesday, February 7th
Deer Creek, MT

"Aahhhh!" Heather groaned through clenched teeth as she puffed in and out in short bursts, trying to manage the pain. "It hurts so much. Isn't there anything I can take?"

"Hang in there, Heather," Jane said, holding the girl's hand and rubbing her arm. "My first baby was born natural. I know how bad this hurts, but you'll get through it."

Carol squeezed Heather's leg reassuringly. "I'm sorry, but I don't have anything to give you. You're real close though," she said. "You'll just have to tough this out." Carol dipped her hands in the bowl of hot water, then dried them on a towel draped across her legs. "Let me check you again. Maybe we can have you start to push." Carol reached under the blanket spread across Heather's legs to check the dilation.

Heather locked her eyes on Carol, anxious and exhausted. "What do you think? Can I push yet?"

Carol looked hopeful. "I think," she said, trying to sound confident, "that you're not going to get any more effaced than you already are, and you seem fully dilated."

Jane flashed a smile at Heather, while Jennifer let out a whoop.

"Thank heavens," Heather said, relaxing a little and feeling a huge sense of accomplishment. "I never thought you'd say that. What do I do?"

Carol pulled the thin blanket, which was only needed for privacy since David had successfully heated the house to over eighty-five degrees, off of Heather's legs, then positioned a stack of towels nearby and lit two additional candles. Ty had found the LPN at home, too sick and weak to be able to assist, leaving just the women of the house upstairs with Heather, while Ty and Jane's husband, Gordon, waited in the basement with the children, ready to be called on if needed.

Carol moved quickly to arrange things around Heather's legs. "Let me get set up. It should just take a minute or two. Once I'm ready, I'll have you start pushing when you feel the next contraction coming on. If all goes well, we should have this baby delivered in just a few minutes. You excited?"

Heather groaned as another contraction began. "I'm excited to… have the pain…be over. Being a m…mother scares me… right now."

Carol wiped her own forehead with a wet towel. "This will be nice having the patient tell me what's going on and be able to help. Usually my patients just moo a lot or try to kick me." She tucked a shower curtain liner under the end of the box spring, placed a bowl of water to one side, towels on the other, said a quick prayer, and smiled. "Alright, Heather. I'm ready. Tell me when the next contraction begins, then start to push, but not too hard to begin with. I'll have you push along with the contractions. Alright?"

Heather nodded in relief and waited. "Okay, I can feel it beginning."

Carol felt Heather tense up. "You're doing fine. You know how hard your contractions have been. Match your pushing to the contraction, so you're pushing the hardest when the contraction peaks, then ease back with it."

Heather grunted and began to push, panting hard as she did so.

"That's good, Heather. I can feel the baby's head coming towards me."

Heather bore down for thirty seconds, then held it. "The contraction's ending," she gasped. "What should I do?"

"Ease back on your pushing, okay. And take some good, deep breaths. Pushing like that is hard work."

Carol coached Heather through a few more contractions, until the baby finally descended enough for her to grasp the baby with her fingers. She used both hands and tried to gently pull. "Just a little bit more, alright."

"Aaaahhh!" Heather yelled again at the end of a contraction, sweat running in streams down her face. "It's so hot in here."

"The head is crowning, keep doing it. I think I can deliver the head with the next contraction, but it'll require another good, hard push from you."

Heather nodded, and waited, taking a sip of the water Jennifer offered. Ninety seconds later she felt another contraction building. "Here it comes!"

Carol guided the baby's head as Heather tensed. "Remember, a long, hard push on this one." Heather's legs flexed, and Carol once again felt the baby descending through the birth canal. "You're doing great," Carol encouraged. "It's coming! Keep it up."

Jennifer and Jane knelt on either side of Heather, encouraging her as she struggled with the pain of the delivery. "I can't do it," Heather blurted, her strength giving out.

"You don't have a choice," Carol said sternly. "The nose is out, push hard!" she demanded, her voice rising to a shrill pitch in the otherwise quiet house.

Heather tensed again, took in a deep breath, gave a powerful push, and held it as long as she could.

"You did it!" Carol cheered. "The head is out; you can relax."

Heather sunk back into the pillows, breathing hard, unable to talk. Jennifer once again held the cup to her lips. "Here, drink this," she said. "You're doing wonderful."

Carol used a clean rag to wipe blood and fluid from the baby's face. Gray, waxy vernix matted the baby's hair tight against the scalp, and she dabbed at that while waiting for the next contraction to begin. "The hard part is over, Heather," Carol said, smiling at the new mother, beads of sweat glistening on her forehead. "The baby looks small. I think we can get it all the way out on the next contraction."

Heather closed her eyes. "This is so hard," she mumbled. "Is it a baby or a basketball?"

Jane laughed and rubbed the girl's hand. "It hurts like the dickens, doesn't it? You'll forget the pain though and probably have a couple more kids. I did."

Heather shook her head. "This cured me. You're looking at an only child." She caught her breath and grimaced. "Contraction!" she said.

Jane and Jennifer both leaned in to help support Heather as she bore down, and Carol described the birth as it happened. "I've got one shoulder...doing good...other one's out," she said as she carefully pulled on the child as it emerged. "I see the cord...now it's coming out. I've got him!" she said triumphantly. "Oh, wait. I mean I've got her. You have a baby girl. Congratulations!"

Heather collapsed back in exhaustion, too tired to speak. She smiled and tried to see the baby in Carol's arms.

"She's beautiful, Heather," Jennifer said. "You should be so proud. You're our first new mom since everything happened."

"You told me if it was a girl you wanted to name her Madison," Jane said. "Is that still what you want?"

Heather nodded weakly as Carol worked on the crying baby, its tiny, frail cries filling the living room. Jennifer slid over and helped cradle the baby while Carol wiped her clean, then wrapped her in a blanket before handing the bundle carefully to Heather. "The cord is still attached, so don't pull too hard."

Heather snuggled the baby tight to her chest and kissed her on her head. "She seems so tiny," she said. "Any guess how much she weighs?"

Carol ignored the question as she tied strings around the umbilical cord two inches apart.

"Spencer, my last one, was a little over eight pounds," Jennifer chimed in. "Madison looks smaller than he was. I'd guess maybe six and a half, or seven pounds at most."

Jane nodded. "Her color is good. Nice pink cheeks."

The baby's cries quieted, and she began to root around.

"She wants to nurse," Jane suggested. "You probably won't have any milk yet, but you should put her on."

"The cord's cut," Carol said. "So she's not tethered to you anymore. You should still have some contractions to help deliver the placenta, but they won't be as strong. I'll cut the cord closer to her bellybutton when you're done nursing."

Heather shifted the baby and pressed her to her left breast, which Madison quickly responded to, trying to latch on. "Ouch. That hurts a little," Heather said, wincing and wiping several strands of hair off of her face. "I can't believe it's over. It's been such a long pregnancy."

"Here you go; eat this," Jennifer said, handing Heather a piece of bread. "Your milk should come in in a couple of days. It's not as bad as childbirth, but it can sure get uncomfortable. Kyle liked it because it made my boobs bigger, but I never looked forward to that part of motherhood." Jennifer paused, looking around at the women grinning at her. "Okay, not sure why I shared that with you. Don't let that leave the room, alright?"

The women laughed. "He's not the only one," Jane responded. "I think it's universal."

Carol continued to work on Heather, with a large bowl between them, positioned to catch the fluids and afterbirth as she pulled gently on the umbilical cord. "If we were in a hospital, they'd be drawing blood, running tests, and taking samples. All that stuff makes a country vet's head spin. It's much simpler with animals."

"Some people bury the placenta under a tree," Jane said. "My grandmother was originally from Sweden, and she always told us to bury it under a fruit tree if it was girl, or under a nut tree if it was a boy. We never did, though. The hospital always kept it. Said it was medical waste."

"Well I don't want it," Heather said as she shifted Madison to her other breast and tried to help her latch on. "That all seems kind of gross."

"You know," Carol said, still focused on the afterbirth. "It's not unusual for animals to eat the placenta after they've delivered. There are actually a lot of amazingly healthy components to it. Animal placenta's are used in cosmetics and medicines; they…" Carol looked up to see all three women staring at her, wide-eyed. "You're not that interested in hearing this, are you?"

They shook their heads in unison. "I am not eating mine," Heather stated. "I don't care how hungry I get."

Carol nodded and went back to her work. It was another ten minutes before the placenta was finally delivered, sliding quietly into the bowl. "Placenta's out," she announced.

It was now well past midnight, and all in the room were tired. Gordon was asleep in the basement, and with things going smoothly, Ty had left before the baby had been delivered. Emma had come upstairs to check on the delivery on a regular basis, but she too had drifted off to sleep an hour before. Madison slept peacefully on her mother's chest, leaving just the four women still awake.

"I'm exhausted. Can I go to sleep?" Heather asked.

"How are you feeling?" Carol asked, still focused on taking care of Heather and wearing a worried expression.

"Just really tired. Why?"

"Jennifer, I need you," Carol said, her tone tense.

Jennifer moved down by Carol and noticed the placenta floating in the bowl in several inches of blood.

"Go get me another bowl," Carol whispered. "Quick!"

Jennifer hurried into the kitchen.

Heather rose up on her elbows. "Something wrong?"

"You're bleeding more than you should. How do you feel?"

"Just tired, like I said, and weak. I just had my first baby, you know."

Jennifer returned from the kitchen, handing the bowl to Carol. "What now?" she asked, the color draining from her face.

"I want both of you to massage her abdomen," Carol said, motioning to Jennifer and Jane. "Push pretty hard. Heather, your uterus hasn't meshed back together. You're losing quite a bit of blood. This might hurt a little."

Jennifer saw fear darken Heather's eyes.

"What's happening?" Heather asked, her voice rising.

"We've got to stop the bleeding. Try to relax."

Jennifer and Jane pressed on Heather's abdomen. It was soft and pliable, having lost most of its muscle tone during the pregnancy. Heather grunted in discomfort.

"That hurts," Heather whimpered, visibly worried.

"I don't care. Keep doing it!" Carol demanded. "There's still too much blood. Heather, try and tense your abdomen. Do keggles, something. Try to somehow tighten up your internal muscles."

Heather grunted and strained, trying to help, but the blood flowed unabated.

"What do we do?" Jane mouthed as she continued to knead Heather's stomach, watching the bowl fill with blood.

Carol shook her head and looked around the room. "I don't know." Panic filled her voice. "Someone give her a drink of water!"

Jennifer grabbed a cup and helped Heather drink as Jane took the baby and laid her on the box spring beside her mother.

"I feel dizzy…like the room is starting to spin," Heather announced. "What's happening?!"

Jennifer and Jane looked anxiously at Carol. "Keep pressing on her," Carol insisted. "You're losing too much blood, Heather. I can't get it stopped."

"You're the doctor! Help me!"

"I'm trying," Carol snapped back. "But I don't know what else to do. I don't have any drugs to give you or IVs or anything." She raised her hand for the massaging to stop, then leaned forward and pushed her hand up into Heather's uterus.

Heather screamed. "That hurts," she cried, twisting sharply on the bed.

Carol probed inside the patient. She'd never done anything like this to a human before, but she'd had her arms in plenty of animals and knew what healthy tissue felt like. She quickly felt along the wall of the uterus. The first side she checked felt healthy and strong, but as she slid her hand to the other side, she felt a jagged ridge and a cleft about an inch wide and several inches long.

Heather cried out as Carol probed the tear in her uterine wall.

Carol tried to pinch the two sides of the wound together, but there was nothing solid to grasp, and the flesh slipped from her grip. Blood ran over her fingers like a faucet opened halfway as she continued trying to close the gash, an impossible task with no surgical tools.

Heather was crying and flexing her hands. "My fingers are tingling. Can't you help me?"

Carol pulled her hand out and a gush of blood followed. She caught most of it with the bowl, the rest splashing onto the shower liner stretched over the floor. She picked up a rag lying nearby and wiped at the blood.

"What can we do?" Jennifer asked, leaning forward to resume massaging.

"You're going to be alright," Carol said, taking a deep breath and trying to smile. "Jane, why don't you hand Heather her baby. That will help her relax and slow the blood flow." She looked at Heather, who was glassy-eyed and tugging on her blanket. "You hold Madison. She needs to be with her mother."

"Oh, thank heavens," Jennifer said, relieved. "I was really worried there for a minute." She smiled at Heather and dabbed some sweat from her forehead before turning back towards Carol, who was still catching the blood draining from Heather and looking scared.

"I need another bowl," Carol whispered calmly. "Can you get that, please, Jennifer?"

Jennifer stood, her legs shaky, and ran to the kitchen. She found an old ice cream bucket and hurried back to where Heather lay.

She handed it to Carol, who looked pale and worn out. "Can I get you anything else?" Jennifer whispered.

"A miracle," Carol whispered as she shook her head, tears welling up in her eyes.

"I'm cold," Heather said, rubbing her baby's back with one hand while flexing her other hand in front of her face. "Am I going to be alright?"

The room was still well over eighty degrees, but Jennifer found a blanket and draped it across Heather. "You have a beautiful baby," she said, forcing a smile. "You did so good tonight."

Heather smiled feebly. Her pale lips blended into her ghostly white face. "She is beautiful, isn't she?" She saw something in Jennifer's expression. "Am I okay? I feel so cold...so tired."

Jennifer knelt down and kissed her forehead. "You're a new mother. You're perfect. Now just relax. Get some rest."

Heather looked over at Jane, whose cheeks were streaked with tears. "Thanks for helping us today. You're like a mother to me."

Jane patted her hand. "And you, like a daughter to me. Just close your eyes and rest."

Heather smiled, kissed Madison on the cheek, and closed her eyes as Carol blew out the two flickering candles on the table beside her.

CHAPTER THIRTY-TWO

Tuesday, February 7ᵗʰ
Deer Creek, MT

Kyle whistled. He wasn't good with lyrics, but he could whistle a tune, and it helped pass the time and fill the silence as he rode. Garfield had grown accustomed to his whistling now and no longer jumped at the sound. Considering the horse's age, Kyle wondered if Garfield could jump at much of anything anymore.

That he had a horse was something to be grateful for, despite the fact that Garfield was old, worn down, and not too far removed from the glue factory. But had his route not followed the river most of the way, Kyle wasn't sure how well having a horse would have worked out, with Garfield's constant need to stop for water. Whether that was a Garfield thing or a characteristic of horses in general, Kyle, the inexperienced horseman, wasn't sure. He thought back to traveling through Texas, when he went days without a water source beyond the jugs in his wagon. A camel might have worked, he mused, but he was sure a horse wouldn't have lasted more than forty-eight hours.

A pheasant spooked from some bushes on the near side of the road, and Kyle quickly reached for his shotgun. Before he could get it aimed, the bird had disappeared into the trees, and Kyle reluctantly holstered the weapon.

A thin layer of fresh snow that was sure to melt before noon covered the ground, and Kyle scanned ahead for any signs of geese or pheasant that might supplement his dwindling food supply. A few yards ahead he saw what looked like a set of human footprints trailing across the road.

"Whoa, Garfield," he said, pulling back on the reins. He surveyed the area, spotting a thin wisp of smoke rising from somewhere further up the side of the mountain. Kyle reached for his shotgun but was stopped by a voice from the west side of the road.

"Raise your hands above your head!" the voice commanded.

Kyle looked for the source, his head twisting side to side.

"You understand English? I said raise your hands!"

Kyle slowly raised his hands. "I haven't done anything," he called back, hands up. "Just let me go on my way."

"Keep your hands above your head. There are three guns aimed at you. If you do anything sudden or unexpected, it will be the last thing you do. Understand?"

Kyle's heart raced and his hands shook a little. So far he hadn't sensed life and death desperation in the people he'd met. Yes, they were scared and hungry, but in this part of the country the population was thin, water was abundant, farms and ranches dotted the valleys, and wildlife was everywhere. He'd seen quite a few fresh graves, some at cemeteries, but most of them close to houses or farms, so he knew that the area hadn't escaped the impact of the EMP. Still, there wasn't that deep desperation he'd seen in so many other areas. "What do you want?" Kyle called out.

"I'll do the interrogating here, if you don't mind." A tall, skinny man stepped from behind a stand of trees, their thick trunks concealing him until now. His military-style weapon was pressed tight to his shoulder, ready to fire. "Why don't you get down off that horse so we can talk, eye to eye."

Kyle eyed the stranger nervously. "How do I know I'll be safe?"

"I could ask you the same question, and seeing as you wandered into my territory, I think I have first right to find out what you're up to. Capisce?"

Kyle took a deep breath and climbed down. "I'm just passing through. No intention to cause any trouble," he said as he dismounted. He stepped away from the horse with his hands still above his head.

Two more figures slipped from the woods and took up positions near Kyle, rifles ready. "What's your name?" the first man asked.

"Kyle Tait. I'm from Deer Creek, just a little east of Missoula."

"Little far from home, aren't you?"

Kyle nodded.

"Get lost on your way home from church?" The others laughed, but didn't comment.

"It's not Sunday, is it?"

"Not. It's not Sunday. What are you doing here?"

"I'm going up to check on my parents. They live in Moyie Springs."

"You waited five months, then left home at the end of January to check on your folks two hundred miles away? You take me for a fool?"

"No, I don't. There's a little more to the story than that, but that's the short version."

"You running away from problems? Kill someone or something?"

"I was accused of something I didn't do, but couldn't prove it. It was leave town or be killed. I chose to leave."

The man stared at him for a long time before responding. "What are you doing off the highway on this road? We don't like outsiders much, that's why we're here."

Kyle heard a noise near his horse and saw that one of the other men had approached Garfield and was inspecting the load. "I come this way a lot, well, not this road, but the highway. My GPS took me this way once and dead-ended me at the river. Since I'm on horseback, I thought I'd save a couple of miles and cross the river with my horse. I'm hoping to get to Moyie by Saturday."

The man lowered his gun, but kept it aimed at Kyle. "It's dangerous out here, you know."

Kyle nodded. "I've had my share of run-ins. You don't need to tell me that."

"The problem we have is if you're a bad guy, and we let you go, it's like we're linked to whatever you do."

"But if I'm not," Kyle said. "And you do something to me, then you're directly responsible for that."

"But no one will ever know about it if we do, will they?" the man replied, his voice carrying a calm indifference that unnerved Kyle.

"No," Kyle said, pausing. "I guess they won't. I suppose I'm at your mercy, aren't I?"

"Search his stuff," Kyle's interrogator instructed one of the other men. "See if there's anything that indicates a problem." The man motioned Kyle over to the side of the road and gave him a push. Another man followed at a distance while the third went through Kyle's bags.

"Looking for anything in particular?" Kyle asked, watching the search.

The man beside him shrugged. "It's hard to say, but you know it when you see it. Had a couple of guys come through here with an unusually large amount of women's jewelry, some of it with blood on it. That wasn't right."

"What did you do with them?"

"The man thought a second. "Did you know that pigs will eat just about anything?"

"That sounds like a confession, and a threat."

"You can take it how you want. Let's just say that those two won't be bothering anyone else."

"So you just sit out here on the side of the road and execute the people you think are a danger to society?"

The man gave Kyle a dismissive look. "There is no society right now, friend. And what would you have us do when we find scum like that? The thing that makes society possible is for civilized people to live without fear of dirt like that. We're safe. Got us a nice compound and just need access to the river down here. Otherwise, we're pretty independent. But others around here aren't as prepared. The least we can do is cull some of the riffraff who make life difficult for peaceful folk." The man shot a thick stream of tobacco juice onto the ground near his feet. "You getting nervous?"

"No more nervous," Kyle said, "than I have been every minute of every day since the country went down the toilet. As long as your friend there isn't scared by a little bit of food and some dirty underwear, I should be on my way in a few minutes."

The man stepped close to Kyle, his face just inches away, breathing his tobacco-laced breath directly in Kyle's eyes. "You think we're wrong to do this, don't you?"

The man at the horse was opening Kyle's clothing bag. Kyle bit his lower lip and cocked his head to the side. "You know what? I have no idea what to think anymore. I was put on trial and convicted for something I didn't do, but I'm not mad at them for doing it. They're all just as scared as I am, trying to survive from one day to the next with nobody else to rely on to do the difficult things." He shook his head. "I guess we all just do what we can, and hope for the best. It's not like the authorities can do much right now."

The skinny man looked at Kyle, a poorly concealed smirk on his face. "You think the authorities are going to help you?" He let out a grunt. "Don't get me started." He turned to look at the man by Garfield and yelled. "We don't have all day, Wyatt. You see anything wrong?"

Kyle turned too.

The man shrugged his shoulders and held out his hands. "Seems clean. I don't see anything suspicious."

"Well then," the skinny man said as he lowered his gun. "Looks like you're free to go. Sorry for the delay, but we just can't be too careful. Good luck with the rest of your trip, and I suggest you stay off the back roads."

Kyle walked the short distance back to Garfield, patted him on the neck, then climbed into the saddle.

The three men stood ready at the edge of the road, watching him closely.

Kyle smiled and nodded, his pulse starting to slow. "Thanks for being reasonable," he said, then spurred Garfield and continued down the road.

CHAPTER THIRTY-THREE

Wednesday, February 8th
Deer Creek, MT

Jennifer never imagined that the death of someone she'd known for only twelve hours could impact her so much, but losing Heather, after spending such an intense evening together, had left everyone numb and heartbroken. Jane and Gordon had finally gone to sleep in the basement while Carol tossed and turned on the couch for most of the night. Jennifer paced the floor in the kitchen after a sleepless night of holding the baby, who was acting hungry once again.

Heather's body, covered with a blanket, lay on the living room floor in much the same position she had been when she passed. The women had helped Madison nurse a second time while Heather was unconscious but still had a faint pulse, but that had been four hours before. Despite Carol's best efforts, Heather's heart had stopped shortly after that, and now the young mother's body was cold and lifeless.

Jennifer heard a sound in the living room and saw Carol sitting up on the couch. She stepped around the corner and gave her friend a reassuring smile. "So, what do we do now?"

Carol glanced down at the body, closed her swollen and bloodshot eyes, and tried to rub some of the tired away. "I couldn't even save her in my dreams. I feel like I've been run through a meat grinder."

Madison screeched, and Carol looked at the baby, then up at Jennifer. "Holding her didn't bring any milk down, did it?"

Jennifer shook her head wearily from side to side, and smiled tenderly at the baby she bounced in her arms. "No such luck, and she's not happy right now. She wants to eat."

"Jane told me there are no nursing mothers in Clinton, so we need to go visit Allison Powell. She's the only one I know who's nursing. She was just starting to wean her baby when the EMP hit, but changed her mind when she realized she wouldn't be able to get any formula or baby food. I think her son is about fourteen months now, but he still nurses." Carol glanced down at Heather's sheet-covered body, then back up at Jennifer. "We can try cow's milk if we have to, but for Madison's sake, I pray Allison will nurse her for a few weeks, hopefully longer."

Jennifer avoided looking at the corpse. "I forgot all about Allison. She doesn't come out to meetings much, so she slipped my mind. I'd already thought about sending David to the ranch for some milk. While he's doing that, I'll go find Allison and see what she says."

Carol rocked the baby while Jennifer woke David and gave him instructions, then got dressed to go out. Once David was on his way to the Shipley Ranch, Jennifer wrapped Madison in a blanket and hurried off to the Powells.

The house the Powells lived in was one of the older ones in Deer Creek and wasn't technically in the subdivision, but rather on one of the lots that had existed before Bryan Shipley had pieced off a portion of his ranch to create the Deer Creek community. Being outside of the subdivision, the lot didn't have the same restrictions that would have prohibited the older doublewide trailer the Powells lived in, as well as the junky old cars parked around the side of the house that always drew complaints.

Right now Jennifer didn't care about building codes or property rights or any of the other issues that muddied the community's relationship with the Powells. She had Madison, helpless and hungry, who would be fighting for her life if she couldn't get the food she needed. Jennifer knocked firmly on the door, then stepped back and waited. She heard the footsteps of a small child running to the door, then saw the handle turn and the door pull open. A little girl with long dark hair, dressed in dirty sweat pants and t-shirt, looked at her from the doorway.

"Hi. Is your mom here?"

The little girl nodded, bouncing her head quickly, but she didn't move.

Jennifer waited. "Could you get her?" she asked the motionless girl.

"She's sleeping," was the reply. The girl had a runny nose, and she wiped snot on her arm, smearing it across her face where the dried remains of previous smears still clung.

"I'm sorry, but it's really important."

The girl stared at her, then turned and ran off. Jennifer stepped inside and pushed the door closed behind her. She waited nervously at the door, bouncing Madison in her arms and rocking her from side to side, trying to keep her quiet. She heard voices in a back bedroom, then someone coming towards the door.

Allison Powell was rubbing her eyes as she came around the corner. She was dressed in an old, yellow robe that was cinched loosely around her waist, with flannel pants and wool socks. Her long, curly red hair, matched the freckles that covered both cheeks and her forehead. "Hi," she said simply when she saw Jennifer.

"Hi Allison," Jennifer said, shifting nervously. "I need your help."

Allison stopped as soon as she noticed the baby. "What?"

Jennifer raised Madison in her arms so that Allison could see the baby. "This is Madison Jones. Her mother died giving birth to her early this morning." Jennifer made eye contact with Allison, her eyes pleading. "You're the only one we know who can feed her."

Allison crossed her arms tightly across her chest. "What about regular milk. I'm sure you can find someone with baby bottles."

"We're looking for that too, but you know that mother's milk is better for her."

Allison let out a long, deep breath and looked at Jennifer with tired eyes. "Come, sit down," she said, indicating a couch that had seen better days. Allison sat in a rocking chair that faced Jennifer, slumping back into it. "I don't think I can do it," she said, after an uncomfortable period of silence. "It's hard enough with Caleb, and he's my own."

"I know it's a lot to ask, and I wouldn't if there was anyone else who could do it, but her mother's dead, and she's hungry." Madison had started to cry, and was trying to find something to suck on. "Please, couldn't you try it for a couple of days, at least until we have a chance to figure something out?"

"There's no one else?"

Jennifer shook her head. "No one that I know of. Please!"

Allison looked wearily down at the baby, then back at Jennifer. "I just don't think I can. I'm sorry, but...."

"You can't say no," Jennifer interjected. "Look at how tiny and helpless she is. Please, Allison. I'm begging you. We'll bring you some extra wood, or food. Whatever you need." Jennifer, exhausted from being up all night, fought to control her emotions.

Allison closed her eyes and rubbed her forehead. "Alright," she said, finally. "I'll do it. But I can only promise a couple of days, and I'll need some help. Caleb and Alyssa already take up a lot of my time, and with this one, I just don't know if I'll have the strength to feed two."

Jennifer wiped away a tear of relief. "Thank you so much." She carried the baby over to Allison and laid her in Allison's arms. "She's a beautiful little girl."

Allison loosened the belt on her robe. "She's tiny. You forget how small they start out. Hope I don't drowned her; Caleb has a big appetite." She positioned Madison at her nipple, rubbing the baby's cheek with it. Madison lurched for it, latching on without too much difficulty, and began to suck vigorously. "I sure wasn't expecting this when Alyssa woke me up, not that we get a lot of people stopping by." She stroked Madison's head. "How old is she?"

Jennifer thought a second. "About ten hours. Last night was kind of a blur."

"What happened to her mother?"

Jennifer relayed the events of the delivery, and Allison listened as she nursed, filling Madison up without having to switch her to the other breast. "Hope Caleb doesn't mind sharing. He's used to a monopoly on these things," she said as she repositioned her robe.

"Thank you again," Jennifer said as she took the baby back. "Is your husband here?"

"No. It's his day with the militia. He won't be home 'til later. He's sure going to be surprised. So what kind of help can I get? I was barely hanging on with two kids. Adding another is going to push me over the edge."

"My family will help," Jennifer quickly offered. "In fact, I was thinking that maybe your family could move in with us at Carol's. It would be a little crowded, but we could make it work. I need to be with my kids, and my daughter, Emma, is too young to stay here by herself, but if we're all there together, my kids and I can help with your kids, and we have wood, a warm house, and Carol and Grace to help as well. I know it's not perfect, but I can't think of a better option right now."

"Let me talk to Curtis before I agree to anything. I don't even know how long I can do this. Leave Madison here for now, but any help would be appreciated."

Jennifer stood to leave. "I'll go talk to Gabe and some others from the council. Maybe they'll have some ideas."

CHAPTER THIRTY-FOUR

Friday, February 10th
Northwestern Montana

The first shot sailed over Kyle's left shoulder, whistling by so closely he thought it might have nicked his ear. Before he could react, a second shot caught him in the chest, six inches below his left shoulder, knocking him backwards off his horse and into the snow and growth on the side of the road. Kyle blacked out momentarily before coming to in severe pain and struggling for breath. He watched as Garfield, spooked and confused, ran wildly in the direction of the shots.

Finding that his left arm was useless, Kyle rolled onto his back and brought his right arm around. He felt a clean hole in his jacket where the bullet, the cause of such unbelievable pain, had struck.

He'd started out early that morning after spending the night in the barn of an abandoned house near the river. He'd cooked pheasant for breakfast, filled his water containers, and headed off just after sunrise, hoping to reach his parents' place by noon the next day, assuming Garfield held up and nothing unexpected happened. Now he unexpectedly lay on his back in the weeds, dizzy, struggling to breathe, arm numb, and unsure of why he'd been shot and by whom.

That the snow wasn't stained crimson with blood he owed to Frank Emory and his safety lecture, and the Kevlar vest Frank had given him. Because the vest was bulky and uncomfortable, Kyle hadn't worn it once he'd cleared Missoula, but after being held at gunpoint by the survivalists, he'd changed his mind and begun wearing it again. Staring up at a gray sky and waiting to catch his breath, Kyle was grateful he'd changed his mind. Frank had warned him that if he were shot while wearing it the impact would hurt like hell, and it did, and that it'd probably break some ribs, but at least he'd be breathing and not bleeding out all over the ground.

Whoever shot him was good. The flash had come from at least six hundred yards ahead, and to be so close on the first shot and nail him on the second, the shooter was practiced and comfortable with their weapon. Kyle tried to clench his left hand, but his fingers responded minimally, quivering and barely balling into a loose fist. He forced himself to let his head fall back in the snow and to relax, to focus on the trees swaying back and forth overhead in the breeze and on the branches and the birds that flew lazily by, anything to help him think about something other than the pain.

It seemed like an hour, but was more like just a minute or two, before he was sure he was going to live. Kyle rolled slowly onto his stomach and started to assess his situation. He edged gingerly up the bank and peered down the road. Garfield was about eighty yards away on the side of the road, still antsy and unsettled and moving further away. He scanned the direction the shots had come from, but saw nothing in the way of people or movement.

Kyle slid back down the shoulder of the road and did a quick inventory, finding he didn't have much more than a knife, his handgun, and a short length of rope on him. Everything else he'd brought on his journey was tied to his saddle or in the backpack secured to the horse, now eighty yards away and moving towards the shooter.

Kyle continued to work his left arm, clenching his fingers and flexing at the elbow. It was still numb, but feeling and movement were slowly returning, to the extent that his arm no longer felt like a dead appendage hanging uselessly from his shoulder. Taking his pistol from the ankle holster, he ejected the magazine and counted the bullets. He'd used it that morning to scare off a coyote, firing a couple of warning shots before the young animal dashed off into the bushes. That left him with eight rounds to work with. He plugged the magazine back in the gun, released the safety, and began to plan.

Since he had fallen between the road and the river, Kyle needed to get across to the forested hillside where the trees would provide cover. He ducked low and backtracked, working in the direction he'd come from to a curve in the road that would shield him from view. Once he was sure he was out of sight, he dashed across the road to the protection of the trees.

The forest was thick with pine trees, but only a thin undergrowth of patchy scrubs and nameless ferns covered the forest floor, enabling Kyle to move freely through the trees, though his vision was limited. Kyle knew that with only a handgun he was at a disadvantage, so he ran uphill to try and at least get on higher ground than whoever had shot him and improve the odds somewhat.

Once he felt he was high enough, Kyle turned north and hurried along the mountainside, running as fast as he dared while trying to minimize noise. Because the forest was densely treed, he'd lost sight of the roadway, forcing him to guess at his location relative to his horse and the shooter. The further he went, the more uncertain he became, until he eventually slowed his pace, stopping every few seconds to listen. His mind raced. What if, he thought, the shooter was doing the same thing – circling up high and trying to come in behind him?

A branch snapped up ahead, and Kyle froze in his tracks, holding his breath for a long time, even as his lungs screamed for air. He waited, eyes and ears straining for any hint of movement. After a long, silent moment of nothing, Kyle slowly let out his breath and stepped closer to a tree, watching and waiting. His thoughts flashed back to Colorado, when the tattooed man had trapped him on the side of the road. The same tensions and emotions flooded over him. Kill or be killed. Lose and die forgotten. Or win, and all you get is the chance to do it all again the next day. He hated what life had become.

Kyle cautiously resumed his advance, moving more carefully now, wary of any sound or movement. He descended at an angle, a thirty-degree drop from his highpoint, towards the general area of where the shooter might be. Proceeding from tree to tree, and using the skills he'd been taught in the Deer Creek Militia as a counter offensive to an assault from the tree line, although with only one man and one pistol, the strategy was greatly modified. Reach the cover of a tree, drop down, wait, peer out quickly for signs of threat, count three, peer quickly from the other side, wait, then carefully move around the tree, exposing yourself slowly as you looked more thoroughly for the enemy. If everything was clear, then select the next place of cover, check for obstacles, and make the move.

If done correctly and efficiently, you could move to a new cover spot every thirty-five to forty seconds, depending on how far away the next place you selected for cover was. Of course that was in training, with no threat of return fire. Kyle's current pace was noticeably slower.

Kyle had been moving forward in this fashion for ten minutes when he caught a glimpse of the road far below through a break in the trees. He paused where he was, studying the forest and what he could see of the road, watching for any sign of someone tracking him or movement in the opposite direction. Reassured he was alone, he proceeded onward, adjusting his course to drop more directly towards the road.

Nervous, he moved forward, selecting the thickest trees for cover, each time having to force himself from their protective shelter and into the open, risking his life with every move. He'd dropped down to about fifty yards above the highway when he heard Garfield snort some distance back. It gave him a feel for where he was, but also strained his nerves further, knowing he was between his horse and the shooter, and that it wouldn't be far, or long, before the situation was resolved, one way or another.

Kyle leaned back against the tree and uttered a short prayer, something he found himself doing more often, then slowly crept towards a fallen tree ten yards below that he'd selected as his next point of concealment. He reached it and dropped down, breathing hard. The trunk of the tree was large, more than three feet in diameter at the base where he was hiding. The root cluster had torn out of the ground and stood over six feet in the air, the tree having had the misfortune of growing in a rocky patch of ground that had forced the roots out and not down.

His cover was excellent, the tree providing a thick wall of wood and branches to conceal him along with a decent view of the road below. He even caught a glimpse of Garfield, who was now grazing calmly and alone on the side of the river. Kyle knelt down and scanned the area again, peering over the trunk, studying the road, and watching for anyone moving along it. With the fallen tree providing such great cover, Kyle decided he would wait things out. If nothing happened before dark, he'd retrieve his horse and make a quick dash out of there, and if something happened before then, well, he'd just play that out as it happened.

He waited twenty minutes, with every sense on edge and ready to react, but there was nothing. He was about to find somewhere to relieve himself, a need he'd had since arriving at the tree, when he heard the snap of a branch, a sound too loud to be natural.

Kyle shrank back against his cover, his brain filtering out the sounds of wind and water and birds, listening for any additional signs that would indicate a person – a cough, a sneeze, footsteps, voices, anything that would let him know whether to relax or attack. He gripped his gun in both hands, ready, but not anxious to shoot, especially when there was a good chance he could be shot in the exchange.

Hearing nothing, Kyle silently shifted, turning his body so he could look through a gap in the roots of the tree. Moving his head slowly to the side, he peered through a two-inch opening in the direction he expected the shooter to come from and where the noise had originated.

He choked off a gasp as two figures, bundled in hats and heavy coats, with rifles in hand, moved stealthily through the trees no more than fifteen yards away and heading towards him. His heart skipped, and it was all he could do to keep from jumping up and running, so strong was his urge to escape. He stayed motionless, not wanting his movement to draw their attention.

Kyle was confident he hadn't been seen, as their attention was focused towards the road and away from where he was, and they would likely have been more evasive had they known he was there. Suddenly, one of the figures motioned towards the fallen tree, and they began moving towards him. Kyle drew his head back slowly, his thoughts racing, trying to decide what to do. He could hear their footsteps, careful and methodical and cautious, drawing closer.

One handgun against two rifles was bad odds, even with the element of surprise. Kyle extended his legs, gripped the gun a little tighter, placed a shaking finger on the trigger, and rolled against the fallen tree, tucking under it as much as he could while trying to silence his breathing.

Dirt crunched and twigs popped, sending shockwaves through Kyle's body as the footsteps drew nearer.

"See anything?" The voice was low and wary.

Kyle placed them no more than five feet away, just the other side of the tree he hid behind. He listened for a reply that didn't come, the question likely just eliciting a shake of the head.

"Keep watching. I need to take a leak," the voice instructed.

Kyle lay still, too scared to blink, cold sweat running down his back. He heard the sound of a zipper, then splashing only a couple of feet from his head. They were using the other side of his cover as a toilet. If this had been paintball, they'd have had a good laugh about it later. But the reality was, at least one of them would likely be dead before lunchtime.

He waited, not daring to move, as the splashing became intermittent, then stopped. Pine needles crunched as the man stepped away. Kyle lay still, trying to determine how quick and silent he could be getting to his feet. However fast it was, he was sure it wouldn't be faster than they could turn and pull a trigger.

There was a different voice, softer, feminine. "You think he's dead?"

"Pretty sure. You aimed too high, but my shot hit him in the chest. I saw him go down. If I hit the heart, he was done almost immediately. If I missed the heart, then he's had plenty of time to bleed out. We're good."

There was a pause in the conversation, then a question from the woman. "Should we just take the horse and be done, or do we have to make sure he's dead?"

"I know you hate it, but you always confirm your kill. That's why we're taking our time and going this route. The body can take some pretty serious damage before shutting down. We don't want an unexpected bullet coming between us, do we? Let's just do this. Stay close, and keep your head up."

Kyle listened as they walked away, their footsteps growing fainter. He waited, giving them time to move further away before rolling from his cover and getting back into a kneeling position behind the tree.

The two figures traveled sideways across the hill, their attention focused on the road and trees in front of them, their backs to Kyle. He had to act before he was discovered and while they were still close enough for his gun to be accurate. Shooting someone was terrible. The thought of shooting someone in the back, a man or a woman, was hard to fathom, yet here he was. The people were still close, a hundred feet or so, and were big targets he was sure he could hit.

He raised his gun, aimed at the larger of the two, clenched his teeth, put pressure on the trigger, then hesitated. Part of him wanted to run away and just escape, but he needed his horse and everything on it. The targets were getting further away, becoming smaller. Kyle shook his head briefly, whispered "God forgive me," and began to fire. He pulled the trigger quickly, firing three times before the target reacted, falling forward and down in a violent, jerking spasm.

Kyle heard a scream and fired at the second figure as it launched sideways behind the cover of a tree. Kyle fired again, sending a chunk of wood spinning away and leaving a blonde gash in the tree where the bullet struck. He lowered his head and watched the figure, but could only see a sliver of her arms and legs that wasn't hidden by the tree.

The body on the ground was motionless and made no sounds of distress or pain. Kyle guessed the man was dead, as his shots had been well grouped in the center of the man's back, likely taking out his spine and vital organs. Kyle's eyes jumped back and forth between the figure on the ground and the one hiding behind the tree.

"Please, don't shoot," the woman begged. "It wasn't my idea to shoot you."

Kyle stared at the two people, and the thought suddenly came to him that there could be others, perhaps more traveling along the road or further up the hill. He grew more nervous, stepping in closer to the fallen tree that concealed him. "How many of you are there?" he called out.

"Just two," came the reply. "It's just me and Christopher."

Kyle looked around. He wanted to believe her, but knew that he shouldn't. He listened and waited, trying to hear anything unusual. If there were more people, they'd certainly know where the action was.

"What are you going to do?" the woman asked.

"I don't know," Kyle shouted back. "I thought I was going to kill you without having a conversation first. It would've been easier that way."

"Please don't," she pleaded. "I…I'm sorry we shot you. I tried to stop him."

"Sounded to me like you took the first shot."

"I had to. He insisted that I do it. Said he always…" she paused.

"Always what? Shot people?"

There was no response.

"Toss your gun out from behind the tree," Kyle ordered.

"If you're going to kill me, I should at least hold onto it. It gives me a fighting chance to get out of here."

"I didn't say I was going to kill you."

"You didn't say you weren't."

Kyle swallowed. "Fine. I won't kill you."

"How do I know?"

"You don't know, alright?" Kyle was getting angry. He didn't want to debate this woman. "All you know is that I have the upper hand, and if you don't come out, you're likely going to die. Understand?"

Kyle walked closer to the woman, keeping the tree between them as he waited for a response. "What are you going to do?"

"Alright, just a minute." He could see her lifting the strap of the gun over her head. "Where do you want me to put it?"

"Toss it over on your partner."

"Are you serious?"

"I am. Sorry I don't seem too sentimental, but he tried to kill me."

The weapon was tossed from behind the tree and landed on the lifeless body.

"Now what?"

"Throw your coat over there as well."

After a few seconds, the woman had removed her coat and tossed it from behind the tree.

"Raise your hands, and come out where I can see you."

"Don't shoot," the woman pleaded as she emerged cautiously from behind the tree. Without her coat, she was left wearing brown canvas pants, hiking boots, and a green, long-sleeved, waffle-knit shirt. A brown wool cap covered her head. Her hands and legs were shaking visibly, and she held the tree for stability. "Now what?" she asked.

"You have any more weapons?"

She shook her head.

"Lift your shirt, and your pant legs, so I can be sure."

She gave him an odd look, and Kyle noticed her striking features – dark, almond-shaped eyes, full lips that turned down at the corners, a long, thin nose, and rose-colored cheeks on alabaster skin. "I don't trust you," he explained. "Nothing personal, but I have to be careful. You should understand."

She smiled at him, though she looked terrified. "I'm Stacy," she said. "What's your name?" She reached down, grabbed the hem of her shirt, and pulled it up, lifting it over her head."

"Whoa, hey, that's plenty," Kyle protested. "I just want to make sure that you don't have anything tucked in your waistband."

One hand held her shirt, and she rested the other on her hip, which was shifted seductively to the side. "Now my pants, right?"

Kyle stared at the woman standing in front of him shirtless, wearing just a plain black bra that was pushing her large breasts together. Her cap had fallen off, and long, dark hair cascaded over her shoulders, contrasting vividly with her soft, pale skin. "Like what you see?" She forced a crooked, seductive smile, and leaned her head forward. "I used to dance. Made good money, too. The guys really liked me."

"Put your shirt back on, then lift your pant legs," Kyle said, trying to look her in the eyes. "I'm not looking for a performance. Just want to make sure you're not going to shoot me in the back."

Stacy dropped her shirt to the ground and began undoing her belt. She bit her lower lip, closed her eyes, and flipped her head, tossing her long hair over her shoulder. "You have any money?"

Kyle was unnerved by the situation in front of him – one of the most beautiful women he'd seen, undressing in the woods while her boyfriend lay dead on the ground just a few feet away.

She pulled the belt from her pants with a snapping sound, winked at Kyle, then started unbuttoning her pants.

"I said to just lift your pant legs, not undress."

"You like it better this way though, don't you?" With her fly undone, she worked her pants lower, shifting her hips from side to side and revealing powder blue underwear. "If I'd known I was going to be performing, I would have worn something that matched."

"Stop!" Kyle yelled, firing a shot and bringing the performance to a halt.

Stacy stood still with her pants around her knees, her bare skin glowing in a shaft of sunlight that filtered through the trees. "What?" she asked, her voice shaking but with an innocent, schoolgirl look on her face. "Does this bother you?" She turned to the side. "There might be something in my bra, you know."

"I'm sure there is," Kyle replied, "but likely no room for any weapons. Put your clothes back on. Now!" He looked down at Stacy's gun lying across the man's body and climbed over the tree towards it.

"You coming to check if they're real?" She attempted to sound seductive, but there was too much fear in her voice.

An uneasy feeling swept over Kyle. He stopped and looked at her closely.

Stacy grabbed the bottom of her bra cups. "I'll give you a peek, so you know I'm not packing."

Kyle looked closer, noticing her shaking hands and fear-filled eye that flicked beyond him up the hill. He spun quickly, seeing movement two hundred feet away, then a flash. The bullet struck him in the chest almost in the same place he'd been hit earlier, knocking him backwards. The impact was less severe, but his wounded ribs screamed in agony, and he cried out as he fell down.

"He's wearing a vest!" Stacy shrieked. "Shoot him in the head!"

She lunged for her rifle, but with her pants around her knees, she tripped and fell to the ground before reaching it.

Kyle, still holding his pistol, took aim at Stacy, not twenty feet away, and pulled the trigger. She screamed as a bloody wound opened up on her white ribs, but continued struggling forward on her knees, trying to reach the rifle just a few feet away. He shot her once more, hitting her again in the side, spinning her around onto the ground.

"Stacy!" a man shouted from the hill above them.

Kyle rolled over and saw the man running towards him. He fired a shot in the man's direction and heard the bullet strike wood. The man kept running. Kyle continued pulling the trigger and chunks of wood splintered off trees between him and his target, then he heard the click of an empty chamber.

Kyle glanced over his shoulder at Stacy's rifle, just a few feet away. He scrambled to his feet and dashed for it. A gunshot sounded, and a bullet whistled by. Kyle dove towards the dead man and used his good arm to grab the rifle, a .223 that was an updated version of the first gun he'd owned and matched the one that lay partially under the dead man, and which was blessed with a large magazine that Kyle prayed was more than just decoration. As Kyle scrambled for cover he noticed that Stacy's eyes were still open, but dim, and she was watching him with desperation.

The man drew closer, darting between the trees for cover and bringing the gap between them to an uncomfortably close distance. Unsure how many bullets he had, Kyle waited for the right moment to take his shot, hoping he had a least one bullet to work with.

"Stacy!" the man yelled again, a heart-wrenching plea.

Kyle heard the despair in the man's voice, recognizing that he was emotionally frantic. As the man bounded closer, Kyle slid across the ground towards Stacy, drawing up behind her. Blood continued draining from the large open wound in her back, a sight that would have sickened him in times past.

He rested the barrel of the rifle across his left forearm and just above Stacy's underwear-clad hip, and waited, his finger poised on the trigger, ready to shoot when the opportunity arose. He saw movement and fired, missing, but not by much. The man dropped to the ground and rolled, then bounced back up and kept coming. Kyle fired again and missed again. Stacy tried to shift beneath him but was too weak to move much. The man was getting closer, making Kyle more anxious, knowing he didn't have unlimited ammunition.

Kyle kept the sight of the rifle on the man as he rushed forward through the trees. The man fired wildly towards Kyle, and the shot flew far overhead.

Stacy mumbled something, but Kyle, focused on the onrushing man, failed to understand her. He flattened himself to the ground, getting as low as he could behind the woman this man was rushing madly towards, watching the man approach through the sights of the gun. The man didn't slow at the fallen tree, instead leaping onto it with one foot and launching himself through the air, landing thirty feet away.

As his feet hit the ground, the man paused for a brief second with his gun extended, unwilling to take a shot towards Stacy. That was all Kyle needed. He pulled the trigger several times in rapid succession, the bullets punching a tight cluster of holes in the middle of the man's chest, dropping him in a heap on the ground.

Kyle waited, breathing heavily, unsure whether it was all over or if someone else would come charging down the hill in a suicide rush like this one. He raised himself up on his knees, ears ringing from the gunfire, eyes scanning the area for anyone else intent on his destruction. He got to his feet and went to the second man, now lying motionless in the dirt. Kyle pressed his fingertips to the man's neck, then pulled him over onto his back.

He was young, somewhere in his mid-twenties Kyle guessed. A thin, blonde beard and a crooked nose were his only distinguishing features. His eyes were open, and Kyle, never comfortable looking at the dead, released his grip on the man, then quickly patted him down, finding nothing of value besides a magazine for the handgun.

Kyle crawled back to Stacy, who was half-conscious and watching him. "Is there anyone else?"

Stacy bobbed her head up and down. Kyle, unsure, knelt down beside her. "Who?!" he demanded, placing his ear near her mouth.

She struggled to speak. "My...brother...log cabin...up the... dirt road."

"Thanks for the warning," Kyle said, not sure if he believed her. He leaned back to look around, searching for this brother who might be coming his direction. He felt something on his wrist and looked down to see Stacy's hand. Fresh tears filled her eyes as she tried to explain.

"No…young…please help," she pleaded, barely getting her words out.

Kyle knelt closer, sensing she was finally sincere. "Say again?" he asked.

"Little brother…cabin…please. Help." She coughed, spraying blood on his face.

"Is there anyone else there?" he asked, wiping away the blood.

A barely perceptible shake of her head indicated no. She swallowed, obviously in pain, and closed her eyes for a second.

Kyle reached out and touched her shoulder. Her skin was soft and warm, and she opened her eyes at his touch. "What's his name?"

She grimaced. "Collin," she said. "Collin Lee."

"Is the cabin close?"

She closed her eyes and nodded slightly. Kyle could see her struggle for breath. He rose to his feet and walked over to the first man, grabbed his gun then searched the man, again finding nothing but additional ammunition. He went to the second man, grabbed him by an ankle, and dragged him next to the other two, then took Stacy's hand and placed it in the palm of the man who'd been so desperate to save her and whose devotion to her was obvious, even under threat of death.

Kyle was surprised to see Stacy open her eyes, still clinging to life. When she saw what he'd done, she smiled and mouthed the words "thank you."

"You're welcome," he said, then took her jacket and lay it across her shoulders. He knew it was pointless, that she'd be gone in a few minutes. In fact, he was surprised she was still alive, but that didn't matter. Regardless of what had occurred, a life was still a life and deserved to be treated with dignity.

"Good bye," he said as he stood, trying to sound sympathetic. "I will check on Collin, and I'm sorry." He noticed that she flinched slightly at the mention of her brother, then he turned and walked cautiously towards the highway.

CHAPTER THIRTY-FIVE

Saturday, February 11th
Deer Creek, MT

Jennifer kept an eye on the Dutch oven in the fireplace, lifting the lid occasionally to stir the wheat. Grace's store of grains was a life-saving resource for both her family and the community, and Jennifer knew she should be grateful to have access to it, but it was hard to get too excited about another meal of whole grains, flavored with a pinch of salt and a dash of sugar.

At least Spencer had finally stopped crying each time wheat was served, having come to the realization that something, no matter how plain and repetitive, was better than the hunger pains he felt when he had nothing to eat. David and Emma had long ago accepted their plight, and while they didn't talk about it much anymore, Jennifer knew they both wanted, more than anything, the foods they loved – a bowl of Fruit Loops, a hot dog or hamburger, some chocolate ice cream – not the constant repetition of a subsistence diet.

Jennifer had never been a connoisseur in the kitchen. While she considered herself to be a better than average cook, she was not one to labor over meals or obsess about flavors and techniques. Now when she had extra time in her days, flavor and variety was something she thought about and longed for, and the lack of it was driving her crazy, like a powerful itch in the middle of her back that was just out of reach.

Jennifer's knowledge of wheat, prior to her introduction to Grace's food storage, had been limited to whole wheat bread and the white flour she baked with. A wheat berry sounded like a healthy fruit you might find growing in the wild next to a patch of raspberries, not a dried, hard grain that farmers harvested from their fields. When Grace and her seemingly never-ending stream of cans filled with stored wheat had moved into Carol's house, Jennifer had expected to find flour in them.

Grace, seeing Jennifer's confusion when she first opened a can, explained that they were looking at an actual kernel of wheat, the thing that flour was derived from when it was processed at a mill. Jennifer had asked why she hadn't just bought flour instead, saving the trouble of grinding it down. "Flour only has a storage life of about a year, but wheat will last decades, even centuries if it's stored well," Grace had said without any sense of ridicule, going on to explain that if temperature and oxygen levels were controlled, the wheat would still provide nutritional benefit even when it was decades old.

Nutritional value aside, Jennifer longed for the day she could stop by Costco and pick up a fifty-pound bag of flour or, better yet, stop by a bakery and pick up loaves of fresh-baked, white bread, or a chocolate sheet cake, iced with thick buttercream frosting, and a gallon of ice-cold milk to wash it all down.

She closed her eyes and daydreamed for a moment, then shook her head to bring herself back to reality and the wheat berries that had started boiling. She lifted the lid of the Dutch oven and stirred. Just a few more minutes she thought, then she'd let it simmer while she woke the children, and they got ready for breakfast. As she placed the lid back on oven, she heard a noise at the front door.

Jennifer pulled her robe tight around her, then hurried upstairs to see who was there. Carol emerged from her bedroom just as Jennifer opened the front door to find Curtis Powell holding baby Madison. His face was rigid and unfriendly.

"Come in," Jennifer said, swinging the door open. "It's cold outside."

Curtis kicked the fresh snow off his boots and stepped inside, then held out the baby. "Here," he said, thrusting Madison towards Jennifer. "You need to take the baby back."

Madison was awake, but not crying. She was wrapped in a pink blanket that Jennifer had retrieved from her old house two days before, her first time being there since Kyle's arrest. Going back had been harder than she could have imagined, not only with the bloodstains in the bedroom carpet, but also because of the dead girl that had been found in the basement. She'd hurried in, found the box of clothes and blankets from when Emma was a baby, then retreated in a rush like she was escaping from Chernobyl.

"I was going to come over this morning," Jennifer said, taking the baby. "I was just cooking now and..."

Curtis interrupted her. "It's not about the food, or the help. The two babies are too much for Allison. She was struggling before this, physically and mentally. The pressure of caring for Madison, it's too much. I'm sorry. I really am, but I have to think about my family and do what's best for them. We just can't help you with her anymore."

Words escaped Jennifer as she looked from Curtis to the baby, then back to Curtis again. "What are we supposed to do? There aren't any other options, you know. No one has baby formula, and Allison is the only one who's nursing."

Curtis shook his head. "Don't put that responsibility on us," he said, his voice stern. "That's not fair. This isn't our problem or our fault. We did our best to help, but it didn't work out." He looked at Carol, who stood close to Jennifer, arms folded. "Listen, maybe, maybe there's a way to, you know, to just let her..." he was having a hard time finding the right words. He stopped and thought a second, then continued. "Maybe you can just let her die." He let out a deep, distress-filled breath and tried to smile, but couldn't. "I know it sounds really cold, but she's only three days old. She doesn't know anything. If her mother had died a week ago, she never would have been born. Maybe she wasn't supposed to live."

Jennifer looked at him, aghast. "You can't be serious!"

"You know," he said, gathering resolve. "Like the Romans did when they didn't want the baby, or like the Chinese do; they just leave it in a rice field. Call it a late term abortion, if that makes it easier. Nobody asked for this baby, and no one will blame you if you do something about it. Say it died of natural causes, and everyone will give you a hug for trying. There are plenty of other things for us to spend our energy on right now. This baby will just take food from people who need it more and who've earned it."

Carol shook her head. "We won't do that, Curtis. Tell Allison thanks for helping."

He grabbed the door handle and paused. "We're not bad people. You have to understand how tough things are, and not just for us. It isn't wrong to look out for the good of the majority. This baby and a few other people are just a drag on the community. We don't have the luxury to waste so much energy on them. When times are good, I get it. You can look out for the weak ones. But right now..." He stopped and shook his head.

"What would you have us do?" Carol asked, shocked by the gall of his suggestion.

Curtis shrugged and shook his head. "I don't know; you're the doctor. If we just don't feed her, it would only take a couple of days. This baby, and some of the older people, are just takers, a burden on the rest of us. It's time someone said what a lot of people are thinking. We've got to make difficult decisions."

"That's murder," Jennifer said, glaring at Curtis and cradling Madison.

"It's not murder. I'm not saying to shoot them, just ignore them. Let nature take its course."

Jennifer shifted the baby to her shoulder. "When did she eat last?" she asked, unwilling to look Curtis in the eye.

"Less than an hour ago, but there wasn't a lot of milk. Our boy had eaten before the baby woke up, and he drained Allison pretty good." He opened the door and let himself out. "I am sorry, but it's time to face the reality of our situation," he said and closed the door behind him.

Jennifer turned to Carol, flabbergasted. "Can you believe him?" she asked, trying to control her anger, her voice shaking. "This poor baby. At least they brought her back to us alive." She rocked Madison and kissed her on the forehead, causing her to stir.

"Don't let it upset you, Jennifer. We asked a lot of them. They're young and have a lot on their plate." Carol took the baby from Jennifer. "I think I smell something burning."

Jennifer ran downstairs and returned a minute later, toting the Dutch oven full of cooked wheat. She placed it in the kitchen sink. "Good thing you have a sensitive nose. I don't think we lost too much." She retrieved a stack of bowls from the cupboard and set them on the counter. "So what do we do? Talk the Shipleys into giving us milk every day?"

Carol nodded. "We do, but it needs to be goat's milk if possible, not cow's milk. Some of my clients raised their children on that exclusively."

Jennifer paused. "Goat? Are you sure?"

Carol nodded. "Mother's milk is best by a long shot, but there's a growing community that swears that goat's milk is the next best thing."

"Does the Ranch have any dairy goats?"

"They do," Carol said. "Not sure how much they're producing now, though."

"Any idea where we can get more baby bottles?" Jennifer asked, dreading the need to go begging once again.

CHAPTER THIRTY-SIX

Sunday, February 12th
Moyie Springs, ID

It was just after noon when Kyle led Garfield towards the checkpoint on the east side of the Moyie Canyon Bridge. The sky was overcast, and a light snow fell intermittently, just enough to dust the highway and give the area the feel of winter. He'd seen guards as he approached the checkpoint, three people with rifles slung across their backs, who, when they saw him, became active. Two retreated, one inside a high-end motorhome parked at the end of the bridge, the other behind an embankment of dirt and timber that formed an elevated defensive position.

Kyle approached with a rifle slung over his shoulder and a handgun stuck in his belt, but his arms held to the side. He waved when he got within earshot. "Hello!" he called out.

The man that remained at the barricade waved back and waited for Kyle to approach. "What brings you to these parts?" the man asked when Kyle was close. He held his rifle in his hands, though still pointed at Kyle's feet. A gold sheriff's badge was pinned on his coat.

Kyle smiled nervously and took a look around. "I've come to check on my parents, Gene and Sandra Tait. They live in town here." He noticed a rifle aimed at him from behind the embankment and a woman watching through a slit in the curtains of the motorhome.

The sheriff, a tall man with broad shoulders and a weathered face, stroked his scrubby beard while sizing Kyle up. He sniffed, shrugged his shoulders. "I don't recognize the names. Where do they live?"

Kyle pointed southwest across the canyon, towards the facing hillside. "Over there, on the hillside. They have a bed and breakfast with five small cabins. Call it Moyie Manor. They've only owned it a few years, so you might not know them."

The sheriff nodded. "I know the place, though I don't know them. Bad time of year to be traveling, isn't it?"

Kyle nodded. "I'd have come sooner, but I was in Houston when the EMP happened. Took me a while to get home."

The man looked at Kyle wide-eyed. "You walked here from Houston?"

Kyle nodded and explained his situation, with the exception of the trial in Deer Creek, and the sheriff responded warmly. "Welcome to Moyie Springs," he said. I'm sheriff Greg Pratt, one of the leaders of our militia here. I'd just come over to check on my team when we saw you coming. If you want, you can walk with me. I was just about to head back across the river."

"That would be nice. Haven't had much conversation lately."

"Your son not much of a talker?" Greg asked, indicating Collin sitting in the saddle.

"He's not my son, and no, he's not much of a talker. His name's Collin."

Greg furrowed his brow and eyed the boy for signs of distress, but the boy just clung to the saddle, his eyes locked on the bridge ahead of them. "He been with you long?"

"Just a couple of days. His mother died in an accident, so he was left all alone. I haven't been able to get him to talk. Not sure if it's because of the messed up state of his world, or if there's something wrong with him, but don't count on an answer."

The sheriff studied Collin for a minute, then waved the other two guards over. He gave them instructions, then he, Kyle, and Collin set off to cross the bridge. They'd only gone a few feet when the boy cried out and grasped at Garfield's neck with both arms, his eyes filled with terror. The bridge they were about to cross spanned a deep ravine, deep enough that it made Spencer and Emma nervous to cross it in their car. Kyle recognized the same fear in Collin's eyes.

"You want to get down?" Kyle asked, extending his arms towards the child.

The boy nodded and lunged for Kyle, grunting as he dismounted. When his feet hit the pavement, he turned and headed back away from the bridge. Kyle, bruised and still sore from being shot, grimaced and rubbed his chest and shoulder.

"Collin!" Kyle called after the boy. "We're not going that way. You need to stay with me." He motioned to Garfield. "Come hold onto the stirrup and walk beside him. He won't let you go over the edge." Kyle watched Collin think about the idea. He couldn't imagine what the boy was going through, with everything and everyone he knew stripped from his life.

After the events with Collin's sister, Kyle had kept his word and gone in search of the cabin where her brother was supposed to be. He found a narrow dirt road and followed it through the trees for a little over a mile, finally coming across an old cabin with smoke rising from the chimney. Kyle waited in the bushes for half an hour, watching for any signs of life. There were a few noises, but nothing indicating a group of people, so he crept closer, peered through a window, and spotted Collin reading a book on the couch, but no one else.

Taking a deep breath, Kyle knocked on the door then retreated, taking cover around the side of a shed. Kyle could hear the door being worked, and watched as the boy pulled it open and stepped outside, curious and cautious at the same time. To

Kyle's eyes, the boy was just a little younger than Emma, probably nine years old, with dark hair that had grown long enough to hang down in his eyes. The sweater he wore was oversized, but his jeans seemed two sizes too small. His dark eyes darted nervously around.

As the boy turned to go back inside, Kyle called to him loud enough to be heard, but not so loud as to scare him. "Collin, Stacy sent me."

The boy jumped and retreated inside the doorway.

"It's okay," Kyle said, stepping slowly from behind the shed, his empty hands held out to his side. There was no verbal response from the boy. He just stared at Kyle, gripping the doorknob, uncertain what to do.

"Is Stacy your sister?" Kyle called out, trying to sound friendly.

Collin nodded slowly.

"She asked me to come and help you. She was worried about you. Are you alright?"

Collin nodded his head, the movement barely perceptible, but he still refused to speak.

"Are you hungry?"

The boy shook his head slowly from side to side.

Kyle smiled, trying to reassure the child, but he was anxious himself. He'd debated the merits of keeping a promise to a dead woman who'd tried her best to kill him, and had himself talked out of it three times before finally deciding to find the cabin and at least check things out. Had Kyle seen any adults, he would have left without a second thought. He had feared an ambush, but now, faced with a lone nine-year old boy, he wasn't sure what to do. To abandon the boy would mean almost certain death. To take him along would mean delayed travel at a minimum, and who knew what other problems would arise.

"Is there anyone in the house with you?" Kyle asked, carefully scanning the area, but seeing nothing.

The boy shook his head, the movement so slight Kyle could barely discern it.

"Listen," Kyle continued. "There was a bad accident, and the people who were here, Stacy and her two friends, they're not going to be able to take care of you anymore. I'm really sorry." Kyle watched for any change in expression, but Collin just held onto the doorknob, not moving.

Kyle extended his hand and took a step forward. "How about you come with me?" he said, trying to sound as safe as possible.

The boy's head snapped back, and he ran inside, throwing the door shut behind him. Kyle heard the deadbolt lock, and he swore under his breath, recognizing that helping Collin was going to mean a serious delay. He walked to the door and knocked softly on it, trying not to frighten the boy any more than he already had. "Collin," Kyle said. "Please. I'm here to help you. Your sister isn't coming back."

He waited, but there was no response. He went to the window on the front of the house that he'd peeked through earlier and noticed the screen was torn and the window wasn't latched. Kyle pulled off the screen and tugged the window open, but didn't want to terrify the boy, so he didn't climb through. Kneeling down by the window, Kyle called for the boy. He could see Collin peering at him from behind a kitchen cabinet, eyes so wide he thought the poor child's eyeballs would just tumble right out of their sockets.

"Collin, my name is Kyle," he began, telling him about his kids, the things he'd seen on his trip, and anything else he could think of that would put the boy at ease. When he started talking about Garfield, the boy seemed to show some interest. Finally, after almost an hour of one-sided conversation, Collin unlocked the front door and let Kyle inside.

Upon entering, Kyle noticed the doorframe was splintered inward and didn't totally secure the door. The cabin was furnished with a couple of couches, an old TV, a woodstove, and a kitchen table with four wooden chairs around it. Written in marker on the wall above the table was what looked like a scoreboard. There were three entries:

1 @ 75yds

2 @ 200 yds

1 @ 300 yds

He guessed he was meant to be the next entry, the new record, 1 @ 600yds, and likely would have been if not for his vest. He thought briefly of adding an entry of his own, 3 @ 20 yds, but concerned about further compromising what little human dignity he was fighting to retain, Kyle left the wall blank.

Collin followed Kyle through the house as he searched it. A back bedroom was littered with discarded backpacks, the contents strewn on the floor. He wondered who the owners of the backpacks were and what had become of their bodies while he continued searching the old cabin, gathering what little he could find that might be of assistance, which didn't amount to much beyond a few cans of food, ammunition, and some clothes for the child.

Only after again explaining to Collin that his sister had died and promising that he could see her and say goodbye, along with the promise that Collin could ride Kyle's horse, was Kyle finally able to convince the boy to leave the cabin and come with him. Collin still had not spoken but did reward Kyle with a faint smile as Kyle described some of the funny things about Garfield. With that small victory, they trudged down the dirt road, Collin trailing ten paces behind, to where Kyle had tethered Garfield.

The boy shed a few tears when he saw his sister's body, but was indifferent to the two men who lay beside her. Kyle asked who they were, but Collin didn't say. He just stared at his sister's lifeless body. Kyle waited for a few uncomfortable minutes before finally insisting that it was time to leave, and to his surprise, Collin came without resistance. Kyle had initially debated whether or not to let the boy see his sister, but had figured the poor child couldn't be any more scared than he already was, and at least having seen Stacy dead, he would know he couldn't go back to her.

With Garfield's age and the weight of the load he was already carrying, Kyle decided to walk so that Collin could ride. The pace was a little slow, but likely no slower than it would have been with both of them riding, plus Collin seemed to find comfort in being on Garfield, something about the large, docile creature giving him a sense of security.

They walked until late that night, the moon lighting the way, until they found a pickup truck with a fifth wheel camper on the side of the road, giving them a good place to sleep for a few hours. After gathering handfuls of young pine needles for breakfast, they departed early the next morning.

Now they were just a couple of miles from his parent's place, and Kyle was getting more anxious by the minute, anticipating and dreading what he might find when he arrived.

"What kind of vest is it that you're wearing?" The sheriff's voice startled Kyle, bringing him back to the present.

"I'm sorry. What was that?" Kyle asked.

"Your vest. What kind is it?"

Kyle paused, not sure what to tell the sheriff and not wanting to cause any problems this close to his destination.

"Look," the man said. "I can see the bullet holes in your jacket, and you're favoring your left arm. You don't act like law enforcement, so I'm asking you about your armor. Not trying to trick you or anything, but we do try to be aware of who's coming into our community."

"Sorry," Kyle said, glancing down at the holes in his jacket. "I don't know much about it, just that it works. A friend gave it to me before I headed this direction. He was military and border patrol, so he probably got it from his work."

"You're still sore from being hit. Does it have anything to do with your companion?"

Kyle nodded, explaining what had happened in as tactful a manor as possible, and promising that he wasn't there to make trouble. By now they were most of the way across the bridge, with the town ahead of them looking relatively peaceful. "How are things going here, sir?" Kyle asked.

"Just call me Greg, and actually, things are pretty good, at least compared to most places. We're a small community, but we have the essentials—farms, food, some medical capacity, along with a secure location." He nodded at the bridge they had just crossed, then pointed across town. "The river's a natural barrier, so between the bridge here and the one in Bonner's Ferry, we have natural choke points to defend. There's only one big road coming from the north and no big population centers across the border in Canada, so no reason for significant threats to come at us from that direction, though that road is still guarded, in addition to the bridges."

"Any problems to this point?"

Greg shook his head. "An uptick in crime for the first month, but we've been lucky. We're an isolated agricultural community with lots of arable land, water, wood, infrastructure, a sawmill with more wood than we can use in a decade, a jail, and schools. I could go on." He stopped and looked at Kyle. "Listen, we know how lucky we are, so we don't want people coming in and messing things up. Visitors get escorted through town and sent on their way if they don't have a reason to be here. I'll be the one going to your parent's place with you. If you are not who you say you are, don't expect to be able to stay. If you do have a connection, welcome to Moyie Springs, but remember, we don't tolerate much. We have enough information about what is going on in the bigger cities to know we want none of that here. If you step out of line, you'll be dealt with harshly. Do you understand?"

Kyle raised his hands defensively. "Loud and clear. I have no intention of messing things up for my family. You really don't need to worry about me."

"Good." the Sheriff said. "I've got better things to do with my time."

They reached the far side of the ravine, with Collin still clinging tightly to the stirrup, and Kyle walking beside Greg. Another RV was parked just past the end of the bridge, and Greg told Kyle to wait while he went to the vehicle. The door swung open, and two armed men emerged, eyeing Kyle while they talked to the sheriff in hushed voices. Kyle talked to Collin while they waited, then hefted him back up on the horse. Eventually Greg returned, and the other two men retreated back into their RV.

The clouds had cleared away, and the sun was warming things up, causing the thin layer of snow on the road to melt off and mists of steam to rise in the cool air. "We good?" Kyle asked.

Greg nodded. "Just giving them a heads up. This side of town is pretty quiet, not many people coming through, so they're curious. There are a lot of long, cold, boring days out here."

Greg followed Kyle's lead, cutting back south along the top of the ridge that overlooked the river.

"What brought your parents here?" Greg asked as he scanned the far side of the river.

"Retirement. They were both teachers, retiring after thirty years in the profession. Mom taught fifth grade, and dad taught high school science. He still substituted here to keep busy. Mom grew up in Sandpoint, and loved the area. Dad is from Seattle, but had no desire to return, as big and crowded as it is anymore."

"They chose well to not retire in Seattle. Much lower survival rates there. Lots of fighting going on."

"Is there military involvement?" Kyle asked, his ears perking up.

Greg shook his head. "Nothing like that. Just too many people in too small a space with too few resources, and no sense of community for that matter."

"I've worried about other countries coming over, especially to cities on the coast. You hear of anything like that?"

Greg laughed. "No. No invasions, at least not yet. To me, it wouldn't make sense for anyone to do that, at least not yet."

Kyle looked at him, surprised, and Greg continued. "First off, why put yourself in the middle of anarchy? A military force would have to restore some law and order, which would be a major drain on their resources. Anyone smart will just sit back and let us fight it out, then see what and who's left when we're all done. Hell, if the Chinese landed on the West Coast, it would give people someone to fight instead of each other. Probably do more to unify us than our government has in the last six months."

"You don't think they want our land or our stuff?"

"Nope," Greg said, shaking his head vigorously. "We're so far across the ocean it would be cheaper for them to manufacture it than to come over here, fight for it, and ship it back. Most of it probably came from China in the first place. They don't need the land because their people don't know to want what they don't have, and besides, we took out most of their command infrastructure and have promised to drop the big one on them if they try anything, and they know we're desperate. In other words, we should be good, if you consider our current status good."

Greg smiled at Kyle. "You wonder what we talk about during the long, boring shifts at the end of the bridges?"

"Let me guess," Kyle said, rubbing his chin. "Politics?"

Greg laughed, the first indication of humor he'd shown since they met. "Got it. My theory is that China just needs to hold tight for a few years until we're ready to start buying again. We'll have to replace everything, and I mean everything. Every factory owner in China is going to be crazy rich in a few years, just like America got after World War II when Europe had all their stuff bombed out and had to buy it from us. Amazing how things cycle through history."

"From what I can see, this isn't too bad a place to be, up here out of the way like you are." Kyle turned to make sure Collin was doing okay, then continued. "You have everything you need to survive and can spend your guard time discussing politics instead of fighting off the bad guys."

Greg nodded, smiling. "You're not far off. Not many places in America I'd rather be right now, that's for sure."

A strange beeping sound startled Kyle. Greg reached down and pulled a radio Kyle hadn't noticed from his belt and spoke into it. After a short conversation with a guard at another checkpoint, the radio was replaced and Greg turned his attention back to Kyle. "There's always something," he said, dismissing the call.

Kyle shook his head in wonder. "Okay, how do you still have radios? I thought we lost everything like that back in September."

Greg shrugged. "We lost most things back then, but not everything."

"What? You just happened to find some radios that worked?"

"No, guess we got a little bit lucky. There are a few preppers in the area, myself being one of them, at least to a degree. I read an article on a blog once that said microwave ovens make a good Faraday cage, and…"

"A farawhat cage?"

"A Faraday cage. It's a device that protects electronics from an EMP, so they aren't affected by the electrons or whatever it is that causes the damage. There are different things that'll work – metal trashcan, steel cabinets, whatever. A microwave is just one of them. Anyway, I had a few old radios and a couple old microwaves I didn't use, so I wrapped the radios in foil, stuck them in one of the microwaves, and forgot about them. When all this happened, I pulled them out, popped a couple of batteries in, and they worked."

"Where'd you get the batteries?"

"Batteries are cheap, and they last a long time, so I always kept hundreds of them on hand. Just had to be sure and rotate them."

"I'd say that seems like a lot of trouble, but obviously in hindsight, it wasn't."

"Not everything worked. I had an old cell phone and my first ipad that I stuck in there too. They work if you want to play games, but with no cell systems, I can't communicate with them. There are a couple guys in the area with HAM radios though, so we're not entirely cut off." He looked up ahead at a log home with a business sign hanging out front. "That's it, isn't it?" he indicated with a lift of his chin.

Kyle sucked in his breath and nodded. "It is."

CHAPTER THIRTY-SEVEN

Wednesday, February 15th
Central Montana

Rose stared towards the west, her heart pounding as she watched the figure in the distance drawing ever so slowly nearer. Encountering a stranger out in the middle of nowhere made her chest tighten and her breathing difficult. She tried telling herself to relax, but it didn't work, as she couldn't find any reason to convince herself she was safe. Reining Smokey to a halt, she pulled out her gun and peered through the scope.

The figure was still a long ways off and appeared to be a man wearing a dark coat, jeans, and a backpack, trailed by a small dog that had to trot to keep up with the walker's long strides. "What do you think, Smokey?" she asked.

Smokey didn't reply. He just dropped his head to graze on the knee-high, brown grass, concerned only with finding something more to eat and oblivious for the moment to any tension Rose felt.

She glanced back at Blitz, still plodding steadily along after all these miles. "You two good with this?" she asked, trying to summon her courage as Smokey gave a good shake.

Rose kept her rifle in her hands and spurred Smokey, mildly reassured by the fact there were few vehicles for someone to hide behind. Smokey tugged on a final tuft of grass and set off again, resigned to his fate of nonstop walking. Rose felt the familiar tug on the saddle as Blitz was roused into action, and the small procession was once again on its way.

A little under fifteen minutes later, the man was close enough to communicate, which he did with a wave. Rose returned the gesture, but still held her rifle tightly in her right hand. "Breathe deeply," she told herself, feeling the tension in her chest ratchet up another notch. To her dismay, the man began heading across the median in a line to intercept her. She had seen a few people over the last week, but only two had made any attempt to communicate, and then with just a wave.

Rose mentally urged Smokey onward, willing him to hurry and get past this unwanted stranger, but without any physical prodding, Smokey maintained his steady pace, unconcerned with the approaching man. Rose's hands shook. She grabbed the saddle horn and squeezed it tightly, clenching her jaw to steady her nerves.

"Hello!" The man's greeting was carried on a stiff wind which blew in her direction.

Rose waved but didn't speak, certain her voice wouldn't carry that far. She stopped Smokey, took her gun in both hands and aimed it in the general direction of the man, then waited.

After crossing the median, he leapt nimbly over the rail on the south side of the road, not more than forty feet away. Rose's finger rested on the trigger. She was sure he could sense her anxiety, and it was obvious her rifle was aimed at him, yet he made no attempt to reach for the rifle slung over his back.

"Good afternoon," he shouted, one hand cupped to the side of his mouth. He continued walking towards her, though his pace was slower and his hands were held out where she could see them. "Nice day today, isn't it?" His smile was warm and friendly, non-threatening.

Rose nodded. "A little windy for my taste, but at least it isn't too cold." He stopped a dozen feet away, too far to grab at her. Rose kept a firm grip on her rifle.

The man nodded, turned partway into the wind, and held up his hand to test it. "The wind is nice for me at least. Helps push me along. I'm sure you feel it more than I do, riding into it."

Rose smiled and felt her chest loosen slightly, but still maintained the grip on her gun. The man turned back to her and smiled. He looked young, maybe twenty, and was either clean-shaven or didn't have much of a beard yet.

"Where you headed?" Rose asked.

"Minnesota," he answered with an optimistic grin. "You?" His eyes were bright blue, his complexion clear, and he had a slender build.

"Missoula. Looks like I'll get there first." Rose studied him, still wary.

The boy shrugged. "More than likely. I've got a lot of miles to go, but I'll get there eventually. I passed through Missoula a few days ago. With the horses, you should be there soon."

"Do you have food?"

"Some. My pack is mostly food, and a couple changes of clothes. I try and shoot what I need or work for it when I have the chance. Churches have been helpful."

She noticed a handgun tucked in the belt of his pants and tensed up. Though he'd done nothing to threaten her, the weapon still worried her. "You had many problems on your trip?"

"A couple," he said while nodding. "But nothing too serious. I ran track at UW, so I've been able to outrun everything to this point, sometimes literally. I'm not carrying much, so no one's wanted to waste a bullet on me I guess. Hoping my luck continues. You?"

"Don't ask," Rose replied. "Things I don't want to think about, much less discuss."

"I'm sorry to hear that. It's sad how far we've fallen, isn't it? Hopefully the rest of your journey will be smooth." He glanced up at the sky to the bank of clouds slowly closing in on them.

"Weather looks like it's going to change soon. I guess I should let you get on your way."

"Probably best," Rose agreed, assessing the clouds herself. "Have a safe journey and be careful, okay?"

He smiled again, a broad, bright grin lighting his face, deep dimples denting his cheeks. "I'll try and be safe, Ma'am. Thank you." He crouched down and rubbed his dog's head. It was a small, mangy looking thing, half-starved, but happy. The dog wagged its tail and licked the boy's hand. "Good luck to you too," he said as he started past her, his pace brisk and energetic.

Rose watched him stride by, confident, unencumbered with fear. "Hey, Minnesota," she called out to him when he was thirty feet past.

He stopped and turned towards her, the smile still on his face. "What is it, Missoula?"

"Thank you."

He looked puzzled. "Thank you for what?" he asked, sincerely curious.

"Thank you for restoring a little of my faith in humanity," Rose answered, giving him a smile and a wave as she gently kicked Smokey in the flanks.

CHAPTER THIRTY-EIGHT

Thursday, February 16th
Deer Creek, MT

Jennifer quickly tied her bootlaces and slipped on her jacket before pulling the door open and letting herself out. The brisk morning air momentarily took her breath away as she put on a hat and pair of gloves, then quickened her pace towards the Shipley Ranch. She covered the mile and a half to the ranch in fifteen minutes, though without a working watch or clock to consult, she just knew it took awhile.

Once at the ranch, she only needed five minutes of milking time, as there was only one of the three females in milk, that one being a fortunate consequence of an early pregnancy resulting in two kids being born in late September. Still, all of the goats needed to be fed and tended to before milking, if for no other reason than to keep them occupied so she could milk uninterrupted. The two other females had recently had their babies and would soon be producing milk for the community, so it was important to keep them all healthy in order to grow the herd size.

The Shipley's had four mature Nubian goats, three does and a buck, which were valuable for both milk and meat. The goats had always been like pets, remnants from kids' 4H projects, and Bryan's wife, Katie, enjoyed having them around, finding them to be better companions than Bryan's dogs, with the added benefit of weed control. Additionally, the goats' natural diet was much cheaper than the truckloads of dog food Bryan's dogs consumed. Now, however, the goats had become one of the most valuable possessions in the community, especially since the cattle the Shipleys raised were Angus and not a dairy breed.

In exchange for a quart of milk each morning, Jennifer had volunteered to take care of the goats, a task which included feeding the small herd, cleaning the pen, washing the milk containers, and caring for the animals, something Carol, a thirty-year veterinarian, and Katie coached her on as needed. Once the kids were weaned, there would be all three does to milk, but Jennifer, now accustomed to the work, was confident she could have the milking done in less than ten minutes, five if she really got good at it.

Emma usually helped with the animals each day but had been coughing through the night so had stayed in bed. Jennifer was glad for the opportunity she usually had to work with her daughter, as it gave them time together plus gave Emma something good to do, helping her state of mind. Emma had nearly returned to her old self after Kyle's return, but then with his banishment she'd sunk back into a funk that once again worried Jennifer.

Madison's arrival had changed things, however, helping all of them, but especially Emma, to focus on something else and to forget, for portions of each day at least, their own problems and how much they missed having Kyle there. Emma glowed when she held her little sister, as she now referred to the baby, beaming proudly as she fed her and even willingly changing diapers and rocking the baby when she cried. Jennifer continued having nightmares about the night the young mother died, but recognized that good was coming from the new life that had been brought into their home.

Jennifer offered more help to the Shipleys than just tending the goats, knowing the value of the milk she received far outweighed the work she provided, but her repeated offers were graciously declined. "Help with the goats," she had been told, "and take good care of the baby." Jennifer choked up a little when she thought about the kindness of others, especially when there were dire needs in every home.

Jennifer worked quickly through the chores, lost in thought as she finished up the milking. She rubbed the doe affectionately, pleased the animal hadn't stuck her foot in the bucket like she had the day before. Jennifer poured her portion of the milk into her quart container and the remainder in a pail for the Shipleys, washed the milk bucket, delivered the Shipley's milk, and headed home. The sun had cleared the mountains and was quickly warming things, giving her hope for a warm, sunny day that would get them out of the house and not require them to burn too much wood. Two days of colder than normal temperatures and running a steady fire all day had made her anxious for a break from that routine.

She skirted along the upper edges of the creek bank as she walked home, noticing that the water levels were climbing a little higher each day, slowly filling the small reservoir the community was in the process of creating. Under Craig Reider's direction, a dam was being constructed across the creek with the hope of providing extra irrigation water in the summer when the creek flow slowed. Despite the fact it was being done with shovels and wheelbarrows, the work was proceeding quickly.

The base of the dam was twenty feet thick and built with salvaged concrete from sidewalks and driveways of vacant homes, then back-filled with gravel. A dirt and gravel mixture was being dumped on top of that, filling in the cracks and keeping the water backed up behind it. When completed, the dam would measure nine feet high and pinch off across a section of the creek that was no more than thirty-five feet across. Two sections of twelve-inch irrigation pipe ran through the base of the dam and would be used to allow water to flow through once the reservoir filled, but until then, they were blocked off in order to fill the lake.

Hurrying to get the milk back to Madison while it was still warm, Jennifer offered a curt smile as she passed two men with rifles slung over their shoulders who were pushing wheelbarrows loaded with shovels and rakes towards the dam.

Jennifer had just reached home when she heard a ringing in the distance, like a church bell, a sound that at first she couldn't place. Then, like a kick to the stomach, the realization hit her. Someone had shot the truck hood that hung from the tree outside the militia house, the one that David had had so much trouble hitting a few weeks before. Someone had sounded the alarm.

She bounded up the steps and burst through the door. Emma quickly looked up at her while rocking the baby. David raced up from the basement, a rifle in one hand, his boots in the other. "Here, make a bottle," she said, handing the milk to Emma and grabbing David as he brushed past her. "Where are you going?" she demanded, her voice strained.

"You heard the alarm, Mom; I have to go!"

"No, David! I've already lost your father. I will not allow you to go. Just stay here and help me protect your brother and sisters."

David looked at his mom, no fear in his eyes. "Mom. I can do this. My friends are out there. I need to go help."

Jennifer squeezed his arm harder, looking him in the eyes, and felt her chin quiver. "But David, if something happens, I don't know what I'll do. I don't know if I can take it."

"I'll be careful, Mom. I promise. But I have to go. There aren't very many of us, so everyone's needed. Besides, it's probably another false alarm. The guys on day shift are too jumpy."

Jennifer's grip loosened, and David pulled away, his face calm. He grabbed his jacket from the front closet and a backpack with three loaded magazines, pulled on his boots, and hurried to the front door. "I do know this isn't a drill, Mom, so have your gun ready. Hopefully it is a false alarm, but if it's not…," he stammered. "Be ready, just in case."

David flew out the front door and was gone before the sound of the slamming door quit echoing through Jennifer's mind, her maternal fears imagining every conceivable threat her son was off to face.

Emma had the bottle filled and was back on the couch holding the baby close and watching her mother. "I'm scared, mom," she whispered. "Is he going to be alright?"

Jennifer tried to fake a smile. "I hope so, Em. I really, really hope so."

CHAPTER THIRTY-NINE

Thursday, February 16th
Deer Creek, MT

David flew down the street, running as fast as he was able with his gun in one hand and his backpack thrown over his other shoulder. He spotted men coming from two other streets and was overtaken by a man on horseback who galloped past, shouting words of encouragement.

A garage a half-mile from the militia house, designated as the mustering point after the previous incident made it apparent that the militia house was too close to potential threats, was his destination. David, breathing heavily when he arrived, listened to the men already present as they speculated about the situation, though none of them really knew much of anything.

David was standing off to the side and trying to catch his breath when someone shouted to quiet the group. Voices quickly went silent, and everyone strained to hear, listening for anything out of place. David heard a low rumbling just as someone blurted out "engines!" Another man confirmed it. "I heard it too. It sounds like more than one."

A nervous murmur rumbled through the twenty men who were gathered. Craig Reider, now standing at the front of the group, spoke. "Listen up! Sean has gone ahead to the militia house to find out what he can. He said the rest of us need to be ready for action as soon as he gets back."

Craig spent the next few minutes confirming weapons were loaded and ready and everyone was primed to shift into action once Sean returned. David was focused on Craig's instructions when someone alerted the men. "Here comes Sean, and he's moving pretty fast." David turned towards the militia house and saw Sean sprinting down the street. Sometimes the militia jogged around the area to get in shape, but never a full on sprint, and it scared him.

David felt a hand grab his shoulder, startling him. He jumped as he turned and saw Ty Lewis giving him a reassuring smile.

"How you doing, David?" Ty asked, his eyes on Sean sprinting towards them.

"Alright, I guess," David answered, his attention re-focused on Sean as well. David tried to swallow, but his mouth was dry, like at the end of an August football practice. He licked his lips and waited for Sean to reach them.

Sean didn't break stride or slow down, arriving at the mustering point less than two minutes after he was first spotted. The ragtag groups of soldiers watched in silence as Sean hurried towards them.

Sean slowed to a walk just in front of the garage, fighting to catch his breath as he stepped in front of the group. "Okay...I'm sorry, but this doesn't look good... From the upstairs window..." he took a couple of deep breaths between each phrase, pushing himself to relay the information as quickly as he could. "I could see a...dump truck and maybe a tour bus...coming down the freeway from Missoula. ...with the spotting scope, I could see damage to the vehicles ... looked like bullet dings. We won't know until they get here...but they don't look friendly."

The men shifted anxiously from foot to foot. David was nervous as well, though maybe less so than some of the others, he thought, since he was one of the few people in the group who had actually shot a weapon in combat. Most of the men had done nothing more violent than take down a deer in hunting season, and some of them not even that.

"This is what I need," Sean said, finally able to talk without stopping for air. "I need four men to head to the barricade on the road from Missoula on this side of the river. I don't expect anything to happen there, but we need to be ready just in case. You come and back us up if we get into trouble by the bridge." Craig indicated a group he had formed before Sean's arrival, and the men started to leave. Sean called them back, instructing them to wait until all assignments had been made.

"I want twelve men for the barricades by the bridge, six on each side. You're our first line of defense. The crew from the militia house already has four men there, so that'll give us sixteen, plus there are two more upstairs with bigger weapons." Craig walked through the group, picking out people as Sean spoke, including Ty, who still stood beside David.

More militia members continued to arrive while Sean gave directions. David estimated that their numbers had grown to over thirty. "I need four to head south to the Shipley Ranch. I don't anticipate any trouble there, but make sure Bryan and his boys are armed and ready, just in case. Who has the horse?"

A hand was raised, and Sean pointed at the man. "Is it fast?"

The man nodded. "She's young, but she can move."

"Good. I need you to stay close to the militia house. Be ready to run messages and respond to gunfire anywhere it's not expected. Who's a fast runner?"

No one responded, so David hesitantly stuck his hand up.

"David, I need you to take the back way to Clinton as quickly as you can. Let them know what's going on over here. You can take one of the bikes, but with the snow, I don't know that you'll be able to ride the whole way. You may have to do some of it on foot. See if they can offer any help, then come back this way down the freeway if they get a group together. That's a lot of distance to cover, but we need to get word out. Wait and talk to me before you take off."

David nodded, feeling his heart already begin to race.

Sean counted heads. "You six, divide yourselves between the bunkers along the river. Two in each. Stay there unless instructed to reinforce somewhere else. Craig, you stay here. As more show up, I want you sending half of everyone to us at the bridge, then spread the rest out to reinforce." The deep, steady rumble of the engines was increasing, as was the sense of dread that hung in the air.

"Alright!" Sean said, raising his voice. "This is what all our drills have been about. We get a chance to protect our homes. I don't know what's in store, hopefully it's a false alarm, but remember, we don't have unlimited ammo, so if it comes to shooting, shoot to kill. No pray and spray out there, and don't waste bullets on someone who isn't a threat. Stay where you're assigned, unless you're directed to leave or you can't hold your position. I don't know how big this group is that's coming in. It might be just a couple of folks who are lost, but I doubt it."

David looked around at the nervous faces. The group was mostly men in their thirties and forties, though there were a few women and several men whose hair was solid gray. His legs trembled, and the memories of the night on the mountain came rushing back, adding to his anxiety. At least this time I'm not the only one who knows they're coming, he thought.

Sean continued speaking to the group. "We need to hurry and get into position. I know most of you have never shot a man before, and it will be really difficult if it comes to that. Remember, these people have come here, to our homes. We're not doing anything more than defending ourselves, and we'll do whatever we have to do to defend our families." He scanned the group, noticing tension, fear, and nervous resolve in his men.

Someone in the group shouted out, "Try and imagine them with antlers, they'll be easier to shoot that way." Sean smiled and several let out a low chuckle.

"Are we ready?" Sean called out, his voice growing stronger. The group responded half-heartedly, so he repeated, as loudly as he could. "I said, are we ready?!" This time the response was surer, with men waving their rifles in the air, shouting, and cheering.

"Alright!" Sean rallied, his rifle held over his head. "Then get to your posts, and keep your heads down!"

The group broke up quickly, with men and women scrambling in different directions. They were all nervous, but there was a confidence as well, earned during the past weeks of training and drilling with the militia.

David went to Sean and tapped him on the shoulder. "What do I need to do?"

Sean grabbed David by the elbow. "Have you been the back way to Clinton before?"

David shook his head.

"There's a wood bridge about five miles up that you can get across on. Get there fast and let them know that it looks like an armed group of men are heading through the valley. Have them gather their forces and at the very least prepare a defense. If you hear gunfire and there's any way they can afford to send reinforcements, have them send men our way through the hills on the North side of the freeway. We'll take any help we can get, and let them know that if these guys are bad news and head east, we'll trail them and help push them past Clinton. Just don't get south of the freeway, I don't want any friendly fire issues."

David made mental notes and nodded at each instruction. "Got it," he said when Sean finished. As he turned to leave, David felt a tug on his jacket and turned back.

"Thanks for your help, David," Sean said warmly. "You didn't have to do this, you know."

"I know," he said. "But we're still a part of this community."

Sean patted the young man on his shoulder, then motioned towards Clinton with his head. "You better get moving."

CHAPTER FORTY

Thursday, February 16th
Deer Creek, MT

Ty joined the men assigned to the barricades by the bridge, found a place, and took cover. Over the past three months, the militia had worked hard to build two large fortifications on both sides of the road that led across the bridge. The barricades were set back about fifty feet from the river and angled at forty-five degrees to the road and consisted of long embankments that were flanked by ditches in the front and rear. The ditches were shallow but wide, and the dirt that had been excavated from them, along with a variety of other material, had been used to make the earthen berms that rose six feet above ground level and were capped with large tree trunks that lay horizontally along the top.

From where he knelt, Ty could see the dump truck and an old bus exiting the freeway and maneuvering around the dead cars the militia had placed in the roadway to slow and deter approaching vehicles. Tensions were high with his group, all of whom were watching the vehicles approach as they took cover behind the mammoth tree trunk.

On the far side of the river, the approaching vehicles came to a stop and shut down their engines, and a group of eighteen people, some dressed in military-style fatigues, exited the bus, joined by two men who climbed out of the dump truck's cab. Sean had taken up a position a few feet away from Ty and let out a low whistle. "These boys mean business," he said, loudly enough that everyone in their bunker heard. "But they don't know who they're dealing with, do they?" he continued, his voice rising.

One of the men from the bus retrieved a white flag and held it over his head, waving it back and forth for a few seconds, then began walking towards them across the bridge.

"Everyone hold your fire!" Sean called out, loud enough for the men at both berms to hear. "Let's see what they have in mind before we do anything. I want everyone to stay down low so they can't see what our forces are like, except for a couple people at each berm. You can stick your heads up, so they'll see you. The rest of you stay out of sight."

Ty stood up, volunteering to be visible, and saw the two oldest men at the far berm stand as well, one holding only a .22, the other a handgun. He nervously held his semi-automatic, wondering if it would look too staged if he dropped his rifle and held only his hunting knife. Peering through his riflescope, Ty saw the men on the far side of the river venturing off in groups of two and three to check the abandoned vehicles, but knowing they wouldn't find anything, as he'd been on one of the teams that had salvaged everything of value and pushed the vehicles into their current positions. Even the fuel tanks at the freeway exit's gas station had been drained with a siphon hose months ago. Nevertheless, the brazenness of the outsiders made Ty's heart beat a little faster.

Once the messenger arrived on their side of the river, he raised a piece of paper in the air, and Sean motioned for Ty to retrieve it. Ty set his weapon down and climbed down the front side of the barricade, then hurried forward to retrieve the note. The messenger sneered confidently at Ty, assessed the men at the barricades, then quickly retreated back across the bridge.

Ty trotted back and handed the note to Sean, who unfolded the paper and read it to himself before reading it aloud.

We have no intention of harming anyone, if we don't have to. Our demands are simple. We require 10,000 rounds of ammunition, 500 pounds of beef, 100 MRE's or equivalent, and 500 pounds of wheat, beans or other grain. In exchange, you get to live.

You have 10 minutes to agree to our proposal, after which you will have 2 hours to fulfill our demands. If you choose to resist, we will, like we've done in other towns, kill who we need to and take whatever we want, women included.

We are professional soldiers trained to survive. Our group includes Army Rangers, Navy SEALS, and Green Beret.

Choose wisely.

Sean folded the paper back in half and looked at the militia members around him, their numbers having now swollen to twenty-two between the two barricades. "I'm sorry folks, but I have no intention of agreeing to their terms. Any objections?"

One of the men near Ty spoke up, his voice shaking. "Some of us, maybe a lot of us, might get killed if we fight them. Sounds like they're a lot more trained than we are."

Sean shook his head. "I don't buy what their note claims. In my experience, no quality soldier I know would go around the country preying on the weak. Maybe some washouts or wannabes, but no one who was actually a Ranger or a SEAL would. Trust me."

Ty felt a great deal of apprehension, and could tell by the expressions of others that they did too.

Sean looked around, seeing the same, and held up his hand with the note in it. "I know most of you have never taken fire, and it's a pretty scary thing. But this isn't just about us. If we don't stand up to them, where will they be tomorrow? What happens when they ask something of a community who just can't do it? We've got what they want, so they might take it and move on. Or they might decide they want more, until they've completely drained us. Then what?" He shook his head. "Some places may have given them what they want, but I say no."

"If we can just pay them to go away, why not do that? Seems safer, if you ask me," one of the younger men implored, his face pale, his hands trembling.

Ty shook his head vigorously. "I don't want to get shot, and I sure don't want to see any of you get hurt, but we have to say no. We're strong enough to take them on and win. Besides, if we give in to them today, what will they want when they come back in a month? They'll suck us dry and attack when we're weaker. I'm not willing to purchase temporary security at the cost of long-term survival."

"But they might not come back," the first man insisted. "If we give them what they want, they said they'll leave us alone."

One of the older gentlemen spoke up. "We can't trust people who use these kinds of tactics. If we give them our supplies, we'll just show them we're weak and afraid, and they'll push us as far as they can. If we don't fight them today, we'll have to fight them some point down the line. I say we man up and get it over with, before there are fifty people getting off that bus."

Sean looked at the twelve faces surrounding him at his barricade and smiled grimly. "This isn't my decision, but this group here is going to have to make the call because we don't have time to survey everyone. What do you say? Those in favor of surrendering our resources to these bandits, say 'aye.'"

Ty looked around, saw a lot of nervousness, but no one spoke.

"Those in favor of defending what is ours, say 'aye.'"

Ty was joined by most of the others in a vote to defend. A couple of folks abstained from voting, but it didn't matter, the decision had been made.

Sean took a deep breath. "All right then. We need to get into position. If you're not ready to shoot, get on it quick. Make sure your magazines are full, on your person, and ready to go. Find a position you are comfortable firing from, then wait for my instructions. Any questions?" No one said a word. "Alright. I'm going to give some directions to the folks in the house and on the other side of the road, then answer the letter. I'll be back in a few," Sean advised as he hurried off to the militia house.

Ty watched from his position on the barricade as the invaders stood in small groups and calmly waited for a response. Five minutes later, Sean returned and climbed on top of the highest position on the barricade. Taking the letter in his hands, he raised it above his head and tore it into pieces, then tossed the pieces into the breeze.

Ty quickly turned and watched the men across the river, who, seeing the response, were assembling themselves before the last scraps of paper fluttered to the ground. They huddled for a moment then broke apart, most heading for the dump truck. Ty counted four men climbing into the bed of the truck, while another man got in the cab and started it up. The engine rumbled ominously as it roared to life, and thick, black smoke billowed from the exhaust stacks.

The dump truck pulled forward a few feet, then stopped and began backing up, turning so the rear of the vehicle faced away from the bridge. At over a thousand yards away, Ty watched as the truck stopped, and metal plates were handed from out of the back of the truck to the men waiting on the ground. The men secured the plates to the sides of the truck, providing protection from bullets for the tires and engine. Near the back, pins were pulled, and hinged metal plates used to protect the rear tires were swung down.

Anderson West, positioned close to Ty, let out a low whistle. "Doesn't look like this is their first rodeo, does it?"

"No, no it doesn't," Ty replied, feeling a lump growing in his throat. "But they haven't dealt with us before, have they?" He heard footsteps and saw Sean running back to his position from the other bunker.

"Look at the bus!" Anderson said, pointing. "I don't like the looks of this."

Two men were dragging someone off the bus who had their hands secured behind their back and was fighting back against his captors. It appeared to be a teenage boy, but Ty couldn't tell for sure. The men pulled the boy out into the middle of the road where everyone at the barricades could see them. "This is bad…" Ty began, but before he could finish his thought, one of the men pulled out a handgun and shot the boy in the back of the head, then let the lifeless body slump to the ground.

Gasps ran up and down the barricade as Sean attempted to reassure the men. "Okay folks, now we know who we are dealing with. That was meant as a warning, but let it harden our resolve. These people are evil." Sean picked up his rifle and leaned against the thick tree trunk that lay along the top of the berm. "We can take them, but it's going to be a fight. Wait to shoot until I tell you to." He looked through the scope on his rifle and fired a shot.

One of the men who had just executed the boy went down, clutching his upper thigh. The others scattered.

"You want us to fire?" someone called out.

"Not yet. Save your ammo. I'm dialed in good on the long shots. There'll be plenty of shooting to do in a few minutes."

Sean took aim and fired another shot but didn't hit anyone. The dump truck pulled behind the bus, and the wounded man was dragged behind the vehicle.

"Alright," Sean yelled. "I need a volunteer. Gonna be dangerous, but important."

"I'll do it," Ty said, his voice shaking. "What do you need?"

Sean handed a small, heavy satchel to Ty and spoke rapidly. "There are four grenades in there. I need you to get under the bridge, quick as you can. Hide there and wait for the dump truck to get to this side of the river. When it does, carefully pull the pin and toss the grenade in the back of the truck. The bridge is forcing them to stay together, so most of their team will be in there. If you can get it in there, this will be over."

"That's it?"

Sean nodded. "Yeah, but once they see you and realize what you're trying to do, you need to be ready for a lot of lead flying your direction."

Just as he was about to leave for the bridge, Ty felt someone pull on his jacket. Turning, he saw Luther Espinoza kneeling beside him, also listening to Sean's instructions. "Give me the bag. I'll do it." Luther's left arm was still in a sling, damaged from the first firefight the community had had. "I can't use a gun very well, but you can, and you're a good shot. You'll be more help on this side of the berm than I will."

Ty paused, conflicted about what he should do.

"Hurry," Luther said, reaching for the bag. "I need to get there before they see me."

Sean nodded. Luther pulled the bag from Ty's hands and crept to the end of the berm. "How many of these babies do I have again?" he asked.

"Four, but only use what you need to," Sean answered.

"Pull the pin and toss, right?"

"Affirmative," Sean said, then scrambled to the top of the barricade to watch what was happening across the river.

Luther ran across the road to the other berm, ran the length of it, then ducked through some bushes to conceal himself as he scurried towards the bridge, his fifty year old body not as agile and quick as it once was.

Luther had just scrambled under the bridge when they heard the truck's engine rev and saw it emerge from behind the bus, its wheels now well protected on all sides by the steel plates. The truck maneuvered in the road until it was positioned to come across the bridge backwards, then, with gears grinding, it lurched and began to slowly move towards them.

Sean directed the men, spreading them out to present smaller targets. He shouted loudly enough to be heard by the groups hidden behind both berms, "Keep your heads down. They're going to try and get past us shielded in the bed of the truck. If Luther doesn't drop a grenade in on them, we need to take out the driver. Shoot at whatever you can, but it'll likely just be headshots. They won't expose much more than that. Watch your fire if they dismount, and make sure you're not shooting at someone on our team. Remember the drills. No more than three shots in a burst, and make them count!"

Ty's hands shook as the truck approached loudly. He said a silent prayer and thought about his wife and what she'd do if he didn't come home, and whether she'd hold up if another member of their family were lost.

"You doing okay, Lewis?"

Ty looked to his right, where Anderson was still crouched. "I'm a little nervous, to be honest."

"You're braver than I am. I feel like I'm going to wet myself."

Ty nodded. "Alright, I admit it. I'm so scared I can hardly breathe. I'm trained to be a school teacher, not a soldier."

Anderson nodded. "Well I'm a builder and a lot more comfortable shooting nails than people."

"I tell you what," Ty replied. "There were a few things about teaching that drove me nuts, but I'd take a lifetime of those headaches over one day of this."

Anderson kept his aim on the approaching truck. "I feel the same way. I'd much rather be facing a building inspector than getting shot at. If I ever get to building again, I'll plant a sloppy wet kiss on the first inspector to walk on the jobsite."

The truck continued its slow advance towards them, the cars placed as barricades on the bridge forcing it to slowly wind its way towards them, a process made more difficult because the truck was coming in reverse. Every person in the militia, their eyes just far enough over the top of the tree trunk for them to see, watched nervously.

"We need to build this up, make it taller," Sean muttered under his breath, referring to the barricade. "It'd be nice to be able to shoot down into the back of that truck."

The berms had been built as a defense against pedestrians and pickups, not armor-reinforced trucks. From their positions, height wise they'd be able to shoot into the side windows of the cab, but not over the sides of the bed, giving their attackers an advantage. Building the berms higher had been considered at one point, but effort had instead been spent on improving their defensive positions along the river.

Out of the corner of his eye, Ty noticed one of the men scamper down behind the barricade, get on his knees, remove his hat, and begin to pray. The man was joined by three more, all offering up silent prayers before returning to their positions. Ty thought about doing the same, but worried he'd be too frightened to crawl back up the bank. Instead, he stayed in position, kept ahold of his gun, and uttered a few words under his breath.

Sean whistled and waved over the man with the horse, who was waiting in the driveway of the house closest to the militia complex. The man bent low and rushed forward, pumping his arms hard with the exaggerated movements of someone forcing himself to do something he didn't want to do.

"Get back to my brother. Tell him to send everyone this direction. I don't think these guys have split up, so I want the rest of our guys to take up position at the house where you've been waiting, just in case they get past us. You wait there too, but be ready to ride for reinforcements. Got it?"

The man nodded, spun on his heels, and raced back to his horse. Ty heard the sound of hooves on the road at the same time the dump truck hung up on an old Ford pickup not more than fifty yards away. They watched, rifles ready, as the truck worked forwards and backwards, unsuccessfully trying to disengage itself.

"Be ready!" Sean hollered, his eye pressed to the scope of his rifle.

A head popped up over the side of the truck to peer down at the old pickup and was met with a hail of bullets from both defensive positions as Sean yelled "Fire!" From Ty's vantage point, it looked like numerous silver dings appeared in the side of the truck and at least two of the bullets found their mark, snapping the man's head quickly back then forward as he was hit from both sides, a spray of blood misting out over the truck.

"Hold fire!" Sean yelled. "But stay ready!"

Gunfire ceased, leaving just the sound of the big diesel engine on the bridge. A voice from the truck shouted instructions, and after a short pause the truck engine revved, then jerked violently backwards. The clamor of metal tearing and rubber screeching pierced their ears as the bumper was torn from the pickup and bounced onto the road.

"They're going to be mad!" Sean yelled. "They have two men down, and we're not hurt yet. Hang in there."

The truck continued backwards, coming faster. A gold-colored Toyota Camry, the last vehicle on the road, was knocked out of the way as the truck smashed into it in a crash of breaking glass and crunching metal, then came to a stop twenty-five yards in front of the barricades. With the screech of sliding metal, the back gate of the truck swung down, revealing the barrel of a tri-pod mounted machine gun. In front of it, a large metal plate with two small openings, one for the barrel, and one for the operator to peer through, concealed the gun and the operator, along with the rest of the crew.

As Ty took in this surreal image, several men popped up in unison on both sides of the truck, making their heads and rifles visible. With a sudden flash of weapons and an explosion of sound, the air was filled with the deafening noise of gunfire and the acrid smell of gunpowder. Bullets flew in every direction, spitting up wood and dirt all around Ty and the others as they ricocheted off rocks and trees. Ty fired off two quick shots, then dropped behind the heavy log that protected him, feeling the thud and vibrations of bullets striking the opposite side.

Ty mentally tallied the three shots he had fired so far. He slid a few feet to the side and rose up with his rifle at his shoulder, just as he'd been trained. He quickly found a figure in his sights, one who was aiming in his direction, pulled the trigger two times, and saw the head snap backwards. He ducked back down as the air erupted once again with the rapid, heavy thuds of the machine gun, taking deep breaths while listening to the impact of bullets striking the militia house.

A stream of bullets traced a pattern across the second story of the militia house, punching a series of holes through the old wooden walls. Ty rose up and fired a couple more rounds, then noticed the machine gun swung his direction. "Get down!" he shouted, dropping and rolling down the bank as the heavy thuds of the bullets struck the tree, sending wood chunks raining down.

Somewhere close to him a person screamed and rolled down the bank with blood pumping from a wound in his neck. Ty turned and saw Anderson West, his hands clasped to his throat, writh-ing on the ground as one of the women from the team rushed over to him. Ty closed his eyes to block the image and waited for the pounding of the bullets to slow, then scrambled back to the top of the bank. He peered over the top just as the machine gun swung towards the opposite berm. The chaotic sounds of warfare engulfed him – guns firing, soldiers yelling, bullets impacting, and men screaming – every nightmarish thing he could have imagined, and more.

He quickly raised his weapon and aimed at the machine gun. With the gun pointing away from him, he could see the arms of the operator through a gap in the plate by the barrel. He took quick aim and pulled the trigger, pausing just long enough between shots to fine tune his accuracy. On his third shot, he hit his target, just as the machine gun resumed firing, seeing the hand holding the weapon disappear and blood spurt from the stump that remained. As he turned his attention to the bed of the dump truck, he was struck, knocking him backwards down the dirt bank, his cheek and shoulder throbbing with pain.

Ty took a brief moment to determine if he was dying, searching for wounds but not feeling any blood. He sat up and looked for his gun, finding it at his feet with a large chunk missing from where a bullet had struck it. He picked his gun up and quickly tried to chamber a bullet, but the action wouldn't work and he threw the useless weapon onto the ground.

Anderson was being treated, but Ty could tell that his friend was either dead, or dying. "I need a gun," he shouted over the din before grabbing Anderson's weapon, a black semi-automatic with a banana shaped magazine, and scrambling back up the slope, numb to the danger.

He crawled to a gap where no one was positioned, raised his head, and saw a flurry of activity on the bridge. Luther was crawling slowly towards the truck with the satchel slung over his shoulder, a trail of blood extending out behind him. With a flash from the other side of the river, Luther collapsed forward writhing in pain.

Ty screamed out Sean's name and scooted towards him, trying to get Sean's attention. "They're shooting Luther from the other side of the river," he cried. "You gotta take them down."

"Cover me!" Sean yelled as he raised his rifle, searching for the shooters on the far bank.

Ty lifted his head and scanned the side of the dump truck. The machine gun swung back towards them, and Ty pulled Sean down just as the firing began. They waited a few seconds before popping up again, their ears ringing from the barrage. With the machine gun swinging away, Ty once again zeroed in on the arms of the man at the controls. His second shot drew blood, though not as dramatically as before seeing as Anderson's gun was a smaller caliber than his own.

A head rose above the edge of the dump truck, and Ty fired at it. He missed, but a silver divot appeared along the edge of the truck, and the man dropped his weapon and clawed at his eyes. His second shot found its mark, and the man dropped from sight.

"Got him!" Sean exclaimed after his weapon discharged, then quickly turned his attention back to the closer threat.

The shooting continued in a steady, indistinguishable roar for three or four minutes, then slowly died down as the return fire from the dump truck diminished. Sean called out for his men to hold fire. A brief moment of silence was followed by moaning and crying, along with banging sounds from inside the back of the truck. Then, to everyone's relief, they heard the transmission grind into gear.

"Luther's on the road," yelled Ty as the dump truck began moving towards Luther's twisting body. Ty rose to his feet and ran along the top of the berm, leaping over stunned men as he sprinted towards the river. With steel plates covering the side doors of the truck, he needed to get ahead of it to be able to take out the driver through the windshield. Gunshots rang out and bullets whistled past him, but he kept running, seeing in his peripheral vision the truck closing in on Luther, lying injured on the road.

Two gunshots came from close by, then all gunfire ceased, leaving only the sounds of the truck's engine and Ty's feet pounding the dirt. He drew even with the front of the truck, which was crawling forward in low gear, then began to get ahead of it, but it was only a few feet from Luther, who, wounded and bleeding heavily, was unable to move to the side.

Ty pushed himself to his limit, gasping for air but desperate to stop the truck. He turned as he ran, seeing he didn't have the angle yet, and pushed harder, raising his gun to his shoulder. The truck was shifting gears when Ty finally had the shot he needed. He planted his feet, aimed, and pulled the trigger in rapid succession, shattering the windshield with the truck less than ten feet from Luther. Ty kept shooting until he ran out of bullets. The driver slumped forward as Luther rolled over and lobbed one of his grenades over the cab of the truck.

In the fresh silence Ty heard the clang of metal striking metal, followed by frightened shouts and a deafening explosion, but the truck continued to roll forward.

"Move, Luther!" Ty shouted, unable to stop the truck. There was a sickening, hollow thud and a scream, as the front wheel struck his injured friend. Ty dropped to his knees in shock. The dump truck careened forward, bounced off the rail on the side of the bridge, then collided with the same blue pickup it had tangled with earlier before finally coming to a stop.

Overcome with emotion, Ty tried to stand but his legs buckled. Tears streamed down his cheeks, and sobs wracked his body as he looked at the broken form in the middle of the road.

Sean gathered a group of men, and they approached the idling truck, now jammed against the railing. A gunshot from the back of the truck sent everyone diving for cover, but no one in the truck showed his face. Sean's team waited thirty seconds after the gunshot, then resumed their advance.

Ty watched as they skirted around the front of the vehicle and yanked open the driver's door, ready to unload a volley of bullets, but the driver was already dead. With the others providing cover, one of the men climbed into the cab and turned the engine off, then they waited, listening for sounds of life from the back.

While Sean's team waited, several of the better shooters at the barricades trained their rifles on the far side of the river, scanning the area for any additional threats. The remaining members of the militia tended to the wounded while trying to deal with the emotional repercussions of the short-lived battle.

Ty heard shots and turned back to the truck in time to see one of their men standing on the roof of the cab, firing shots into the bed of the vehicle, and then it was quiet. Fifteen minutes after the first shots were fired it was all over.

CHAPTER FORTY-ONE

Friday, February 17th
Moyie Springs, ID

Kyle knelt in front of the grave marker once again, trying to reconcile his emotions and guilt at not having been there in their time of need, weighed against the awareness that, under the circumstances, it was a miracle he'd made it at all. The lightly falling rain mirrored his mood, with hardly enough moisture to justify an umbrella but threatening, with dark, rolling clouds filling the valley, to turn the drizzle into something more torrential at any minute.

"We should probably head back, Kyle."

Kyle turned towards his father and nodded. "You're right. No sense in getting any wetter than we need to." He stood and put his arm across his dad's shoulders as they left the cemetery. "It's still a shock to me that she's gone. I always thought she'd live forever. Last time we talked everything was good. I never imagined it would actually be the last time I spoke to her."

Five days previous, Kyle had walked up to the front door of his parents' house, unsure of what to expect. He had imagined every possible scenario while traveling. One second he feared they'd both be dead, then the next he'd convince himself that they were doing fine, then that they'd be at death's doorstep, and he had arrived just in time to save them. Worst of all, he feared he'd frighten them, and they would unleash a volley of bullets that would cut him down after having walked thousands of miles.

The walk through Moyie Springs with Sheriff Pratt, and the orderly situation he observed, had increased his hopes that all would be well, so it had been heartbreaking when his dad tearfully welcomed him home with the news that Kyle's mother had succumbed to a stroke just before Christmas. Her blood thinning medication, which she'd taken for years, had run out in early October, and shortly thereafter, she had suffered a series of strokes, the last one, three days before Christmas, proving fatal.

Since his mother's passing, his dad, Gene, had been struggling, and was in a deep depression when Kyle's knock sounded. The gun propped beside Gene's recliner was there for defensive purposes, he promised, but Kyle worried, based on his father's state of mind, that it might be put to another use some point in the not too distant future. Their reunion, however, had snapped Gene out of his melancholy, and each day Kyle had seen an improvement, to the point that he was close to again being the jovial grandpa Kyle's kids knew.

They were halfway home from the cemetery when his father broke the silence. "You can't imagine how much I miss your mother." His voice, full of emotion, was nearly drowned out by the sound of rain on their umbrella.

"I know. You two were inseparable. How many years were you married?"

"June would have been forty-one." He rubbed his eyes with the back of his hand. "Sorry to get all weepy on you, but I haven't had anyone to talk about it with."

"You're fine, Dad. I'm sorry I wasn't here for you sooner."

"That last month was the hardest. She couldn't do much of anything except lay in bed. I spent most of my time taking care of her, but she just got weaker and weaker." He paused, but Kyle just listened. "I knew she was going to die. I could get her to drink water, but she wouldn't chew anything. Even the doctor at the hospital told me it would just be a matter of time."

"Was she in pain?"

Gene shook his head. "Not that it seemed, but she couldn't communicate, so I don't know. I hope not. I tried to keep her comfortable. That's when we moved out to one of the rental cabins. It was smaller and had the wood stove. There wasn't so much to take care of or keep warm. I could just focus on her. I'd comb her hair and rub her arms and her legs. She didn't talk, but I could see in her eyes that she knew what I was doing. That was something I guess." He laughed. "I tried to paint her fingernails for her once, but I wasn't very good at it. Just made a mess of her hands."

Kyle smiled as he wrestled with his own emotions. "I bet that made her happy. We all knew how much she loved you. I wanted a marriage like yours when I married Jennifer. We're not there yet, but we're trying."

"Don't sell yourself short, Son. I never walked home from Texas for your mother."

"But you would have if you needed to. You know it, and don't say otherwise."

Gene smiled and shrugged his shoulders. "You're right. I suppose I would have walked as far as I needed to for her. Florida to Alaska, if that's what it took, though I'm glad I didn't have to. My hips would have made it tough."

"Are they still bothering you?"

He nodded. "They are, but I think a replacement is out of the question now. The best our doctors can do is sew a few stitches or give recommendations on how to stay healthy. I hear they've done a couple minor surgeries, but it's only the essential stuff —removing bullets, or delivering babies, that kind of thing. At this point I expect I'll die with the hips I was born with. Guess that's the way God designed it."

The Bed and Breakfast was in sight, and they could see smoke billowing from the cabin's chimney. Gene motioned to the cabin. "You haven't said what you plan to do with the boy."

"I don't know what to do," Kyle said, shaking his head. "He doesn't talk, I don't know where he's from, and I killed the only family that I know he had. I've been trying to think of something, but I'm at a loss."

Gene put his hand on Kyle's arm. "If we can't figure anything out, let him stay with me. I spent a lot of years with kids, and I think it would be better for me than being alone, since I'm pretty sure you're going to head back to your family at some point."

"Are you sure?"

"I am," he said decisively. "I've thought about it for the last couple of days. I need to have someone around, and he can't take care of himself. Plus, I think he's on the verge of opening up. I can see it in his eyes when I talk to him. There's a spark there that's gently flickering back to life. He even smiled at me this morning. If we get something better figured out for him, that's fine. But if not, I'll take him."

"That would be good for him to have someone that cares. I don't think he was in the best environment where I found him."

They reached the cabin and pushed the door open. Collin was reading in a chair by the window and looked up when they came in.

"We've got lunch, Collin," Kyle said, holding up a slab of venison he had purchased at the market. "You like deer meat?"

The boy shook his head vigorously. "No," he said, defiantly putting the book down on his lap.

Gene looked at Kyle and whispered, "He speaks."

Kyle turned back to Collin. "I'm really sorry, but it's what we have. What do you like?"

"Pizza."

Kyle stopped in his tracks. Gene's eyes opened wide. They had tried to get Collin to talk for the five days since arriving in Moyie, but they had never gotten more than a grunt out of him when he was awake. During the night he would talk in his sleep, but that was it.

"I think I can get some flour at the market tomorrow and try to make a pizza," Gene said. "Is there anything else you like?"

The boy looked up at the two men, the wheels in his head turning. "Hamburgers," he said hopefully. "And spaghetti."

"Oh, those are delicious, aren't they?" Gene crossed the room and sat in a chair facing Collin, eager to engage the child. "I like broccoli and carrots. Do you?"

Collin shook his head. "No, they're gross, but I like corn, and Corn Flakes."

Gene peppered the boy with questions about food, discovering his preferences on anything a person could eat—Chinese, Italian, Mexican, candy, snacks, fruit, and on and on. They talked about food for thirty minutes, with Kyle listening while he stewed the venison in a pot on the woodstove.

Kyle indicated to his father that the food was ready. Gene stood and smiled at the boy. "Lunch is ready," he said, "but I wonder if I can ask a favor?"

Collin nodded cautiously.

Gene bit his lower lip. "My wife died a few weeks ago, and it's been really hard for me. I miss her a lot, you know. Anyway, she would always give me these big, long hugs. I wondered if you would do me a favor and give me a hug, to help me not miss her as much."

Kyle held his breath, watching, waiting to see how Collin would respond.

Collin looked nervously around the room, then up at Gene, and nodded. He stood and moved to Gene with his arms out wide.

Gene knelt in front of the boy and embraced him, tears streaming down his cheeks. "Oh, thank you, Collin. This makes me feel a lot better. It's really hard when you lose someone you love, isn't it?"

Kyle's eyes blurred as the boy's head bobbed vigorously up and down against Gene's shoulder. They held their embrace, arms wrapped tightly around each other, both crying, until Kyle finally broke the silence. "The food's going to get cold, guys," he croaked out. "Let's eat."

CHAPTER FORTY-TWO

Monday, February 20th
Deer Creek, MT

J ennifer escorted her brood through the front door of the house and instructed them to go downstairs and change out of their good clothes, then read or play quietly so she could take a nap on the upstairs couch, hoping to get rid of a headache that had been tormenting her for two days. Their family had just returned home from the funeral service for the men killed on Thursday, while Carol and Grace had gone on together after the service to help tend to the injured men, each recuperating in their own homes and attended to by their families. Six had been wounded, three seriously, but Carol was only really worried about one of them, a woman who had taken a bullet in the stomach.

Four Deer Creek men had been buried. All were given hero's farewells for their willingness to protect the community, no matter the cost, and Jennifer was emotionally and physically drained. She couldn't remember a more difficult period in her life than the previous three and a half weeks. She had thought the first weeks after the EMP were tough, and they were, but now they seemed comparatively easy.

Kyle's arrest, near execution, then banishment, the death of Madison's mother, caring for the baby under tough conditions, the assault on the community, and the possibility of losing her son as the gunfight raged within earshot – after all that, the funeral was almost a break. But even then, to see the grief of families who had lost husbands and fathers just added even more to her own emotional toll, and she felt like she was reaching her limit.

Thursday's battle had been a complete nightmare. She'd waited inside during the confrontation, trying to focus on the baby, who still didn't love goat milk but would eventually finish her bottles. Jennifer had tried the milk and didn't love it either, but the Shipleys had assured her that it was fine, if not delicious, so she forced the milk, the baby's best hope to stay alive, on Madison. When the shooting had started, it terrified her, knowing that not only was David in immediate danger, but the community as a whole was on the brink as well.

As the shooting had built to a crescendo, with hundreds if not thousands of shots fired, she was sure that there wouldn't be any survivors, and thinking of David injured, bleeding, and alone, ripped her heart out. Sending your son off to war was one thing. Sending him to war and listening to him die was something altogether different. The fighting seemed to go on forever, and Carol, Grace, and Jennifer, along with the children, had knelt in a circle and prayed until the guns went silent.

As soon as the shooting was over, the women had rushed to the bridge, searching frantically for the injured and, more specifically for Jennifer, David. No one had known where he was when she got there, the regular militia units having been split up. She had headed across the bridge, having just passed Luther's twisted body and fearing the worst, when Ty had called her over to where he sat with his wife, nervous tremors still wracking his body.

He'd just explained that David had been sent to Clinton for reinforcements when gunfire erupted out on the highway towards the east. Sean had quickly dispatched a squad to investigate, of which Jennifer insisted on being a part, and they hurried down the highway to find David and some men from Clinton carrying

DAUNTING DAYS OF WINTER

the bodies of two men in fatigues who had fled. Jennifer was so overcome with emotion when she saw David that she had to be helped back to town.

The rest of the day was spent recovering from the assault. Deer Creek had lost four men: Luther at the bridge, Anderson West at the east berm, and two men in the militia house, cut down by the machine gun when the walls of the house had proved to be inadequate protection against the heavy weapon.

None of the group that had attacked the town appeared to survive. A total of twenty-two bodies, all of them men ranging in ages from early twenties to late forties, had been buried in a mass grave on the north side of the river. Sean had reported at Friday's militia meeting that more than two dozen weapons, forty-one thousand rounds of ammunition, a moderate amount of food, silver, gold, fuel, and an assortment of crowbars, sledge hammers and other tools had been recovered. There were no plates on the bus or dump truck, but a registration document in the bus indicated an Oregon origin.

None of the men had identification, at least beyond a variety of tattoos and scars, and Jennifer's heart broke a little for the mothers and wives who would never know what happened to their loved ones, even though she was glad the men were dead.

She had just drifted off to sleep when a knock sounded at the front door. Jennifer sat up and looked out the window, rubbing her eyes. A man and a woman stood on the porch, with a pair of horses out by the street. She got up from the couch and opened the door as Emma came upstairs with Madison, who had just woken.

The man turned as she opened the door, and she recognized him from the community. "Hi, Tom. Can I help you?"

He smiled. "Hi Jennifer. This lady here, Rose, is looking for your husband. I told her he was gone, but she wanted to talk to you."

Jennifer looked closely at the woman, but didn't recognize her. "Hi," she said. "You're looking for Kyle?"

The woman smiled and nodded. Her face was weathered, but pretty, her teeth white and straight. She was tall and thin, with sandy blonde hair that spilled out from under a water-stained cowboy hat. "Yes. He's a friend. I needed some help, so I came here."

It was chilly out, and Jennifer could see that the woman was tired and cold, so she invited her in, then went to the kitchen and filled a cup with warm water. After sending Emma downstairs with the baby, she handed the cup to Rose, who had perched on the edge of the couch. "Here. We don't have coffee or tea, but the water is safe and warm. Tom said your name was Rose?"

"Yes. Rose Duncan. You're Jennifer, right?"

"I am. I'm sorry, I don't recognize you at all. Should I know you?"

The woman shook her head. "No, we've never met, but I know a lot about you, though Kyle didn't tell me you were expecting. I only knew about your older children."

"The baby's not mine," Jennifer explained. "Her mother died, and I guess I've kind of adopted her. How do you know us so well?" She looked at Rose warily, not comfortable with her level of familiarity.

"I can't believe he didn't tell you about me. I helped him in Wyoming when we had a big snowstorm back in October. He stayed with me for several days, before the roads cleared and he got back on his way. You don't know how glad I am to find out that he made it safely. I've worried about him for the past four months."

Jennifer's mind raced back over the details Kyle had told her about his journey home. She thought she knew about most things, but Rose Duncan's name was unfamiliar.

"Maybe he didn't tell you about me. I'm sure there were a thousand other things that happened along the way. It's nice to meet the woman a man would walk two thousand miles for. You're just like Kyle described."

Jennifer let out a puff of air. "I'm so sorry. I feel like I've let you down. Do you have family in the area? You've come an awful long way. There must something else that brought you this direction."

Rose shook her head. "No. Just Kyle."

Jennifer's mind was racing, trying to recall what Kyle had said about the storm. She thought back to the meeting where Kyle had spoken to the community and remembered someone asking about it. If she remembered correctly, Kyle had said that he'd been saved by an older woman, but…

"He showed up in my yard in the middle of that terrible blizzard. Would have frozen to death if my dog hadn't alerted me…"

This woman wasn't older, maybe a few years, but not what you think of when you say older. Why hadn't Kyle said anything about Rose?

"He stayed for four days, so we really got to know each other. He told me all about your family. Then when my homestead was attacked and my dog killed, well, it sounds strange, but Kyle was the only person I could think of to go to, after what I had done for him and all the time we'd spent together. I know it sounds silly, but here I am."

Jennifer felt herself go cold inside, like someone had pulled a plug in her heel and let all of the life in her just drain out. "So, you're saying you spent four days with my husband, then decided to follow him halfway across the country?"

Rose nodded. "I guess so. It sounds kind of creepy when you say it that way, but I guess that's what it boils down to."

"Can you excuse me for a minute?"

Rose nodded, smiling politely. "Do you have a bathroom I can use? After so long on the road, it would be nice to use an actual bathroom again."

Jennifer indicated down the hallway. "There's a bucket of water in the bathtub; use that to flush."

She hurried downstairs to where her kids were playing a game of Risk. "Emma, I'm going out for a minute; take care of the baby. David, you help her."

"You okay, mom?" David asked as he rolled the dice. "You don't look very good."

"I'm fine." Jennifer went back upstairs, grabbed her coat off of the arm of the couch, and let herself out. She walked, trance-like, down the street, her mind churning over her conversation with Rose. Why would a woman, she wondered, follow a man five hundred miles across two states, on horseback, under such trying circumstances? The question repeated itself over and over in her mind, and none of the answers she came up with were good.

She thought back to when she was a young girl, and her mother had learned about her father's indiscretions and the things he did while he was on the road. At the time, she couldn't understand why it was so devastating for her mom, why she cried alone in her bedroom at night, even weeks after the revelation.

At that age, when boys weren't that important, she had just thought it was because her mother was too fragile to handle rejection or disappointment, and that her mother was too dependent on her father. But after she married Kyle, Jennifer knew what it meant to give yourself to someone else. It was more than just sharing a last name and an address. It was letting them into your heart. It was putting all your weaknesses and vulnerabilities on the table and trusting them to still love you. Marriage was not being able to see a future without your partner in it, knowing that someone loved you, in spite of your silly mess-ups or odd little personality quirks. It was being the only one that belonged in that particular place in their heart, forever, no matter what happened.

It wasn't finding out that you were just there for when they needed something, at their convenience, to be used interchangeably with whoever else might come along. She had never fully understood what her mother had experienced, until now. The wound was bitter, and painful, and devastating.

Jennifer walked numbly along the top of riverbank, picking her way past the boulders that dotted the bank. The water was low this time of year, but it was cold and still deep enough to be dangerous. She wanted to cry, but no tears came. The day had left her feeling so hollow she wasn't surprised there was nothing left.

She looked out across the water, swift, cold, and deadly, and she crawled down to the edge, dropping her head into her hands. "You've done it, God. I've wondered for the past five months where my breaking point would be. Thought maybe I was tough enough to deal with whatever you threw at me, but I was wrong. I've endured separation, indescribable fear, evil, more death than I ever hoped to see, losing my husband twice, nearly losing a son, and now you have to rip my heart out too?"

A sob escaped her lips, and she shuddered, losing her grip on the rock and sliding down to the ice at the water's edge, her legs splashing in up to her knees. The water was icy cold, causing her to jerk involuntarily, but she left her legs in, the temperature rapidly making them more and more numb. "Do you even care about me? Do you even know I'm alive, or did you just wind up this world and step back to watch it all fall apart?"

The river was rocky near the shore, then the bottom fell away to a deeper section where David liked to come and fish, though he never caught many to speak of. She estimated the water to be at least five feet deep, maybe six, not necessarily deep enough to be deadly, but fully dressed and with the cold temperatures, it could be dangerous. She didn't have her gun, it was still on the floor beside the couch, but at least this way, her death could look like an accident.

Ten, fifteen minutes tops, she thought, and she would have no more worries, no more disappointments, no more struggles, no more anything. It could all be over. How nice it would be to not go to bed with your stomach hurting from hunger, or have to worry about what tomorrow might bring. If there was a heaven, maybe she would still make it. God embodied love, and surely He would understand what she'd been through. If hell was where she ended up, how could that be any worse than this. In fact, maybe it would be better, since she wouldn't be cold or hungry. And, if there was nothing at all, well then there would be no struggles, no heartbreak, none of the crap that life seemed so happy to jam down your throat every day.

She stood up and reached out to swirl her hand in the water. It gave her goose bumps up and down her arms and across her back. She looked out to the deeper water, wondering how cold it would feel and how long it would hurt and if drowning or hypothermia would take her first. She took a step forward. The water was deeper and came up to her thigh. She gasped as the cold gripped her legs and the current tugged at her. She paused and looked around, knowing someone from the militia might come by and see her at any moment. She began to cry, wanting so much for all the pain to go away, but scared to take another step forward.

Jennifer heard laughter off in the distance that reminded her of Spencer, her pure, loving, little ray of sunshine whose enthusiastic hugs at bedtime melted all the troubles of the world away. Then she thought of Emma, and how much Emma mimicked her mother in wanting to be grown up and in charge, but how much she still craved her mother's love and approval. David flashed before her, with his broad shoulders, his courage, and the emotional rock he had been for her through so many challenges. How can I do this to them? She shook her head, trying to clear it, to think straight. What am I doing, she asked herself.

"I'm not done yet," she gasped, her jaw tight from the cold. She moved back towards the bank, her legs numb and unsteady.

She stepped in a hole in the rocks, sinking up to her waist in the water. Shrieking from the cold, she grabbed at the ice ledge lining the side of the river to steady herself, but her fingers slipped off, causing her to lose her balance. The current nudged her, and she teetered back and forth as she fought to regain some stability. As she felt her foot slipping deeper into the water, she lunged forward and grabbed ahold of a large, exposed root on the bank of the river, clasping it tightly with both hands.

The root was thick, dry, and secure, and she clung to it while she caught her breath and regained her footing, then slowly pulled herself out of the water, her legs weakly pushing her body forward. Slowly climbing up the bank, Jennifer flopped over the top edge with a gasp of relief. She rolled onto her back and closed her eyes, letting out a breath and shaking her head slowly from side to side. In the distance she heard a horse approaching at a gallop, its hooves beating hard on the dirt path. Jennifer sat up to get out of the way, shielding the sun from her eyes to see who was approaching.

"Jennifer!"

Still numb and out of breath, she watched the horse come to a stop. Rose dismounted and rushed towards her. Jennifer wondered briefly if Rose had a gun and had come to eliminate the competition permanently.

"Jennifer, are you okay?"

Jennifer nodded, avoiding eye contact. "I'll be fine. You don't need to worry about me. Kyle isn't here, you know. The community…"

"Jennifer, stop, please. You weren't there when I came out of the bathroom, so I waited for you. When you didn't come back, I began to think and realized what this must seem like. I was so tired from traveling and too excited to have made it that I didn't explain things the way I should have. And, I forgot to tell you the most important thing."

"Are you pregnant?"

Rose laughed. "No, I'm not pregnant. I haven't had sex in almost a year, though heaven knows I tried with your husband. I'm embarrassed by what I did, but Kyle loves you. You need to know that. He refused to cheat on you even though I gave him the opportunity. That's why I came here, because he's one person I know I can trust. I just knew he was a decent man and thought he might help me."

"You had nowhere else to go?"

Rose shook her head. "It's pitiful, but true. My kids are too far away, my parents are dead, and my husband is gone, plus it was over with him anyway. I needed somewhere to go where I could be safe, or at least where I could trust the people around me."

"So you're saying you came here because Kyle wouldn't sleep with you?" Jennifer blinked, fighting back tears that were a little freer in coming than they had been earlier.

Rose wavered a little. "I guess so, though that sounds bizarre. I came here because I wanted to be somewhere I felt safe. With what I knew of Kyle and what he told me of the community, I thought I'd find that here. I'm so sorry. I should have explained that first thing."

Jennifer closed her eyes and took several deep breaths. "Thank you for clearing that up. I've been teetering near the edge emotionally for a while, and this nearly pushed me over. It feels good to be pulled a few feet back away from the brink."

Rose reached out and grabbed Jennifer's hands. "I truly am sorry. I wish there was something I could do for you."

A thought came to Jennifer and she looked at Rose. "Would you be a character witness for Kyle?"

"Of course. Whatever you need."

"Come with me."

They returned to the house, where Jennifer put on dry clothes. Then the two women hurried across town, with Jennifer explaining to Rose what had happened to Kyle. When they reached their destination, Jennifer knocked sharply on the door. A young boy of about twelve answered. "Is Sean here?" Jennifer asked.

The boy nodded and turned. "Uncle Sean," he called out. "There's someone here for you."

Jennifer waited for Sean to appear, bouncing with nervous energy. It was only a few seconds before she heard his voice.

"Hi, Jennifer. What brings you by?"

Jennifer smiled more fully than she had since the day Kyle had first arrived home. "Sean, I have someone here you have to talk to. Someone who will swear that Kyle would never do what he was convicted of. I want you to meet Rose Duncan."

CHAPTER FORTY-THREE

Thursday, February 23ʳᵈ
Moyie Springs, ID

The wooden door was old, with its green paint faded and peeling in long, thin strips. It rattled on its hinges and seemed like it might fall into the house when Kyle knocked on it. He took a step back, cleared his throat, waited, and listened. Thanks to bad directions, a slow horse, and the remote location, it had taken him three days to find this house, which could have been longer if not for Garfield's patient service. The resilience of his loyal steed, even though Garfield had seen better days, was a blessing.

Kyle couldn't hear anything from inside the house, so he stepped forward and knocked firmly on the door again. Having spent so much energy locating it, he refused to give up and go away.

The last few days in Moyie Springs had been most interesting. Collin had finally begun talking and, once Gene had gained the boy's trust, had opened up about everything.

Collin's story had come out in drips and drabs over the course of a few days, to a point where Kyle and Gene had been able to put together enough pieces to make sense of it. Though there were still lots of holes to be filled in, they had learned, firstly, that Collin was from Seattle, where he had lived with his mother.

Collin related how the lights in their apartment building went out one day and never come on again. They stayed in their apartment for a week, never going outside, just living on what little food they had, until the stench from the toilets forced them out, at which point they walked across the city to where his sister, Stacy, lived.

While staying with his sister, increasing local violence forced the three of them to abandon her duplex and travel out of the city and seek out Christopher, an old boyfriend of Stacy's. After they had been there for a while, Collin's mother disappeared and Christopher had become more violent towards Collin, hitting the boy if he asked for food or water, and forcing Stacy to protect him.

The three of them, Stacy, Collin, and Christopher, eventually moved further out of town, to where Andre, a friend of Christopher, lived. There they had hunted and fished and eaten things they could scavenge. At some point, Andre had acquired a working vehicle, and they had driven further away from the city, ending up at the cabin where Kyle had found them, surviving on deer meat, tree bark, and food taken from strangers. Collin recalled that Stacy hated how mean Christopher had become, and that she had spent more and more time with Andre, who seemed to like her a lot.

Collin didn't know how long they had been at the cabin when Kyle found him. He had just said they were there a long time, that they were hungry a lot, and that Andre and Chris fought about him and Stacy, and sometimes Christopher would hit them both, at least until Kyle had shown up.

What the complete story was, Kyle didn't know, but he was glad Collin was out of the situation. The last few days, Collin had spent a lot of time with Gene, even calling him grandpa, and smiling and laughing. Today they were going fishing and pheasant hunting, building a relationship that Kyle recognized was good for both of them.

There was still no answer at the green door. Kyle had stepped forward to knock on it one more time when it was thrown open with a slam. A man stood beyond the door, a shotgun leveled at Kyle. "What do you want?" the man demanded.

Kyle pulled his hands back, raising them helplessly over his head. "I'm sorry to bother you. I'm looking for Roman Bakowski. I was told he lived here."

"I'm Roman Bakowski. What do you want?" The man had an accent like a Russian gangster's from the movies, a low, guttural growl of a voice that was heavy on the letter w and rolled around in his mouth like he was chewing marbles.

"My name is Kyle Tait. I was told that you have a HAM radio, unless there is another Roman Bakowski around."

"I the only Roman Bakowski in the area. Who told you I do the HAM radio?" He still held the shotgun leveled at Kyle, but his demeanor eased up a little, and the scowl on his face was softening.

"My friend, Frank, said there were people in the area with radios. The sheriff told me about you and where you lived, but it was hard to find. Frank does HAM radios. Said I should look someone up so I could talk to him."

"I don't know a Frank. I talk to lot of people on my radio. Why would he tell you come here?"

Kyle gave an edited version of how he'd come to the area and explained that Frank was the closest one to his family who could communicate out of the area.

"So why I should help you? What have you done for me?"

"I have silver," Kyle said, holding out a silver quarter.

Roman looked at it and scoffed. "Why do I need silver? You have gold?"

Kyle felt his wedding ring on his finger, spinning it around a couple of times. "Just my wedding ring, but I…"

Roman cut him off. "You married?"

Kyle nodded.

"Keep ring. Your wife kill you if you give it to me. I take the silver."

Kyle handed him the coin, an old 1962 quarter.

Roman held it out in front of him in the light, squinting. "You giving me twenty-five cents?"

"But it's silver, an old one; it's worth more."

"I know it's silver, but it still say twenty-five cent. This all you have?"

Kyle stuck his hand in his pocket, fished out another one, and handed it to Roman. "Here. Can you help me?"

Roman sighed. He'd lowered his gun and now looked at Kyle more closely, his bushy, silver-flecked eyebrows dancing on his forehead as he tried to focus. "I need my glasses. Pretty blind without them. Was sleeping when you got here. You lucky I'm not so cranky."

"Sorry I woke you."

Roman shrugged and led Kyle into the house, groped around on the kitchen table until he found his glasses, then led Kyle out the back door to an old barn behind the house. "You like rats?" he asked as he forced the barn door open.

"Not especially."

"Then we are good, because I only have mice here." He let out a hearty laugh and propped the door open. "Come. Sit down here," he said, pointing to a bale of hay positioned in front of an old desk. "I go start generator. What is friend's address, where he talks?"

Kyle handed Roman a piece of paper with a series of numbers that Frank had written down for him, and Roman studied it as he walked to another door that led out the back of the barn.

Roman was gone a few minutes, then Kyle heard the roar of a generator. A small fluorescent light flickered on above him, and Roman returned.

"I don't think I know this Frank person. What you want to tell him?"

"I need to see if he's had any contact with my family or town and make sure everything is okay. I've been gone for almost a month now."

"That's it? You just want to say 'how's it going?'"

"Well, I don't have a script. I just want to see how things are for my family and my friends there."

"Okay. If that what you want, we get to work." Roman's fingers flew expertly across the keypads and dials on the old radio. After thirty seconds of adjusting, he grabbed the mic and keyed it. "This Big Polack looking for Silver Fox, Frank Emory. Over."

"How do you know his name is Silver Fox?"

Roman shrugged. "I call all Americans on the radio Silver Fox. It's good American name. You have problem with that?"

"No. Just thought maybe you actually knew Frank or something."

Roman chuckled, wiped something from his eye, then continued to adjust the dials. "Shhh. This hard work."

Kyle waited patiently as Roman worked for another fifteen minutes, adjusting dials and talking into the microphone, but there was no success.

Roman finally got up without saying a word, walked outside, and shut off the generator. He returned with a grim look. "How far away is this Frank guy?"

"Maybe three hundred miles, a little less probably."

Roman slapped his forehead. "I need to adjust antenna. This set up for Poland, for longer distance. You come back in week. I adjust antenna and keep trying your friend, Frank. Write down what I should tell him."

Kyle took a pen from his pocket and wrote a short note with a number of questions in large, clear letters. When he was done he handed it over.

Roman took the note and read it over, mumbling to himself as he did so. "Alright, got it. You school teacher?"

Kyle shook his head. "No, why?"

"You write very big." He shrugged. "Come back in seven days, alright?"

Kyle nodded. "I'll be back in seven days."

Roman grabbed Kyle by the shoulder and spun him back around as he was about to leave. He smiled widely. "Good deal for fifty cents, no?"

Kyle returned the smile. "Good deal for fifty cents."

CHAPTER FORTY-FOUR

Saturday, February 25ᵗʰ
Deer Creek, MT

"**A**re you sure about this?" Ty asked, with daylight fading as he peered from the cover of a fir tree at a neighboring house.

Sean nodded. "I've been watching him all week, as much as I can, plus I've stopped by twice, but he won't talk to me. There's definitely something that's not right."

"Are the three of us going to be enough?"

Sean shrugged. "There's just one of him, so I hope so. I've never seen him with a gun, and we're armed, so it should be pretty simple." He paused and waited. "I can see him through the window. He just went into the back. Let's move while we still have light." Sean motioned with his hand, then he, Ty and Craig emerged and hurried in the direction of their target.

Ty ran to the side of the house, and Sean and Craig approached the front. Craig concealed himself to the side of the door while Sean banged on the door with his fist. "Dale, I need to talk to you. Open up, please!" There was no response, so he pounded on the door again.

"You sure he's home?" Craig whispered.

"I saw him through the window. I'm sure of it." Sean reached out and tried the door, but it was locked. "I'm going to check around back. You wait here," he muttered, and had just taken a couple of steps away from the door when there was an explosion of sound behind him, and a hole was blown through the top of the door.

"Shotgun!" Craig yelled, diving from the porch for cover. "You okay?" he asked as he rolled up against the front of the house. "I thought you said he didn't have a gun."

Sean had fallen to the ground and rolled to the side. He felt the back of his head. "I'm fine. He missed me. You?"

"My ears are ringing, but that's it. Now what?"

"Get off my property, Sean!" Dale's voice carried through the hole in the front door. The sound of a shotgun being pumped followed it. "If I see you near me again, I'll blow your head off!"

"This makes it a little more complicated, but confirms my suspicions," Sean whispered to Craig as he quickly crawled toward the front of the house, situating himself beside Craig under the living room window. He found a large rock, hefted it in his hand for a few seconds, then tossed it through the window above him. Glass shattered and crashed to the ground. "Dale, you're just making this worse!" Sean cried out. "Come out and let's talk. I don't want anyone to get hurt."

The shotgun blasted again, and what little glass remained in the window exploded outwards. "I've got nothing to talk about. Just get away from me, understand? You're a make-believe-cop, and I don't recognize your authority."

"Keep talking to him," Sean said to Craig. "I'm going around back. If he doesn't come out in a couple of minutes, fire four shots, five seconds apart. I'll try and get the door open with the sledge hammer while you do that."

"What am I supposed to say?"

Sean shrugged. "Make something up. Just keep him by the front door." He patted Craig on the shoulder and scrambled towards the back of the house. He could hear Craig yelling at Dale to drop his weapon as he reached Ty at the side of the house.

"You said he didn't have a gun," Ty said as Sean passed.

"I didn't know, alright. The kid surprised me. Come with me to the back."

"Am I going to get shot?" Ty asked. "I told my wife this was just routine business. She'll kill me if I get hurt."

Sean laughed. "You can stay back. I just need your eyes."

The two men hurried to the back of the house and quickly climbed the stairs to the back door. Ty held his pistol in one hand, and a sledgehammer in the other. Sean's shotgun was at his side as he reached out for the doorknob, grabbed the cold metal, and twisted. Finding no resistance, he turned the knob the rest of the way and carefully pushed the door open. "Wait here," he whispered to Ty, then crept into the house. The back entryway was covered in mud and smelled of rotting meat. As he crept into the kitchen, he saw a skinned rabbit spread over the kitchen table and a bucket on the floor filled with feathers and fur.

Sean spun around as Dale's voiced boomed from the next room. "If you don't leave, I'll shoot you. I promise!"

Dale's threat was followed by Craig's voice, sounding distorted and strained. "I don't want a shoot out. Put your gun down, and we can work this out."

Sean let out a deep breath and reached for the table to steady himself, knocking a knife perched on the edge of the table to the floor in the process, where it bounced with a metallic clang. Sean paused, listened, aimed his gun at the door that led from the kitchen, and waited.

"Just come outside, Dale. This is the last time I'm asking!!" Craig's voice sounded through the house.

There was no movement, so Sean moved towards the door and slowly pulled it open, exposing a cluttered dining area beyond which he could see the front door with a hole blown through it.

The living room was past where he could see. He pulled the door wider and was about to move forward when he felt cold metal pressed against the side of his face.

"You ever hear of the Castle Doctrine?" Dale asked in a whisper.

Sean closed his eyes, swallowed, and nodded.

"Then you know it means I can shoot someone who comes in my house, and not be charged with anything."

"Please don't, Dale. I have a son."

"I don't care."

"What's it going to be?" Craig's voice carried through the broken window at the front of the house.

"Is that your brother out there?"

Sean nodded.

"I'm going to kill him next, you know." He pressed his rifle harder against Sean's cheek. "I see your gun moving. Drop it right now."

Sean dropped his weapon to the ground. "Please, Dale. Don't make things worse."

"Worse? How could things get any worse? The country's screwed, my mother's dying, and you want to arrest me. Don't you?"

"I wanted to talk to you, and your mother."

"I'm not stupid. Get on your knees and beg. You only have a few seconds left to live, and I want you to die like a coward."

Sean slowly knelt and clasped his shaking hands in front of himself. "Please, Dale, don't do this. I beg you."

Dale smirked as he raised his weapon. "You can go to hell and wait there for your brother. He'll be joining you soon."

There was a gunshot and a flash, and the small kitchen was filled with an ear-shattering roar of sound.

***

Emma's eyes opened wide as Grace carefully brought the cake up the basement stairs. The words "Happy Birthday Emma" were written in blue, contrasting sharply with the white icing that covered the cake.

"Mom," Emma gasped. "Is it real?"

Jennifer nodded. "It's beautiful, isn't it?"

Emma's eyes glowed, her head swiveling slowly to follow Grace as she carried the cake around the table. "I can't believe we have a real cake, Mom."

Grace grinned. "Believe it, Emma. Made from scratch like they did it when I was a little girl, so it might taste a little different than you're used to."

"Is that real frosting, too?"

Grace set the cake down in front of Emma. "I didn't have powdered sugar, but I did the best I could. Should still taste pretty good."

Spencer reached out, jabbed a finger in the icing, and snatched it back before Emma could stop him, then plunged it quickly in his mouth. As he swallowed, his expression was one of near ecstasy. "It's good!" he declared.

Emma cast him an angry glare, but refrained from saying anything. "There aren't any candles to blow out, so can we just cut it now?"

Grace grabbed a knife and began cutting the cake. "I had to cook it in the Dutch oven, which is why it's round," she said as she sliced it into pie-shaped pieces. "But it baked up just as well as in a regular oven. I've gotten pretty good with these old Dutch ones. Here." She placed a piece of cake on a plate and set it in front of Emma. "You have the first bite, and tell us how it is."

Everyone watched as Emma quickly cut off a bite with the edge of her fork and scooped it into her mouth. She chewed slowly, closing her eyes as she did so. "It's sooo good," she said, tilting her head to the side. "I forgot what cake tasted like."

"I want some," Spencer said, anxious to get in on the celebration. "The big piece." He pointed to a slice of cake that was a shade bigger than the others.

"That's for David," Emma said. "He's bigger, and he works harder than you do." She slowly put another piece of cake in her mouth and gently bit down on it. "I'm going to make this last all night," she announced. "It's delicious."

Jennifer took a bite and groaned. "I think we're all going to be sick tomorrow. Our systems will be in shock."

The group savored the cake, speaking little, just slowly, deliberately, taking one precious bite after another. When the cake was gone, it was time for presents, and Emma eagerly received each gift with a hug and a smile. The presents were simple and unwrapped, though Jennifer had found a few recycled gift bags that had been put to use. Emma's gifts included a pretty, pink, oval-shaped rock that Spencer found and polished, a figurine that Jennifer had recovered from their old house, and a "get out of chores" coupon from David. Her friend, Britney, gave her two books, and Carol presented a bracelet with charms from Mexico, Italy, and several other countries she'd visited, while Grace gave Emma a hand-stitched quilt.

"You don't have to give that up, you know," Jennifer said when Grace brought the quilt out for Emma. "That's supposed to be for your granddaughter."

Emma pressed the quilt against her chest, giving her mother a pleading look.

"I want to give it to Emma," Grace said. "I'll just make another one for Tabitha. It's not like I don't have lots of time."

Emma's squeal of delight was cut off by a knock at the door.

Carol answered the door, finding Sean and Gabe on the porch, and invited them in. "You missed all the cake," she said as they surveyed the scene, "but you can help us sing Happy Birthday again. It's Emma's birthday today."

"That's great," Gabe said. "I didn't know it was your birthday, young lady. How old are you?"

"I'm eleven," Emma answered in a sing-songy voice. "Look at my new quilt."

Sean let out a low whistle. "That's really nice. Who'd you get that from?"

Emma pointed across the room. "Grace gave it to me. She was making it for her granddaughter, but she decided I could have it."

"That was really nice of her," Gabe said. "How about we sing, then Sean and I need to talk to your mother. We have some good news."

Jennifer's ears perked up, and Sean gave her a reassuring smile.

The group sang a rousing rendition of "Happy Birthday", then Jennifer grabbed a jacket and went out on the front step with the men, her curiosity barely contained.

"What's up?"

Gabe looked at Sean and motioned for him to be the spokesperson. "We know Kyle isn't guilty of the rape, or the murder, or anything."

"That's it? It took you this long to realize that? I've known that since the day you took him into custody. Now he's who knows where, and you come tell me this?"

Gabe reached out for Jennifer's arm and squeezed it softly. "Jennifer. I'm sorry for what has happened to you. I really am. What you don't know is that we know who did it. We have a witness. Kyle can come home."

Jennifer placed a hand on her chest, taking a step back. "You're saying that he…" She struggled to find the right words.

Sean stepped forward. "We're saying that if he was in jail, we'd be unlocking his cell right now. We'll let the people in Clinton know in the morning, but he's absolutely, one hundred percent innocent. He didn't do anything wrong."

"How'd this happen?"

Sean sighed, pursing his lips. "It's a long story."

Jennifer looked closely at him. "Is that blood on your neck?"

Sean rubbed his neck and nodded. "I thought I'd cleaned it off, but it's not mine. Our friend Ty Lewis saved my life, like he did you and Kyle on the mountain."

Jennifer's hands began to shake. "What happened?"

"That's not important right now. We're here about Kyle." Sean paused to gather his thoughts. "That whole thing never sat right with me, you know. Kyle just didn't seem like the kind of person to do what he was accused of, but everything, and I mean everything, pointed to him. After Rose vouched for his character, I went back over to Dale's to talk to him again. He was the last one to see the girl alive, but he wouldn't hardly talk to me, just kept to the same story, and wouldn't let me talk to his mother, Lois, either. Got real nervous when I asked to see her."

"Lois hasn't been around at all lately. I'm not sure if you knew that," Gabe said. "We all thought she was sick."

Jennifer shook her head. "I didn't know. When this all happened to Kyle, I quit working at the school, and that was the only place I ever saw her."

Sean nodded. "When I went back home, my sister-in-law told me Lois had only been to school one day since the murder. After that, Dale would come by every few days and make an excuse for her, which made me suspicious."

"Dale did it, didn't he?" Jennifer's lips were trembling.

Sean nodded. "Yeah, it was him. I went back over to Dale's house with Craig and Ty. When Dale wouldn't open the door, we took matters into our own hands. We probably violated the Constitution, but we found his mother. She was locked up in a room in the basement. Dale was keeping her prisoner and slowly starving her to death, because she knew what had happened and was going to tell us."

"I thought she told you she'd seen the girl leave."

Sean nodded. "She did. I interviewed her myself, and she was pretty adamant about it. Assured me the girl was fine when she left. Turns out that Dale had threatened to kill her, and himself, and whoever else he could hurt if she told me anything. He assured her that no one would get blamed for it. Apparently he didn't know that the house he put her in was yours. He just knew it was empty. The rest was just a bad coincidence for Kyle. When Dale found out, with the bad blood between them, he just went along with it."

Jennifer shook her head. "I can't believe Kyle was almost executed, and that I almost died, because of this. When is Dale's trial going to start? I want to see him humiliated like Kyle was."

"There isn't going to be a trial, Jennifer."

Jennifer glared at Sean, the starlight sufficient for both men to read her thoughts. "You'll drag Kyle through the mud, but not him?" she shouted, unable to contain her rage. "I can't believe this. I hate this town."

Sean held up his hands. "Jennifer, stop," he interrupted. "Dale's dead. There can't be a trial. It's taken care of."

Jennifer paused, and she looked to Gabe, who nodded. She felt herself get dizzy and reached for the railing.

Gabe shifted nervously from foot to foot. "I'm so sorry, Jennifer. I feel responsible for this. We tried to do our best, we really did, but we obviously failed pretty tragically."

Jennifer rubbed the sides of her head in an effort to ward off a headache, then dropped onto the frozen steps. She sat in silence, with neither Sean nor Gabe knowing what to say. Finally Jennifer spoke. "It's okay, Gabe. I went a week or so trying to hate all of you, but I wasn't very good at it. Leah's dad's face kept coming back to me, and I think I would have been just as demanding as he was. I just hate the situation we're in, not being able to know."

She looked at Sean. "Why did he lock Lois up if she went along with him?"

"She said she came home from school and confronted him. Told him how someone else had been arrested. He panicked and hit her. When she woke up she was secured in her little prison. She said he was trying to make her death look natural, so we wouldn't figure it out. Thought if he could get rid of her, then he was safe as long as he didn't out and out kill her. Another week or so and he might have gotten away with it."

"Now," Gabe said. "The big problem we have is letting your husband know he can come home. Do you know where he went?"

"He went to his parents' place in Idaho. It's three hundred miles from here."

"How can we get word to him, any ideas?"

Jennifer shook her head. "He promised to come get us in April and take us up there if the situation is good. I don't know any way to get ahold of him sooner."

"I do."

The three adults swung around to see David standing in the snow by the corner of the house, a huge grin on his face.

"Dad told me where to find a guy with a radio."

CHAPTER FORTY-FIVE

Saturday, March 3rd
Moyie Springs, ID

"**C**ome in. Come in, my friend." Roman's grin lit up his face as he ushered Kyle into the front room of his modest home. "You are late, but congratulations are for you, you know."

"Did you get ahold of Frank?" Kyle sensed something in his new friend's mood and was hopeful that Roman had gotten news from Deer Creek that would be helpful.

"Yes, yes. I talk to Frank yesterday, finally. Have very nice conversation."

"What did he say?"

"Said that you can go home, and that you have new baby girl."

"He said I have what?"

"He said it is girl. Congratulations."

Kyle shook his head. "No, that can't be right. Was he talking about my daughter Emma? It was her birthday last week."

Roman frowned and tugged on his chin as he consulted his notebook. "No. Says new baby girl. You think it was going to be baby boy or something?"

Kyle sighed. "No, I think maybe you talked to the wrong person. My wife wasn't pregnant. I don't think you spoke to Frank, or at least not the right one. Can we try again?"

"You have more money?"

"I didn't bring any with me. I didn't think I'd need it."

Roman looked at Kyle, perplexed. "I not have much gas, you know. Took long time to get Frank. I pretty sure he the right one. You know David?"

Kyle nodded. "He's my son."

Roman smiled triumphantly. "See. I got right guy then. Frank say that David come talk to him few days before. Said you are free man." Roman paused and looked at Kyle sternly. "You killer or something?"

"No. I promise you that I'm not. Just in the wrong place at the wrong time. Is my family safe?"

"Frank say they all safe. But he did say new baby girl. You sure your wife not pregnant?"

"I'm positive. What else did he say?"

Roman went over the short list of questions and smiled at Kyle when he was done. "Not bad for simple Polack, no?"

Kyle smiled, his head swimming with the news. "You did wonderful, Roman. I can't thank you enough."

"That silver buy me good food, so I am good. Congratulations on everything, that you can go home, and baby girl. I loved my baby girl."

Kyle shook his head and grinned. "I think you've somehow got that message mixed up. I was home a month ago, and I'm positive Jennifer wasn't pregnant."

"Humph," Roman grunted. "Let's see. You talk to me, I talk to Frank, who talk to David, who talk to Frank, who talk to me, who talk to you. Could be some confusion, but I think not."

"There's obviously some confusion there."

"I don't think so. I pretty sure you have new baby girl. That good thing, you know."

"No, you're wrong." Kyle let out an exasperated laugh. "There has to be a language issue or something."

Roman stiffened a little. "You not like my English?"

"I'm sorry. Your English is really good, but maybe you misunderstood something that was said. How long have you lived here?"

"I am in America three years and five months now. Know only just a little bit of English when I get here."

"You really are doing great with it. Where did you come from?"

"I come from Poland. That's why I Polack."

"Oh, that's right. I forgot you'd said that. How'd you end up in Northern Idaho? It a long way from Poland."

"You want me tell you the story?"

Kyle nodded. "Sure, I'm curious. Idaho is such a long way from home for you."

"I tell you story then. Sit down. It take little while." Roman pointed to an old leather couch pushed up against the far wall and waited for Kyle to sit. "Comfy?"

Kyle nodded.

"Okay. Where to start?" He thought for a second then smiled. "You know Ronald Reagan?"

"I was too young to vote for him, but I know about him. Why?"

"Ronald Reagan come to Poland when I am younger. My father, he talk about Reagan all the time after he came to Poland. Said Reagan helped make Poland free, so I can get good job and vote like an American. After that, as I grow up, I always think I should go to America, to live there, but I never do. Anyway, I get married. Very nice girl and very beautiful. Polish women are very beautiful, you know."

"I didn't know that, but I'm glad to hear it. Thanks."

"You are very welcome. Anyway, I get married, and I have job, and then we have children, first a boy, and then baby girl, like you."

Kyle shook his head, causing Roman to laugh heartily.

"So then I have wife and children, but no money, because family is very expensive in Poland. So I think I never get to come to America, only see it on TV, but that okay, because at least I have job and family. I can be happy in Poland. No problem. But then my life change. Malina, my wife, she have job cleaning offices at night so we have money and can buy a house maybe, not live in apartment forever. Anyway, one day, Malina taking kids to school in the morning, and she very tired, she work very hard, you know, and Malina," Roman paused and wiped at his eyes, swallowed, and looked away. After a short silence he continued, struggling to tell the story. "I am sorry." He cleared his throat. "Malina very tired, and she fall asleep while driving, just for short moment. There was red light. She went through and hit truck, which make very big fire." Roman waved his hands over his head mimicking a large explosion.

Kyle wiped tears from his own eyes. "I'm so sorry, Roman. I can't imagine losing my family like that. It must have been very difficult for you."

Roman rocked back and forth in an exaggerated nodding motion, looking out the window for a long minute to compose himself. "Yes, very difficult. Very difficult. After few months, life not so good. I want to kill myself, but then I think, maybe I go to America instead. We have money in bank for house, and I get little bit from insurance, so I can do it. I buy picture book about America, and look at different places. I grow up and live in Warsaw, which is very big city, and very old, and very crowded. Not so nice, I think. But Idaho, it has trees, and mountains, and lakes, and not so many people. Very beautiful, like a dream for me, so I pick here."

Roman paused, and Kyle wasn't sure if the story was complete or if Roman was gathering his thoughts. "How have you liked it so far?" he prodded.

Roman thought a second. "Idaho pretty good. Very nice people, and better than killing self, but I rather have Malina and my children." He wiped away a lingering tear. "But here, at least I don't see place of crash every day. I just keep the good memories, so that is better."

CHAPTER FORTY-SIX

Sunday, March 11th
Western Montana

Kyle unfastened his belt and dropped his pants, then squatted back against a fallen tree for support. As was their morning routine, Garfield was tethered to a tree on the riverbank while Kyle retired to the woods for his daily constitutional. Being early spring, large enough leaves were as yet unavailable, so Kyle had piled several strips of birch bark nearby and was proceeding with the work at hand.

Bracing himself with his elbows, his mind wandered back over the past couple of weeks. To his relief, his father was doing much better, and Kyle, despite the loss of his mother, had had a remarkably encouraging visit. Moyie Springs was weathering the situation amazingly well. It had a good community structure, a barter market was established, basic healthcare was available, and defenses were secure. The fact that there were no major population centers close by was a benefit as well, although what news was coming through from the cities indicated that at this point the worst of the anarchy had burned through, and those who had survived were now in the process of reestablishing some kind of stability.

Collin was also in good hands, having bonded deeply with Gene over the past week and showing signs of being a normal ten year old boy, not a war vet with PTSD. Ideally, Kyle would have liked to find the boy's family but only knew that his mother had disappeared after their first move from Seattle. It later came out that Collin's dad was a career military guy, who, despite what seemed like regular attempts, had only been able to see Collin once or twice a year after divorcing Collin's mom. At least if Collin wasn't able to be with his own family, Kyle's dad was a good person to be with.

As a father himself, the thing that haunted Kyle the most about Collin's situation was what Collin's father must be going through. A seemingly decent parent separated from his kid and unable, for the foreseeable future, to contact him or even know of his well-being. Kyle had experienced a version of that for eleven weeks, the longest eleven weeks of his life, but at least he'd had a pretty good idea where his kids were and knew they were in a safe community. For any parents who traveled or had family in cities that fell apart, Kyle imagined the anxiety would be beyond description.

Kyle was fumbling with the strips of bark when he heard a strange noise from near the river, then Garfield let out a stressed, high-pitched squeal. The noise unnerved Kyle, and he paused before reacting, listening for it again. It took only a few seconds before a deep, rumbling growl rolled through the forest, setting the hairs on the back of his neck on end. Kyle jerked his pants up and hitched his belt before grabbing his handgun from the tree he'd been leaning against.

Kyle had wandered away from Garfield in search of bark but could clearly hear his horse, panicked and frantic, neighing in desperation and thrashing against the reins that secured him to the tree. Gun in hand, Kyle dashed through the forest towards the highway, using his arms to shield his face from the branches. He burst onto the road and began to sprint towards Garfield.

The bear was on the far side of the horse, no more than twenty feet away and approaching at a run. Because Garfield was bucking and thrashing so wildly, it made shooting at the attacking animal too risky, so Kyle fired two shots, hoping to frighten the bear off. Whether or not the bear registered the shots, Kyle couldn't tell. The animal kept charging and was now just steps from the horse.

Kyle, still fifty yards away, yelled as he ran, trying to draw the bear's attention from the meal that had been so generously secured for it by the side of the river. Kyle had only taken a couple more steps and was still yelling, when the bear reared up and swiped at the horse, its powerful black paw swinging down in a blur towards the terrified animal. Garfield continued to spin and kick, but being tethered to the tree, his frantic efforts to evade the bear were futile. The tree whipped from side to side with the horse's tugs, but both the rope and the tree held firm. Garfield spun away from the strike, revealing a long gash with bright crimson streaks of blood on the horse's rear haunch.

The animals separated briefly, and Kyle hurriedly fired off a shot, but it was poorly aimed, and despite the size of the target, he didn't expect he'd hit the bear. Lightning quick, the bear struck again with the single-minded determination of an animal recently emerged from months of hibernation driving it forward. The second blow, aimed at the horse's head, staggered the animal, and the sound of the impact resonated in Kyle's ears. The next swing was aimed at the neck, but somehow Garfield avoided it, though Kyle could see streams of blood on the horse from the cuts to his face and rear. The combined sounds of the injured horse and the attacking bear all but drowned out Kyle's shouts as he ran towards them.

With the animals still too close together and Kyle still too far away to shoot accurately, he just kept running, desperate to get to his horse before the bear killed him or maimed him further. The bear continued to attack, undeterred by Kyle's appearance or the gunshots, the prospect of fresh meat too tantalizing to resist. The bear lunged with his mouth and clamped down on the back of Garfield's neck, then twisted violently back and forth, viciously tearing the flesh and dragging poor Garfield to the ground.

Kyle was closer now. With the animals on the ground and thrashing less, he had a better opportunity to get off a clean shot. He skidded to a stop and raised his gun once again. Even with the bear's teeth sunk deep in his neck, Garfield was still fighting, and with the two heads close together, it meant Kyle had to take good aim. His first shot was slightly high, splashing into the river behind them. He was pretty sure the second shot caught the bear in the shoulder but passed through, as there was another splash in the water, though this time Kyle finally got the bear's attention.

The bear released its hold on Garfield and rose up on its hind legs. Kyle fired again, hitting the animal in the chest. It roared and swung its head furiously from side to side, and Kyle quickly fired again, hitting it somewhere in the upper body. At thirty yards, and from the shoulder of the road looking down on the animals, which were below him on a slight decline near the river's edge, he wasn't sure where exactly the bullet had hit. Kyle had once read an article that told of a grizzly bear in Alaska that had killed and eaten three people. When the bear was finally killed, authorities found it had been shot more than a dozen times with three different weapons. Here he was, alone on the side of the road, firing 9mm bullets into a five hundred pound black bear, and the thought that he was just making the bear angry crossed his mind. He fired again, then took a few steps back towards the forest, hoping at least for a little cover if the animal came after him.

The bear's attention was drawn back to Garfield, who still had a lot of life left and was struggling to get back on his feet. The bear lunged at the horse again, slashing its stomach and opening a long gash that bled profusely. Kyle was halfway across the road and had just shot at the bear again when the creature reared up, bellowed at him, then spun and retreated towards the river. The bear crashed into the shallow water, splashing loudly as it crossed to the heavily wooded hillside.

Kyle fired at the bear once more as he hurried towards Garfield, dropping to his knees beside the bloodied animal, which was now trying to get back on his feet as blood pumped in streams from multiple wounds onto the ground. Garfield whinnied as Kyle rubbed the horse's head. "I'm so sorry," he stammered, unsure what to do.

Garfield reacted to the touch, pulling away and trying to rear, but restrained by the reins still tied to the tree. Kyle pulled out a knife and slashed the leather straps, freeing the horse, who pulled away and somehow managed to stay on his feet, the muscles in his legs and sides trembling from the shock of the bear attack. Garfield struggled to walk, staggering on the rocky ground. Kyle led him by the reins to the road where the surface was flat and stable, then tried to inspect the wounds of the skittish animal.

He glanced over his shoulder to where the bear had disappeared into the trees on the far side of the river, but saw no trace of it, then turned his attention back to his horse. "Doesn't look good, Garfield," he said, as he watched a severed artery on the back leg pump out a steady stream of blood. Kyle applied pressure on the vein, trying to close the wound, but Garfield pulled away. "It's okay, boy," he soothed, running his hands along the length of the animal. Kyle was not much of a horse person, but over the last few weeks he'd grown more and more attached to the animal as they'd traveled, and he'd formed a close bond with the horse.

Kyle released the straps of the saddle, then gently lifted it from Garfield's back and set it on the ground. Blood dripped from the horse's face and ran down three of his legs. Kyle looked helplessly at Garfield, trying to see some way he could help the poor horse, but uncertain what could be done, even if he were able to get it to a vet. They'd passed a house a mile back, but there was no assurance the resident would be willing or able to help, or that Garfield would even be alive when he returned.

The blood was running so fast that it pooled on the road by Garfield's hooves, the horse's orange hair now mostly matted and dark with blood. Garfield eyed Kyle, flicked his tail weakly from side to side, and let out a pitiful whinny. The horse staggered forward, and Kyle walked along beside him, tenderly rubbing his neck and leading him slowly along the road. They walked back and forth on the road for ten minutes until Garfield began to lose strength, finally lowering himself to the ground and sprawling over onto his uninjured side, his legs kicking weakly in front of him.

Kyle knelt beside him, certain it was only a matter of time before the horse passed on and not willing to abandon him before he took his last breath. Leaning back against an old Ford Taurus on the side of the road, Kyle stroked Garfield's head, while the animal emitted pitiful noises as his life slowly drained away. Garfield's eyes closed, but his chest still expanded and contracted weakly, his breaths becoming more and more shallow.

Kyle closed his own eyes and exhaled noisily, the adrenaline draining from his body and leaving him tired, especially after a poor night's rest. He reflected back to the same time last year. Mid-morning he would be at work, maybe out directing repairs or a new power installation, often in areas not too far from where he currently was. He'd driven this road many times for work or to visit his parents, an easy and scenic four-hour drive on a Friday after school, with most of the sights flying by too quickly to be seen or appreciated. He knew where all the public restrooms were along the way, had stopped for fuel at many of the gas stations, and felt like he could almost do the trip with his eyes closed. In all that time he'd never considered walking it, at least not before September.

Garfield let out a loud snort and jerked his head. Kyle glanced down sympathetically. "Hope there's a horse heaven my friend, cause you've sure earned the right to get in." The horse's eyes were open, and he lifted his head and looked around, panicked. Kyle tried to gently force the animal's head down, but Garfield resisted, fighting against Kyle's pressure, becoming more and more stressed. Then Garfield tried to scramble to his feet. "What's..." Kyle began, then heard the growl of the bear again, close.

Kyle leapt to his feet and spun around, drawing his pistol as Garfield thrashed on the ground, his hooves pawing for traction on the asphalt road. The bear was coming from out of the trees a few yards downstream on their side of the river. Kyle fired two quick shots at the animal, then heard the chamber click empty. With the bear just a few feet away, Kyle ejected the magazine and pulled a second one from his pocket, jamming it in quickly, something Sean had insisted the militia members practice until it became second nature. The magazine clicked in, and Kyle worked the action to chamber a round as he skirted around the back of the car, the bear now just steps away, the sound of its claws on the road making Kyle's blood freeze in his veins.

The bear let out a high-pitched roar as it lunged towards Kyle. Kyle spun and fired into the animal just as it struck him and knocked him backwards onto the ground, then landed on top of him, knocking the air from his lungs. The bear reared back and took a swipe at Kyle's head with a giant paw, which Kyle was barely able to dodge. The animal, now astride Kyle, had him pinned to the ground as it roared in pain and fury. Kyle shot again as he struggled for breath, virtually pressing the muzzle of his gun against the bear's chest before pulling the trigger, but it only seemed to make the animal angrier. The bear lunged forward, its jaws gaping wide and aimed for Kyle's throat. Kyle stuck his left arm in front of his face, and the bear clamped down on it, twisting hard to the side. Kyle fired again but was jerked by the bear, causing him to miss his mark. The agony of the bear's teeth clamped tightly on his forearm sent unbelievable jolts of pain through Kyle's whole body.

Kyle screamed when he caught his breath, momentarily startling the animal. With the bear caught off guard, Kyle ignored the pain and used his arm, which was still in the Bear's mouth, to steady the animal's head above him while he jabbed the gun against the throat of the animal. He knew he had only a few seconds before the animal overpowered him, and having no desire to be a part of the beast's food chain, Kyle pulled the trigger in rapid succession, angling the barrel so that the bullets would travel upwards into the animal's skull.

On the third shot the animal stiffened, its jaws briefly clenching tighter on Kyle's arm, then falling slack as the bear slumped forward, landing hard on top of Kyle. Kyle gasped as the full weight of the bear, warm and musky, pressed him flat against the highway. Its fur pressed against Kyle's face and smelled like an old rug that had been left in the backyard for a summer. Kyle worked his right hand free and fired one more shot into the animal, still fearing it might somehow revive and succeed in separating his head from his shoulders.

Finally confident the bear was, in fact, dead, Kyle lay his gun down and began extracting himself from under the animal. He grabbed the bear's furry head with his left hand and attempted to pull it to the side, but sharp jolts of pain ran through his arm and forced him to let go. Realizing he only had the use of one arm, Kyle pushed with his good arm while thrusting up with his right leg, rocking the bear's carcass and sliding out a little each time he rocked the animal.

After numerous attempts, he finally rolled free from under the animal, panting for air and covered in blood. Kyle crawled away from the bear and lay on the road, cradling his left arm while carefully moving each of the fingers on his left hand to see if they still worked. Finding them functional, he carefully removed his jacket and rolled up his shirtsleeve, revealing a series of puncture wounds on the top and bottom of his arm as well as some deep gouges on his left shoulder.

Garfield had somehow gotten to his feet during the struggle and was breathing hard and wheezing, having staggered away from the bear and towards the river, his legs, like a newborn animal trying to negotiate his first steps, barely strong enough to hold him up. "Be careful, old boy," Kyle called out as the injured animal descended the bank to the water.

The horse slipped on a boulder and dropped to his front knees, letting out a pitiful moan as he fought unsuccessfully to regain his footing. Kyle stood up, found himself similarly shaky-legged, and slowly made his way to the horse. "Just wait, Garfield," he implored as he bent to stroke the animal's head, then descended the slope to the river. Blood covered his hands, arms, and face, and he washed it off before taking a drink, then cupped his hands and scooped some water from the river. He retraced his steps back to the wounded animal and trickled the water onto the horse's tongue.

Garfield responded to the cold liquid, lapping at it as best he could. Kyle repeated the process until Garfield no longer responded to the water, and he rolled over onto his less injured side and laid his head on the ground, resuming his slow, rhythmic breathing. Kyle walked back to the saddle on the ground and fished out an old undershirt, wrapping it tightly around his arm in an attempt to stem the bleeding. He doctored his various wounds, then followed the trail of blood on the highway back to the dying animal.

Garfield lay immobile on the ground, his chest no longer moving, his limbs still. Kyle rubbed the horse's nose. "I'm so sorry, friend," he said as he dropped beside him. "I'm so, so, sorry." He gazed at the animal in silence, Garfield's mane fluttering in the wind the only movement.

Kyle returned to where he'd set the saddle and stared down at it. All of his possessions were attached to it, along with some deer meat and a few other food items his father had sent. The next town was over five miles away, with an unknown number of homes along the way. He plopped down, leaned back against the saddle, and reloaded the magazines for his pistol, now uncomfortably short on ammo. He had his backpack, but somewhere along the way, he was going to have to find someone willing to trade a saddle for a duffle bag or, better yet, a bicycle, and hopefully a few other supplies to help him get home. He rested for a long time until, somewhat recovered, he stood up, grabbed the saddle by the horn, hefted it onto his back with a grunt, and once again began the journey home on foot.

CHAPTER FORTY-SEVEN

Monday, March 19th
Deer Creek, MT

David opened the door and leaned outside. "Mom, Grace says that dinner is ready. You should come in now."

Jennifer looked at David, her face betraying the mixture of emotions she was experiencing.

"No sign of dad?" he asked, knowing what was on her mind.

She shook her head. "Nothing. I've been watching for the last two hours, and still nothing."

"He'll be okay. He made it from Texas; he can make it from Idaho."

Jennifer swallowed, though the lump in her throat made it difficult. "You're sure dad told Frank he would be home on the sixteenth?"

"Yes, Mom. You've already asked me that multiple times. And I'm sure. He'll probably be home tomorrow. He's on horseback, so, you know, it's tough to predict how long the trip will take."

"Thanks, David," Jennifer said with a half-hearted smile. "I should be the one reassuring you, not the other way around."

"Let's go eat. It's spaghetti. Grace used some more of her food storage stuff. It looks like real food, but she says the sauce is from powder, and we don't have mushrooms, or cheese," he thought a couple seconds, "or real hamburger, or butter, or peppers, or..."

"I get it David. It's not like real spaghetti."

He nodded with a grin. "Well, it isn't, but it still looks and smells pretty good, especially compared to all the wheat and bean stuff we eat most of the time."

Jennifer stepped inside, and David followed her to the kitchen. A big pot on the table was filled with spaghetti and sauce that had been stirred together. Carol, Grace, Emma and Spencer were already seated, with Spencer eyeing the food ravenously.

"Looks good, doesn't it, Spence?" Jennifer said as she sat down.

Spencer nodded, keeping his eyes locked on the food. "I love spaghetti," he muttered.

Grace smiled. "I'm glad to hear that little Spencer," she said. "I'll have to make it more. I've been trying to pace our food use, but we'll be able to start growing a garden again soon, so maybe I don't have to hold back as much."

"That would be nice, wouldn't it?" Jennifer said.

Spencer nodded, still focused on the food.

Grace offered a blessing, then they began to eat. Jennifer watched as her children attacked the food and felt a pang of guilt cut through her as they devoured the meal, so obviously hungry, yet so rarely complaining. Jennifer picked at the food on her plate. She was as hungry as the rest, but her stomach was too tied in knots to eat much. "Slow down, David," she said. "You should try tasting it a little bit before you swallow."

"David swallowed and kept shoveling. "Sorry, but this is real good, and I'm pretty hungry."

Jennifer returned the smile, but inwardly she wanted to cry. Her kids were all skinny and dirty, as well as smelly, if the truth was told. And their father was missing. It all tore at her heart every time she thought about it.

Jennifer had just taken a mouthful when Carol spoke up. "Did anyone hear the big news today?" she asked as she looked expectantly around the table. No one answered, so she went on. "I was checking on Craig Reider's daughter this morning, she's been sick, and anyways, she told me that her uncle is getting married."

"Who's her uncle," Emma asked, looking up from her food.

"It's Sean, from the militia, isn't it?" David said, looking at Carol.

Carol nodded. "It is Sean, and he's engaged."

"Who's he marrying?" Jennifer asked, only half listening to the conversation but still curious about the answer. "Someone from Clinton? I don't think there's anyone in Deer Creek, is there?"

Carol shook her head. "It's not Clinton, and it's not Deer Creek. She's from Wyoming."

Jennifer's jaw dropped. "You mean he's marrying Rose?"

Carol nodded and grinned widely. "That's what I mean. Apparently he asked her last night, and she said yes."

"I didn't even know they were dating," Jennifer said, before taking another forkful of food.

"How do you even date around here? It's not like you can go to a movie, or a restaurant or anything." David wiped the corner of his mouth with the back of his hand. "I did see them talking a few times. How long has she been here?"

"It's been about a month," Jennifer said, doing the math in her head. "She got here a couple of weeks after your dad left."

"Don't you have to know each other for a long time before you can get married?" Emma asked, scraping the last bit of food into her mouth.

"There aren't any rules, Emma," David said. "If you knew anything about love, you'd know that."

"Like you know anything about it," Emma shot back. "Or are you still in love with Amy?"

David went red in the face and stared daggers at his sister. "Just shut up, Emma," he said as she laughed at him.

"Kids," Jennifer said, raising her hands. "No fighting at the table, or anywhere else for that matter. Just cut it out. And David's right. There aren't any rules for falling in love."

David gave Emma a smirk, which she just ignored. "So why do people get married, anyway?" Emma asked.

"Because they love each other," Spencer said, joining the conversation.

"But they already love each other. They don't need to be married to do that. Do they, Mom?"

Jennifer shook her head. "Of course not, sweetie. I love you and your brothers, and we're not married."

"So why do people get married?" Emma asked her mother, curious.

"Ahh, I guess, it's just more of a tradition, than anything." Jennifer stammered, looking around the table for help with the question. "It's just what we do."

Grace raised her hand. "Mind if I chime in?"

Jennifer nodded, grateful for the help.

Grace addressed Emma directly. "Do you plan to get married someday?"

Emma shrugged. "I suppose. That's what we do, isn't it?"

"It is, but marriage has been changed a lot since I was a little girl." Grace looked around the table and smiled. "You probably don't want me to bore you with my story…"

"Please, tell us," Jennifer said. "It would be nice to hear about you and Chuck. Looking back, I wish we had spent more time with their grandparents, having them tell their stories. It's a shame we found it so easy to just send the kids off to watch TV while the adults visited."

Grace nodded in agreement. "You kids up for a story?"

David and Emma nodded. Spencer looked at his mom, hoping to be excused from the table. He was met with a stern look, so he closed his eyes and leaned back against his chair.

Grace laughed a little. "I'll try not to drag it out too long, but maybe my story can help explain what I think about marriage. I grew up in a pretty small town in Southern Idaho, a town called Grace, just like me. It was almost as small as Deer Creek is, small enough that everyone knew everyone else. One summer in the early sixties, a boy shows up that I had never seen before, a Charles Turner from Cleveland, Ohio. In a little town, it's pretty exciting when someone new comes around, especially when they're as handsome as he was. I had just finished my junior year of high school, and back then, most girls thought about marriage instead of college, so I was pretty excited about Mr. Turner."

"Was it love at first sight?" Emma asked, listening carefully.

"No," Grace said, shaking her head slowly. "It wasn't love at first sight. Love takes time to grow, but it was cute at first sight, at least for me."

Spencer wrinkled his nose. "What's cute at first sight?"

"Cute at first sight is what most people experience, but they call it love. I was definitely smitten with Charles. He seemed so wonderful to me, and I did think it was love at the time, but so did a lot of other girls, which didn't make him very popular with the boys. Anyway, somehow I won the Charles lottery, and before I graduated from high school, we were engaged."

"Oh, my," Jennifer said. "You two didn't waste any time, did you?"

Grace blushed a little. "By today's standards we didn't, although Sean and Rose make us look sloth-like. But back then, we weren't too far out of the norm, especially for small towns. And I might say, marriages back then lasted a lot longer than they do now, so it wasn't bad."

"Guess I'll give you that. How long were the two of you married?" Jennifer asked.

"Fifty-two years," Grace answered with glistening eyes. "Fifty-two wonderful years. And when we married, we both expected it would last. Divorce wasn't really an option. I'm not saying it was a walk in the park. My dad was pretty upset about our romance. Charles was from far away, he was three years older than me, and he wasn't of our faith, so my family tried really hard to discourage me."

"Did you guys elope?" David asked, also drawn in by Grace's experience.

"Oh, no. Nothing like that, though we did talk about it a couple of times. No, my dad realized my mind was made up, and he kind of liked Chuck anyway, so he convinced my mother that they should give us their blessing."

"Did they come to your wedding?" Emma asked.

"Did they ever. We got married at the end of June, just after I graduated, and my parents planned the biggest wedding you could imagine. I thought they might do something little because I was being a bit of a rebel, marrying an outsider and all, but it was just the opposite. I think it was the biggest wedding Grace, Idaho had seen to that point."

"If your parents weren't real happy, why'd they do it? That doesn't make sense." David pulled his knees up close to his body and wrapped his arms around them to keep warm.

"I asked my dad that before our first daughter got married. He laughed and said it was to keep us on our toes."

"Why did he want you on your toes?" Spencer asked, looking puzzled.

"It doesn't really mean to be on my toes. He just wanted us to be thoughtful about it. He said he wanted everyone to know who had promised to take care of his daughter, and he wanted us to know that everyone knew. Said a marriage vow isn't just to one person. I thought about that a lot as my own daughters married off, and it makes a lot of sense. You see, when people marry, it's not just something you do on a whim because you like some-one, though that's what a lot of people seem to think. Marriage is a promise you make to the person you marry and, almost as important, to your community and the families, that the two of you have committed to supporting each other and your children."

"Why do they care?" Emma asked, leaning forward and resting her chin in her hands.

"Because back then, who do you think would take care of me if Chuck didn't?"

Emma shrugged, but David answered. "Probably your family and your neighbors, wouldn't they?"

Grace nodded. "Back then, it was pretty important to the community that there weren't very many single women, or orphans, because the community would have to help take care of them. So, as you can imagine, there was a lot of pressure for families to stay together. My dad wanted to make sure Chuck understood the family's expectations, so he made sure everyone in town knew who was committing to his daughter. "

"Good thing it's not like that anymore," David said. "The government helps with that."

"But it is like that again, isn't it, David," Jennifer said, rubbing his shoulders. "We're back to where we where a long time ago. I think that's why I worry about your father so much. If he doesn't make it back, we're…" she started to choke up and paused for a second to compose herself. "We're going to have a hard time."

"Dad's coming back, Mom. Stop worrying, please. Plus, I'm still here."

"Yes, David, you are. But at some point, you're going to get married and have your own family, and you won't want to still be taking care of your old mother."

Grace tapped the table gently with her hands. "I didn't mean for this to become a downer. Like I said, marriages are good for the community, both for the reasons we talked about and because they're a celebration. It's a happy time. I think this wedding will be good for us, especially coming out of winter. There'll be dancing, and food, and everyone can come together and celebrate."

Carol stood up from the table and grabbed her plate. "Yes, it will be good for us. As the designated doctor in this town, I can assure you that people need something to celebrate. I'm no psychiatrist, but it can't do anything but help. Now, on that note, it looks like everyone is done. Whose turn is it to help me with the dishes?"

Emma stood grudgingly and picked up her plate. "It's my turn, again. Boy, do I miss the dishwasher."

"We have a dishwasher, Sis," David said, smiling. "It's named Emma."

Emma glared at her brother and was about to throw a fork at him when Jennifer grabbed her arm and stopped her.

Spencer laughed, then grinned at David. "Tomorrow the dishwasher's named David," he said, then tried to dodge as David grabbed him and began to tickle him. "Stop!" he shrieked, fighting back against his brother.

David wrestled Spencer to the ground, tickling him as he shrieked uncontrollably. "Tell me you're sorry," David demanded.

"I'm sorry!" Spencer cried, as he tried to peel David's fingers from his side. "I'm sorry," he repeated when David didn't stop.

"Hey! I thought I heard someone say I'm sorry!" came a deep, male voice.

Everyone stopped and turned.

"Kyle!" Jennifer cried, dashing across the room and throwing her arms around her husband.

"Dad!" the kids cried, running to him as well.

"Don't squeeze too hard," Kyle said. "You don't want to break me right off the bat."

Jennifer released her grip and stepped back. "You've had me worried to death," she said as she looked him over. "What happened to your jacket? It looks like it's been through a paper shredder."

Kyle smiled at her as he hugged the children. "I missed you, honey. It's good to be back."

"I missed you, too, Kyle," she said, then kissed him tenderly on the lips. "What happened to you?"

"It's nothing to be worried about. Let's just be happy we're back together, alright?"

Jennifer was about to respond when Madison began crying in the next room. "David, can you go get the baby?" she asked, then turned back to Kyle, who was staring at her wide-eyed.

"What did you just say?"

Jennifer laughed. "Oh, congratulations. You've got a baby girl."

Kyle shook his head. "Something's not adding up here." He looked at Carol for answers.

"Congratulations, Kyle. You should be very proud," Carol said, grinning widely.

David returned carrying Madison. "Do you want to hold her?" he asked, extending the baby to Kyle.

Emma pulled the blanket away from Madison's face as Kyle took her gingerly in his arms. "She's beautiful, isn't she Daddy?"

Kyle nodded. "I think I need to go back to Idaho and apologize to Roman." He looked at Jennifer. "How?"

Jennifer stepped back to her husband and wrapped her arms around him. "I'll tell you my stories, if you tell me yours."

CHAPTER FORTY-EIGHT

Saturday, April 7th
Deer Creek, MT

"I don't think they could have picked a better day," Jennifer said, squinting in the sunlight.

Kyle nodded. "It's wonderful, isn't it?" He looked around at the gathering crowd, with everyone wearing the best they had and carrying lawn chairs as they filled the field for the wedding ceremony. Emma, David and Spencer were all seated nearby.

The wedding had originally been scheduled for inside the town meeting hall, but with such pleasant spring weather, the site had been changed to the town park, a grassy field on the edge of the newly filled reservoir, lightly shaded by a row of freshly budding cottonwoods that towered over the creek. David, Emma, and some of their friends had brought the Shipley's goats, along with shovels, to the park during the past few days to eat the grass down, creating a nice, green, if slightly irregular, pasture for the ceremony to take place.

"You want to hold Madison?"

Kyle nodded and took the baby from Jennifer. He smiled and made faces at her, eliciting a smile. "She smiled!" he exclaimed excitedly. "That one was a real smile; I'm sure of it."

"Spencer got her to smile yesterday. I thought I told you that?"

"I don't think so, or maybe I don't remember. I was so tired when I got home." He gently rubbed Madison's cheek. "She sure is a pretty baby, isn't she?"

Jennifer nodded. "It's such a tragedy her mom is gone. She'd be so proud."

"At least Madison's alive and healthy, although I think she made goat noises at me when I fed her her bottle this morning."

Jennifer slapped him on the shoulder. "She does not make goat noises, and thank heavens we have access to those animals, or she might not be alive. Have you seen Rose yet today?"

Kyle shook his head.

"She's beautiful. She modeled her dress for me yesterday and she looks absolutely stunning."

"I still can't believe she followed me here. I think I was more surprised by Rose than by Madison when I got back."

"Are there going to be any more women from your travels showing up this summer?"

"Maybe one."

Jennifer turned to look at Kyle, her eyebrows raised.

"If the wife of that black bear tracks me down."

Jennifer laughed out loud, drawing the attention of the family sitting in front of them. She elbowed Kyle in the ribs. "Probably just as well I didn't know about Rose. It would've put a worry in my head that didn't need to be there."

Some of the wedding guests turned to look beyond the seating area, and Kyle and Jennifer did the same. "I see her," Kyle said. "She's on her horse."

Jennifer stood to watch as the wedding procession moved towards the guests, while Kyle bounced Madison on his lap. "Did I tell you when I went to Frank's yesterday that we got ahold of Roman," Kyle whispered loudly.

"No, you didn't. What did he say?" Jennifer asked as she watched the bride approach.

"He just laughed at me. Told me that I need to be more willing to trust a Polack."

"Sounds like he's a nice guy."

"He is, but he seemed lonely. Not sure how many friends he has. Must be hard for him, being isolated and with no family around." Kyle stood as the wedding party reached the guests.

"This all seems so surreal, don't you think?" Jennifer asked as two ladies helped Rose, dressed in a white wedding dress donated by a neighbor and modified for the occasion, down from her horse. Sean followed close behind his bride on his own horse, dressed in a gray suit that hung loosely on him, a bright red necktie adding a splash of color.

Kyle bounced the baby in his arms. "First wedding I've heard of in the last seven months. Can't imagine it's a regular occurrence these days. It feels good, though, like we're not in such a crisis anymore."

"Rose is beautiful, isn't she?"

Kyle paused. "Is it safe for me to agree?"

Jennifer laughed. "Yes, you're allowed to agree."

He nodded. "She looks very beautiful today. I think leaving her house was the hardest part of my trip from Texas."

"I said you could agree. No need to add that last bit."

Kyle laughed this time. "But I did leave, because you weren't there."

Jennifer smiled at him. "Brownie points."

Kyle nodded at Sean as he walked down the aisle between the groups of chairs. Gabe, clean-shaven and dressed in a loose, black suit, waited at the front of the gathering on a platform that had been built for the occasion. He smiled broadly as he watched the couple approach.

Rose, escorted by Sean's niece, and Sean, escorted by his son, stopped in front of the platform and Gabe stepped forward, clearing his throat. "Friends," he began, "This is truly a special occasion, not just for this couple, but for our community as well. We've been through an awful lot these past few months. Many times we probably wondered if we would make it this long, if we could ever be happy again, or if life would ever regain some semblance of normalcy. Today is an assurance that all of those things are happening. There is life, happiness, and some normalcy.

"Sean and Rose's union, and the fact that we're all here to celebrate it with them, tells me that we still see a future, one filled with hope and better days. It's much like the world of nature we see around us, coming back to life with the buds on the trees, the green grass growing beneath our feet, the calves we've been blessed with on the ranch, and the warm weather we're enjoying. It all reinforces the same message – that life renews, that after seasons of cold and hardship there is a newness of life, a reassurance that things will improve, and today, that renewing is taking place for the couple you see before you.

"Before they exchange rings, Sean and Rose have asked to share their vows."

Gabe motioned to Sean, who stepped onto the platform and pulled a piece of paper from his suit pocket. He smiled at the crowd, making eye contact with many of the wedding guests, then turned to face Rose, drinking her in with his eyes. After looking down at his notes, he began. "Last year at this time, I was a single father, lonely and struggling to survive in an indifferent world that rushed by and left me exhausted. The first week after everything collapsed, with all the chaos, I didn't think I would live to see another year. For a while, I tried to make things as normal as I could for my son's sake, but I was in a world I didn't want to be in. We escaped the city and came to live with my brother, Craig, and his family and found a community that welcomed us in and put us to work. It was, and is, wonderful, and we are very grateful.

"Here, I wasn't as lonely as before because I had friends and family surrounding me. I didn't even know I was missing something until I met you, Rose." Sean wiped at his eyes and nose, and cleared his throat. "When I first met you and you smiled at me, I thought my heart was about to fail. I now know it was something inside me that stirred back to life that day – the desire to have a companion and a best friend, someone to share my life with, to help me through my struggles, and someone who I can help with theirs. I know things won't be easy, but I pledge my love, my life, and everything that I am to you."

Sean stepped down and embraced Rose before helping her onto the platform. She wiped her own tears away and smiled radiantly at Sean. After taking a minute to compose herself, she began to speak. "I think I should have chosen to go first," she said as she fought her emotions. "I want to tell all of you how grateful I am to be here. You've taken me in and accepted me under such difficult circumstances. I can't express what that means to me."

She turned to Sean and smiled, her face glowing and radiant in the soft spring sunshine. "And I want to tell you, Sean, how happy you've made me. When I came to Deer Creek, I was just hoping for an opportunity to be part of a community that would give me a chance. I wasn't looking for, or expecting to find, a friend and a love like I've found in you. It's not often in life that we get do-overs, and I know we haven't known each other very long, but I pledge to you that I will try and be all that you hope I am. I promise to love you and stand by you, no matter what life has in store for us. I'm so much happier today than I ever imagined I could be. Thank you so much."

Gabe beamed as he helped Rose step down from the platform. He directed the couple to hold hands, then performed the wedding ceremony, a short, simple, yet emotional affair that concluded with Sean taking Rose in his arms and kissing her passionately. Then, cheered on by their friends and neighbors, the newlywed couple sauntered hand in hand back down the aisle to their horses.

In the midst of the cheering, Kyle heard a vaguely familiar sound. He looked at David, who had turned pale and nodded confirmation. "Everyone!" Kyle shouted above the din of the crowd, his voice rising in alarm. Another man towards the front was waving his arms for attention as well. Kyle yelled again. "Everyone, please!"

The applause died quickly as attention turned towards Kyle. "I'm sorry," Kyle began, "but I…"

The alarm rang at the militia house again, cutting him off.

"Gentlemen! Militia members!" Sean shouted as a silence fell over the group. "You have absolutely no idea how sorry I am to say this, but you need to grab your rifles and gather at the assembly point as quickly as possible." He pulled Rose towards him, hugging her and kissing her deeply. "I'm sorry," he said, then ran and mounted his horse, turning it towards the assembly point.

Kyle handed Madison to Jennifer with an apologetic look, and he and David ran for their home to retrieve their weapons.

Jennifer spun around, taking in the scene of despair that had quickly engulfed the community. Most of the men, and some of the women, were already running for their homes. The balance of those left behind were scared and dazed, the last assault, not yet two months old, still painfully fresh in their memories. What had been tears of joy were now replaced with fear and worry.

"Emma! Spencer! We need to get home now!" Jennifer shouted as she grabbed Spencer by the hand. "Hurry!"

CHAPTER FORTY-NINE

Saturday, April 7th
Deer Creek, MT

"**D**avid, I want you to wait here!" Kyle shouted down the stairs as he ran for the front door, rifle in hand. "If things get bad, you can still help defend the town from the house and protect everyone here."

David bounded up the stairs. "It's okay, Dad. I'm coming. I'm not afraid to do this. Besides, I'm already bigger than some of the men on the militia. Let's just go."

"But I'm not okay with this. I don't want you to go. I don't think I can handle it if anything happens to you."

"Mom was this same way, but if we don't keep them from getting into the town, then I'm not going to be able to stop them here. Mom and everyone else will be in trouble. Let's go."

Kyle swallowed hard and threw his necktie on the couch. He knew they didn't have time to argue. "Then promise me you'll be careful. I love you too much to have anything happen to you."

"I promise," David said as he hurried out the door, then rushed to the assembly point with his father beside him.

When they arrived, Sean was already speaking with three of the other leaders from the militia. Sean glanced over as David and Kyle arrived, then did a quick count of their numbers. "Gather in quickly folks. We need to hurry."

Kyle looked around and saw at least forty people already there, with at least a dozen more heading their direction.

"Alright," Sean began. "We'll do this like we did last time, but hopefully with none of the casualties. I've been talking to Rob here, and it looks bad. He was up in the nest and is the one who spotted the caravan. Says there are at least eight vehicles, and they look beefy. Possibly military."

One of the men in the group spoke up. "That's a good thing if they're military, isn't it?"

"We don't know. Could be good, or it could be really bad. If the wrong people have that kind of firepower, we're in for a long, difficult day. They're on the freeway side of the river, so they'll have to come across the bridge if they plan to pay us a visit. I want twenty people at each barricade. We've expanded the barricades, so you need to spread out. I don't want anyone closer to their neighbor than they have to be."

The sound of engines in the distance became more noticeable, and the group shifted nervously.

Sean continued. "I don't know what to expect. We've got the machine gun from February's raid, and our defenses are reinforced, so we're in better shape." Sean kept talking, hoping that as more men trickled in, it would help settle the nerves of the militia members. "I don't know about you folks, but I'd much rather make a stand with a trained group in a fortified location than not. I know most of us don't want to be here doing this, and if you think you're better off taking these people on one by one at home, you're welcome to leave. Otherwise, our best option is together at the bridge."

His offer was met with silence, but no one left, so he continued. "Gabe, I want you positioned here directing people. Send a couple east, and a couple south. Everyone else, I want at the bridge."

Gabe nodded and moved to intercept some of the latecomers.

"I'm going to take the east barricade with this half of you," he motioned with his arm to divide the room, indicating the group to his left. "Craig will take the west barricade with the rest of you. If they come in hostile, we'll do everything we can to stop the lead vehicle on the bridge. With the obstacles already out there, if we plug things up with the lead vehicle, that should bring them to a halt and make them reconsider, or at least get them on foot." He paused and looked over the group, then held up his hand. "I don't know if I should say this or not, but I will anyway." He looked each of them in the eyes. "If this gets out of hand, if we get overrun, get back to your families. Get them up in the hills. There are the valleys south of here that most of you have probably hunted in. We'll gather there if we have to."

There was silence in the group, though several heads bobbed up and down. Sean smiled confidently and clapped his hands. "Time's short, people! Let's do this!"

Sean ran for the barricade, the members of the militia close on his heels. The short distance to their defensive positions took no more than three minutes to cover, but most of the group was breathing hard and sweating when they arrived, a combination of age, exertion, and nerves. Kyle crouched midway along the barricade, with David immediately to his right. He looked at his son and said a silent prayer.

"Hey Sean!" a voice called from the opposite barricade.

"What?" Sean shouted back from the centermost position of the barricade as he peered over the top.

"Was this the plan for your honeymoon, or did you have something a little more romantic in mind?"

Sean laughed nervously, as did most of the men around him. "Rose wanted to do Hawaii," he shouted, "but I thought an armed confrontation at home would be more exciting." He paused. "Right now I'm thinking we should have gone with her plan."

"Well," said the man at the opposite barricade, "be sure and keep your head down. It'd be a shame for Rose to miss out on her wedding night."

Sean bit his lower lip and smiled, but Kyle could see more than a hint of fear on his face. "I'll do what I have to do," he called back. "Let's all of us do what we need to do to go home today."

A murmur of agreement rolled along the line as men readied themselves for the unknown foe. Kyle saw movement across the river on the freeway, and Sean lifted his binoculars to get a better view. "What do you see?" Kyle asked.

Sean studied the vehicle a little longer before lowering his glasses. "It's either really good news, or really bad news. We'll know in a few minutes. There's a military vehicle in the lead, an M1117 Guardian. I drove one in Iraq. It's an armored vehicle on wheels, essentially a tank without tracks. They don't come with a big crew, but they don't need it. That thing, with three preschoolers who know how to use it, can take us out. The ammo we're shooting is just going to bounce off it."

"Can't we shoot out the tires?" one of the men asked.

Sean shook his head. "It can run for miles on flats, so that won't slow it down at all." He paused a second and raised his voice. "I need a couple of people under the bridge with grenades. Any volunteers?" Sean looked around to see a couple of nervous hands raised in the air. "Put your hand down, David. I'm not sending you."

"I don't have a family," David protested as Kyle spun to look at him, shaking his head.

"You have a mother who's been through a lot, and that's enough," Sean replied. "No one doubts your courage, but you're not doing it." Sean pointed behind David. "Ty, you sure you're up for this?"

Kyle heard his friend speak up as he approached Sean. "Luther took my place last time. I'll do what I need to do to keep my family safe."

"Okay, then you'll go, plus Anthony over there." Sean indicated another man with his hand raised. "I want the rest of you to quickly move that dump truck. Get it the rest of the way across the road, then push some of these cars up beside it. Lets give them four or five layers to get through. We can at least stop them for a minute or two, give Ty and Anthony a chance at crippling them." Sean huddled with the two volunteers, instructing them on how to most effectively use the grenades against the armored vehicle, while the other men rolled the roadblocks into position.

With forty pairs of hands and the vehicles pre-staged, it only took a couple of minutes to have the bridge from the freeway blocked six vehicles deep. With the exception of Ty and Anthony, now concealed under the bridge, the militia members were safely back behind their barricades when the first of the military vehicles rolled to a stop on the north side of the river.

"What do you think, David?" Kyle asked his son as they watched thick exhaust billow from the rear of the lead vehicle. "These good guys or bad guys?"

David's hands shook as he handled his weapon. "I hope they're good guys, but I don't know. It says US ARMY on the side, so maybe that's a good thing."

"Hope so. But if I was a bad guy, I'd put that on there, too." Kyle looked at Sean, who was standing and watching the situation. "Can we shoot out the windshield?"

Sean shook his head slowly. "Just be wasting our ammo if we tried. The thing's built for combat zones. Hope our friends under the bridge are on target if they come in hot. Really wish we had some ammo for Rusty's 50 caliber. That would get their attention."

No one emerged from the Guardian, and after idling for thirty seconds, it kicked back into gear and slowly approached the bridge.

"Everyone down low!" Sean ordered. "That machine has some pretty powerful weapons. If they're pointed at you, you'd better be as low as you can get."

The men collectively drew in their breath as the wheels of the machine rolled onto the bridge. Every man in the company waited, searching for any vulnerability in the machine. Kyle spotted what appeared to be bullet dings in the side door, but with the distance separating them, he couldn't be sure.

Compared to the usual quiet of the community, the dull roar of the vehicle's engine was eerie and threatening, like the growl of some ancient demon that was to be fought off by villagers with their sticks and stones. "I don't want anyone shooting until there's something to shoot at, understand?!" Sean looked to both barricades as he shouted his orders. Only a few people still stood. The rest were hidden behind felled trees, boulders, and whatever other cover had been built into the barricades over the past months.

The men, visibly scared of the approaching threat, murmured their assent. Everyone waited and watched, an overpowering sense of dread settling on them as the sand-colored vehicle rolled slowly forward.

"Tell Mom I love her, if I don't make it. And Emma. And Spencer too."

Kyle could see David's eyes glistening and wondered why his own weren't as well. "You can tell them yourself, David. We've come through too much to have this be the end. We'll just be careful and smart, right?"

David nodded stiffly, his hands and arms shaking as he leaned against the thick tree in front of him.

"Do you know how much I love you? How proud I am to be your father?" Kyle slid over and wrapped his arm around his son's shoulder. "Dads don't tell their kids that often enough, especially as they get older. I want you to remember that, though, no matter what happens today. You understand?"

David nodded. "I do. But thanks for saying it. I'm proud to have you as my dad, too." David looked at Kyle and smiled, then glanced back at the road. "They've stopped," he said, motioning with his head towards the military vehicle.

Kyle slid back to his spot along the barricade and aimed his rifle at the vehicle, which had stopped a hundred feet from the tangle of vehicles pushed together in anticipation of its arrival.

"It's retreating!" someone shouted from the far barricade as the vehicle revved and began to move backwards, its wheels turning and angling the door away from the blockade.

The men let out a suppressed cheer, then the vehicle stopped at a forty-five degree angle to the road. The engine shut down and everything became deathly silent. Even the birds and breeze were still.

After ten seconds of complete silence, the groaning of metal on metal was heard. "I think they're opening a hatch," Kyle whispered to David as they strained to see what was happening just a stone's throw away. A door squeaked on its hinges as it swung open, then banged with a dull thud against the side of the vehicle.

"No one fire!" Sean shouted. "Let's see what's happening here."

A pair of boots hit the ground and moved to the front of the vehicle, where a soldier in full combat gear paused, then came forward carrying a US flag on a six-foot pole. He approached the bridge slowly and formally with the flag aloft, then stopped halfway between his vehicle and the blockade of cars on the south side of the bridge and waited expectantly.

"Kyle. Craig," Sean shouted. "Come with me out to meet this guy." Sean moved from behind the barricade towards the cluster of cars.

Kyle slung his rifle over his shoulder, climbed over the top of the barricade and moved towards the bridge, as did Sean's brother, Craig, from the far barricade.

"Be careful, Dad," David whispered as Kyle descended the bank. "I love you, too, you know."

Kyle turned and smiled at his son, then ran ahead and climbed onto the closest car, carefully stepping across the hoods of the vehicles to where Sean was waiting on the bridge, jumping down from the back of a white pickup a step ahead of Craig.

Sean smiled, his face awash with relief. "I think we're going to be alright, gentlemen. Let's go talk to this soldier and see what he has to say."

The three men advanced side by side towards the soldier, their nerves settling, their confidence building with each step. They stopped five feet from the soldier and Sean extended his hand. "Sean Reider," he said. "Militia leader."

The soldier stepped forward with his hand extended. "Private First Class Lance Castillo," he responded as he shook hands with Sean.

Kyle noticed the soldier appeared nervous as well, despite being well armed and clad head to toe in body armor.

"I assure you that we are here peacefully," PFC Castillo said. He was all business now as he spoke, his face betraying little emotion beyond a slight quiver in his voice. "I must receive an assurance of a peaceful response before Sergeant Chandler will speak to you."

Sean smiled. "I can assure you that we want to avoid conflict at all costs. We won't shoot if you don't."

PFC Castillo nodded and signaled to the vehicle behind him.

Kyle noticed all of the weaponry aimed at them, then a man stepped from the vehicle. He appeared to be in his mid-forties and was dressed in a desert-camo uniform with various insignias on one of the sleeves. His stride was quick, and he approached the group with a subdued smile.

"Sergeant Chandler," he said as he shook hands with each of them, his grip strong and assured. When introductions were complete the Sergeant stared at them for a moment and rubbed his chin. "I must say," he began. "This has to be the best dressed militia I've seen this year. I'm flattered by the greeting."

Sean held up his hand and spoke with a grin. "It's my fault. We were at my wedding when we were informed of your arrival."

Sergeant Chandler nodded. "I'm sorry for the interruption. I would guess we probably have your families pretty worried right now, don't we?"

They nodded affirmatively.

The sergeant continued. "We'll make this quick then, so you can get back to your celebration. I'm here on behalf of the US Government, such as it is. As much as we'd like to, right now it is impossible for food of any consequence to be supplied. Last estimates given were for a minimum of eighteen months before food supplies, in any significant quantity, could be made available. My personal opinion is that eighteen months is a pipe-dream if you're thinking of grocery stores being stocked, but I won't share that."

Sean turned to his brother. "Go get word back that there's no threat. Tell them they can go back home."

Craig nodded as he turned to head back to the barricades.

"When food does become available," Sergeant Chandler continued. "It will be the cities, or whoever is left there, who will get it first. Rural areas are going to be down the list."

"That's not right," Kyle protested, speaking out before catching himself.

Sergeant Chandler held up his hand to ward off the complaint. "Not my decision. It's simply a matter of logistics. It's where the most people can be helped the soonest, not that it helps you any. However, if I were you, I'd thank God you're not in a city right now. We're stationed in Ft. Lewis, near Seattle, and I can assure you that you're doing better here than the bulk of the population."

"I'm sorry for the interruption," Kyle apologized with embarrassment.

"That's fine. I've heard worse. The biggest thing you have going for you is land, plus here you have water, so you're doubly fortunate. We've been commissioned to deliver seeds. I have a convoy of trucks a short distance back, and on my word, one of the trucks will stop here and unload a pallet of seeds. These are seeds, not food. Do you understand the difference?"

Sean nodded.

"This will be the only delivery you get this year, and a condition of our delivering this to you is that these seeds are to be planted, and food produced. There will be more than enough to provide for your community, as long as you farm them carefully." He placed a lot of emphasis on the word carefully. "If you do not, then a lot of you are going to go hungry." He looked at Sean and Kyle again. "From the looks of it, you're not starving, so you can do the work. For your sake, and for the country's sake, farming needs to become your profession for the next few years. That and soldiering, because as of yet we don't have a police force to offer you."

"I don't suppose you have any weapons for us?" Sean asked. "Or ammunition?"

The inquiry was met with a laugh. "My apologies for laughing. No, I don't. If you want to know the truth, I was instructed to collect as many weapons as I could. Washington is worried that there have been too many shootings. I told them they could kiss my posterior on the weapons thing. The last things people are going to turn over right now are their guns, and I don't blame them, nor am I about to disarm them. All I can tell you is to not waste your ammunition, because fresh supplies aren't going to be available for a long time. Do you have any questions to this point?"

Sean shook his head.

"How many people are there in your community?"

"437 at last count."

"Was that 537?"

"No, 437."

"I thought I heard 537, because the pallets are broken down by town size, and 537 would be a good number of people to have."

Sean raised his eyebrows. "That's right. I thought you asked how many adults we have. There are 537 total with kids, and animals."

Sergeant Chandler nodded. "I thought so. I'll let my transport drivers know to leave a class C pallet for you. I know this is pretty quick, but we do need to keep going. There are five loaded semis under my authority that have to get delivered before heading back to base for the next load. I know this is not what you want to hear, but I can't emphasize this enough: you are on your own. If you let your crops fail, your people are going to be hungry. It's as simple as that. There are no food stamps or any kind of welfare for you to fall back on. Those days are over and will not return for a long time. There won't be any emergency supplies flown in if you get in trouble. I recommend you get everybody working with shovels and hoes, assuming you have those things. Use sticks if you have to. For the time being, you are your own police force, your own justice system, and your own military, so don't wait around for someone else to come along and take care of you. I'm working with a limited crew myself.

"I wish I could be more positive, but it's better that I be brutally honest. I wouldn't expect another delivery of seeds next year, but these seeds are non-hybrid, so you can save and dry what the plants produce to grow again next spring. These plants will take a little more work and be a little more fragile than what you're used to, but they'll probably taste better and, more importantly, reproduce. Just make sure you save seeds. Good luck." He extended his hand, then spun on his heels and started towards his vehicle. "Oh, one more thing. Our trucks are well defended, so don't do anything that we'll all regret, and congratulations on the wedding." With that, he strode away, followed closely by PFC Castillo.

Kyle and Sean watched in silence as the military vehicle started up and pulled away. In the distance, they could hear other vehicles approaching, then saw a drab green semi-truck emerge from behind a stand of trees.

Kyle put his hands on his hips and felt a shudder run through his body. "I think in some ways I feel worse than I have in a long time," he said as he turned to see the last of their own militia members leaving the barricades and hurrying back to their families.

"Why's that?" Sean asked.

"Because he put into words what I've feared for some time but was hoping to be wrong about."

"And that is?"

"That we really are on our own. I mean REALLY on our own. Our government, which we'd become so dependent on and which seemed so powerful, when it gets right down to it, really is unable to do much for us besides deliver a load of seeds, for which I am grateful. But it kind of pulls the mask off that whole charade, doesn't it?"

Sean smiled and nodded. "It does in a way, Farmer Tait. But who's more to blame? The ones who perform the charade, or the ones who buy the act when they should've known better?"

Kyle sighed. "Ouch. That hits a little close to home. Hopefully I'm a lot wiser, if I ever have the chance to fill out a ballot again."

Sean patted him on the back. "Don't worry, Kyle. We're going to be all right. A country isn't great because of its government. A country is great because of its people, and there are plenty of us around who aren't willing to throw in the towel."

Continue reading for a sample chapter from Ray's first book, 77 Days in September

77 DAYS IN SEPTEMBER

BY

RAY GORHAM

Available now from <u>Amazon</u>, <u>Barnes & Noble</u>, <u>Kobo</u>, and <u>iBooks</u>

CHAPTER ONE

Friday, September 2nd
George Bush International Airport, Houston, Texas
15:40 EST

Kyle worked his way down the aisle of the airplane, squeezing past the other passengers as they struggled to jam their oversized carry-ons into already too-full overhead bins. "Excuse me...pardon me...thank you," Kyle mumbled as he passed, irritated that his flight was already thirty minutes behind schedule. Kyle re-checked his boarding pass for his seat assignment, 26F, then scanned the numbers above the seats. 23... 24... 25... 26. A balding man in his late fifties who, by his tan face and comfortable attire, looked like he'd come directly from a golf course, sat in the aisle seat, the two seats beside him empty.

"I'm sorry to bother you," Kyle said, making eye contact with the man and motioning to the seat by the window. "I need to slip by. I'm in that seat."

The man nodded and rose, and Kyle squeezed past and dropped into his seat, then pushed his carry-on into the cramped space in front of his feet.

"Guess I won't be lying down for my nap today," the man said warmly as he settled back into his seat.

"Not unless you plan to put your head on my knee," said Kyle.

"I'm pretty particular about whose knee I lay my head on, and you're not nearly pretty enough. Guess I'll just have to lean the chair back this flight."

Kyle laughed. "My name's Kyle Tait. It's nice to meet you."

"I'm Ed Davis," the man said, extending his hand. "I guess we're neighbors for the next couple of hours."

"I guess so," Kyle said as he shook Ed's hand. "You headed home?"

"No, I'm heading out. I've got business meetings next week in Denver. Heading up early to visit my daughter and her family. You?

"Heading back home to Montana"

"Montana? You're a long way from home. What brought you to Houston?"

"Hurricane Elliot."

"You came for the hurricane?"

"No," Kyle said, shaking his head. "I came because of it. I work for Western Montana Power. It's a slow time of year, so they farm a few of us out to help in other areas."

"Hmm. Well thanks for helping. How'd things go?"

"Overall, pretty smoothly. As you probably know, the damage didn't end up being quite as bad as they'd anticipated, but the utility companies like to keep us around so the local folks can take care of their families. I helped in Louisiana after Katrina; it was my first time working out of town. Now that was an experience!"

"I'll bet. We were affected by Katrina here too, but more by the refugees than the weather. Can't imagine what it must have been like over there."

"It sure made me appreciate Montana more. The occasional blizzard doesn't seem so bad anymore."

"I don't know about that. I'm not one for the cold. I think I'll stick with the annual hurricane."

"The cold's not that bad. You get used to it after awhile."

"Have you lived in Montana long?"

Kyle nodded. "My whole life, except for a couple of years in Oregon when I was little. I love it there."

"I've heard it's nice, but I think I'd miss the city. Doesn't Houston have about five times the population of your entire state? I don't know if I could adjust."

"Sure you would. We lived in Missoula for a few years, but even that started to get too big for us. You begin to appreciate your space when you have it. This past spring we moved about fifteen miles out of town to a newer community with lots of space. We still have neighbors, but you don't hear them, and the kids have plenty of room. As long as you've got a four-wheel drive for the snow, it's great."

Ed gave an exaggerated shiver. "I think I'm too old for a drastic change like that." He turned his attention back to his magazine and the conversation lagged. Kyle checked his watch, wondering why the plane still hadn't moved from the gate. All of the passengers appeared to be on board, and the attendants were busy preparing themselves for the flight, but the jet hadn't moved.

Kyle pulled his novel out of his carry-on just as the pilot's voice came over the PA, offering apologies for the late departure and a promise that they would be underway as soon as possible. Kyle wanted to hear an estimate of when they would actually be getting underway, but the captain didn't offer any specifics.

Digging his cell phone out of his carry-on, Kyle pressed the speed dial for home. After four rings he heard Jennifer's voice. "Hi. You've reached the Tait family. We can't get to the phone but leave a message, and we'll call back."

Kyle waited for the tone. "Hi, Jenn. It's me. Just wanted to let you know that I'm late getting out. It's about quarter to three Houston time, and we're still waiting to take off. I'll call you from

Denver and let you know if there are any problems with the connection. Talk to you soon."

Kyle turned off his phone and dropped it into his carry-on, then opened his book and began to read.

Atlantic Ocean, 175 miles east of Cape Hatteras, North Carolina 15:42 EST

Clouds hung low over the water, and the flags on the mast snapped out a slow, steady rhythm in the light wind as *Carmen's Serenade* rolled ever so slightly in the swells of the North Atlantic. Captain Jibril Musef, Jim to the crew, stood on the bridge of his container ship and stared down at the body of his first officer. Blood had stopped pumping from the deep gash in his neck and the body was already beginning to take on a waxy, artificial look.

"I'm sorry, my friend," Jibril muttered as he knelt down and wiped the blood from his knife onto the carpet. "Your life won't have been taken in vain; I promise you." He stood, slid the blade into the sheath that was strapped to his side, and stepped towards the forward window of the bridge. In the center of the main deck below him, four members of his crew worked feverishly to open the oversized container that had been carefully located in the center of the ship.

Jibril heard the door to the bridge open and he turned in the direction of the sound. His chief mechanic, Amman, stood at the door. His eyes moved from Jibril to the body on the floor, and then back again to Jibril.

"Is it done?" Jibril asked, noting the streaks and splatters of red on the man's arms and hands.

Amman nodded. "They are all dead. We can proceed without interruption."

Jibril nodded but showed no emotion. "That is good. Help the others on the deck. I'll be there shortly."

Amman turned obediently and left the bridge, the door clicking behind him as it closed. Jibril walked over to the computer terminal and quickly began to type. *The container will be delivered today as scheduled.* He clicked on the transmit button and watched as the computer indicated the status of the message. When the message had been sent, Jibril exited the bridge for the last time and began a rapid descent of the stairs.

Taking the steps two at a time, he reflected on the past decade. Two long years as the engineer's assistant had finally been followed by a rapid rise through the relatively few positions that exist on the large container ships. After two years as a first officer, Jibril's handlers had been comfortable with his progress and promoted him to captain of a ship they had purchased the same month he made his first voyage as the engineer's assistant. Patience marked their efforts in every way, and after thirty-one long months as captain, a courier finally informed Jibril that the mission for which he had trained and waited for twelve years, four months, and twenty-two days was ready.

Since taking the command of this ship, Jibril had slowly transitioned his crew, gradually bringing on the experts he knew were essential to the mission's success. From the stairs he could see his brothers working at the container that would change the world. He paused for a minute to admire the sight, said a prayer of thanks, and rapidly descended the final flight of steps and hurried to where his men were working.

"Any problems?" he asked.

Amman was working at a control panel and didn't look up as he replied. "No. It is all proceeding as planned. We will be ready early."

Jibril stroked the smooth, cold skin of the missile. "Today is a good day, my friends. Allah is watching. Be faithful." A motor whirred and gears engaged with a thud. Jibril stepped away as the nose of the rocket began to lift into launch position.

Pacific Ocean, 40 miles west of Newport, Oregon 16:00 EST

Dae Hyun checked his watch. Five seconds, he thought to himself, then silently counted the time down. At exactly 4:00 PM EST, Dae's fishing boat began to shake, and a deafening roar pounded his ears. At the far end of the boat, orange flames erupted from the opening in the deck as the rocket it had previously concealed leapt skyward. His crew watched with pride, but no one on the boat cheered. They all knew the world was about to change.